WILD WATER

JAN RUTH

WILD WATER
Copyright Jan Ruth

THIRD EDITION 2016

Published by Celtic Connections.

This publication is written in British English. Spellings and grammatical conventions are conversant with the UK.

My son; for his patience with all matters technical.

John Hudspith Editing Services;
for super sharp crossing and dotting.

JD Smith Design; for beautiful insides and outs.

FOR PAUL

Chapter One

Jack

As Mondays went, it was the worst Jack could ever remember.

It wasn't a pleasant feeling, waiting for something, or someone, to come and blow you apart, but in retrospect it was exactly how he'd felt. The second Monday in December was probably the catalyst, when Jack began to wonder exactly why he felt so uneasy.

'I'm not sure I like you in that tie any more,' Patsy had said to him just that morning. An innocent, almost banal remark, but if he eliminated 'in that tie', did it leave the truth? Or did it just mean he was stressed and slightly paranoid?

Christmas traffic was already building into a vortex of road rage on the bypass into Wilmslow. Negotiating the Cheshire set, with their oversized off-roaders and top of the range executive cars, ensured Jack remained in a bad mood. He swung onto his private forecourt and the windows of Redman & Son, Estate Agents and Property Management twinkled with tasteful white lights and sprigs of holly.

He managed to smile at the cluster of staff making coffee, but went directly to his office, purposefully avoiding the weekend gossip. On his desk was a tower of paperwork waiting for urgent attention but his concentration was sapped by miscellaneous rubbish. Maybe it was a combination of being forty-three and having to endure Christmas when it no longer appealed to him. Someone had tied shockingly loud pink tinsel around the litter bin, reminding him that Christmas was indeed coming – so were the in-laws and lots and lots of bills.

There had been a statement in the post this morning for Patsy's credit card, which he had never opened before, and goodness knows what had prompted him to do so this time. There was an entry for almost a thousand pounds' worth of underwear. Some of it, black and see-through, was lying in tissue paper in an old vanity case. Charlotte, his seven-year-old daughter, had discovered it the previous day at the bottom of Patsy's wardrobe while on a forbidden forage for dressing-up clothes.

Through the open door of his office, Jack could hear Clare, his receptionist, reading out loud from a magazine. 'It says here that men who like animals make better lovers.'

He ran a hand through his untidy dark blond hair and scanned the new work that had materialised since the previous week. There was a Barbie-decorated fax from Lottie – as Charlotte called herself – because according to her brother, the dictionary described 'Charlotte' as a pudding filled with stewed fruit. 'Daddy pleese pleese can I have a puppee for Christmas?'

On top of the old fax machine was a photograph of Patsy and their three children. It was a few years old because Lottie was a baby, and Patsy was laughing in that natural, carefree way she had back then. He could remember taking the picture. She'd been crying with laughter – or had she just been crying? How odd that crying and laughter were so physically close. Did it follow, then, that happiness and sadness were almost the same? And love and hate?

There was a burst of sudden laughter from the staff as they argued about whether it would improve Clare's love life if she bought her boyfriend a gerbil for Christmas.

'Is no one doing any bloody work today?' Jack yelled

from his desk. After a short silence, there was a lot of weary sighing, followed eventually by the tentative sounds of phone calls and guarded conversations. Jack didn't know which was worse: the innocent remarks or the feeling of alienation.

He picked up an envelope penned in a familiar hand and tore it open while reading a long list of trivial messages that should have been dealt with by the Sunday staff. Normally, he had a good sense of humour but this morning he saw it as irritating and unprofessional to be informed that one of their tenants had broken a dishwasher by trying to steam fish in it.

Jack glanced through the letter instead. It was a plea for immediate leave from Jean, the company secretary of thirty-five years. Apparently she needed a hysterectomy, which she could have next week due to an NHS cancellation, followed by five months with her daughter in Australia for recuperation. It ended apologetically, mentioning the fact that she hadn't taken leave for two years, but Jack was too mortified to take it in and found himself checking the handwriting for signs of forgery.

It was a joke. It had to be.

His telephone buzzed, and Clare's modulated voice came over the line from reception. 'Your mother's calling long-distance from Spain.'

His parents had been on holiday in Majorca for the previous three weeks because it was always quiet that time of the year for sales, but the lettings and management side of the business in Wilmslow was suddenly manic, and Jon Kelly, who ran the whole operation for Jack, had been sent to manage the North Wales branch in his parents' absence.

The thought that Leo and Isabel were still in Spain instead of on their way home was disconcerting. Jack was beginning to feel overloaded. He lit a cigarette quickly and pressed speak on the keypad.

'Jack, is that you?' Isabel said shrilly, as if being

abroad meant she had to shout. She sounded as high as a kite, which was totally out of character. His father on holiday and with nothing much to do was enough to make even the terminally depressed seem cheerful.

'Jack, your father's gone and done something exciting. Well, for your father anyway.'

'Yeah?' he said cautiously, unsure whether he could cope with exciting, and sat down on the edge of his overflowing desk, trying to remember whether Patsy had ever worn the black body stocking he'd found in amongst the secret lingerie stash. It wasn't anything he'd bought her. He preferred her in light shades because she had long chestnut hair and pale skin like porcelain. The previous Christmas he'd given her cream Italian lingerie and she'd worn it beneath a wrap-around satin dress the colour of her green eyes. It had clung to her body like a beautiful, poisonous vine.

'Jack, are you listening? I said we're buying a villa in Puerto Pollensa.'

'That's great, Mum. Put Dad on, will you?'

Actually, Jack didn't think it was great at all. There was a lot of scuffling and whispering as the telephone changed hands, and then his father's gruff voice came over the line.

'Jack. I need you to go to Conwy for a few days next week. I've something coming on the market and I want you down there,' he said, not waiting for any kind of response. 'I've already got a buyer. I'll email you all the details later. Jean can manage Wilmslow if you put Jon back in lettings,' he went on, then trailed to a halt, as if remembering that his son had a life outside the office. 'Patsy and the kids OK?'

'Yeah … great.'

When Jean came in with a tray of coffee, he was thumbing through a pile of parking tickets and a speeding fine, wondering if he could persuade Jon to stay in Conwy. After all, he was a single guy with no ties, and they were paying him a lot of money. The thought of being a hundred miles away in a North Wales town on top of everything else was filling him with a feeling close to panic.

'Are you smoking again?' Jean asked, then looked at his desk in exasperation, searching for a small free area in which to deposit a cup. 'You haven't smoked for twenty years. There's a ban now as well.'

'Jean,' he said, holding up the letter. 'We need to talk about this.'

'Yes,' she said awkwardly, and pushed the ashtray to his side of the desk.

It was well after ten before Jack found himself back on the bypass, heading for a nine-thirty meeting with Marlow Homes. No doubt Jean would be on the telephone now, apologising for him running late and smoothing the way. Jean was fifty-something, a bit tweedy maybe, but smart and capable of running the operation in Jack's absence. She was irreplaceable.

There had been no way round the gynaecological problem. She was determined to have everything taken out as soon as possible. 'You're so lucky being a man,' she'd said with a sigh, and the rest of the female staff had immediately rallied on her side.

'Yeah, men don't have to put up with periods,' Clare had said with a sassy smile, and Jack had replied, 'Yes they do: periods of bloody insanity.'

Then they'd all just laughed at him.

He thought briefly about contacting Leo and getting him to come back, but it felt a bit pathetic and he couldn't ruin his mother's holiday. This was the first time in years his parents had spent time together and after everything his father and the business had put her through, she deserved her villa in the sun.

There was no sun in Wilmslow. The December

darkness fell early, but the town remained fully employed in the business of making money. It was stockbroker belt, full of social climbers trying to be middle class, and middle class pretending to be something else. Then there were the small-time television personalities, a few well-known faces from the sporting circuit and a smattering of titled gentry. At times, Jack wasn't sure where he fitted in. Much as he sometimes disliked the town's contrived personality, it had a constant turnover of property and Jack always got a buzz from doing the business well.

By the end of the day, he returned to the office marginally more optimistic having received instructions to sell Barbary House, a huge Gothic mansion belonging to some ageing third-rate rock star from the sixties.

'Put it on at six-nine-five, no board,' he said to Clare, handing her the specification details and a set of keys, then managing to give her a smile. 'Sorry I was in a mood earlier.'

'So what's new, boss?' she said brightly, then added, 'Actually, you do look more wrecked than usual.'

Clare was a lot more decorative than Jean, being younger, blonder, and a lot less tweedy. Jack liked her a lot. She'd worked for him for a long time, and was now more or less immune to his moods and tempers.

'You would tell me if there was anything wrong with this tie, wouldn't you?' he said.

'Jack, don't you think you're becoming a bit paranoid about your ties? I'm sure you said something similar last week.'

'Yeah, yeah, probably. Don't give it another thought.'

Inside his office, Oliver, Jack's son, was swinging round in his leather chair and drinking a can of Coke. The computer was making a lot of alarming, explosive noises. Every so often an American voice said, 'That's real cool shootin', dude! Wanna hit me with that one again?'

'Ollie, what are you doing here?' Jack said, dumping

his bag and a pile of Marlow Homes brochures onto the floor. 'I thought Mum collected you on a Monday?'

'So did I, she didn't show.'

'Did you phone her?'

'Yeah. Phone was switched off. Can I have a Big Mac?'

It was well after seven by the time Jack pulled onto his drive, behind Patsy's silver Mercedes Sports. When he saw the battered Volvo parked next to it, his spirits drooped. It belonged to Sonia Adams, one of Patsy's staff from the beauty salon. As far as Jack was concerned, the woman only just fell short of being a nymphomaniac. She'd gone through dozens of relationships, all wildly unsuitable and all of which had been sobbed over at his kitchen table while she consumed vast quantities of his gin and whisky.

Jack slid his laptop and a briefcase full of paperwork onto the hall table and was greeted by Lottie, standing at the top of the galleried staircase in a baggy swimsuit and a pair of Barbie wellingtons. Sonia's daughter, Freya, was completely naked and showered with talcum powder. There were clothes strewn all over the banisters and something was dripping from one of the chandeliers onto the pale blue carpet, foaming into a dark brown sludge as it travelled down the stairs.

'Daddy!' Lottie shouted, 'We're playing strip Barbie.'

'That's nice, love,' Jack said, with as much patience as he could muster. 'Maybe you and Freya should get dressed now.'

'Her name's Fred, not Freya!' Lottie shouted angrily and threw a pair of Barbie knickers at him.

Oliver catapulted them back, and laughed with derision. 'Ugh, you two are *so* sad.'

Against his better judgement, Jack marched into the sitting room and sloshed a lot of whisky into a glass. The gin bottle was missing and he could hear shrieks of laughter and low mutterings in the kitchen. At least there was no sobbing. He lounged back on one of the cream sofas and waited for the alcohol to hit his system, which didn't take long as he hadn't eaten since breakfast. When he glanced around the room he was aware of certain subtle changes.

Because the house was so big – a six-bedroom Victorian property on the edge of Prestbury golf course – they had always employed help, but Patsy was so fussy she usually ended up sacking them. The latest one hadn't been replaced, and a vase of dead flowers sat in a film of dust on the fireplace. The heavy swag and tail curtains were tied back unevenly, leaving one of the tassels trailing across the limed oak floor. It didn't faze Jack very much; it was more the lack of care which was significant.

Rather than announce his presence in the kitchen, he poured himself another, slightly smaller drink then showered for a long time.

Over the rush of water, he could hear Lottie arguing with her brother, gradually winding him up. 'Well, Mummy has done something bad and only Fred and me know what it is. Stupid Liver doesn't know.'

'Shut up, Puddin,' he said, then more harshly, 'Sod off, will you?'

There followed a good deal of theatrical screaming, a loud thud, then something that sounded like a small child crashing down the stairs. Jack dashed out of the shower, fumbling for a towel and falling over Patsy's handbag and hairdryer on the floor, amazed that she and Sonia were still gossiping and drinking gin in the kitchen while everything else felt like it was spiralling out of control. By the time he had reached the landing, Jack's mind was on fast forward, already calling the ambulance and trying to explain to social services why the children weren't being supervised.

It turned out to be two empty golf bags filled with

rubbish from the kids' bedrooms. Lottie and Freya were standing in the hall, surrounded by the debris, knowing he was going to explode.

'Clear all that crap up right now and go to your room!' Jack yelled. There was a short silence as they took it in; then Lottie gave him a knowing smile.

'Daddy,' she said sweetly, 'we can see your todger.'

His heart now pounding unnaturally fast, Jack abandoned the shower and dressed in denim jeans and an old T-shirt, then studied himself carefully in the full length mirror. For a stressed-out forty-something with possibly disturbed children, all the inner turmoil didn't show – well not yet, anyway.

At just under six foot with a natural athletic build, he had a tendency to put weight on easily, especially if he didn't keep swimming. For as long as he could remember, although he always struggled to keep it that way, he'd worn a size sixteen collar and trousers with a thirty-four-inch waist. Of late, his clothes felt slightly loose. Like everything else in the house, they were well made and co-ordinated and carried the required label, but then Patsy was in charge of them, otherwise he'd probably slob around in tracksuit bottoms and a washed out T-shirt.

Jack peered more closely at his face: tired, same as yesterday, grey eyes, hair not too tidy. His late summer tan from Italy was fading and he needed a shave and a haircut. But was that enough to stop someone loving you?

Resisting the urge to go through Patsy's Gucci handbag or search the clutter on the dressing table, Jack made his way downstairs. He could hear Lottie and Freya singing breathlessly in the playroom as they practised some sort of energetic dance routine. There was the usual pounding bass from Oliver's den.

That he should feel nervous about entering his own kitchen was faintly ridiculous, but the feeling wouldn't go away. The reasons soon presented themselves when Sonia stood on her toes and embraced him tightly, for much longer than Jack thought was necessary, then glued her red cavernous mouth onto his face.

'Jack, you smell delicious as usual.'

'It's soap,' he said as politely as possible, and pulled her arms down from his neck. She gave him a petulant frown but grinned at Patsy and helped herself to another gin and tonic.

Patsy was chopping some sort of unappetising vegetation on the granite worktop, but when his eyes left the food to look at her, he almost passed out. Her hair, which had always been a chestnut curtain reaching almost to her waist when she wore it loose, was sheared to within an inch of its life. But by far the most alarming aspect was the colour, not far off pillar box red.

Sonia smirked. 'Jack, your jaw is dragging on the floor.'

For a long minute, he couldn't speak. He was gutted, and it was hard to hide. Patsy's emerald eyes met his and there was just enough defiance there to make him feel uncomfortable. When he did speak, his voice came out as little more than a whisper. 'Please tell me it's a wig … Patsy?'

Her classically featured face, always skilfully made-up, looked away from his. She continued chopping. Her nails were painted the same angry red as her hair.

'Have you eaten?'

'Why didn't you collect Ollie?'

'Because I was at work,' she answered evenly, in the same condescending tone she used on Lottie when trying to avert a tantrum.

'You close the salon on Mondays.'

'Not in December. We open six days a week. It's our busiest time of the year.'

'That's right,' Sonia butted in cheerfully. 'I've never waxed so many bikini lines.'

‘Why was your phone switched off?’ Jack said, keeping his eyes on Patsy.

‘I forgot to take it with me.’

‘Ollie came to the office. We couldn’t contact you.’

‘I did tell Oliver, he must have forgotten,’ Patsy said, determined not to lose her temper in front of Sonia, who was watching the exchange with avid interest. ‘Look, I don’t know what all the fuss is about,’ she went on. ‘Call Oliver down, will you? I’ve made you both a salad.’

‘There’s no need. Ollie had a Big Mac and I’ve got no appetite.’

Patsy stopped chopping and slicing then, and for a moment it seemed she held the knife like a weapon before throwing it down. ‘Well, that’s just great, Jack!’ she said.

The early part of the evening went much the same way. He didn’t often bring work home, but with Jean’s imminent departure and the unavoidable trip to Conwy the following week, Jack felt under pressure to clear some of the backlog. He set up the laptop on the mahogany coffee table in the sitting room because he wanted to watch *The Money Programme* as well. After a couple of hours, he became aware that Patsy was watching him from the doorway.

She looked at the whisky bottle on the table and the files and computer printouts all over the floor, and folded her arms. ‘You know you’re a workaholic? Just like your father.’

‘What’s that supposed to mean?’ Jack said, keeping his eyes on the screen, an unlit cigarette dangling from his mouth.

‘It means you never stop thinking and breathing the business.’

‘I can’t afford not to. And anyway,’ he said, finally meeting her eyes, ‘it’s never stopped you enjoying the profits.’

She slid out of the room with an expression he couldn’t

quite decipher. On the one hand she was right, it did take over sometimes, but because he was so conscientious, it was impossible to get off the treadmill. His success was down to him being centre stage – he was always available to talk to, to sort out the problems and the complaints.

Everything relating to property had endured bad press for the last few years, and Jack had found it increasingly difficult to keep ahead of the opposition, to sustain the energy he put into every tiny detail. It was demanding and required a high level of motivation. He needed Patsy on his side, he needed her emotional support and it always affected him when they were estranged. Once she'd left the room and he was reminded of their rift, his concentration evaporated.

After a while, he silenced the television and Patsy's voice was just about audible on the bedroom telephone extension. The conversation sounded serious, almost like a monologue. If it was a girlfriend or someone from the salon it was usually punctuated with some laughing and shrieking. Resisting the urge to pick up the phone and listen in, Jack waited till he heard her run a bath, then dived up the stairs and dialled 1471. The usual computerised female voice came over the line. 'You were called today at eight fifty-seven p.m. The caller withheld their number. Please hang up. Please hang up.'

Jack hung up. Even the bloody telephone was conspiring against him. He waited until the blood stopped pounding in his ears, then went into Lottie's room. She was already in bed, wearing her Barbie pyjamas and talking to Dudley, her toy dog.

'Daddy, can you do Dudley for me?'

For ten minutes, Jack made the toy dog bark and wag its tail and experience things only a real dog could dream about. When he was exhausted from trying to think of new adventures for a Basset Hound, he pulled the duvet over Lottie and put the dog to sleep in its basket.

‘Daddy,’ Lottie began, all serious, ‘are you cross with Mummy about her hair?’

‘No, I’m not cross with anyone.’

‘You were before, on the stairs. Fred has seen this sort of thing before and she knows what to do because her daddy is a doctor,’ she said gravely. ‘Close your eyes and put your hands out, I’ve got something to help you.’

Jack closed his eyes obediently, until he felt something flutter into his hands. It was a plain brown paper bag. He smiled at her earnest face. ‘Lottie, there’s nothing in it.’

She looked at him with exasperation, retrieved Dudley and put the bag over his bald muzzle to demonstrate. ‘Next time you think you’re going to yell put this over your mouth and breathe really deeply, like this.’ She took several deep breaths, her eyes fixed on his.

‘Why?’ Jack said, loving every moment. Lottie was at her best like this.

She stopped panting and then dropped her voice to an eloquent whisper. ‘It’s to stop you from hooping and venting.’

Jack laughed. ‘You mean hyperventilating.’

Bored with this line of thought, she suddenly flung her arms round him and covered his face with tiny kisses, begging him for a puppy again. Jack tumbled her about till she was breathless with giggles.

Lottie had been an unplanned child. Sometimes she was as wild as she could get without being naughty, but she enraptured Jack with her odd ways and her big personality. She always gravitated towards her father, despite his hit and miss discipline, or maybe because of it. If she was ill at school, it was Jack who got the phone call, never Patsy. If she wanted to go swimming, it was Jack who had to take her because Daddy pretended to be a big fish under the water. With Mummy, she had to be ladylike and never, ever scream.

Oliver wasn’t quite the opposite, but he preferred to

argue and compete with Jack. He used to talk to Patsy, but now he frequently gave his mother the cold shoulder, and at times his attitude verged on total disrespect. Patsy said his arrogance stemmed from Jack being too lenient.

He stuck his head round Oliver's bedroom door and cringed at the mess. Other than the light from the computer screen, his room was a black pit. Oliver's face was just discernible, intent on the complexities of Cyber City Cops. Unlike his sister, he had not inherited his mother's colouring and was closer to Jack in terms of his hair and eyes, only Oliver's hair was bright blond, slicked down with too much gel.

'Homework all done, Ollie?' Jack said.

'No, there's no point.'

Jack sat on the unmade bed with its jumble of clothes and CDs and his foot came into contact with a beer can. He suddenly realised that he was only on borrowed time with Dudley the dog. This stuff was much harder.

'Why's that?' Jack said quietly, not really expecting to find out.

'I want to do property management with you.'

Jack was puzzled at how adamant Oliver had become over this. In truth, he didn't have a problem at all with his son wanting to be part of the family business. Despite his faults, Oliver had exactly the right kinds of personality and skills for the job, and it would do him good to learn some practical skills for a change. Oliver'd had education rammed down his throat since he could walk and talk. Ryle's Park had been Patsy's idea. Jack had always expressed reservations about private education. He didn't trust the privileges money could buy, and now it was as if Oliver had reached saturation point with it all and was standing at the crossroads looking for an alternative.

'Is all this because you think it would be an easy ride, being the Managing Director's son?'

'No,' Oliver said, sullenly.

'OK then, I'll think about giving you an interview,' Jack said, and placed a book about simultaneous equations in front of his son. 'In the meantime, it doesn't give you license to sit and do nothing with an expensive education.'

'Yeah right,' Oliver said and rolled his eyes.

'I mean it, Ollie. You don't get past the door if you can't apply yourself to a few exams.'

Nothing could have been further from the truth. Of all Jack's staff, there was only Jean who had any formal qualifications, yet it was Clare and Jon who had the qualities he most admired. They both had the kind of skills no one ever sat exams for; they had empathy and humility, only listened with half an ear when he was in a bad mood, and enjoyed the same sarcastic sense of humour.

Jack's ideas of interviewing prospective staff were unorthodox. They consisted of a pub lunch, concluded by half a day of following him around the office and out on the road, with Jack landing the unsuspecting candidates in various difficult situations. If they could think on their feet and laugh at his jokes, he usually employed them. Oliver would be a part of this team. He had a lot to learn from them, but Jack reckoned it would be an interesting two-way process.

Jack sat in the semi-darkness of the conservatory until past midnight, staring at the gently floodlit garden, with its oak trees and the rolling lawn that edged the golf course. When he couldn't stay awake any longer, he climbed the stairs.

Patsy was flicking through a magazine on the bed. She wore his dressing gown and looked up with reproachful eyes when he entered the room. With her clown-like haircut, she looked naive and vulnerable, and he just wanted to hold her. He wanted *her* to hold him.

'You don't like my hair, do you?' she said quietly.

'I loved it the way it was,' Jack said, kicking his shoes off. 'I just wish you'd talked to me first.'

'You mean I need permission to get a haircut?'

He sat on the bed and put his watch and a lot of loose change on the bedside table. 'No, course not, it doesn't matter,' he said, not wanting another fight, and pulled her into his arms. 'It'll grow on me. Hopefully, it'll grow on you.'

But she didn't smile. Jack slid his hands under the dressing gown and hung his head over her shoulder. 'Pats, I've had a really lousy day at work,' he said, feeling the soft warmth of her pampered body under his hands. He missed the luxurious feel of her hair, not being able to bury his face in it. 'I need to talk to you.'

'Well I don't want to,' she said firmly, and began to unbutton his shirt and tug at his belt. 'I don't want to talk about your day at work. I want you to make love to me.'

For a moment, Jack was a little surprised. It was rare for Patsy to initiate anything sexual and she would never be direct enough to say it, despite her up-front behaviour the rest of the time. It was always Jack who had to make the running, to second guess her feelings, and even after twenty-odd years of marriage, he still got it wrong. This aspect of her used to fascinate him, but he was beginning to grow weary of it. Maybe it was the onset of middle age.

Patsy shrugged the dressing gown off and pulled him across the bed, kissing him and folding her legs round him. His wife was so beautiful; it used to be possible to feel aroused just by looking at her. Once upon a time, she only needed to laugh and smile and throw her arms around him. It had been enough. Now there was something different in her demeanour, something desperate. Sexual dominance didn't faze Jack at all, but it didn't really sit well with Patsy. She lacked the passion and the sensitivity to carry it off. Whatever it was, he couldn't respond to her. Her physical attraction wasn't enough anymore. There was a big gap between mind and eye. The more Jack wondered about it, the less inclined he felt to make love.

‘What’s the matter?’ she whispered.

‘Hell, I don’t know. I just feel a bit stressed and I’ve had too much to drink, that’s all.’

‘Well, it’s never bothered you before,’ she said starchily, and extracted herself from his arms. ‘You’ve been out of it on whisky and it’s never made any difference. You and Danny used to joke about it.’

‘My brother is half my bloody age,’ Jack said, wondering why she’d brought his brother into this conversation. ‘What is this? Go on, have a go. Make me feel as shitty as possible.’

She turned her back on him then, which was worse. After a few minutes, he said, ‘Pats, I’m sorry. I do love you.’ When she didn’t reply, Jack resigned himself to staring at the ceiling.

As Tuesdays went, it was the worst Jack could ever remember. It seemed that barely an hour had passed before he was woken by the sound of Patsy retching in their en-suite. She staggered back to bed and lay curled on her side, this time facing him. He rubbed his face and put a hand out to her, noticing that the clock said five-thirty.

‘What’s the matter, Pats?’

‘Jack,’ she whimpered, ‘Get me a cup of tea, will you? Please … put sugar in it.’

Although he was a light sleeper, it took Jack an age to come round and then blearily find his way into the kitchen. While he was waiting for the kettle, he was struck by the idea that she may be ill and felt stupid for not having thought of it before. Worried sick in case it was terminal, he went slowly back up the stairs, convinced he was right because it so obviously explained the change in her behaviour. Patsy gave him an odd look when he started to tell her about their private health plan.

‘Jack, I don’t need to go into hospital,’ she said irritably, removing his hand from hers so she could drink the tea. 'For goodness sake, it was something I ate.'

Eventually, the colour returned to her face, and she began to get dressed, pulling on the white tunic she always wore for the salon. Then she went to sit at the pine dressing table, which looked like the cosmetic counter in Harrods, and began to apply her natural look.

'Is that a good idea?' he said from the en-suite, 'Going in to work?'

'I've told you, we're fully booked,' she said, deftly applying lipstick before snatching up her handbag. 'I've got appointments an hour earlier than usual. Will you be a love and drop off the children for me?'

Jack said nothing and started shaving. When the foam gradually disappeared, his face still looked white, but then he'd not had any dinner the previous night and only four hours of restless sleep.

Considering the dawn start, it was difficult to believe he was running late. Oliver refused to get out of bed, and Lottie was a ball of unfocused energy.

'No, Daddy, not those tights, we're not allowed,' she said, trampolining across the bed. 'Can I have peanut butter and tuna sandwiches today?'

'Lottie, get some clothes on and brush your hair.'

'Can I have Mummy's big silver hairbrush?'

'Yes, yes! I don't suppose she'll be needing it,' Jack said, sweating by now, looking at the clock and trying to find Lottie's school uniform. Lottie settled herself at Patsy's dressing table, smeared her mouth with orange lipstick, and pulled everything out of the drawers looking for the coveted hairbrush.

Scattered on the floor, under an assortment of scarves, belts, and jewellery boxes lay a small packet. Jack stooped to pick it up and turned it over in his hands. It looked like a pregnancy testing kit.

'Daddy, shall I wear my hair in one big bunch or lots of little ones?' Lottie said, frowning at her reflection.

'Daddy? *Daddy*?'

Jack slipped the packet into his trouser pocket and pushed everything back into the drawers. On automatic, he drove to Oliver's school in Adlington, then back to Lottie's school in Prestbury. When she got out of the car, Jack was horrified to see she had several untidy ponytails sprouting out of her head and Patsy's make-up plastered clown-like all over her face.

She kissed him emphatically. 'I love you, Coco. Bye-bye,' she said in one of her funny voices. 'I hope you've got that old bag.'

Jack pushed his car well over the speed limit down the winding Cheshire lanes and arrived at the office in a tense state of anticipation. Several people on the forecourt, which was shared with the stuffy solicitors next door, sniggered at him. Totally rattled, Jack allowed himself to be steered to the mirror in the staff room to discover his face imprinted with dozens of Lottie's colourful kisses.

'So who's the appreciative lady?' Clare said, scrubbing at his face with tissue paper.

'Lottie.'

'She's quite a handful, that one.'

'It's OK, you don't have to be polite,' Jack said. 'They always say that at parents' evening. What they really mean is, "she's very clever but weird, and please can you take her somewhere else?"'

Throughout the morning, Jack left three messages on Patsy's mobile, with no response. When he rang the salon, Sonia told him, a tad sarcastically, that Patsy was with an important client. Tim, his oldest friend and the accountant for both Redman Estates and Patsy's salon, rang to cancel lunch.

'Come to dinner then, you and Margaret,' Jack said, feeling the little packet under his hand. He felt a desperate need to talk and Tim was his only option.

'I'll have to get back to you on that one, Jack,

Christmas and all that,' Tim said. 'Look I'm sorry, mate, but I have to fly, I've got to get into Manchester.'

When he tried the salon again, he had the feeling Sonia was enjoying fielding Patsy's calls, rather like Jean did for him.

'Sorry, Jack, she's doing a full body wax and a pedicure,' she said, then sounded like she was reading some kind of diary. 'Er … after that, she's got a pubic tint at three and then –'

'A what? *Are you winding me up?* Look, just put my wife on the phone. It's important.'

After an age of waiting and listening to the background hum of female chattering, Jack hung up, convinced now that she was avoiding him. Determined not to be fobbed off any more, he spent almost an hour trying to get into Bramhall. Every direction he tried there were either queues of traffic, Father Christmas floats, or council workers trying to erect trees in the middle of the road.

Patsy's salon, In the Pink, occupied a prime position in the centre of the village. A three-storey Georgian building sandwiched between a boutique and a bank, it was richly decorated with expensive soft furnishings. Jack waited obediently in the little reception area. Patsy's taste was evident in the silk-covered Queen Anne chairs, the little bottles of oils, and the wind chimes. Everything was so chic and understated but it all served to make him feel clumsy and uncomfortable. Maybe it was something to do with female power, Jack thought.

Presently, he was greeted by one of the staff. She was straight off the set of *Footballers' Wives*, with her perfect tan, sharp nails, and white teeth. Her smile slipped ever so slightly when she saw him there – or was he imagining it?

'Oh, hi, Jack,' she said. 'Patsy's on top floor.'

Cursing, Jack bounded up both flights of stairs and burst into the little office. Tim almost swallowed his cigarette. 'Jack! What are you doing here?'

Chapter Two

Jack

At the end of an intense week, Jack found he didn't mind speeding down the motorway to North Wales after all. Oliver had finished school for the Christmas holidays – his private school was always a week ahead of Lottie's – and Jack had the idea of taking him along to Conwy. Patsy had agreed, but for odd reasons.

'Fine,' she'd said. 'A week working in your father's cold little office at this time of the year will put him off estate agency for good. Then maybe he'll realise why he's at Ryle's Park.'

'I haven't got a problem with him wanting to work in the company,' Jack had replied tentatively, but Patsy had flared up and they'd argued bitterly over Oliver's future.

'I don't want him turning out like you and Leo,' she'd said. Confused by this, Jack hadn't broached the subject again; he needed to think about it. He needed to think about quite a few things, and the opportunity to be a hundred miles away from everything and everybody was a lot more attractive than he'd imagined.

The approach to Conwy was via a bridge across the river. After the endless grey ribbon of road, the sudden image of the decaying, medieval castle was strangely uplifting, as if it still offered a stronghold. There was a busy straggle of stone cottages around the quay, where boats plunged and reared in the fierce wind and choppy water. Wailing gulls circled the rigging or rode the foaming swell. Beyond the mouth of the estuary, away from the protection of the harbour, the open sea was dark and restless till it became one with the black horizon. The rain had stopped, and a dying winter sun brooded behind the mountains of Snowdonia.

Welcome to the Walled Town, a sign said.

They passed his father's office, which bordered one side of a little cobbled square with an old fountain and a Christmas tree with half its lights out, struggling to stay upright in the wind. Jack checked in at the impressively historical King Edward Hotel, and the girl at the desk handed him two keys.

'Dinner is from seven. Oh, and Mr Redman, there's a message from Mrs Redman.'

Jack took the slip of paper from her, but hesitated opening it in front of Oliver. None of the messages he received were good these days.

They found rooms seven and eight on the first floor, a single and a double. Everything was oak panelled and creaked a lot. Oliver threw himself on the single bed, complained about the springs, and flicked the television on. Jack left him to unpack and no doubt investigate the minibar. Once in his own room, he read the few lines scribbled on hotel paper. It took him a few moments to realise the message was from his mother in Spain, and not Patsy. After a few attempts, he managed to speak to Isabel.

'Don't worry but your father has had a little flutter again,' she said.

'You mean another heart attack?'

'No, nothing as serious as that but they won't let him get on the plane till they've done some tests.'

'What tests? How long are you going to be stuck there?'

'Jack, I honestly don't know. Leo said if it's going to be a problem, just close the Conwy branch for now.'

'Close it? We're talking about the same fella, aren't we? Big balding guy with a cigar?'

His mother laughed, but there was little humour in it.

Jack slept badly. The bed was strange and the gulls were up and about too early. He made some coffee and peered through the leaded windows into the narrow street below. All the buildings were crooked and everything rattled in the wind. He dressed in black jeans, a plain shirt, and a ski jacket. From his limited experience, his father's office was nearly always freezing. Oliver made an appearance, ready for action in his shades, geared with his mobile phone and a clipboard.

'I want to do the notes for any market valuations.'

'Right, but Ollie …'

'Yeah?'

'Ditch those shades and get a couple of sweaters.'

They walked to the office, leaving Jack's Aston Martin at the hotel. Like his business suits, not only was it the wrong image but totally unsuitable for negotiating hill tracks up to farms. Jack struggled with a big bunch of keys to open the unfamiliar door of the shop. Inside, he could hear the telephone ringing, and it continued to do so until he got to it.

It was Leo, sounding far away and crackly. 'What time do you call this?'

'For Chrissakes, it's only twenty past eight!' Jack said, and mouthed to Oliver to find a kettle and a heater. 'How are you, anyway?'

'Get the diary on screen. I need to go through a few things with you.'

Jack rolled his eyes in despair. His father had already suffered one heart attack and the whole point of moving to North Wales had been to semi-retire. Leo had tried to for a while. The local estate agent had sold them Harbour House, but Leo had ended up buying his office as well, and so the whole business had started again. After two years of letting him build up what had been a failing company, and then selling Harbour House for twice what he'd paid for it, Isabel had had enough. She was tired of living in a hotel and finding herself 'between properties' yet again, so she'd dragged Leo to Spain for a respite and a consolidation of plans. Anyone who knew Leo didn't blame her in the slightest.

'There aren't many appointments,' Jack said, relieved. He knew the current market value of most roads in Cheshire, but his father's patch always gave him a headache. The properties ranged from smart little mews houses near the golf course to riverside pads with fishing rights, or derelict farmhouses with several acres of agricultural land.

'There's only one I'm interested in,' Leo said. 'Smallholding called Gwern Farm. Belongs to a certain Miss Williams. You know her, went to school with her.'

'You mean Anna?' Jack said, 'Anna Williams?'

'That's her. Boy, did she have a crush on you.' His father laughed then had to stop to cough. 'Anyway, few years ago, she inherited that place of her grandfather's but it's falling down and she can't manage it. She's on her own with a kid and a load of bloody dogs.'

'What's it worth?'

'A mint. Most of the buildings are grade two listed,' Leo went on, warming to his subject. 'I've got a buyer lined up, an American hotel chain and it's solid cash, I've checked it out. Details are on file. In the meantime, get yourself down there and get some nice pictures for the office window, some aerial views.'

'Aerial views? How the hell am I supposed to get aerial views?'

'There's a ruddy great mountain outside. Stand on that.'

'So, if I get this in the bag can I go home to civilisation?'

'No. Was that your mother's idea?'

Oliver plonked a mug in front of him with a grey looking liquid in it. 'What can I do now, Dad?'

'Find Gwern Farm on that map and put a red circle round it.'

Just after nine, Leo's only member of staff arrived. Gina could speak fluent Welsh and knew every address within fifty miles of Conwy. She was about nineteen, with long legs and blonde hair. Oliver went out for more hair gel. Although Gina explained in detail to both Jack and Oliver where Anna Williams lived, they were less confident of finding the place once they'd left the town. Leo's old Range Rover obligingly climbed the mountain pass, where sheep wandered down from the open hillside and ragged ponies stood in the middle of the road.

'Check that map again, Ollie,' Jack said, changing to a lower gear and flicking the wipers on to full speed. Rain and sleet flew in all directions and it was almost impossible to see any turnings, let alone a concealed entrance with a broken sign.

Eventually, they found the turn, more by luck than design, and bounced into a rough potholed track swamped with mud. It climbed for about a mile between foothills running with leaping white water. A pair of buzzards circled in and out of the low cloud.

'Cool,' Oliver said, squinting up at the sky. 'This place is wild.'

Jack glanced at him thoughtfully. This was a part of Oliver he didn't know, but it struck a chord in him.

Gwern Farm materialised alongside Llyn Gwyllt, a cold looking expanse of water the same shade of grey as the sky. The main property was a Welsh farmhouse with assorted outbuildings and a smaller cottage close to the lake.

They left the Range Rover in the yard and were immediately set upon by a pack of well-muscled gun dogs. Strong and boisterous, they almost knocked Oliver flat.

A voice called them away. ‘Benson! Here!’

The dogs surged towards a woman standing in the farmhouse doorway. She shooed the animals inside, then came towards them, her head down against the weather. Her body was wrapped in what looked to be a man’s full-length overcoat and she wore a pair of dung encrusted boots. When she lifted her head there was a slight hesitation before she smiled.

‘Hello, Jack …’ she held out her hand. ‘I was expecting your father.’

Everything Jack remembered about Anna Williams came flooding back the moment he saw those eyes. She was still the same natural Anna, tall and curvaceous with the same dark tumble of curly hair. When he touched her hand, the physical connection sent him back in time, to when he was fifteen, tongue-tied, and unable to stop looking at her.

She offered them a drink. The kitchen was big with an untidy jumble of old mismatched furniture, worn from years of use. It had original beams, and the floor was Welsh slate. Jack slumped into one of the overstuffed chairs near the open fire and watched Anna make tea at the Aga, the dogs at her feet.

She wore a long wool skirt and several sweaters with holes in them, echoing the dreamy, hippie style of their schooldays. Jack put his head back and closed his eyes, and he could see her lying in the long summer grass, his first love. ‘My gypsy’, he used to call her.

‘What’s the matter with you?’ Oliver hissed at him.

‘Nothing!’

‘Shall I measure the kitchen then?’

‘What? No, not yet,’ Jack said irritably.

‘It’s great to see you,’ Anna said, passing him a chipped mug decorated with hunting scenes. ‘It must be more than twenty years.’

‘Twenty-five. The last time I saw you, you danced

barefoot at my eighteenth.'

'That's right!' she said, laughing as she met his eyes with a blunt curiosity. 'Patsy was seventeen, and pregnant with Chelsey.'

'Chelsey is twenty-four now, living in London with her boyfriend.'

Suddenly, inexplicably, Jack felt the pain of losing the closeness he'd had with Patsy for all those years. Had it really been that long? How could anything once so tenacious be slipping away? But then, how did anything slip away? Seeing Anna again had triggered a different slant on his feelings. Love seemed simpler then – or was it because the passage of time cleverly lost all the negative parts? Maybe he'd lost part of himself along the way?

She showed them the rest of the farmhouse. Although built of solid stone, it was damp in places, and rattled and moaned with draughts; and although spacious with three reception rooms, it was overfull of furniture, books, stuffed animals, and birds in glass cases. Some of it was valuable and in need of restoration, but a lot of it was sentimental memorabilia. Anna said very little, opened doors where necessary, and watched his face, trying to read his thoughts.

'I can't bear to throw anything out,' she said.

Normally, Jack advised vendors to get rid of any clutter, but he found himself without the right words. The clutter belonged here, every dusty picture, broken vase, and silent clock. He followed her up the stairs, watched by the eyes staring out of several ancestral portraits. The five bedrooms seemed more functional, but the washbasins and baths were all in the styles and colours of the sixties. In the master bedroom, he moved the faded brocade curtains back from the window and a dead moth fell out. The brown, heather-clad hills stretched for miles in every direction, broken only by dead pinkish bracken and a few leafless trees bent by the wind. It was bleak and powerful, and Jack felt drawn to it.

He let the curtain fall back and, in an attempt to be more focused and professional, lifted the edge of the threadbare carpet and saw the beginnings of dry rot in the floorboards. When he looked up at her face, he let the carpet fall back, then stood up and dusted his hands.

'Shall I make a note of that, Dad?' Oliver said.

'No,' he said, his eyes still on Anna.

'What you need to note are the restless dead,' a voice said behind them. It was a boy of about Oliver's age. 'No point in selling this place to anyone who's scared of ghosts.'

'This is my son, Josh,' Anna said. 'He's doing his best to put anyone off buying.'

'Have you actually seen any spooks then?' Oliver said to Josh, deeply impressed by anything supernatural.

'Yeah, loads. I've got all the sightings recorded on my laptop.'

'Cool … any chance of having a look?'

Oliver and Josh disappeared into one of the bedrooms and Anna showed Jack the attic. It had been converted to an artist's studio, and was in stark contrast to the rest of the house; mostly bare with whitewashed walls and an easel. A modern window was set in to the eaves, giving the space some natural light.

'This is what I do,' she said simply, indicating the mess of paints and brushes and stacks of paintings leaning against the wall. She'd always been the creative one at school, but these were outstanding, beautifully detailed watercolours. The cruel prettiness of the landscape leapt off the canvas.

'I get quite a few commissions, mostly local properties and pets,' she said. 'Then there's B&B in the season, but that only runs Easter to September.'

'And it's not enough, right?'

'No, it's not enough,' she said quickly.

Anna took him outside before the light failed. There was a listed barn and a dairy, some broken farm equipment, and a lot of hens.

'How many acres altogether?' Jack shouted above the wind.

'About twenty,' she shouted back.

He followed her to the little cottage by the lake. At first, Josh and his ghosts had amused Jack but now he had changed his mind. The water was like ink and full of moving reflections, the only relief being long islands of dead grasses. There was a rich sense of ancient atmosphere here, haunted, even. Anyone with half an imagination could take it all very seriously.

'Mind your head,' Anna said, pushing open the wooden door. 'It was built for the Celt stature.'

It was a two up two down, still with an old inglenook fireplace, a bread oven, and a boiler. Next door was another little box-like room, with the original Adam fireplace and a black kettle.

'This was the parlour,' Anna said with a curtsy. 'It was used for receiving the minister, or the laying out of corpses.'

Fascinated, Jack said, 'What's the history behind this place?'

She told him it had been in her family for generations and probably dated back to 1850, lived in until her great grandparents built the main farmhouse, her home. For a moment, she was swept up in her heritage, obviously in love with every brick and stone.

Jack knew her well enough to understand what it all meant to her. She'd always been deeply aware of having no family to speak of. She'd lost both parents when she was tiny and was brought up by a – not unhappy – combination of foster families and grandparents. This farm, and what it represented, were her roots. In fact, it probably went deeper than that; it was the branches and the leaves as well. He could imagine her flourishing here, caught up in the ethos of it. It was all so Anna.

He followed her up the few stairs. There were two bedrooms, both with their original fireplaces, decorated recently with corn dollies. Through the little weathered windows lay Snowdonia, now a dark mass of shadows in the dying afternoon, although the lake still shivered with light.

'No wonder the American is interested,' Jack said, turning from the window. She looked at him briefly, then hugged her coat tighter and looked down at her boots. 'Some of it is listed. He won't be able to do too much damage.'

'You're sitting on a goldmine, you know that, don't you?' he said.

'Yes. The American has been here twice, offering lots of money. I keep sending him away and he thinks it's because I'm stalling for more.'

Jack looked at her thoughtfully. 'You don't want to sell, do you?'

After a moment she looked up. 'I have to,' she whispered.

Jack drove back to the hotel in contemplative silence, realising he'd made no notes whatsoever, although he couldn't stop thinking about everything.

Oliver said, 'Josh reckons there's this woman, right? She drowned in the lake over a hundred years ago and floats in through the cellar … such a cool place.'

Jack's mobile had a missed a call. He recognised the number, but the reception was so poor around the farm he waited till they were back at the hotel before he tried calling Tim. Margaret, Tim's wife, answered.

'Actually, Jack, it was me who was trying to get hold of you.'

At first, he presumed it would be about arranging the aforementioned dinner, but she sounded odd, tearful. This wasn't entirely unusual. Tim and Margaret had been trying for a baby for years, and the latest treatment was taking its toll. When Jack had burst in at the salon, Tim had been in the same tense, scatter-brained state.

'What's wrong?' Jack asked.

'Oh, Jack,' she said, catching her breath. 'You're Tim's oldest, closest friend. You would tell me if there were anything going on, wouldn't you?'

'Like what? What do you mean?'

'I'm at my wit's end. I think Tim's having an affair.'

'I'm sure you're wrong,' Jack said, unconvincingly, but he arranged to meet her because he couldn't think of anything else. When he rang home, Maria, their part-time child-minder, picked up.

'Where's Patsy?'

'You've just missed her. Some office party,' Maria said cheerfully. 'She looked a million dollars in that Vuitton dress you bought her.'

'Put Lottie on will you?'

Lottie was sulky because he was away with Oliver. 'When are you coming home?' she said in a little lost voice. It never failed to get to him.

'Soon. Friday teatime. I sent you something in the post today.'

'A puppy? I hope you remembered to put some holes in the box. Maria and me are making chocolate crispy cakes.'

'Save me one, will you?'

Wednesday was the most fantastic clear day, with eggshell blue skies and soft, damp air. A chocolate crispy cake came in the post. On impulse, and because there was nothing more pressing to do, Jack decided to go up to Gwern Farm, to do the job he should have done a few days before. He left Oliver in charge of a mound of photocopying, happily chatting up Gina and answering the phone as if he were a property tycoon.

On the drive up, it was as if he was seeing it for the first time. The mountains seemed less oppressive, the running water was no longer foaming and bouncing, even the birds were less predatory and more in tune with the change of atmosphere. Anna was tossing hay into a big pile for the wild ponies. She was wearing jeans this time, and not quite so many sweaters. Her hair was twisted into an untidy bun and pushed under a tweed cap, but it kept falling down.

'Are these part of the fixtures and fittings?' he shouted to her, indicating the ponies. She spun round, pleased to see him. 'Jack! You didn't say you were coming up this morning.'

'Great day. I can't believe how different it looks.'

'No two days are ever the same up here,' she said, and turned back to the ponies. 'They're not in very good condition, so I feed them from now till the spring.'

'Out of your own pocket?'

She grinned at him, biting her lip. 'They only have to look at me through the kitchen window in the wind and rain, and here I am, interfering with nature. I'm either a control freak or just too soft for my own good.'

'I wouldn't say that exactly,' Jack said, taking the rake from her. 'Have you got time for a walk?'

'Sure.'

Anna called up the dogs, and they climbed the well-worn flanks of Maen Esgob.

'The American has been here again. He wants to turn the house into a hotel.'

He couldn't see her face but the contempt in her voice was unmistakable. 'And?'

'He's pushy. I don't want to deal with him. I told him to contact my agent.'

'Fine. That's what you have an agent for. I could tell him you would prefer to sell locally.'

She turned to face him then and searched his eyes. 'Can I do that? I'd much prefer it.'

'Of course. You don't have to take the first offer. We can keep him dangling a while yet.'

As they climbed higher, the landscape revealed complex differences. Looking down the valley, the mountains became more glacier-like. To the east, the broken towers of Conwy Castle were just visible at the head of the estuary, and behind them was the sea, a deeper blue where it merged with the sky. Anna stopped at a rocky outcrop that afforded a natural viewpoint and pointed out the names of the ranges. 'The one in the foreground that looks like it's sprinkled with icing sugar, that's Drum, then Craig Hafodwen, and Foel Lus. The high peak, the really snowy one, is Cefn Maen Amor.'

'You say those names with feeling.'

'It's an attractive language, expressive.'

They continued along the ridge, the dogs running in and out of the heather and bracken, disturbing sheep and chasing the scent of rabbits. They ran back and forth to Jack, pushing at his hands, bringing him dead birds, sticks, and old bones.

After an hour or so, a track led them back down towards the lake, through a belt of dense firs. The Labradors threw themselves into the water and swam like giant otters. Jack thought about his daughter and how much she'd love this. He told Anna about Lottie and her puppy obsession.

'I've a border collie about to give birth. You're welcome to one of the pups,' she said.

'No point, Patsy won't have animals in the house. Besides, there's no one at home.'

She looked at him knowingly for a fraction of a second, then changed the subject. 'How are your parents? I've got to know them again since they moved here.'

'Marooned in Majorca.'

'That's not so bad at this time of the year,' she said, but when Jack outlined the reasons why, she became more serious. 'Leo needs to retire properly. He drives all over the country in that Range Rover, six or seven days a week.'

'I know. It's just the way he is,' Jack said, watching a heron poke around the marshy grass by the water's edge. 'I thought he was mad, you know, setting up here again, but now I'm not so sure.'

Back at the farm, Jack got on with the considerable task of writing up the notes that would go to form a sales brochure. When he suggested an interior photograph of the kitchen range, Anna hurriedly went to move all the clutter out of the shot. There was a half-dead seagull in a box, trays of seedlings, cereal packets, paintbrushes, and cats darting across the windowsills.

'Creative people carry poetic license,' she said, laughing and shooing the cats away. Jack's mobile rang, and although the signal kept cutting out, Oliver was just coherent.

'Dad, where are you? You've been ages. Guess who's turned up here?'

'Good or bad news?'

'Excellent news!'

Jack couldn't think of anyone that would fall into that category. 'Come on, Ollie, who?'

'Uncle Danny.'

Only women and children thought of his much younger brother as 'excellent'. When he rang off, Jack told Anna about Danny.

'He's either after a loan, he's crashed the car Dad gave him a fortnight ago, or he got someone pregnant again.'

'A real pillar of society,' Anna said, passing him some coffee. 'By the way, you're sounding like your father.'

'Huh. Dad disowned him years ago,' Jack said. That wasn't strictly true, but Jack frequently found himself a buffer against Leo's age and failing health, especially where Danny was concerned. Despite their differences,

Jack loved his wayward brother, but surrogate father was a position he didn't always relish and certainly not now.

'How long are you in Conwy for?' Anna asked.

'I've got to go home for Friday night, to dress up as a woman for the office party,' he said, shoving all the paperwork and camera into his case. 'Then I expect I'll have to come back on Saturday with both kids. Patsy's away on some Christmas thing and Maria booked the weekend off ages ago to take Auntie Nelly to the chiropodist …' he trailed to a halt when he caught her smirking.

She was leaning against the Aga with her head on one side. Her hair had all but come loose and her hands were clasped around a coffee mug. Something tugged at his insides.

'I'll get a copy of the brochure to you by the end of the week,' he said, closing his case.

'I don't want flowery rubbish in it.'

'I don't do flowery.'

Outside the office, Danny's wreck of a car was parked across the pavement, partially blocking access to the National Trust shop next door.

Inside, Danny was as exuberant as ever and embraced Jack in a bear hug. 'Hey, brother!'

He was wearing the scruffiest denims Jack had ever seen, held together in places by gossamer threads, with a couple of large holes across the backside. In sharp contrast, over his white T-shirt was an expensive black leather jacket.

'So that's where my jacket got to,' Jack said.

'You gave it me ages ago! I beat you at snakes and ladders and you had no cash,' Danny said, and flashed Gina one of his cocky smiles. He was a natural flirt.

'I don't remember that,' Jack said, noticing that Gina was flustered with the photocopier, already under Danny's spell. 'Don't believe anything Dan says,' Jack told her. 'He's *not* a balloon scientist or an out of work actor. He's a twenty-six-year old drop-out still trying to pass his law exams. And don't make arrangements to go out with him, anywhere.'

'Oops!' she grinned.

This didn't surprise Jack. His brother was never short of female company. He had an endless supply of charisma that always got him out of trouble, no matter how outrageous his behaviour. Some girl had once explained to Jack that it was because Danny had a nice bum and made everyone laugh. 'And that's it, is it?' Jack had replied, stunned.

'So. What's with the visit?' he said, shoving Danny's feet off his desk and removing him from the swivel chair.

'I've come to help,' Danny said, perching on the edge of Gina's desk, tipping out the expensive wrapped biscuits meant for clients. 'The olds are still away, aren't they? You're short-staffed and I'm short-cashed. So I'm all yours for the Chrissy hols,' he said, letting Gina unwrap a mint chocolate for him. 'I went round to your mansion in Prestbury first,' he went on. 'Patricia told me you were running two branches and she hardly ever sees you except when it's time for another argument. Tim was there, cooking the books. What in God's name has Patsy done to her hair? Anyway, she told me to bugger off, as usual.'

Jack kept his eyes on his computer screen. It had bothered him for a long time that Patsy had taken a sudden dislike to Danny. They'd always flirted with each other in an open, funny sort of way, but this complete change of heart was disconcerting. What really bothered him was the idea that Tim was in his house when he was absent. He tried to dismiss the thought and turned to Danny.

'Are you serious about helping?'

'Yeah, I need somewhere cheap to stay though, unless you're paying – in which case, I'll stay at the hotel.'

‘Find yourself a B&B,’ Jack said. ‘You can work till Dad gets back but Gina’s in charge and you don’t do any market appraisals.’

‘Yes, boss,’ Danny said, jumping off the desk and saluting Jack. They all sniggered, except Jack. Gina would have no chance of being in charge of anything except the kettle. After a short while, Danny and Oliver went out to find a B&B and buy chips. A long time later, they both returned in high spirits and smelling of beer. Oliver had a bag of plastic reindeer horns, which lit up and flashed, so naturally Danny had a set slung round his crotch.

‘Did you find anywhere to stay?’ Jack asked.

‘Yeah, great place. Amazingly sexy landlady,’ Danny said, fixing a set of horns to Jack’s head. He switched them on and everyone laughed. It was only when it was time to lock up that Jack realised where Oliver and Danny had been most of the afternoon.

‘Oliver showed me this place, up in the mountains,’ Danny said. ‘Cheaper than the others, with dinner thrown in. She’s even giving little dogs away.’

‘He means puppies,’ Gina said unnecessarily.

‘Gwern Farm, Anna Williams’ place,’ Jack said, slowly removing the keys from the door.

‘Bloody gorgeous scenery,’ Danny said, getting into his car. ‘Even the outside is worth a look. Don’t waste the battery on that reindeer.’

Full of moody resentment, which was childish and out of character, Jack managed to march all through the hotel lounges to the bar before Oliver reminded him his horns were still flashing. Later, in his hotel room, he remembered to call Jean. It was her last day in the Wilmslow office and Jon and Clare had taken her out for a Chinese. Under the circumstances, Jack’d had to come clean about Jean to his father because he knew Leo would want to be involved. In the end, they’d sent her sixty roses and quite a lot of spending money for Australia.

'It's very generous of you both,' she said to Jack.

'I still think you're only doing this to get out of the vicars and tarts party on Friday,' Jack said, then added more seriously. 'You know there's a job for you when you get back.'

Jean laughed, but he could tell she was touched.

Jack wished sixty roses and a cheque could sort out his personal relationship with the same ease. He wondered idly whether the current rift with Patsy was why he felt so drawn to Anna, but the idea of that made him feel nervous. Feeling lonely, he rang home but there was no reply. Eventually, Patsy answered her mobile.

'Oh, it's you,' she said. She sounded half-asleep.

'Where are you?'

'Sainsbury's,' she said in a bored voice. 'I'm doing a big shop.'

'Don't forget it's the office party on Friday.'

'Can't wait.'

'If you feel like that, don't bother on my account!' Jack said, annoyed he couldn't talk to her properly because she was in the supermarket. He heard her sigh.

'Patsy, I'm sorry. I feel a bit fed up. I love you,' Jack said, rubbing his eyes.

'Yes, I know,' she said, rather resignedly and rang off, leaving Jack feeling a lot worse and wishing he'd not bothered.

On Friday, as Jack was preparing to leave the office and head home, Anna's ancient Land Rover pulled up at the bank opposite. She reversed it perfectly into a tight space, jumped out with Benson the black Labrador in close tow, rummaged for something in a big leather bag, then went in to the baker's. Jack watched her come out and cross the little square to go in the butcher's, then the post office. Benson came out wagging his tail and carrying a newspaper. Everywhere she went, someone stopped her to talk.

Jack found his concentration severely taxed and kept looking up from the computer and the telephone to check where she was. After a while, she came across to the office and Benson tipped over the litter bin.

'Thanks for sending Danny,' she said with a beaming smile, tugging at Benson's collar and trying to scoop back all the rubbish.

'I think that was down to Ollie.'

'Oh, well, he's good company anyway.'

Jack showed her the draft brochure for the farm, and watched her slowly turn the thick cream pages. She wore no makeup, her hair was damp, and she had very long, very dark eyelashes.

'It looks very expensive,' she said.

'What, the property or the brochure?'

'Both, I think.' She looked at him for a moment, as if weighing up whether to say something. 'I'm having a couple of friends over for dinner tomorrow night. Would you like to come? And the children of course?'

'As well as Danny? Dan counts as five people where there's food and drink concerned.'

She laughed, and made for the door, as if sensing he was hedging. 'Let me know?'

'Anna,' he said quickly. 'I'd like to come.'

Chapter Three

Jack

The outfits for the party had arrived earlier. The women had to go as vicars and the men as tarts. It was an old favourite but never failed to get the party going and was the most voted-for theme almost every year.

Patsy refused to wear the full vicar costume. When she set eyes on Jack, she refused to go at all. 'You're really going like Lily Savage?' she said, watching distastefully as he pulled a red mini-skirt over a pair of tights.

'Yep. That's right.'

'You're Managing Director, Jack. You look ridiculous! No one will have any respect for you after this,' she said, following him round the bedroom as he stuffed his feet into a large pair of court shoes.

'Actually, I think you're wrong,' Jack said, brushing his hair back. 'We all respect each other anyway, more so if we make fools of ourselves sometimes.'

Sitting at her dressing table, he could see her stony face in the mirror. 'Come on, you're the expert, make me look like a woman,' he said, twisting round to face her. 'Or would you rather go as the tart and I'll wear that vicar thing?'

'Is that some sort of joke?'

'Oh, for Chrissakes, can't you laugh at anything anymore?'

But she wouldn't do the makeup, so Jack enlisted Maria's help.

'You need to have a really close shave first,' she said.

Lottie came to assist, thrilled with the naughty messiness of it all. 'Daddy, I want to do the lipstick.'

'OK, you find a nice colour and get me a handbag.'

Coerced by Maria and Lottie, Patsy eventually donned the cloak, but Jack noticed she wore a very short, chic black dress underneath. He put his arms around her, just as the taxi came, and she softened a little towards him. 'I'm sorry I've been moody.'

Jack looked carefully into her face for some sort of reassurance, but all he could think about was the empty kitchen cupboards and all the invisible food from Sainsbury's.

'I don't really understand what's happening between us, but I love you,' he said. 'I've missed being close to you.'

'Don't lose that handbag, it's Gucci,' she said, and kissed his cheek before looking away quickly.

For the previous three Christmas parties, Redman Estates had taken over the clubroom above The Mandarin, a smart Chinese restaurant in the centre of town. They always did a banquet then put a DJ on for the rest of the evening. Patsy hated it, preferring to sit downstairs in the elegant dining room at a window table.

If he was honest, dressing up and dancing wouldn't be Jack's choice of an evening out either, but he felt it fair that on this one occasion in the year, the staff vote should carry the most weight.

Jon, Clare, and some of the other staff were already at the bar. Jack ordered himself a double Scotch and an orange juice for Patsy, and compared tights with Jon.

'There's no way I could suffer these every day,' Jon said, a pint of bitter in one hand and a handbag in the other.

'At least I haven't laddered mine yet,' Jack said, pointing to a big tear on Jon's inside leg. 'Oh, bugger, look at that! Have you got a spare pair, Patsy?'

'I only wear stockings.'

'Oh, Christ. I couldn't cope with them,' Jon said.

Tim arrived, alone and breathless, in a long flowery dress and a silver wig. Sorry I don't look like a tart in this but I left it too late to get a short skirt. They didn't have one in Oxfam that fitted either, so I had to borrow this from my mother.'

'Where's Margaret?' Jack said.

'Sends her apologies, she's not feeling too well. We were at the hospital again yesterday.'

There were a dozen places set at the table and it made Jack feel uneasy to see Margaret's place empty. Patsy seated herself in it instead, and fell into deep conversation with Tim. When the food came, Jack had no appetite. Clare was tipsy and giggly and flung her arms around him.

'Poor bossy wossy, all stressed out,' she said and sloshed wine in the direction of his glass. 'If you don't want that sum dim thing, can I have it?'

'Go ahead,' Jack said, then watched as Patsy picked at little heaps of rice and sipped mineral water with slices of lemon floating in it.

'Why aren't you drinking? Neither of us are driving,' he said, irritated by her stuffy behaviour, as if she was above enjoying herself. 'I know you can't let your hair down anymore but this health food kick is really getting on my nerves.'

'It's better than smoking and drinking myself to death and being pawed by the office bimbo.'

'What did you just say?' Clare said indignantly, but Jack caught hold of her hand under the table.

Always overwhelmingly loyal to Jack, Clare gave him a sympathetic glance and went warily back to her food. Patsy caught the subtle exchange between them, threw her napkin down, and stormed to the powder room.

Once the tables had been cleared away, she reappeared, minus her vicar's cloak, and persuaded Jon to dance with her. Everyone looked like out of control drag artists except Patsy, and the other women looked at her with a mixture of admiration and contempt. When they started playing the slow records, Tim was there again, falling over his long dress in an effort to get to Patsy and hold on to her.

Jack watched like a stalker from the other side of the room, pretending to listen to his maintenance contractor drone on about gas pipe checks, and started to feel disorientated. He'd had too much to drink, nothing to eat, and he couldn't find his shoes or handbag anywhere. Someone grabbed his arm, and made him dance to something so fast his fake breasts dropped through the bottom of his top and rolled across the floor. Everyone in the room was close to hysteria with laughter, except Tim and Patsy, who were smooching and talking.

Patsy was laughing, throwing her head back seductively. The hard knot of tension that had sat in his stomach for several days began to smoulder into a slow anger. Barely aware of what he was doing, falling over the shoes and bags on the floor, Jack grabbed the back of Tim's arm and roughly dragged him round.

For a second, there was a smile on Tim's face but it fell the instant Jack got hold of the front of his dress and pushed him to the floor. Mr Music the DJ carried on regardless, and another merry Christmas song belted out, but no one was listening by then. They were all transfixed by the surreal sight of the two men on the floor.

Tim was tied up in the long dress and trying to protect himself with his handbag, but Jack somehow managed to give him a bloody nose and would have carried on hitting him had Jon not pulled him on to his feet.

Tim, shaken up, looked at Jack, astonished, touching the slow trickle of blood as it crept over his lip.

'What the *hell* was all that about?'

'You and Patsy know what that was about,' Jack said, swaying slightly. His anger had completely gone now, and his skirt had ridden up round his thighs. His staff were open-mouthed, but he just thanked God they were all drunk and wouldn't remember most of it. The only person in the room stone cold sober was his wife.

'I can't believe you just did that,' she said, then calmly went to collect her coat and left the room. There was an uncomfortable minute of silence, then the spell was broken.

Jack ran after her, flying down the stairs and on to the pavement but there was no sign of her. Trying to ignore the shouts and jeers from passing cars, Jack marched to the taxi rank and it was only by promising to pay double the fare that he managed to get home at all.

Maria was waiting in the hall, agitated. 'Patsy's gone,' she said.

'Gone?'

'To the health farm. She said there would be no traffic on the roads now and it would be better than going in the morning.'

'Oh, right, yes, I know,' Jack said, 'See you next week then?'

Maria pulled on her coat, but hovered in the hall. 'Jack, she was really upset.'

'Give my regards to Auntie Nelly! Hope her feet are OK.'

When he heard Maria's car pull away, Jack dived upstairs and spent a long time looking at his sleeping children, then when he felt ready, carefully opened all the wardrobes in the master bedroom, convinced everything would be gone. There was nothing of any significance missing.

Lottie woke him just before six in the morning. 'Daddy, come on! We're going to Wales! Ollie said there was dogs and Uncle Danny!' she said, pulling his head by his hair. 'I'm sooo excited!'

Jack felt like he wanted to die.

'Lottie, go and wake up Ollie and get me some water, please, sweetheart,' he said feebly.

'OK.'

Somehow, Jack managed to stagger into the shower, switch it on, and put his head under the powerful jets of water. He towelled himself dry very slowly, without making any sudden movements. Presently, Lottie brought him a plastic Barbie cup with lukewarm water in it.

'Ollie won't get up. He told me to bog off,' she said, then looked at Jack resting his forehead on the shaving mirror. 'Daddy ... why do you keep saying oh God, *oh God?*'

After forcing himself to consume twice the recommended amount of fizzy tablets and two pints of water, Jack found himself speeding back down the motorway, vaguely aware that he was probably still over the legal limit for driving. They stopped at a service station for breakfast but Jack could only manage coffee, and then had to sit outside because Ollie and Lottie ordered bacon and eggs, fried potatoes, syrup waffles, and doughnuts.

When he glanced in the mirror at the petrol station, he noticed he had a cut eyebrow and some of Patsy's blue eyeliner and mascara was still in place. He looked like someone on the run. A random thought struck him – maybe he *was* on the run.

At the Conwy office, both phone lines were ringing and there was a couple waiting to see him with a complicated-looking surveyor's report

'Look at the bloody state of you,' Danny said, sniggering, 'Dad's on the line, wants to speak to you about interest rates and some mortgage deal.'

'What? Can't you deal with it? Tell him I'm with someone.'

Jack sat down carefully, aware that Mr and Mrs Jones

were staring at him. They pushed a lot of paperwork across the desk, and Jack took a long time to focus on it. In fact, if he looked at it for too long, some of the text merged together.

'We're not paying the asking price any more. The gable end wants re-pointing.'

'Right, leave it with me and I'll get back to you,' Jack said, wishing they'd go so he could put his head on the desk. They went, but slowly, obviously not convinced anything would happen.

Danny smiled and waved reassuringly, then closed the door after them and grinned at Jack. 'Good night, was it?'

'No, it wasn't,' Jack said, shoving the Jones file on top of several others. 'Look, just go and get me some cigarettes and some Alka-Seltzer, then take the kids out somewhere, will you?'

Obviously feeling cheated, Danny disappeared with Oliver and Lottie, and Gina brought Jack a printout of the diary for the day with an anxious little smile.

'I could do some of these viewings after we close.'

'No, absolutely not, remember Suzy Lamplugh and all that.'

Jack refused to let any female staff meet clients at properties, empty or not. Clare had been sexually assaulted a couple of years ago, and just weeks later, some weirdo had locked one of the other girls in a cellar. Danny wasn't really up to the mark with any of it, even if he was available, so basically it meant that Jack had to do everything.

The result was a long list of minor problems with rented flats and houses, a lot of viewings, and four difficult market appraisals, all of which had addresses he couldn't even pronounce let alone have a chance of finding on time.

'Do you think you'll be OK?' Gina asked, handing him a pile of keys, all tagged according to his father's cryptic system, a sandwich from the corner shop, and a makeup remover pad.

By the time Jack had found his final appointment of the day – an empty cottage in the middle of Llanrwst forest – it was pitch dark and he was running an hour and a half late. He was amazed the prospective buyers even turned up, but that was down to Gina who was still in the office, phoning everyone and trying to keep track of where he was.

It was well after seven when he dropped everything back at the office, made a few phone calls, then crawled to the hotel and collapsed into the bath. He must have fallen asleep because the water was stone cold when he came round. Feeling marginally more human, he called Gwern Farm. Danny answered the phone in his usual disinterested drawl.

'Yeah?'

'I'm running late. Tell Anna I'm sorry, will you?'

'Great. We're all eating the bloody tablecloth here.'

He tried calling Patsy for about the sixth time, but her mobile was still turned off and he couldn't remember where she was staying. While he was shaving and getting dressed, Jack tried to assimilate how he felt about everything that had happened in the last forty-eight hours, but it was still too complicated to work out, except that as time went on he felt more stupid. He knew his volatile behaviour got him into trouble, but he just couldn't help himself; he had always worn his heart on his sleeve. Once upon a time, Patsy had loved it. She used to say his fiery personality and his sense of fun were products of playful passion, and it turned her on. Now, it seemed to have the reverse effect. . Last week she'd told him he was immature, and why did he have to be the only father in Lottie's class to swim twenty lengths in a reindeer costume to raise money for school computers? 'All the other parents just make a donation, but you, you have to make a fool of yourself!'

At the farm, Danny answered the door. ‘Good grief, it still lives,’ he said, glass in hand and three days of stubble on his face.

‘I don’t want to talk about last night, OK?’ Jack said, stepping into the porch. The dogs jumped over him, and Lottie was crawling along with them, wearing a makeshift tail made from a draught excluder. She was covered in animal hair.

‘Daddy, I’ve had such a brilliant day and I don’t want to go home,’ she said stubbornly.

‘We’re not going home. Come here and give me a hug,’ Jack said and scooped her up off the floor but she squirmed to get down again, more interested in kissing Benson and holding out his ears.

‘Jack? Come into the kitchen,’ Anna shouted.

‘My daughter is in love with that dog of yours,’ Jack said, plonking down half a dozen bottles of wine in a cardboard carrier.

‘So am I,’ she said, turning from the stove, spoon in hand and smiling, ‘but then he is pretty special. Grab yourself a drink if you can find a glass.’

The kitchen was an even bigger mess than he remembered, but this time there was a gorgeous Italian cooking smell mixed with the slight smokiness of the fire. The sick seagull was sitting up in its box, watching him with beady eyes. Jack looked into his glass of wine and felt strange in Anna’s house with his children, but without Patsy.

Anna introduced him to a big, jolly woman called Hilary, who ran the local pony trekking centre.

‘Call me Hilly, everyone does. I’m hilly when I stand up and hilly when I lie down.’

Then there was Alex, an outdoor type who owned some trout farm. He nodded at Jack and said little, preferring to watch Anna and drink his beer.

The food was good, but Jack knew it would be. Anna

had always been a superb cook and the table was covered with dishes of pepper salad, lasagne, pancake cannelloni, and numerous desserts, all piled over the table with assorted cutlery and dishes. Nothing matched but no one seemed to care, least of all Jack, and everyone just grabbed a plate and hauled a chair up.

'Jack, have you not eaten for a week?' Hilly said, watching him load up his plate.

'No. Just don't talk to me for about twenty minutes. You might not want to watch, either.'

When the allotted time had passed, Anna removed his empty plate and gave him some tiramisu in a cereal bowl. 'You look shattered. Danny said you had a tough day.'

'It was the hangover from hell that did it,' Jack said. 'Anyway, I survived. Thanks for putting up with my family today, the difficult half at that.'

'None of them have been difficult,' Anna said, pouring coffee into chipped china cups. 'Josh and Oliver have been out most of the day and Danny took Lottie into town, then pony riding at Hilly's,' she went on. 'Since then, she's been happy playing with the dogs and feeding the seagull,' she said, then 'Oh, I'm sorry if her clothes are dirty. We had to dig up some worms.'

'I don't care about her bloody clothes,' he said quietly, stirring his coffee.

The way she met his eyes caught him out with one of those awkward, silent moments. Maybe Anna felt something too, because she suddenly got up from the table and went to find a bottle of cognac. When Jack looked up from his coffee again, Alex was staring at him.

They moved into the sitting room and Alex opened the cognac. 'Anna tells me you went to school together.'

'Yeah, long time ago.'

'I know a bit more than that,' Hilly said, squashing next to Jack on the sofa and nudging him with her ample shoulder. 'You jilted her for someone else and broke her heart.'

'Hilly, don't be so embarrassing,' Anna said, trying to change the subject. 'Tell us about those American riders you lost on the mountain yesterday.'

Hilly was funny and entertaining, but after a while Jack wasn't really listening, and neither was Anna. She caught his eye again and the years fell away.

They'd loved each other from being small until they were eighteen. Jack had always stuck up for her when she got called the white witch, because she had three bottles of aromatherapy oil and could do an Indian head massage. Some of the lads called her 'fat Anna' because of her tall, heavy figure and impressive cleavage. Privately, they thought she was rather erotic and would have done anything to get a bit closer.

Jack had got a lot closer. Anna Williams had been the second girl he'd slept with at high school, but it was the first time he'd ever felt deeply in love with anyone. It was weird that he still felt bad about hurting her, after all this time. In fact, he had an overwhelming urge to take her in his arms, hold her, and kiss her. He tried to convince himself that it was only because he was short on affection and feeling vulnerable.

But that theory didn't hold up when she looked at him with those same emotions mirrored in her eyes. He wondered whether it was written all over his face, because as soon as Hilly moved, Danny threw himself down next to his brother with a grin as wide as the channel tunnel. 'Is that right? You and Anna were an item?'

'Yeah,' Jack said.

'She still has the hots for you.'

'Rubbish.'

Hilly interrupted, 'Come on, we're playing Monopoly with real money.'

'This should be right up your street, Jack,' Alex said, swirling his drink round, 'buying property and charging people for landing on it.'

'Jack, lend us twenty quid, will you?' Danny said, opening the board.

During the game, Jack fell into a coma-like sleep. Anna woke him by removing his hand from his empty glass, which was tipping towards the stone floor. He struggled to sit up and rubbed his face.

'Sorry, I'm not very good company at the moment.'

Anna settled herself next to him with the cognac bottle. 'Is something wrong?' she said quietly, refilling both their glasses.

The other three were still playing Monopoly, and it looked like Alex was winning because he was the only one sober enough to concentrate on what he was doing. Danny and Hilly were convulsed with laughter, both trying to dream up the rudest or most complicated rules. Jack looked at Anna's face in the flickering firelight. 'Where do you want me to start?'

'I usually start at the end and work backwards.'

He told her about the party and Tim's nose.

'You've not changed, you and Patsy. You were both always so hot-headed, jumping to conclusions,' she said gently. 'I can't remember how many fights you had with innocent bystanders, let alone with each other.'

'I know, but this is different. I can feel it's different.'

'I'm listening. Convince me.'

Telling Anna made it all more real, but he needed to talk to someone. He gave her a potted history of his marriage, most of it concentrated on the last three weeks.

'Do you think I'm going mad?' he said, realising how desperate it all sounded.

'No, course not. I hope you're wrong though. Almost twenty-five years of marriage and three children is not something you would want to dismiss lightly.'

The game finished with a roar of defeat from Hilly and Danny.

'I should be going,' Jack said. 'Lottie must be dead on her feet.'

'Lottie's been asleep for hours,' she said, then touched his sleeve. 'Come on, I'll show you.'

He followed her upstairs into Danny's twin-bed room, where Lottie lay with her arms round a slumbering Benson. Jack knelt down and the dog licked Jack's face and thumped his tail.

'I'm not ready to go yet,' Lottie said sleepily.

'Anna says you can stay here till morning.'

'Go away then, Daddy.'

It was getting on for the early hours of the morning by the time Hilly made a noisy departure, hugging everyone and obviously impressed with Danny's bum and his sense of humour. Eventually, Jack and Oliver got away too, although with less fuss. Jack glanced in the rear-view mirror as they lurched down the unmade road. Anna was at the door, and Alex was behind her, his arms around her waist.

'Dad, it might be a good idea if you looked through the windscreen occasionally,' Oliver said sarcastically.

Back at the hotel, Jack couldn't get to sleep, and tossed and turned for a couple of hours. He had been more comfortable slumped on Anna's old sofa near the log fire, with purring cats on his legs and an old dog leaning against his feet.

As usual, he woke late with a headache and told Oliver to meet him at the office. It was closed on Sundays so Jack had the place to himself. Once there, he rang the Joneses with the news that he'd got two thousand off the asking price because of the re-pointing, then checked the e-mail. There was an enquiry from someone looking for a smallholding to breed rare goats.

Gina was in the process of sorting through the photographs of Gwern Farm and setting up the advertising. In the original packet were the more personal ones of the scenery, and one of Anna laughing with the dogs. Jack removed these and put them in his case, leaving the serious ones of the interior and the shots he'd taken of the house from across the lake.

Anna was pleased with her draft copy, 'I love what you've done with this,' she'd said to him last night in private. 'The way you've described it; the pictures … everything.'

'I want to attract the right kind of buyer for you.'

Jack slid a copy of the brochure into an envelope with one of his business cards, and addressed it to the prospective goat breeders.

The next message was from his father, presumably left last night, complaining that Jack couldn't be contacted and why wasn't he at the hotel. He managed to get hold of his mother.

'Jack, we've got a flight for Tuesday. Oh, hold on, your father wants a word,' she added wearily.

'What's happening with the Williams' place?' Leo asked.

'It's all set up, but she doesn't want to sell to the American if she can help it.'

'Is she *mad*? Does she know what he's offering?'

'Leave it, Dad. You can't force her.'

Jack knew he wouldn't leave it, but it was up to Anna now and Jack had no doubts she could handle his father.

When he called the farm, Danny told him that Anna and Lottie were down on the beach. 'She wants you to meet her there.'

'Right, I'm heading off when I've picked up Lottie,' Jack said. 'Be here for nine tomorrow and make sure you pay Anna for your B&B.'

'No problem. Anna says she'll accept payment in kind.'

'In your dreams.'

When Oliver turned up at the office looking pale and grumpy, Jack locked up and they headed to the coast in the

Aston Martin. It was one of those mild, blustery December days with a low winter sun. The tide was a little way out, rushing and sliding at the shoreline where it met a bank of mussel shells, seaweed, and white driftwood. There were thousands of chattering oyster catchers riding the wind and diving over the curling surf, and there were a couple of yachts further out, their spinnakers in full sail.

They walked across the hard, rippled sand, and saw Anna throwing stones into the sea for the dogs. She waved when she saw Jack and Oliver, but Lottie was too busy helping Benson dig a hole.

'I hope you didn't mind coming down here,' Anna said when they finally got within speaking distance. 'We let Brian go.' She indicated the empty box and knocked the sand from her hands.

'No, no problem,' Jack said, 'and thanks for yesterday, last night … this morning.'

'Daddy I don't *want* to go home,' Lottie whined. 'I want to stay here with Anna and Benson and Uncle Danny.'

So do I, Jack thought. They walked back slowly along the shore, Oliver skimming stones and Lottie showing signs of developing a full-blown tantrum. When they reached the Aston Martin, she wouldn't get in. 'No. I don't want to!'

Anna promised to send her some pictures of the new puppies. 'I'm relying on you to think of at least six names,' she said, finally settling her into the back seat.

'I want one to be called Snog.'

'Snog the dog?' Oliver sneered.

Jack closed the car doors on Oliver and Lottie and wondered what to say to Anna. He probably wouldn't see her again, and he wasn't quite sure how that made him feel, but then she wrapped her arms round herself and stood some distance from him.

'Bye, Jack,' she said.

'If you get any problems with the American ... or anything ... give me a call?'

She nodded and smiled, and they both knew she wouldn't. Jack pulled away, and through the rear-view mirror saw her standing there, now holding the empty box with the dogs milling round her feet, the wind tugging at her hair.

The drive back was thoroughly depressing and everywhere looked flat and grey. Oliver was moody, Lottie tired and argumentative, and Jack was all those things. There was no sign of Patsy at home and the house was cold and silent.

'Why is there never anything to eat in here?' Oliver said, slamming every cupboard door in the kitchen.

'Where's Mummy?' Lottie said, rubbing her eyes and dragging Dudley by his ear.

Jack threw all their bags into the hall and put the central heating on full.

'Come on, Lottie, come and help me at the supermarket,' Jack said. 'We'll get a Christmas tree. You can choose.'

Cheered by this, Lottie jumped back in the car. However, it was the last Sunday afternoon before Christmas and after the isolation of the windblown beach, Sainsbury's looked to be full of humanity verging on insanity. Jack was tempted to ditch the idea and go for a takeaway, but Lottie was already pushing a trolley and a list written in thick felt pen at him.

'We need some crackers, Daddy,' she said, then stopped him picking up crisp breads. 'No, not those kind! Pulley crackers!'

It was dark by the time Jack had managed to unpack everything back at home, find the decorations in the loft, and make three different things for tea because no one could agree on what they wanted to eat.

Later, while he was running a bath for Lottie, he could

hear Oliver talking to Josh on his mobile phone. He was laughing a lot, in the derisory way that teenagers do.

'Where's Mummy?' Lottie said again, pouring far too much of Patsy's expensive foam into the water.

'I expect she'll be back soon,' Jack said distractedly, half listening to Oliver's side of the conversation. His son obviously intended to make a friend of Josh, a situation that hadn't occurred to Jack. But then, why shouldn't Oliver and Josh stay in touch?

By ten o'clock, Lottie had been flat out for hours. Even Oliver was asleep, but there was still no sign of Patsy. Jack flicked through the television channels and watched *Question Time* without hearing a word of it, aware that the house phone was blinking, telling him there was a new message stored.

Getting himself a large Scotch first and lighting a cigarette, Jack pressed playback. It was Tim. 'Jack, I don't know when you'll hear this, I've been calling your mobile all weekend. Where have you been? Look, mate, just call me, will you? Please Jack. I need to talk to you.'

For a long time, Jack sat in the dark room, looking out at the garden and Lottie's decorations on the tree. The baubles were lopsided and there were big bare gaps. Several chocolate wrappers hung limp on little coloured strings, their innards long gone. 'You will talk to Tim, won't you?' Anna had said, concerned. He rang Tim.

'Jack, is that you?'

'Just answer me one question … are you having an affair with Patsy?'

'*No*! No I'm not. What do you take me for?'

Jack felt weak with the relief. All the strain of the past few weeks came at him in an overwhelming rush and he was lost for words. All he could think was thank God it wasn't Tim. Tim would have been unbearable.

'Are you still there? Jack?'

'Yeah,' he said quietly, 'still here.'

'Look, we can't talk on the phone. Let me see you tomorrow. Remember you arranged to meet Margaret? Well, I'll be there too. OK? Jack?'

'OK.'

Jack disconnected and poured himself another drink. Not long after, Patsy's car purred into the drive. He could smell her perfume first, heavy and slightly musky. She looked tanned and relaxed, in a soft cream raincoat, silk shirt, and leather trousers. She looked in control.

'Had a good time then?' he said carefully.

'Yes.'

'Why was your mobile switched off?'

'I didn't want to speak to you. And I don't want to speak to you now,' she said, grimacing at the Christmas tree and Lottie's homemade dog decorations and knotted tinsel.

Presently, he followed her upstairs. She was unpacking, carefully hanging her clothes with unnatural precision.

'Why don't you sleep in the spare room?' she said evenly, then began to sort through the clutter on the dressing table.

'Is that what you want?' Jack said, sitting on the edge of the bed, 'I'm sorry about Friday night. I got it wrong, about you and Tim.'

She snorted with annoyance, and began to cream something over her face. 'Look, I've told you, I don't want to speak to you. I'm tired and I want to be on my own.'

Jack lay like stone in the spare room. As usual, it took him hours to drop off to sleep and then it seemed only minutes had passed before his watch alarm disturbed him and someone barged into the room. It was Maria, wearing a bright pink boiler suit.

'You frightened me half to death!' she said, aerosol and duster in her hand.

'What time is it?' Jack mumbled, dragging on an old dressing gown.

'Twenty to nine. Patsy left ages ago,' she said, 'I didn't expect anyone to be in here. I've had instructions to clean all the spare rooms.'

She trotted after him into the master bedroom, grumbling that Patsy had given her a long list of cleaning jobs she wanted completing that day. And it wasn't fair, she wasn't a cleaner, she was a child-minder and how could she look after Lottie properly if she had all this housework to do?

'And I don't like to say, but she hasn't paid me for five weeks.'

'Tell me how much and I'll give you a cheque,' Jack said, looking for a clean shirt in the wardrobe.

'You won't find a shirt in there. There's about fifty on the ironing pile. Do you want me to do you one?'

'Would you? Please … and a coffee?' Jack said, screwing up Patsy's list and tossing it over his head.

She grinned at him. 'Right you are then.'

Before he left for work, Jack left Maria a cheque for twice the amount she was due, by way of a Christmas bonus. She was a student doing a course in childcare and fitted them in round college, but Jack felt they sometimes took her for granted. They certainly couldn't manage without her. She was brilliant with Lottie and totally trustworthy, and the way Jack saw things at the moment, he needed a full network of support.

In Wilmslow, all the staff had their heads down, no doubt having discussed the Friday debacle, and unsure how to react to him. Jon followed him into his office and discreetly closed the door behind him.

'Everything all right, Jack? We weren't sure you'd be in.'

'Why's that? Are there any indigestion tablets anywhere?' he said, reading his messages. The most prominent was from the Fancy Dress Company, requesting the return of three boobs and a pair of size eleven court shoes in navy. Jon passed him the medicine box. 'We could do with a replacement for Jean.'

'Let Clare have a go at Jean's job. Put an ad out for another negotiator.'

Clare was apprehensively pleased. 'But I don't know how to do the overseas landlord's tax. Then there's the management banking, and the payroll.'

'Then learn,' Jack said, 'Double pay if you can do it all in a month and train someone to do your job, and all without killing Jon.'

Jack was late for his meeting with Tim and Margaret. They were waiting for him at The Grapes wine bar, close to the office. It was crowded and noisy with parties, but they'd saved a table and already had a bottle of wine open. Tim had a black eye and a sore-looking nose.

'Christ, did I do that?' Jack said, horrified.

'Never mind that,' Tim said, and pulled a chair out.

'I'm to blame for this mess,' Margaret said.

Jack poured out half a glass of Sancerre. 'How do you work that out?'

'Because I put the idea there in the first place,' Margaret said, full of concern and sympathy. She held on to Jack's arm then and looked at him with earnest brown eyes and too much blue eyeshadow. 'Tim wasn't having an affair. He just didn't want to carry on with the fertility treatment, and didn't know how to tell me.'

'We've decided not to try for a baby any more,' Tim said, exchanging a glance with his wife. 'Six years now … it's too much strain.'

'I'm sorry,' Jack said quietly, 'but I'm glad you two are OK.'

When Tim refilled their glasses, he wondered with a stab of jealousy why Patsy and he didn't have enough maturity in their relationship to sort out the big issues. Constant fire and brimstone used to be exciting, now it was just exhausting.

'So, why all the meetings with Patsy?' he said to Tim, hating the fact he needed to ask.

'She wanted the books bringing up to date so she could have the business valued.'

'Why?'

Tim frowned, as if it were a daft question. 'Because she's selling it.'

'Go on.'

'Well, I could never get hold of her at the salon to finalise my report so I ended up discussing it at your house, and then …' Tim stopped when he saw the fog over Jack's face. 'You don't know about any of this, do you?'

Chapter Four

Jack

Jack was torn in two for the remainder of the day. He swayed between wanting to go and confront Patsy at the salon, full of accusation and demanding to know what was going on, but then he reasoned himself out of it and, after a while, was even sympathetic to her behaviour and blaming himself. If he tried hard enough, everything was plausible and Jack was the one overreacting, but then the doubts would kick in again. After living with someone for twenty-five years, sometimes sixth sense was greater than common sense.

Jack didn't want to play detective, but he didn't want to be the last to find out who or what was happening to his marriage, either. What he really wanted was for Patsy to come to him. In this fluctuating state of mind, Jack drove home early to find Patsy's car on the drive.

In the kitchen, Patsy and Maria were crying and arguing. Lottie was as white as a sheet and had a plaster cast covering the whole of her left arm. When she saw her father, Lottie came to him with a deadpan expression, thumb in mouth, and buried her face in his legs. Jack picked her up carefully.

'What happened, sweetheart?'

'I fell off my bike,' she said, and muttered something else but Jack couldn't hear above the shouting.

'For Chrissakes you two, shut up,' Jack said, mostly to Patsy who was doing most of the yelling. Maria, who was doing all of the crying, charged out of the kitchen and slammed the front door behind her.

'Where's she going?' Jack said.

'Home, I expect,' Patsy said, 'I've sacked her.'

'Great move.'

Not wanting to start anything, Jack tried to fill the kettle with Lottie still hanging gibbon-like around his neck. Patsy tried to take her but she wouldn't leave him, and buried her face deeper into his jacket. Annoyed further by this, Patsy busied herself with making herbal tea, banging cups onto the worktop.

'Why have you bought all this rubbish from the supermarket?' she said, throwing out packets of biscuits and crisps.

'Does that really matter?' Jack said, throwing the herbal tea bag out of his cup with the same vigour and spooning in a lot of coffee instead. 'So what happened?'

'I would have thought even you could work that out.'

Her nastiness made him feel almost as miserable as Lottie. He took his daughter to her room, where with the help of Dudley, the story of Lottie's accident came out. Around lunchtime, Patsy had come home to get changed then begun to argue with Maria because she hadn't made a start on the spare rooms. Bored with waiting for Maria, Lottie got on her bike and, not seeing the kerb in time, sailed headfirst over the handlebars.

'I want to sleep with Benson,' Lottie said. 'I want something warm and real.'

'I'm warm and real.'

'I want something with fur all over.'

'That lets me out then, my fur's sort of limited to bits and bobs,' Jack said, trying to make her smile but her little face remained doleful.

'I might have a picture of Benson.'

'Where? I want to see.'

He left her, leafing through the photographs of Gwern Farm, scrutinising every shot in case Benson was in the background. Downstairs, Patsy had calmed down and was crying silently in the conservatory, carefully dabbing under her eyes. She was wearing a silky beige trouser suit with a green shirt, and a lot of chunky gold jewellery. Jack had never set eyes on any of it before. She always used to show him anything new.

'Is she all right?'

Jack sat on one of the squashy chairs and wondered which way the wind was going to blow.

'Maria did nothing wrong.'

'How can you say that? Charlotte was in her care and she now has a broken arm.'

'It was an accident. Call Maria and tell her you were suffering from shock or something. And get a cleaner sorted out.'

Patsy said no, she wouldn't call her, and she didn't have time to go sorting out cleaners. She began to re-apply her lipstick with the aid of a little mirror, then announced she was going back to the hair and beauty convention at The Prestbury Hotel.

Oliver turned up with four lads in a van, one of them much older, with several earrings and a tattoo of a naked woman down the left side of his face. It was difficult not to keep staring. They unloaded a lot of heavy amplifiers and musical equipment onto the drive.

'Dad! Can we use the sitting room for a session?' Oliver asked.

'No chance, garage or nothing.'

After the customary moaning, there ensued the usual thudding bass and electronic caterwauling from the garage as Utopia launched into their set. Whoever was singing wasn't very good, and the lyrics were bordering on obscene. Mr Spencer-Brown from next door was on the phone in no time to Jack. During the conversation, the whole house was suddenly plunged into silent darkness as the electrical circuit overloaded.

Great! It gets better and better, Jack said to himself, finding his way up the stairs with Lottie's little pink torch. In the semi-darkness of the bedroom, he managed to find an old pair of denims then spent an hour scrambling round the loft in the garage with fuses. There was an appreciative noise from the boys in the form of whooping and whistling as the light flooded back, illuminating the mess of cables and equipment, take-out cartons, and cans of beer.

'Dad, Lottie's crying,' Oliver said, standing at the courtesy door into the kitchen. 'She says she feels sick.'

'Christ Almighty!' Jack said crossly, banging his head on the loft access. 'I don't know what evil I must have done in my past life to get lumbered with all this crap.'

The boys sniggered and started tuning up again.

'We need a decent keyboard player and a singer. Can Josh come up?' Oliver said, twiddling with the frets on his guitar.

'What you need is to turn this lot down and kill one of those amps,' Jack said, then dived upstairs to Lottie's room, just as Utopia let rip with another explosion of drum rolls. Almost immediately, the telephone began ringing, followed by the doorbell. Jack ignored both.

'What's the matter, sweetheart?'

'I don't feel very well. My arm is hurty,' Lottie said, white-faced and sniffing.

'I know, it will for a while. Do you remember when Ollie broke his ankle?' She shook her head, then threw up all over the bed.

Eventually, Jack got to the door. It was Chelsey, with about five suitcases and a very tall Caribbean man, also carrying a case and a big food mixer.

'I thought you'd never answer. Dad, this is Trent.'

'Hello, Trent. Hi, love. I wasn't expecting you till tomorrow,' Jack said, kissing her on the cheek and making for the stairs again. 'Look, Lottie's not very well so make yourself at home, won't you?'

'Where's Mum?'

'Search me. I don't bloody know,' Jack said, mostly to himself.

By the time he'd stripped Lottie's bed, stuffed everything in the washing machine, scrubbed the carpet, and made the bed again, Lottie was sitting up, complaining about Jack's choice of bedding and asking for a chocolate and tuna sandwich.

'That's not a good idea,' Jack said, 'you can have a glass of water. Chelsey's here. Shall I send her up?'

'Has she brought me anything nice? I told her I wanted dog-breeder Barbie.'

Chelsey had brought a book about Bob the border collie with barking sound effects and was happy to sit with Lottie to read it while Jack went to see Maria and go to The Taj Mahal Curry House on the way back. On his way out, Jack passed Trent still in the hall, looking uncomfortable.

'If I could just kip on the sofa for a couple of nights, that'd be cool.'

'Sure,' Jack said, not sure at all.

Maria lived with her parents in Cheadle Hulme. She wasn't over-pleased to see Jack, more flustered and embarrassed, but she led him through to the lounge.

'I've come to apologise,' Jack said, 'We want you to come back.'

'I'm not working for Patsy, I can't.'

'Then do it for Lottie and me, please, Maria. I'll see Patsy keeps out of your way. No more cleaning or lists.'

She looked everywhere except Jack's face. Her shiny brown hair, always scraped up into a long, thin ponytail on top of her head, bobbed about nervously.

'Is there something you're not telling me? Maria?'

'It's just ... Patsy's *changed.* I can't get on with her anymore.'

'Huh, you're not the only one.'

'Look, I'm really sorry. I love Lottie but I'm not coming back.'

She was adamant, and nothing he said would sway her. Jack drove away feeling as if he'd seen the second half of a film with a lousy ending. At least Trent had been out for a six pack of beer and a bottle of Scotch.

Patsy didn't arrive home till the early hours. Jack was still awake because Lottie had been disturbing him at regular intervals. He watched his wife go through her precise routine. She undressed in the bathroom and emerged in a long, silky wrap, then rubbed cleanser onto her face. Her movements were brittle and angry.

'Why does the house stink of curry?' she said, pulling the duvet back on her side of the bed. 'And why is there a complete stranger asleep on the sofa?'

Lottie shuffled into the room, rubbing her eyes. 'Daddy, I've got a big hurty again.'

'Come on, sweetheart, you and me can sleep in the big bed in the spare room,' Jack said, anxious to get away from the possibility of another row.

In the morning, Patsy crept into the spare room with a cup of coffee. 'Did you get any sleep?' she whispered, because Lottie was flat out with her mouth open and her one good arm flung across Jack.

'No, not really, but I'm sort of used to it these days,' he said, struggling to sit up.

Patsy sat on the edge of the bed and her mood was different again, apologising for the extra hours she was working, and fretting about Lottie.

'And I hope you've made it up with Tim,' she said, then added casually, 'Did he say anything?'

'Such as? Patsy, we need to talk. I feel like there's something I don't know.'

Her head flew up then and her eyes were scornful, or scared – it was difficult to tell.

'What? Don't be ridiculous! Such as?'

Jack shrugged, already knowing she wasn't going to confide anything.

'Tell me.'

'There's nothing to tell. I'd better get going,' she said, making for the door, her eyes everywhere except on Jack. 'Chelsey said she'd look after Lottie this morning and I'll be home early. There's a lot to do here.'

As a last resort, or maybe because he made no reply, she came back to the bed and kissed the side of his face, but it felt like a cheap cover up, as if by her generous actions and a few well-chosen words she could wipe away the uneasy distrust and keep him sweet.

Jack lay listening to the sound of her car backing out and something Anna had said came into his mind. 'I hope you're wrong. Almost twenty-five years of marriage and three children is not something you'd want to dismiss lightly.'

At the office, Leo and Isabel called in, fresh from Manchester International Airport with bottles of duty free and a winter tan. Isabel held Jack at arm's length and surveyed his face critically. 'You don't look well. You look like you've been smoking and drinking too much.'

'I'm fine, just a bit tired,' Jack said and tried to smile, but his mother was no one's fool and gave him a knowing look.

'We'll be down Christmas morning,' she said, taking the cigarette out of his mouth and kissing him firmly. 'Don't do everything yourself, you know I like to help.'

She meant the Christmas dinner. Usually, Jack and Chelsey did all the cooking. The thought of all the festive cheer, with the explaining away of Maria, and the little nuances that went to make up a relationship, made Jack feel desperate. He never was any good at lying, acting, or pretending.

Tim rang at lunchtime. 'We're dead here, I don't know

about you. Drink?'

'Yeah, give me half an hour, usual place?'

The 'usual place' was a pub on the outskirts of Alderley Edge. Tim was already there, with two pints of beer and two plates of Thai duck sandwiches, the usual.

'I feel I owe you an apology,' Tim said.

'How's that?'

'This business with the salon. Has she, well has she talked to you about it?'

'No,' Jack said, and drank half his beer. 'I don't know what's going on, but I get the feeling I'm not going to like it.'

'All I know is, the Pretty Woman chain intends to move into Bramhall and Patsy reckons she's got no chance against their prices. She wants out.'

Jack wondered what his father would think about all this. Leo had bought the salon building for her when she was eighteen, and Jack had put substantial time and money into the business ever since.

'And that's it, is it?' Jack said.

'It's as much as I know. Apart from she was never at work when I tried to reach her.'

'Do you think she's seeing someone else?' he asked suddenly, watching Tim's reaction carefully, but his friend showed no sign of being shocked or surprised by the idea.

'It's possible,' Tim said with a slight shrug.

'She had an affair just after Chelsey was born, do you remember? I don't think I could forgive her again.'

Tim drank his beer, deep in thought, then reached into his briefcase and slid a gold business card across the table. 'She left that behind once, in my office. I don't want you to jump to any conclusions.'

Jack studied Tim's sensible face and picked up the card. With a frown, he looked at the hairdresser's name and address.

'Do you know of him?' Tim asked, biting into his

sandwich, but Jack just frowned and shook his head.

'I don't know what to do,' he said quietly.

'If you're looking for advice, I wouldn't do anything just yet. It's all supposition. At least get Christmas out of the way, for the kids' sakes,' Tim said, pushing a plate over to Jack.

'Then what?'

'You could wait some more. It might blow over to be nothing. You could confront her, or you could hire a private eye. Depends on how cool you can be. Are you not eating your sandwiches?'

Jack had a feeling he wasn't going to be any good at 'cool.' He went for a haircut first, then, keeping Tim's advice in mind, decided to go to the doctor's for some sleeping pills and anything else that might help. He had to pretend he was close to suicide to even get an appointment because there was a flu epidemic.

Doctor Musgrove, who was close to retirement, looked very critically at Jack and took his blood pressure.

'Why can't you sleep?'

'I think my wife is having an affair with a French hairdresser,' he said, then instantly regretted it, sure that Doctor Musgrove was convinced he was making it up just to get the pills, but his face remained professional and passive.

'Anything else?' he said, starting to make notes.

'I've got a permanent stomach ache like my insides are tying themselves in knots. French knots … chignons, probably.'

'What about your diet, what have you eaten so far today?'

'Just some Barbie Pops.'

He looked up then. 'What is that exactly?'

'Cereal with the chance of a free Barbie picnic set. We've got eight boxes to get through.'

He could tell the doctor was less than impressed with this because he stopped writing for a moment and made a little sigh. 'Do you smoke, drink?'

'Well, yeah,' Jack said, trying to read his notes upside down. 'It's not good, is it?'

The doctor put his pen down then. 'You've got raised blood pressure and very probably irritable bowel syndrome.'

'What's that? How?'

'Stress, anxiety, poor diet, smoking and drinking, I don't think I need spell it out,' Doctor Musgrove said, passing him a leaflet and a prescription. 'Take the white tablets before a meal and I'm giving you a mild sedative, which should help you sleep, but only for two weeks. I want to see you again, Mr Redman.'

When Jack got to the door, the doctor called him back. 'Oh, and Mr Redman,' he said, head still bent over his desk, 'Go easy on the Barbie Pops.'

Patsy was not as sympathetic. 'What do you expect when you eat such rubbish and smoke?'

She was busy stripping the tree of Lottie's efforts and putting the final touches to her designer décor. It was Christmas Eve, and the house looked like something out of *Homes and Gardens* magazine. Jack said nothing, dutifully swallowing his tablet and forcing down some toast.

Patsy's parents arrived in the afternoon. Lottie was already over-excited and couldn't stop chattering. The hospital story was first and the sacking of Maria, then she got on to the weekend in North Wales.

'And I slept with Benson. He smelt of the outside and he had a big, long, pink tongue, like this,' she said, sensually sticking out her tongue. Grandma and Grandpa smiled politely.

'Charlotte, we've all heard quite enough of this,' Patsy said, giving Lottie her warning look. 'I don't know where she gets these stories from, she has a silly imagination,' she said to her parents, who were fussing with their baggage and full of their own importance, much to Lottie's frustration.

'They're not stories, they're real!' Lottie shouted back. 'I keep trying to tell you and none of you will listen!'

'That's enough, young lady,' Patsy said. 'Go to your room and calm down.'

Lottie banged her way upstairs. 'Anyway, she had much, much bigger boobies than you, Mummy!' she yelled, through the banisters, 'And I'm going to *prove it!*'

Jack's heart missed a beat. He read the label on the sedatives but they were strictly for bedtime only.

Cynthia and Harry settled themselves in the sitting room, admiring the swathes of festive foliage and the exotic sprays of cut flowers, and progressed onto the smallest talk ever known to man. Jack tried to bribe them with alcohol so he could have some, but they only wanted tea. During the tea and Harry's yearly rendition of what was wrong with the way Jack ran his business, Lottie burst in with the photographs of Gwern Farm.

'I thought I told you to go to your room, Charlotte,' Patsy said.

'Yes and I've just *been,*' she said, sticking her chin out.

Jack grabbed hold of her and pulled her onto his lap. 'We'll look at them later,' he whispered to her, and slid the pictures into the back pocket of his jeans.

Matters improved towards teatime, when Trent, Oliver, and Chelsey came back from shopping in Manchester. The house transformed into noisy chaos and Jack felt more cheerful, less hemmed in. He watched Chelsey make some complicated-looking meal with chicken and rice. She was tall and slender with Patsy's eyes, but she had not inherited Patsy's classical looks and she was strawberry blonde rather than chestnut.

'Dad, you look shattered,' she said, handing him a

plate.

'Not slept for weeks, too overexcited about Father Christmas coming tonight.'

'You don't really believe all that crap, do you?' Lottie said sweetly, and they all laughed.

'She gets this language off you lot, you know,' Jack said.

'No, Daddy, I get it off you,' Lottie said, lapping up all the attention.

It was after midnight when Jack went to bed, leaving Patsy and Chelsey in the sitting room listening to a carol concert on the television. The strains of 'O Come, All Ye Faithful' followed him ominously up the stairs. On the landing, he could hear Oliver talking very quietly in his room on his mobile again, and tapping something into his computer. Jack stuck his head round the door.

'Ollie, it's a bit late for that. Who are you talking to at this time of the night, anyway?'

'Josh. We're setting up an internet spook watch.'

'Right,' Jack said, closing the door. He didn't want a conversation about Josh. Although the liaison worried him, in some ways it made him feel good, too. When he glanced in Lottie's room, she was sound asleep with Dudley, her plaster cast shining in the dark and covered in felt pen and scribble, not all of it tasteful.

When he came out of the shower in the bedroom, Patsy was looking at the photographs of Gwern Farm. His jeans were where he'd left them, in a messy heap on the floor.

'So Charlotte was telling the truth,' Patsy said coldly. 'I thought you stayed at the hotel.'

'We did,' Jack said, towelling himself dry, 'That's a place Dad's selling. I did the pictures. Those were the end of the film.'

'They're very artsy, not classic estate agent at all,' she said, holding out the photo of Anna laughing with the dogs. 'Especially this one. She's not as fat as she used to be. It's Anna Williams, isn't it?'

'Yeah,' he said, rubbing his hair. 'She inherited that farm of her grandfather's, that place they used to go for holidays sometimes.'

'Why didn't you tell me?'

He threw the towel down and looked her in the eye. 'Maybe because you haven't been around to chat to much recently, and when you have you haven't exactly been receptive to casual conversation?' he said, then realised he was still supposed to be cool. 'Look, I'm sorry. I don't want to talk about this now, about anything.'

She dropped her eyes, obviously in instant agreement, which was disconcerting in itself. It was like they were both scared of starting something deeper, and for the moment it was an effective truce, but it hung between them, adding to the corrosion.

Once in bed though, she slid her arms round him. Jack hugged her back, knowing he couldn't have made love to her if his life depended on it. She was so small, like a little bird, and it was this physical vulnerability and her petite femininity that used to draw him to her. Now she seemed different. She resisted his protection. Maybe she no longer needed it.

In most other aspects of their personalities, they were almost too similar, but when Jack thought about it, even this had subtly changed. They were both capable of fiery, uncontrolled temper, but they used to find an odd excitement in it. Now, they were frightened of it.

Maybe they'd grown apart without noticing. These days, she seemed on the verge of obsession with her looks and the image she presented. Whatever it was, Jack didn't like it very much. The thought of not being able to love her in his mind like he used to – and now it appeared not physically, either – was suddenly too much to contemplate. He reached for the sedatives and reluctantly swallowed one.

It appeared in a dream first. Lottie was roughly pushing his shoulder and screaming at the top of her voice. Then Jack realised it was actually happening. Normally, Lottie's screaming was enough to wake the dead, but even sustained for long minutes, it failed to bring him round. She finally resorted to a glass of water in his face.

'*Daddy!* Mummy says if you don't get up now she's going to be really cross.'

'OK, OK! Go tell everyone I'm getting up now.'

It was after eleven and daylight was streaming through the window. Jack took too long trying to find some clothes and if he rested his head on anything for a second, he fell into an instant coma, presumably because he'd taken the sleeping pill at around three in the morning. At least it'd had some effect.

In the kitchen, Chelsey and Trent were chopping vegetables and peeling potatoes. The oven was already full of turkey and goose.

'Oh my God, Dad, did you and Mum have a heavy night?' Chelsey said, laughing and kissing his stubble.

'Sorry, love, not with it yet.'

'Thanks for the cheque, I can pay off my car now,' she said, whisking something up in a blender. 'Go and sit down, Trent and I can manage here, after all, he is one of the chefs at The Imperial.'

Trent passed him a mug of coffee. 'Looks like you need this.'

Jack managed a smile. 'There is a God after all.'

Patsy was drinking herbal tea alone in the conservatory.

'You're not wearing those old Levi's for Christmas day, are you?' she said.

'I wear a suit every day. I'm not dressing up to sit at home,' he said, looking round for his briefcase then searching inside. He gave Patsy a small box. She looked confused for a moment then took the lid off.

'But I didn't get you anything,' she said quietly, looking at the emerald earrings.

'I bought them in October, when we were in Italy.'

Tears welled up in her eyes. 'I haven't bought you anything, Jack.'

'It doesn't matter.'

In the sitting room, Lottie was in her party outfit, in a sea of wrapping paper. She rushed at him with excited kissing and hugging. Oliver, still in his black dressing gown, was opening the envelope Jack had left under the tree for him. It was as much a present for the neighbours as Oliver. He frowned at the contents for a moment, then grinned and held up the key to the local village hall.

'Cool present, Dad. Thanks.'

Cynthia kissed the air on either side of his face and Harry thanked him for the cigars and bottles of vintage brandy, which Jack knew nothing about. Leo, Isabel, and Danny arrived just as Jack was forcing down some Barbie pops.

'You look terrible,' his mother said quietly. 'What have you been doing, working yourself half to death? And why has Patsy been crying? Have you had a fight?'

'No, stop fussing. She's overwhelmed with what Father Christmas left her.'

Danny heard the last part and butted in, 'Anna was as well. She got this bloody great diamond ring off Fish Face.'

'You mean Alex?' Jack said.

'Yeah, getting married in the summer,' he replied, grabbing a beer out of the fridge. 'She's wasted on him if you ask me.'

'No one asked.'

His father struggled inside with a crate of champagne. 'Jack, grab this lot. Why are there no Redman boards up on that new estate down the bypass?'

'Leo! No shop talk, you promised,' his mother said.

The usual pleasantries and presents were filtered through. Danny gave Lottie a walking, barking dog that lifted its leg and did a real pee. Lottie made him fill it from the hot tap and soon everyone was falling over it and wondering where all the water was coming from. Patsy confiscated it and made Danny mop up the mess.

An expert at female disappointment, Danny produced photographs of the new puppies sent to Lottie from Anna, as promised. Full of awe, Lottie clambered onto Jack's lap to show him. They looked like guinea pigs. There was part of Anna's foot in one of the shots, her hands in another.

Eventually, dinner started. The table was set for eleven, traditionally with Jack at the head, but he suddenly decided it more appropriate to swap seats with Trent, which wreaked havoc with Patsy's seating plan.

'I'm not sitting in the middle of Chelsey bun and Charlotte pudding,' Oliver moaned, moving all the little cards round so that he was next to Danny. Patsy was furious and trotted round to Jack's side of the table. 'Jack! Don't just let him do what he likes.'

'I don't see what the problem is,' Jack said, opening bottles.

'You never do! I can't handle Oliver any more. He says he's not going back to school in January. Are you going to deal with that in the same way?'

'I'll talk to him. Just not today, OK?'

Chelsey had made unusual soup from parsnips and apples, then Trent produced the impressive main course, and for a moment, everyone was stunned.

'What is all this stuff?' Danny said.

Trent stood at the top of the table, brandishing a big spoon and a white smile. 'Roasted roots with herbs, compote of glazed shallots, oven roasted cauliflower and coriander, roasted swede with parmesan, potatoes with crunchy garlic skins, and fluffy mash with creme fraîche.'

Lottie looked faintly disgusted. 'But where are the sprouts?'

Everyone groaned, then laughed.

Leo uncorked the champagne and even Harry and Cynthia began to thaw out.

Jack nudged Chelsey's shoulder. 'Where did you meet Master Chef of the Year?'

'He teaches at college sometimes,' she said, spooning something onto Jack's plate. 'Try this, it's gorgeous.'

'But what happened to that guy you were living with, Mike?'

'That was last week. Dad, do keep up!' Chelsey said, then laughed at her father's expression. 'I am joking! Mike's gone to see his parents in Scotland. I'm driving up there tomorrow for New Year,' she said, then lowered her voice, 'I hope you don't mind about Trent. He's just split with his boyfriend and he would have been on his own.'

'No, course not,' Jack said, topping up her glass.

Chelsey took a sip of wine, then looked at him with a little frown. 'Is everything all right between you and Mum?'

'Yeah, course,' he said and smiled, but she wasn't convinced. 'Chel, it's nothing! Don't worry.'

But Jack knew she would worry. Chelsey was that kind of person. She was deeply caring, a bit gullible sometimes, but she'd never caused any serious worries since the day she'd been born. Jack felt he was going to pay for this privilege with his handsome, rebellious son. He looked across to Oliver, who was giving his mother mutinous looks and kicking his sister under the table.

The pudding came, drenched in alcohol and served with Trent's Christmas ice cream. By now, Leo was roaring with laughter at Danny's jokes and lighting a third cigar. Isabel did her best to put it out and control Danny's language but failed on both counts. Jack looked down the beautiful candlelit table to his wife. She had toyed with her food all evening and barely smiled, let alone laughed. They didn't laugh at the same things any more. She caught his eye and Jack was hit with the sudden, cold realisation that this woman didn't love him either. She was going through the motions, as he was. They were doing this for the people round the table and once they broke the spell, they broke it for everyone.

Jack got up and went into the garden, taking his drink and a cigar, and sat on Lottie's swing. After a while, Danny came out to find him, carrying an almost empty bottle of whisky and another glass.

'Harry and Cynthia want to play charades,' he said in a shrill voice, and minced across the lawn, mimicking Patsy's mother.

'Do they? I've been playing that all day.'

Everyone left on Boxing Day. Harry and Cynthia were first, then Chelsey and Trent, who wanted a lift to the station. His parents were last because they couldn't get Danny to wake up. Isabel pulled Jack to one side while Leo was packing the car.

'The villa in Majorca will be ours soon. I want you and Patsy to have a little holiday, just the two of you.'

Jack waved them off with a tired smile then went and sat in the conservatory and chain-smoked his way through a rather morose classical CD.

In the afternoon, Oliver went to check out the village hall with the rest of Utopia, and Patsy said she was dropping Lottie at a friend's because they were taking her to a pantomime.

'And then I thought I'd look in on Sonia, she's on her own this year,' she said, checking the contents of her handbag. She was wearing black leather trousers and a white angora sweater. She'd removed the emerald earrings. Game over, Jack thought.

He watched her drive off, then stared at the address

book under the phone. An hour later, when he finally looked up Sonia Adams' number and tried it, it was an answer machine. Unable to decide what this meant, he jumped in the car and drove to 23 Alderley Avenue.

There were no cars in the drive, no sign of any Christmas decorations or cards on the windowsill. The curtains were half closed and there was a newspaper hanging out of the letter box. Fairly conclusive, Jack thought. Just as he was getting back in his car, the next-door neighbour shouted across the fence. 'Are you looking for Mrs Adams?'

'Yeah, where is she?'

'She always goes to her sister's in Sheffield. Back next week.'

'Thanks.'

For a while, he drove aimlessly along the empty Cheshire lanes then began to feel angry. At home, he ripped out all the drawers in the dressing table and went through every pocket and handbag in the wardrobe, not knowing what he was looking for but knowing he had to find something. Anything. Then he saw the keys to the salon and snatched them up.

There in less than twenty minutes, he parked across the pavement and tried every key on the fob. As the door fell open, the alarm began to beep frantically. *Shit*! He'd forgotten about the alarm. He punched in Chelsey's birthday, and mercifully, it stopped. At least that had remained the same.

The salon was eerily silent and there was a heavy perfume of oils and lotions lingering in the air. His heart banging, Jack went up the stairs to the little office at the top. Once inside, he sat on the Queen Anne chair at Patsy's desk and pulled open all the drawers with a lot more force than required. In the first, there was a little velvet teddy bear with a chain around its neck inscribed with French words. In the cupboard underneath, he found a file full of telephone bills with hundreds of itemised calls to Paris, and another number, which matched the one on the business card Tim had given to him.

In the antique pine wardrobe where Patsy kept spare tunics and a few clothes, there was a silk-covered box, partly hidden by shoes. Inside were some pieces of jewellery, a handmade Christmas card, and several letters still in fancy envelopes. Jack opened the top one and his hands felt lifeless. He couldn't bring himself to read it, but scanned the pages and although it was painful, there was an odd kind of relief to acknowledge the actual existence of something, instead of imagining it.

Somehow, Jack got back into the car and lit a cigarette. He placed the teddy bear and the card on the dashboard. A few people were about, couples linking arms and children wobbling on brand new bicycles. Normal, family-type things.

Slowly, deliberately, he tore up the beautiful heart shaped card into tiny shreds. As far as Jack was concerned, Christmas was over.

Chapter Five

Jack

Patsy came home just after four. It was dark but Jack hadn't bothered to switch any lights on in the house. She called from the hall. 'Jack, are you in? Why are you sitting in the dark? I'm not stopping, I need to change. Sonia is meeting me at The Plough, then I'll collect Lottie on my way home,' she said, flicking the light on and making for the kettle, but Jack was in her way.

'Yeah? Coming all the way from Sheffield, is she?'

She stopped dead in her tracks.

Jack grabbed her wrist. 'I want to talk to you.'

'What about?'

For a moment, Jack hesitated because there seemed to be too many ways of answering, but he let her go, fumbled in the pocket of his jacket, and threw the small packet he'd found in their bedroom across the kitchen table. It lay between them like a bomb.

'Let's talk about that for a start. It's a pregnancy test with a positive result. I think it's worth a mention, don't you?'

'I know what it is, Jack,' she said, then turned away and looked through the kitchen window. After a long minute, she spoke. 'I … wanted to tell you.'

'Keep talking,' he said, pulling out a chair.

She turned round then, her eyes huge and soft. 'We're having a baby.'

'Huh! *We*?' he said with a humourless laugh, 'I don't think so.'

She faltered. 'What are you saying?'

'I'm saying it isn't mine. I'm saying you're seeing someone else,' he said, getting to his feet and going through the pockets of his jacket. Jack slammed the salon keys onto the table along with the little bear, then pulled out an envelope. Watching her stricken face, he let the remains of the card fall out. The crushed silk flowers and torn words floated gently down like confetti.

'So, you've had a good look through all my things and this is the only explanation you can come up with?'

'Oh, don't tell me you're not up to something,' he said, leaning across the table. 'And while we're on the subject, did you really think Tim wouldn't tell me your plans for the salon?'

'It doesn't matter now. It's already sold,' she said dully.

'I sweated blood and tears to build up that business. I even painted the bloody walls and built the shelves for you, do you remember?'

For some odd reason, this made her eyes fill. 'Don't … don't, Jack.'

'I wonder when you would have told me. Or were you hoping I'd just drop off the face of the earth?' he went on, pacing about the kitchen. 'Then you could neatly erase the past and kick off again with, *Philipe?*'

'I still care about you. It's our baby, it is. Philipe's just a business associate. He's been chasing me, that's all. Please, Jack.'

'No. I don't believe you.' He pushed his face next to hers. 'It only works once and I think we've been here before.'

Jack could instantly recall those same feelings of betrayal as if it were yesterday. She'd admitted to a short affair just after Chelsey was born. He never did find out who it was. It had taken a long time to repair the damage to their relationship, but then the salon happened and she was sweet again.

'How long this time? Six weeks, six months?' Jack said, then when she didn't reply, banged the table. 'Patsy, I can't live with these lies any more.'

'I know. I know I'm hurting you. I'm so sorry,' she whispered, searching her bag for tissues. 'I've known him almost two years.'

Jack was speechless. Two years! The previous two years of his life flashed back and forth as he tried to assimilate how this third person in their lives had affected it. Two years meant birthdays and wedding anniversaries had come and gone. He wanted to strike her. He wanted to put his hands round her slim neck and leave dark bruises on it, like those she had inflicted on his insides.

He felt suffocated with the enormity of it all and went to get some air. He pulled open the door into the hall and Oliver was there, leaning against the wall. Mortified, Jack followed as Oliver turned away, to find a bedroom door slammed in his face. He grabbed his jacket, slammed the front door behind him as he left the house, and began to walk.

Hours later, Tim dropped him back on the drive. Patsy's car was gone and the windows were dark.

'She's probably gone for Lottie,' he said, and let himself out of Tim's car.

'Phone me if you need me,' Tim said.

Earlier, Jack found himself at Tim and Margaret's town house, not realising he'd walked almost five miles. They'd had some visitors, who tactfully left when Jack appeared wet and windswept.

The house was silent and empty. When the clock crept past nine, Jack tried to remember which friend Lottie had gone to the pantomime with but drew a blank. Rather predictably, Oliver's mobile was switched off.

As the night dragged on, he began to feel twitchy and

went upstairs to check the contents of the rooms more thoroughly. He looked in Patsy's wardrobes first. It was impossible to tell if anything had been taken as they were still full to bursting. In Oliver's room, he could find nothing missing apart from his acoustic guitar, and in his daughter's, a row of Barbie dolls stood hand in hand across the bookshelf. Dudley was tucked up in bed, waiting.

At almost ten-thirty, the telephone rang and Jack snatched it up. 'Ollie, is that you?' There was a pause, then a low voice. 'Jack? It's Anna. Oliver's here.'

'Where?'

'He called Josh from the station about half an hour ago and Danny just picked him up. I thought you should know.'

Jack slumped into a chair. 'Is he OK? Can I talk to him?'

'He's very quiet. I gather you and Patsy have had a fight, but beyond that he won't say anything. I'm surprised he managed to get a train here. It must have been the only one.'

Her voice was so calm. 'Jack? Are you still there?'

'Yeah, I'll come and get him.'

'No, no, don't do that. He doesn't know I'm talking to you. I got your number off Danny. Let him cool off first. Leave it till the weekend.'

'I can't let him do this.'

'It's not a problem this end. Do you want to speak to Danny?'

'No.'

'Jack, don't worry about him.'

'Yeah, right,' he managed to say, and disconnected a bit abruptly. After the tense words and the shouting, he was starting to feel pathetically susceptible to her voice. Anna had always been the rock in their teenage relationship, and Jack could remember trying to understand how someone so sensible could privately be so off the wall at the same time. He used to think she was shy and none too confident, but with the wisdom of mature hindsight, he realised that it was probably the other way around.

Seconds later, the phone rang again but this time he had to hold the receiver several inches away because the voice was so loud. It was his sister.

'Merry Christmas, you old tart.'

'Hi, Kate,' he said, looking for his cigarettes.

'What's the matter with you? Can't get rid of the bloody in-laws?'

Jack gave her a brief resumé. At first, she thought it was a sick joke, then realised her brother was totally serious.

'The cow!' she shrieked, which was a typical Kate reaction.

Normally, Jack liked her no-nonsense approach, but right now he didn't want this directness. It was too intrusive, although Kate was probably the best person to talk to since she'd been on her own with three children for the previous three or four years. She'd dealt with everything stoically at the time and it was only now that Jack realised how much he'd underestimated the impact it must have had.

'Are you going to be all right? Shall I come round?'

'No, no need. I was just choosing what to have for the evening; a bottle of Scotch or a packet of sedatives.'

'Jack stop it. That isn't funny.'

'Come on, I'm not serious. She'll be back tomorrow, anyway. There's no way Patsy would leave an entire collection of Yves St. Laurent suits and those Gucci shoes.'

The following afternoon, Jack stared at the Gucci shoes in the wardrobe with a sinking feeling. Every time the phone rang his heart raced uncomfortably. Kate had spoken to him twice already, then it was a stream of friends and business associates inviting him and Patsy out for drinks, or confirming dinners and parties. Jack told them all Patsy was sick and the rest of the family had raging temperatures. It wasn't too far from the truth.

Then it was Tim, checking up on him. 'Has Ollie turned up?'

'A hundred miles away in North Wales,' Jack said, pacing up and down. 'I don't know what to do about Patsy and Lottie. I've called everyone I can think of and I still don't know where they are.'

'Give it till tonight then call the police.'

'Report them missing, you mean?'

'Why not? They'll act after twenty-four hours. I know it was only by confronting her that all this went pear-shaped, but Patsy might have planned this, including getting you in a state so you'll agree to anything.'

'Well, right now it's working! I'd do anything to have Lottie back.'

'Don't, Jack,' Tim said carefully. 'This French guy could be pulling some strings.'

Exactly twenty-three hours after Patsy had left the house, the phone rang and Jack knew it would be her.

'Patsy? *What the fuck do you think you're doing*?' he yelled.

'I'm not speaking to you unless you calm down and stop swearing at me.'

'Don't tell me to calm down, you bitch! Get my daughter back here.'

'I can't do that Jack,' she said, very succinctly, 'we're in Paris.'

'Wh … *What*?' he said, totally thrown.

'I want a divorce. Are you listening? I want it on my terms, and then we'll talk about Charlotte.'

'You want to divorce *me?'*

'That's right. Get yourself a solicitor.'

'Let me speak to Lottie, please Patsy,' he said, but he was talking to air. She'd hung up, like it was a scene out of some cheap drama.

For a moment, unable to take it all in, Jack looked stupidly at the receiver, then hurled it across the room where it fell against the mahogany fireplace. He poured a lot of Scotch into a glass, and sloshed almost as much over the carpet. He'd handled it all wrong, jumped in with both feet as usual instead of treading water.

When the phone rang again, Jack couldn't be bothered to find it, let alone answer it, but the persistent trilling got on his nerves and there was always the chance it could have been Oliver. He had to stick the plastic front back on before he could answer.

'Are you still cool?' Tim said.

'No. Try the other end of the scale.'

Jack outlined the conversation and Tim just grunted. 'Take one of your sedatives and go to bed. Forget about it.'

'I couldn't swallow anything, not even a pill.'

'No chance of an overdose then?'

'I wouldn't give the bitch such an easy option.'

'That's better. And Jack? Don't throw the phone.'

In the morning, Jack had a fully expected hangover and a sore throat. It was Thursday and he was meant to be manning the office. Since there was never much happening between Christmas and New Year, the full-time staff just shared the days out. He dressed in dark blue chinos and a sober shirt and tried to get into work mode.

There was a complaint on the office answer machine from one of the rented properties about faulty central heating. Jack rang the tenant back and rashly promised he'd have it fixed that day, then discovered his maintenance guy had a 'Sorry it's Christmas and I'm not working,' message on his answer phone and there was no reply from his mobile.

When the part-time girl arrived, he decided to go and have a look at Geoff Robertson's boiler himself. It was better than sitting and thinking.

Jack remembered checking the tenant, a talkative, apologetic man in his thirties, into Garden Terrace. When Jack arrived at the dismal little property, Geoff Robertson was in his coat, with two kids on the sofa also muffled up in hats and gloves.

'Sorry about this,' Robertson said, following Jack into the kitchen, 'It's probably nothing really but I'm useless at fixing anything. Sally used to say DIY stood for "destroy it yourself" whenever I tried anything.'

Jack pulled the front off the boiler. 'I think it's just the pilot light.'

'Oh, good. I can tell Sally not to come and get the kids.'

Jack made sure it was fully ignited before he thumped the cover back. 'What was that?'

'The ex-wife. She was going to come and get them because it's so cold.'

'Right …' he said, slowly understanding the situation.

When he was driving back to the office, the idea that Geoff Robertson was painting a picture of his own future thoroughly depressed him. A weekend father living in four rooms was something that happened to other people, wasn't it?

Jack tried Oliver's mobile, and was relieved to hear his usual grunt. 'I don't want a heavy talk, Dad.'

'Neither do I. I'm sorry about this mess,' Jack said, negotiating the busy traffic with one hand, 'I don't blame you for bunking off. I feel like doing the same thing.'

'I can't talk now.'

'I know you're with Josh. I'll come over tomorrow night. Is that OK? Will you tell Anna?'

'Yeah … I suppose,' Oliver said grudgingly.

Later, Tim and Margaret made him go to the town house for dinner.

'I can't eat anything except dry toast,' Jack said, thinking queasily about Margaret's French country cooking.

'Shut up, take your tablet, and don't be so boring,' Tim said affably, handing him a gin and tonic. 'Have you got a cut-throat lawyer yet?'

'No. Just a sore throat,' Jack said, then swirled the ice round in his glass thoughtfully. 'I can't get my head round anything.'

'Leo will know the right guy. Have you told him?'

Jack shook his head and drained the glass. 'He's already had two heart attacks this year.'

Jack did his best to eat Margaret's chicken casserole, dreading the weekend coming. There was Oliver to tackle, and Anna to face, which made him feel more mixed-up than ever because he couldn't stop thinking about her. Then there was Chelsey, and Leo, and Isabel. By far the worst feeling, though, was Patsy's betrayal and Lottie's absence. It made his head want to explode. All the time Tim and Margaret were talking to him, he imagined how he was going to break the news to his parents.

Stupid scenarios kept flashing through his mind. "Oh, by the way, you know my wife of twenty-four years? Well, she's gone and got herself pregnant, more than likely by some French guy she's having an affair with, so she's taken your granddaughter to Paris by way of blackmail. And you know that substantial Georgian building you gifted to her? Well, she's gone and sold it for a handsome profit and told your son he can shove off."

Margaret removed his plate and gave him a piece of toast.

'Look, I am sorry but I did warn you,' he said, squeezing her hand.

'You should look after yourself. You're losing weight. I'm jealous.'

'I wouldn't recommend this as a way of doing it.'

Tim topped up his glass. 'What's it called, The Patsy Plan?'

The following day, when he'd been travelling for forty minutes, Jack rang his parents at the King Edward, where they'd taken a suite of rooms.

'What a lovely surprise,' Isabel said, 'Are Patsy and the children with you?'

'No, Mum, just me.'

As soon as he walked into the lounge bar, his mother asked, 'What's wrong?'

'Can we go to your rooms? Somewhere private.'

Leo immediately assumed there was a problem with the Wilmslow branch.

'This business with the government making the vendor produce a survey, did you read that report Jack?' he said, thumping a bottle of Scotch onto the table.

'I'm still ploughing through it. I don't want a drink, Dad.'

Typically, Leo ignored this remark and sloshed a lot of ginger and ice into Jack's glass by a way of compromise. Jack looked out of the window at the art gallery across the street and wondered how to slot into the conversation that their granddaughter was missing, Patsy was pregnant and wanted a divorce, and a big chunk of the Redman empire had sunk without trace.

In the end, he downed his drink and blurted it all out.

His mother seemed resigned to the facts but shocked by the details. Leo sat stony-faced, then slowly refilled his glass.

'One question. One question only. Have you been faithful to Patsy?'

Isabel shot him a horrified look. 'What a thing to say!

Why are you asking him that?'

'Because I need to know.'

'It's OK,' Jack said, not taking his eyes off his father's face. 'Yes, I have. I have been faithful to her.'

Leo rose to his feet and found a pad and pen. 'You need a solicitor,' he said, scribbling down a name and number. He passed the slip of paper to Jack. 'He's in Manchester. Get yourself an appointment to see him and don't be fobbed off on one of the juniors. I'll pay.'

As he made to leave, his mother became tearful. 'Jack, this is just awful. Let me come back with you.'

'What for? No, Dad needs you here,' Jack said. 'Don't say anything to Chelsey, I haven't told her yet.'

He had hoped he'd feel better once he'd told his parents, but instead, he felt weighed down with the responsibility of their emotions as well.

On the mountain road in the darkening afternoon, the sun was sinking in a tangerine flame behind the Conwy Mountain. Jack called the farm and Danny answered.

'It's me, I'm on my way round. Did Ollie tell you?'

'Is Patsy with you?'

'No. Is Anna there?'

'No. She's out tickling trout with Fish Face – or maybe she's tickling *his* trout.'

At the farm, Jack sat in one of the sagging chairs in the kitchen. A fire crackled in the hearth, and Anna's chocolate Labrador pushed at his hands for attention.

'Make me a coffee, will you?' Jack asked Danny. 'Where's Ollie?'

'Gone into town with Josh and Hilly. That dog wants to make out with you,' Danny said, handing Jack a mug of coffee. 'Look, it's trying to make eye contact now.'

'I've got something to tell you,' Jack said, ignoring Danny's daft banter but giving into the dog and fondling its head and ears.

For once, his brother listened without making a

wisecrack, but then he probably guessed something was coming after Oliver's drama.

'I bet Dad freaked out,' Danny said once Jack had filled him in. He stared pensively at his shoes.

'Come on, Dan, spill the beans. I know there are some. You're as pathetic as I am when you're trying to hide something.'

'She made a pass at me.'

'And?'

'And nothing. She's hated me ever since.'

Jack scrutinised him carefully. His brother might be a bit of a lad, but he was no liar. Danny was genuinely embarrassed, probably for the both of them.

'Forget it,' Jack said.

Hilly came back with Oliver and Josh and a lot of takeout food cartons. Oliver looked at his father with a mixture of shame and adolescent bravado. Once the social chat was out of the way and Hilly had gone, Jack took Oliver into the sitting room.

'I want to talk to you.'

'I don't want to talk to you.'

'Well, just listen then,' Jack said, feeling cross and panicky. He forced himself to speak calmly. Christ, this was difficult. There was no way of easing out the information in smaller, more manageable pieces.

'I don't know how much you heard of the argument in the kitchen but the bottom line is your mother's left me and taken Lottie to France. For the time being.'

'I know,' Oliver sneered. 'Why do you think I'm here? And you missed out the bit about the baby.'

'Oh yeah, that as well,' Jack said softly and looked at the ceiling. It was crumbling and there was a damp patch on the gable end. Over the fireplace was a painting of Benson in the heather, nose and tail to the wind, ears alert. It made him think of Lottie.

'She wanted me to go with her,' Oliver said suddenly.

‘Why did you have to go and have another argument?’ he said, and kicked the iron doorstop. ‘You made them go!’

Oliver took his stunned silence as guilt, and went from the room, needing an excuse to hide the tears and lick his wounds in private.

Danny was waiting for his brother in the kitchen, pouring brandy into mugs.

‘He blames me,’ Jack said miserably, waving the brandy away.

‘What do you expect? You’re the only parent in the firing line,’ Danny said, pushing the mug at him again.

Anna and Alex returned. A lot of wind and rain blew in with them and for a while, the dogs barged about, knocking things over and stealing all the attention. Alex gave Jack a tight nod and set about building up the fire.

‘So, how are you, Jack?’ Anna said, filling the kettle. She leant back against the kitchen range and folded her arms. There was rain in her hair and mud on her boots, and she had a huge diamond ring on her left hand.

Jack put the mug down carefully. ‘I might need some help answering that.’

She held his eyes for a long moment, then when she was sure he was joking, released a sudden smile. Alex stood up from the fire, obviously aware of the empathy between Jack and Anna and the huge grin on Danny’s face.

‘What, if anything, are you doing about the farm?’ Alex said to Jack. ‘We want a quick sale. You spent enough time looking over the place and making a fancy brochure, all of which you’ll charge us for. Where are the buyers?’

‘I’m not charging for the brochure,’ Jack said. ‘Any other business is between Anna and my father.’

‘Let’s not make an issue of this,’ Anna said. ‘Jack’s got enough on his plate at the moment.’

She began to spoon coffee into cups, all of which only seemed to annoy Alex. He grabbed his coat and made for the door.

'Where are you going?' Anna said.

'Home! You're obviously going to be tied up here.'

As an afterthought, he came back to give her a peck on the cheek and a self-conscious hug, knowing that Jack and Danny were watching. 'Pick you up tomorrow, around eight.'

Danny mouthed, 'What a twat,' in Jack's direction.

When he'd gone, Anna said, 'Thanks for not saying anything.'

'What do you mean?' Jack asked, knowing full well what she meant but wanting her to talk about it.

'Alex doesn't know about the American, about our stalling tactics.'

'Why does he want a quick sale?'

'Because the trout farm is already under offer. He wants us to pool our resources, move away from here, and open a restaurant,' she said, plumping up the cushions on the little sofa so that Jack couldn't see her face.

She sat down and looked into her coffee. 'Did you manage to speak to Oliver?'

'Are you doing anything tonight?' he heard himself say.

'Why?'

'Can I take you out?'

While Anna was booking an early table at the Castle View Inn, Danny looked over the top of his newspaper. 'Cod-piece won't like you baiting his girl fish with a big hook like that.'

'What's it got to do with him?'

'Everything. He's getting hitched to her and he's the moody, jealous type.'

The Inn was about two miles down the Conwy valley, flanking the estuary and festooned with a lot of white fairy lights and overgrown ivy. Inside, it was full of bright fires and a genuine oldness. Jack ordered a rare steak and a bottle of Sancerre then allowed himself to study the woman.

She was so natural, and the opposite to Patsy in almost every way. Everything about Anna was soft and rounded, with slow, positive movements. She was a rather private person, and whatever was said to her in confidence never went any further. Her personality appealed to Jack enormously.

When he was younger, he'd liked everything to be up-front. Was this, and the fact that she was his opposite, the attraction with Anna now? Or maybe it was just his vulnerability. They'd always had a strong bond, especially physically. Seeing her again evoked a lot of memories, of what they'd done and how they were together. It had been a sensual rollercoaster ride discovering things about Anna Williams, and about himself as well.

Anna peeped at him over the top of the menu, her smile lighting her eyes. 'Why are you watching me like that?'

'I'm just thinking how good it is to be doing something pleasurable, that's all.'

'You were miles away.'

'Sorry. Actually, I was thinking about when we were at college.'

'Do … do you remember when we got suspended for having sex in the caretakers' shed?'

'Yeah! Course I do. I can still remember the smell of the potting compost and the erotic shapes of the watering cans.'

Dying to laugh, but determined not to lose it in a public place, Anna went back to the menu but she kept looking at him over the top, her eyes dancing with amusement.

The food came and they talked about Josh and Oliver.

'It's amazing how well they get on,' Anna said, buttering a bread roll.

Jack looked at his side salad and removed all the onions. 'He blames me, you know, for this mess with

Patsy.'

'I take it the situation at home is still strained?'

'Do you want to hear about it?'

'Only if you want to tell me. I don't mind listening.'

Anna listened a lot, and made little comment.

'It wouldn't be so bad if Lottie was with me, instead of being dragged across bloody France with her arm in a sling.'

'Come on, Jack, that isn't Patsy's style. She won't have been dragged anywhere. They'll have travelled first class and be staying in a big, swanky hotel in Paris,' she said, finishing a bowl of crème brûlée with relish. 'You should have had some of this.'

Then she caught the look on his face, and covered his hand with hers. She had short, blunt nails, and there were some speckles of paint on her arm. 'I'm sorry,' she said quietly. 'I didn't mean to sound flippant.'

'I know you didn't. I think I'm reaching the stage where self-doubt kicks in.'

'Don't let it kick too hard,' she said, and her eyes locked on to his. They were deep, dark midnight blue, like the lake by Gwern Farm.

'What does Llyn Gwyllt mean?' he said.

She corrected his pronunciation and watched the cream swirl round in her coffee. 'It means wild water. Why?'

'Just wondered.'

It was still only early when they wandered out to the car park. Anna hugged her coat around herself and looked up at the stars.

'I need half a cigarette,' Jack said, leaning against the car and lighting one. 'You don't mind, do you? I seem to have slipped back into the habit.'

'No, I don't mind,' Anna said, looking at the Aston Martin. 'Redman Estates must be doing well.'

'It's OK. I just hope it's still there for Ollie.'

'What do you mean?'

'If Patsy has her way she'll want at least half the business, and that's just the start, isn't it? It's likely to include the house and Charlotte, then it's only a matter of time before I lose Ollie,' Jack said and ground out his cigarette. He felt drained, as if saying his fears out loud made them real.

Anna took hold of his hands. 'I know you. You don't deserve any of this.'

He pulled her closer. Her arms went around him without the slightest hesitation. Jack was touched by the depth of feeling in her embrace and hugged her back. It had been a long time since anyone had put their arms around him in such a way. He didn't want her to stop holding on to him. He felt if she stopped then he'd keel over in the car park. He told her, and she held him tighter.

'I'm falling to bits, Anna,' he said over her shoulder.

'No, you're not.'

When he began to kiss her it was as if she was curious to test the chemistry. He could feel her hands under his jacket and she leant against him with such energy it was like all the years had fallen away. Their bodies knew each other.

Her face was slightly wet, and he kissed around her eyes, not knowing whether it was rain or tears.

'Why is it always the wrong time for us?' he whispered into her hair.

Jack drove back along the dark lanes in a state of hopeless agitation. He knew Anna felt the same because she simply stared out of the passenger window. He picked up her hand.

'Anna, talk to me.'

'You drive too fast,' she said, then turned to smile at him briefly. Her eyes were glassy. 'Jack, it was just a kiss.'

No, it wasn't. 'I know.'

At the farm, Alex's car was there. Anna took a few

minutes to twist her hair back up into its wild knot, just like she used to whenever they'd been together.

'I feel sixteen again,' she said, with a little laugh, then realised the irony of what she'd said. The smile vanished and she fumbled with the car door.

Josh and Oliver were talking about Utopia and making toast in the kitchen. Alex was there, waiting.

'I didn't expect you to come back.'

'Well, I got through my paperwork. Thought I'd come back and have a nightcap with you, but you were out,' he said, looking at Jack accusingly.

'We were reminiscing about the old days,' Jack said.

'Dad, can Josh come back with us for a few days?' Oliver said. He looked belligerent, daring Jack to say no. 'We need a keyboard player for the gig next week and he's a better singer than Tattoo.'

'That wouldn't be difficult,' Jack said. 'No offence, Josh.'

'That's a great idea,' said Alex, clutching Anna around her waist. 'We could spend some time alone,' he said into her neck.

'That all depends on what Jack wants to do,' she said, her eyes boring into his.

Jack said nothing. What he wanted to do didn't fit in with the general order of things, so that was out.

'That's settled, then. I can collect Josh, or he can come home on the train,' Alex said pleasantly, then set about helping the boys load Jack's car with a keyboard and a lot of cables.

'Smart car,' Josh said to Jack, then argued with Alex about the getting home arrangements. Josh looked a lot like Anna, with long, curly hair, olive skin, and dark eyes. Anna had said he was part Welsh, part Italian, but beyond that, Jack realised with a pang of regret he knew little else because he'd always been too busy talking about himself.

She came out of the house at the last minute, with some

of the dogs in tow, and leant in the car window.

'Are you sure about this?'

'Yeah, it'll be good for Ollie, and they'll keep me company,' he said truthfully, recalling the silence of the house and the empty beds. 'I hate being on my own.'

'So does Alex,' she said, glancing back at the house. 'He and Josh don't really get on. They're both hot tempered and jealous.'

'It must be difficult,' Jack said, trying to be impartial but relishing the thought nevertheless.

'It's New Year tomorrow. Do you mind if I call Josh around midnight?'

'No,' Jack said, starting the engine. 'And don't worry about picking him up. We'll sort something out.'

He watched her walk back to the farmhouse, her head down against the horizontal rain.

Chapter Six

Anna

Anna was in Hilly's kitchen, which was only marginally less messy than her own and littered with non-kitchen items such as halters, buckets of bran mash covered with a sack, and tail bandages waiting to be repaired.

'Come on, let's see the ring again!' Hilly said, grasping Anna's hand and pulling a childish expression of jealousy. 'Alex must have sold a lot of fish to get this.'

'It's a family heirloom. It wouldn't be my choice,' Anna said. 'It's far too ostentatious.'

'Oh, don't be so tasteful!' She sank into a chair opposite Anna with a teapot and a tray full of sandwiches and biscuits, and began to pour the tea. 'Do I detect an air of malaise?'

'Something like that. Jack took me out to dinner.'

'Uh huh, so that's what it is.'

'What do you think of Jack?'

'Me? I think he's seriously attractive. He's a mature version of Danny with more power and loads of brass. I mean, what else is there?' she said, tearing open the packet of biscuits.

'Be serious.'

'I am, I am!' she said, her mouth full of crumbs. 'He's not flash either, except for his car, but we'll allow him that because he's a man. He smells gorgeous, so that's another good point.'

'How do you know that?'

'He kissed me goodbye that time he came to dinner at

yours,' Hilly said, then lowered her voice. 'There was a subtle hint of something expensive that could only be detected by close contact with his skin. Now that is classy.'

She went back to dunking biscuits. Anna folded her arms impatiently.

'So that's your complete resume of Jack Redman?'

'Come on, I don't really know him. You're the one with insider information. Anyway, I don't see what your problem is.'

'The problem is,' Anna began. 'The problem is, if I'm supposed to be engaged to Alex, why did I let Jack kiss me in the car park? Why did I kiss him back like my life depended on it?' she went on, then had to stop to find a tissue in her bag. Her eyes were smarting and she had an uncomfortable feeling in her throat, which was making her voice wobble. 'I don't understand where all these feelings have come from. Jack and I finished more than twenty years ago.'

This sort of outburst was unusual for Anna and Hilly was instantly subdued. 'I'm sorry, love, I didn't realise. He's really unsettled you, hasn't he?'

Hilly pushed the tea to one side and went to find a bottle of wine. After a moment of contemplation, she said, 'Was it any good, then, the snog in the car park?'

Anna smiled and wiped her eyes, while Hilly poured the wine. 'You don't think he's playing the sympathy card on you?'

'No,' Anna said emphatically, and drank her wine too quickly. 'No, it's nothing like that.'

'I mean, I feel sorry for him, but you don't really want to get involved with all his problems. At least Alex is baggage-free, if you don't count his mother,' Hilly said, refilling Anna's glass and grabbing a sandwich. 'So, what's this Patsy like then?'

At the mention of Patsy, Anna came back to life and

began to search the contents of her copious bag. 'She was, and likely still is, absolutely heart-stopping. Every male in the entire college wanted her, and I'm not exaggerating.'

'Oh, come on, no one is that gorgeous, not to everyone,' Hilly said. She looked at the photographs Anna slid across the table. Slowly, she stopped chewing. 'OK, you're right, she's stunning.'

They both laughed. Hilly wiped the crumbs off her fingers and scrutinised the pictures more carefully. 'How old are you here?'

'We were about eighteen, nineteen, Patsy a year younger.'

'So what happened?'

Anna had thought about this intense period of her life so many times, but it wasn't easy telling someone else. It all sounded silly and adolescent, so she just stuck to the facts.

Her perception of Jack changed slowly at High School, and losing her virginity to him at some festival in Cornwall changed Anna forever. For two years, they were inseparable and even thinking about that time now filled her with the same raw emotions. Despite the fact that Anna had the nagging feeling she was only on borrowed time with someone as high profile as Jack Redman, she was sixteen and head over heels in love for the first time, so there didn't seem much point in spoiling everything.

Then Patsy had come on the scene. Anna befriended her because she had just moved to Manchester and didn't know anyone.

'So, she became part of our group: Jack and me, a lad called Simon Banks, Tim, and a couple of others I can't remember.' Anna twiddled the stem of her wine glass. 'Everyone was dazzled by her, including Jack, and Patsy made it obvious she was dazzled by him.'

Hilly nodded and turned her mouth down. 'I know what happens next.'

'I suppose they were very alike, ambitious and passionate, always arguing, but they looked right together,' she admitted with a wan smile. She remembered Patsy striding down the street with Jack driving slowly after her, winding the window down, and calling, 'Patsy! Get in the car.'

'No, I don't want to see you again.'

It only ever lasted a day or two at most, and then they resumed kissing and cuddling in the college corridors. Anna saw it coming, but was totally unprepared for the unbearable pain of losing him, not only as a lover but also as a close, close friend.

'You must have been devastated,' Hilly said, unusually sympathetic.

'It was so awful. I failed all my exams, had to re-sit everything a year later. Those two years were the happiest and the most miserable times of my life.'

'Then Patsy got pregnant, end of story?'

It hadn't happened as neatly as that. Anna and Patsy were sharing a house with Simon Banks – and Patsy sometimes shared a bed with Simon. This was something Anna knew for certain because she had caught them once. She could remember word for word the ensuing argument between the three of them.

'Is he on these pictures, this Simon?' Hilly said.

Anna pointed him out. 'Simon was attractive enough, quite a lot older than us but a bit of a loser, carefree and careless, dabbled in things he shouldn't. You know the sort. He was always drooling over Patsy and she loved all the attention. Anyway, the next thing you know, she announces she's pregnant.'

'Go on,' Hilly said urgently.

'The very next week, she's showing off a diamond ring from Jack! I couldn't face any of them after that, so I went away for a while, ran away, I suppose.' Anna took a deep breath. She had to tell the next part carefully.

‘Then, about a year or so later, I bumped into Simon in a club, roaring drunk. He told me he was still seeing Patsy even though she was married to Jack by then and they’d had a little girl, Chelsey. He was full of swagger, boasting about their affair. I don’t know what happened after that.’

Anna could remember the rest of the conversation like it was yesterday, but it was in the past, and it had to stay there. If Hilly noticed her cloaked expression, she had the good sense not to pry.

‘Well, the way I see it is this,’ Hilly said, pulling lettuce out of her sandwich. ‘You have three options. Option one, have nothing further to do with him. Option two, have a sexy fling with him and get any leftover feelings out of your system.’

‘I don’t like that one.’

‘Why?’ Hilly said, meeting her eyes. Anna didn’t respond. ‘Don’t write it off just yet. Option three, just do nothing, stay at Gwern Farm, marry no one, have no plans, and see what develops out of the ashes … Anna?’

Anna looked away first and began to fumble with the photographs, putting them back into their tatty folder. Hilly put an arm around her.

‘It could be nostalgia. No one forgets their first love.’

Anna didn’t trust herself to speak, because her emotions had come to the surface again.

‘Looks like option one, then,’ Hilly said, disappointed, ‘just to be on the safe side.’

‘I have to move on,’ Anna said quietly, ‘with Alex.’

Alex collected her at eight for the New Year’s Eve dinner at The King Edward. Leo and Isabel saw them in the bar and came over. Anna liked Isabel, but found Leo a bit intimidating. He settled his big frame next to Alex. Leo was similar to Jack in some of his mannerisms and the way he cut straight to the point, but sometimes he lacked his son’s sensitivity.

'Let me get some drinks,' Leo said.

'Only if you stop talking business,' Isabel said, sitting next to Anna. 'These people have come out to be sociable.'

'I don't want to talk about the farm,' Anna said then felt a bit silly, but Isabel came to her rescue.

'Of course you don't. Now what's this I hear about Oliver and Josh making friends?'

Anna felt a little lurch at the pit of her stomach. It was odd to think that her son was at Jack Redman's house. Jack Redman. When he'd turned up at the farm out of the blue, she'd thought her heart would leap out of her chest it was banging so hard.

Isabel began to talk about Patsy, and Anna looked at her more closely. She wore no makeup, well-made but rather plain clothes, and very understated expensive jewellery. Jack had the same unusual grey eyes as his mother and the same dark blond hair, although Isabel lightened hers. Jack's used to be a mess all the time, and was always getting into trouble at school because he wore it too long. It was only slightly more under control now.

'I can't forgive Patsy for doing this,' Isabel said to Anna. 'And to take Lottie away like that! It's wicked. Jack is distraught. He thinks the world of that little girl. We all do.'

Just after midnight; once the conga had gone into the street, Isabel announced she was going to telephone Danny, Jack, and Kate.

'What for?' Leo called over the music, 'What's wrong?'

'What about you, Anna?' Isabel said, giving her husband a withering look. 'Do you want a quick word with Josh?'

'I did say I'd call.'

'Come to our rooms, it's quieter there.'

Anna followed Isabel up the sweeping staircase, aware

that Alex was not happy, and sat in Leo and Isabel's lounge, staring at Jack and Patsy's wedding photograph on the fireplace. Despite the huge passing of years Anna still felt oddly connected to this family – perhaps because Leo and Isabel could remember her parents when they'd been alive.

Isabel chatted away to Kate over the phone and her eldest grandchild who was still awake, then tried to contact Danny on his mobile before she gave up.

'Oh, he's probably in bed with someone,' she said, and made Anna laugh with her candid philosophy, 'He thinks because he's switched that phone off I won't guess what he's up to.'

Isabel spoke to Jack for a long time. 'Are you sure you're all right? I'm not fussing. I worry about you.'

She had more or less the same conversation with Oliver, then passed the receiver to Anna.

'Mum,' Josh said, 'I don't want Alex picking me up.'

'Happy New Year!'

'Will you come up the day after tomorrow? I'm playing keyboard.'

'Josh, I can't. I can't leave the puppies and the Land Rover wouldn't make it.'

'Come on, Mum, you know you can. You can leave them with Dan and borrow a car.'

Anna knew she could. She looked at the ceiling, closed her eyes, and took a deep breath. 'OK. Let me talk to Jack about it.'

He came on the line and they exchanged the usual greetings. 'I get the drift Josh wants you to come to this gig,' he said.

'Would that be a problem?'

'No, not this end.'

'I don't know what time I can borrow Hilly's car. I don't even know where you live. You know what I'm like with directions,' she said, chewing her bottom lip.

‘Well, I’ll be in the office all day Tuesday, so go there. You remember where it is?’

‘Yes … yes, of course.’

Anna looked at the receiver after she’d replaced it and wondered about the wisdom of what she was doing. It wasn’t option one, that was for sure.

Alex wasn’t pleased.

‘I’m going to see Josh on stage. I’ve never seen him perform before,’ Anna said, back at the farm. Alex ignored her. She may as well have said nothing.

‘It’s bad enough we spend all evening in the company of his parents without you going down to his house!’

‘Oh, shut up Alex!’ Anna said, and threw her coat across the sofa. ‘Jack and I are old friends. I’ve known his parents for years, that’s all there is to it,’ she said, making for the kettle. ‘Do you want tea or coffee, or shall we have a brandy?’

‘I don’t want anything. What’s this I hear about you having a cash buyer for the farm?’

She turned to face him then. Leo must have said something. ‘I don’t want to sell to the American,’ she said quietly.

‘Give me one good reason – or is it a secret between you and Jack?’

The dogs all cocked their heads and slowly wagged their tails, disliking the atmosphere and waiting for the reassurance of Anna’s voice.

‘You just don’t understand about this place, do you?’

‘No, the bit I don’t understand is you,’ he said, snatching up his car keys.

On Tuesday, Anna left Danny in charge of the puppies. He was sprawled in front of the fire watching a football match, with two of them asleep on his chest.

‘Don’t forget to make sure they all get a feed every two

hours,' she said, checking the contents of her bag and searching the kitchen drawers for keys.

'What do I tell Alex if he calls again? He's phoned twice already and I told him you were going to meet Jack,' Danny said, but she wasn't listening.

'And Porridge needs to have an anti-inflammatory pill at six o'clock,' she said, pulling on an old sheepskin jacket. 'If she won't take it, crush it up in some of that custard. Oh, and don't forget to shut the chickens in!'

'Anna, just clear off, will you?'

Smiling to herself, Anna bounced down the rough track in Hilly's little Peugeot. It was cold, windy, and raining sideways, which was pretty standard mountain weather for the winter. Sometimes it stayed like that till the end of June. She pipped the horn at some sheep in the road and they turned to look at her and rushed in three different directions.

The little town was clogged up with a local produce market, but it didn't take much to bring traffic to a crawl in the medieval streets. The car rumbled over cobbled roads, losing its faint radio signal altogether. The castle and the walls had a handful of visitors walking the battlements with binoculars and pointing across the quay at the leaping, rolling boats.

For a while, the scenery was the winter green and rich brown bracken of the hills, with flashes of opaque water, then quickly lapsed into motorway grey created by concrete. Anna followed the signs to Manchester International Airport. Ten minutes later, she was in Wilmslow and looking for a parking space.

It felt odd, wandering around the shops. She didn't really want to; she was putting off entering the smart-looking offices of Redman Estates on the main road. When she finally pushed open the heavy glass door and approached the desk, a very polished blonde in a black suit and a lacy white shirt told her that Jack was not in the office.

'I'm Clare. Can I help?'

'Not really, it's more a personal call. I can come back later,' Anna said, already trying to escape.

'Oh, he won't be long. If you want to wait I'll let him know you're here,' Clare said, smiling and indicating that Anna sit in the available chair. She picked up the telephone and pressed a speed-dial number.

'Jack? The vendor wants to discuss the claim for the collapsed wall at Tanner's Road … well, Robin Crossly says he won't go higher than four hundred and fifty without the use of the paddocks. What shall I do?' Clare said, making very efficient notes. She looked at Anna. 'You've got a visitor. Anna Williams. What did you say about Craig Road, give the tenant two months' notice?'

Anna listened to the increasingly complicated call and began to feel nervous. Jack was busy, and she felt out of her depth. She should have agreed with Alex and made Josh get the train home.

When the call finished, Clare motioned Anna to follow her to Jack's office. 'He says he's sorry he's not here, but he's on his way back and to wait for him. Would you like some coffee?'

Jack's office was the biggest mess she had ever seen. Amongst the piles of files and correspondence was a small photograph of Patsy and the children. She forced herself not to look at it. When the coffee came, it was the real thing, strong and Italian. She wondered if all his visitors got the real thing.

Minutes later, Jack returned. When she looked at his tired, grey eyes, she knew what her out of depth feelings were all about. There was something about this man that drew her. It wasn't just sexual chemistry; it was the unfinished history and the expectation of some kind of conclusion.

'Hi, sorry I wasn't in,' Jack said. He looked so different

in a dark grey suit that at first it threw her and she didn't say anything. Their lifestyles were at opposite ends of a pole, but this somehow made the attraction more powerful. This was a part of him she sensed, but didn't know. This was his territory. He dropped a briefcase to the floor, and smiled slowly at her.

'I didn't think you'd come.'

'No … neither did I.'

Immediately, both telephones began ringing on the desk and dispelled the awkward silence. She watched as he dealt with the calls and asked Clare for coffee. He looked understandably strained, but remained calmly professional with the clients and friendly with the staff. Anna knew he had a frightening temper but she could tell he was respected here. He had just enough charisma to help him get away with the occasional rough edge. As she drank her coffee, Anna realised she was waiting for him to say they were making a big mistake so she could happily go home with Josh and tell Hilly option one was still the one for her.

'Look, Anna, I don't know why it's so bloody manic in here today, do you want to go to the house and I'll meet you there later? It's The Links, number six,' he said, pulling a key off a fob of about fifty others. 'The boys are rehearsing till five so you'll have the place to yourself.'

The thought of being in Jack and Patsy's house was a bit scary. She hadn't expected it, but Anna had to admit she was deeply curious.

'The alarm isn't on,' Jack said, passing her the key. 'It doesn't work, not since Lottie poured Ribena into it.'

Anna laughed at the serious way he said this, reminding her of other times, when things he'd said weeks ago would suddenly pop into her head and set her off giggling.

The Links consisted of a cul-de-sac of big Victorian houses bordering the Prestbury golf course. Anna recalled Patsy talking covetously about these houses when they were still at college. Although they weren't Anna's style, it was difficult not to be impressed.

Anna wandered through the downstairs rooms, not wanting to touch anything or remove her coat. She liked the kitchen; huge, oak, and contemporary, but mixed with traditional touches like old cooking pots and wall clocks. Through the glass-panelled doors was a long conservatory, full of cascading plants and leather furniture. In the sitting room she found a game of chess on the coffee table, still in mid-play, and Josh's sweatshirt slung over the sofa. Newspapers, laptops, and cables were strewn all over the floor, and a couple of files from the office were emblazoned with Jack's scrawl.

Next to this was a formal dining room, all dark woods and white walls. The curtains were half closed and a film of dust lay on the gilded mirror. The glass-topped table still had the remains of burnt down candles and used napkins spoiling its polished surface, and an overpowering perfume from the dead lilies on the sideboard filled the air. Anna stopped for a moment to inhale the scent of her favourite flowers.

She went up the staircase to the galleried landing, pausing at the long stained-glass window which overlooked the fifth hole of the golf course. Through one of the open bedroom doors she could see some of Josh's clothes, mostly on the floor. Next door was a little girl's room, so beautifully furnished and decorated that Anna just stared at it, especially at the creased photograph of Benson on the bedside table. On the floor, there were some half-opened Christmas presents, an unfinished puzzle, and the little stuffed dog that Lottie had had with her at the farm. This little detail was strangely upsetting, as if the child had been snatched away with no time or thought.

Oliver's room was black, silver, and purple and humming with electrical equipment. A Redman Estates For Sale board hung over the bed, covered with pictures and photographs. Anna glanced in the two bathrooms, one white and pretty and the other dark marble and masculine, and came to the main bedroom.

The door was wide open, the bed unmade and cluttered with Jack's clothes. She didn't want to go into this room, but knew the pull was inevitable. And anyway, who would know?

It was all so Patsy. Anna could feel her scalp prickle by simply looking at the glass bottles of perfume and the choice of décor; all polished woods and vibrant colour. Only the film of muslin over the canopied bed softened the room. She could imagine Patsy striding into this room and flinging open all the wardrobes. The en-suite was like an extension of Patsy's salon, although it looked as though Jack had swept a pile of bottles, false nails, and hairbrushes to one side and filled the resulting small area with male necessities. A faint trace of his aftershave hung in the air.

The house made Anna feel uncomfortable. It revealed too much about its owners. It was solid, held together with the years of their relationship. No way was Patsy going to leave all this without a fight, and she'd want to win. Jack and Patsy's presence was almost tangible, making Anna feel like an unwelcome intruder.

Why was she putting herself through all this? She'd done exactly the same thing before when Jack and Patsy had had their silly misunderstandings and arguments, then had to stand by and watch their passionate reunions. If she clung to any notion that saw her with Jack, she was surely on a path set to self-destruct.

Then she saw the photograph on the dressing table, and took a deep breath. This was the child she had never seen, the catalyst in the triangle of their relationship. Chelsey was not a child now, more a young woman with long, fair hair and her mother's eyes. Anna picked up the silver frame and sat on the edge of the bed to study the portrait more closely, lost in thought.

Insulated by the Victorian walls and heavy furnishings, she didn't hear the soft purr of a car engine or the doors opening and closing downstairs. Anna was only aware that someone was in the house when it was too late. Footsteps were coming up the thickly carpeted stairs.

'What the hell are you doing in my house?' Patsy said. Her voice was low with anger and her eyes glittered.

Anna got slowly to her feet, taking advantage of her height, but the photograph felt like lead in her hands. For a moment they both stared at it.

'You!' Patsy said through gritted teeth, 'You of all people!'

'I'm not here to cause trouble.'

'So why are you here? Did Jack tell you to wait in our bedroom?'

'No,' Anna said quickly, 'I'm waiting for my son.'

'Oh, I see. And you thought you'd have a good look round in the meantime?'

Anna couldn't disagree with her, but she wasn't going to be made to say it. She weighed the frame in her hand and put it carefully on to the dressing table. 'I don't think you have any right to preach morals.'

'What's that supposed to mean?'

'I can't believe you need to ask.'

'Jack had no right telling you our business,' Patsy said angrily. 'And as usual, you've only got his side of the story.'

'I wasn't referring to your present dilemma.' Anna moved round to Patsy's side of the bed, knowing she had the upper hand. 'I was thinking about something that happened a long time ago … it's funny how history repeats itself.'

'Get out of my house, you bitch!'

Anna pushed past her and deftly collected all of Josh's things, then quickly went down the stairs, all control gone.

She felt sick and her legs had gone to jelly. Meeting Patsy like that had to be one of her worst nightmares. She could hear the sounds of cases being pulled out and hangers falling down. As Anna was putting Josh's things into the car, Patsy began to sling bags into the boot of her Mercedes. Then, maybe because she was too strung up, she stopped trying to pack anything and began to throw stuff haphazardly all over the seats; shoes and toys, Lottie's clothes still on hangers.

Just as Anna was about to reverse, Jack arrived, saw Patsy's car, and positioned the Aston Martin on an angle, blocking the driveway and squashing some ornamental shrubs.

'Jack, move your car!' Patsy yelled.

'No. Where's my daughter?'

She got into her car and started the engine. 'If you don't move it I'll drive through it!' she said through a small gap in the window. Jack pulled the door open and dragged her out.

'You can't go anywhere, so go back inside and calm down,' he said, still holding onto her wrist. 'I need to talk to you.'

They glared at each other before Patsy dissolved into tears. Jack let go of her and watched with a set face as she went into the house and slammed the door.

He came over to Anna's car. Anna wound the window down, but he looked mostly at Hillyme mud-splattered paintwork and the coat hanger aerial.

'Tell me where Josh is. I want to go home,' she said.

'What about the gig? You can't go home just because Patsy's had a bloody tantrum.'

Anna closed her eyes and took a deep breath, knowing he was right and that she couldn't let Josh down. He gave her the directions to the village hall.

'I'll meet you there at seven,' he said, not letting her eyes go until he was sure of her agreement.

‘OK, OK I’ll see you there,’ Anna said, and waited for Jack to move his car so she could drive away. In the rear-view mirror, she saw him park bumper to bumper with the Mercedes, which was packed full to the windows, Dudley pressed against the glass like a prisoner.

Prestbury village hall was a large black and white timbered building on the outskirts of the green belt. A poster nailed to the door showed Utopia were the third act. There was no sign of Jack and it was after seven, so Anna went inside and positioned herself at the back, where she could see the door.

It was already hot and noisy, with a practice session in progress and a lot of jostling parents trying to talk over the music, ferrying chairs and drinks. Anna worried that Jack would turn up with Patsy and they’d all have to stand together but he appeared halfway through the second act, mercifully alone, in a denim shirt wrongly buttoned up over a pair of faded black jeans. He passed her some white wine in a plastic cup and since the music was too loud to communicate other than in sign language, mouthed what looked like ‘sorry’ to her. Anna wasn’t sure if he was apologising for the scene at the house, being an hour late, or the plastic cup.

The Street left the stage and the general din diminished into noisy conversation again. Jack leant against the wall and made a joke about needing some industrial earplugs.

‘Anna, I’m sorry about before. I had no idea she’d just turn up like that.’

As she watched him patting all his pockets, hunting for his mobile phone, Anna waited for the news that Patsy had come back to him and the baby was his. She was almost praying for it so she could go home, content in the knowledge that things would return to their pigeon holes as before.

‘I’ve had an idea, about the farm,’ he said, catching her

off guard.

'Like what? What do you mean?'

'Don't look so worried,' he said, glancing at his phone message. 'How would you feel if *I* bought it?'

There was a tremendous drum roll from the stage amongst the sound checks and tuning up.

'Why?' Anna shouted. 'What would you want with a falling-down farm in Snowdonia?'

'An investment. Redman Estates could lease it to you so you could carry on living there as estate manager. I'd be responsible for all the repairs.'

'What do you mean, estate manager?'

'It means whatever you want. I thought you wanted to run a restaurant? Well you could do that at the farm, go upmarket with the B&B. You've got the creative skills,' he said, pausing to look at her. 'And I've got everything else.'

'And what happens when we fall out?'

'You walk away with the cash and I find another manager,' he said, then shrugged and looked back at the stage. 'No one can lose.'

'Where does Alex fit in?'

'With you, if he loves you.'

Utopia walked on to the stage to an uproar of stamping and shouting, whooping and whistling. For a while, Josh and Oliver and the other members of the band distracted Anna. The music was strange to her but it touched something in her subconscious, something new and alive.

Eventually, she glanced at Jack but he was absorbed with watching the stage. His idea was clever, and typical of him. He loved to be in control and it would put Alex at a distinct disadvantage. It had the possibilities of putting them all at a disadvantage if Patsy decided to play more serious games with Jack's finances. Between them all, including the American and Alex, Anna was beginning to feel out-manoeuvred. Before she'd walked into Redman Estates everything had been so simple.

The last track was a cover version of an old Fleetwood Mac song, 'Gypsy'. It was the song she and Jack had danced to many times in his flat. To hear Josh sing a perfectly accurate but sped up version was odd.

'Did you know they were doing this?' she yelled at Jack, almost angry with the feelings it unearthed and the confusing way it was mixed up with her son.

'Yeah,' he said, then frowned at her expression, 'What's the matter?'

Josh and Oliver found them some time later, trailed by a crowd of teenagers and looking hot and sweaty but struggling to hide any excitement because it wasn't very cool.

'Dad, what are you doing here?' Oliver groaned. 'Sardine's picking us up. We're crashing there.'

'Who? Anyway not tonight, your mother's at home. She wants to see you.'

Sulky and subdued, Oliver helped load up Anna's car with Josh's equipment, in between giving his father dirty looks and grinning at some dark girl who seemed bent on following him about. All Anna could see in her mind was Patsy sitting in the conservatory, waiting. She kept the picture there, to keep her emotions focused.

When she was in the driver's seat, Jack made her wind the window down, but it stuck halfway. He put his head sideways into the gap.

'Anna, think about what I said. Talk to Alex about it.'

'No!' she said, more irritably than she meant to. 'It wouldn't work.'

'Why the hell not?'

Because we'd end up in bed together. 'All my life I've let my heart rule my head, especially where you've been concerned. It's time I let my head sort this out!'

'In that case you can see sense in what I'm saying. Who told you that garbage about hearts and heads anyway?'

'Alex,' she snapped, and struggled to wind the window back up. Jack stood back from the car with a hangdog expression, frustrated because he could see an opportunity that wasn't going his way. He was only interested in another business deal. Anna started the engine and Jack shouted something after her, but she couldn't hear, didn't want to. She pulled away, and when she looked through the mirror he was standing in the biting cold wind and sleet, his arms by his side and his shirt flapping about. She tried to talk to Josh but he answered in monosyllables. Every blasted song on the radio had lyrics that sharply corresponded with the triangle between Jack and herself, Patsy and Simon Banks and all the way to the motorway distinctive red and cream Redman Estates For Sale boards were dotted about in gardens. Like the one she had at home.

The dirty, sodden leaves of winter skittered across the beam of the headlights and wet snow splattered onto the windscreen as she negotiated the complex junctions around the airport. Where the North Wales signs started to crop up around Chester, it quickly became a whirlwind of white confusion in the blackness. She flicked on the windscreen wipers to full speed.

'Why did you have a go at Jack?' Josh said, eventually. 'He took us for a Chinese banquet on New Year's Eve somewhere in Manchester with all these other people. Then we went to this weird, late night movie,' he said, turning to look at her. 'Jack's OK.'

'I know,' Anna said, feeling a well of tears throb behind her eyes.

'So why did you go and spoil everything and have a go at him?'

'I didn't, not really,' Anna said, trying to wipe away the silent river of tears that ran down her face, making a mockery of everything she'd tried to tell herself. She couldn't hold that vision any longer of Patsy sitting waiting. All she could see was Jack in the car park, an unshaven, windblown muddle, calling her name as if a business deal was the very last thing on his mind. Damn the man.

As Anna reached for another tissue, the steering wheel felt too light. In fact, everything felt wrong. She grabbed it with both hands and checked all the mirrors, forcing her concentration back to driving. It was a badly lit section of road, but there was nothing travelling behind her.

'Why are you crying?' Josh said moodily.

But Anna wasn't listening any more. She tried slowing the car by moving down a gear, but the road was so greasy there was little she could do to stop the car veering sideways. In the beam of the headlights was nothing but racing tarmac and a bewildering white maelstrom of snow. Josh, suddenly aware of the mood change, sat upright, holding the seatbelt.

'Mum! Do something!'

'I can't!' she said, stamping on the brake. 'Nothing's happening!'

In a panic, Anna yanked on the handbrake, but this seemed to make the slide worse and the screech of tyres added to the sensation of being out of control.

'We're going to crash,' Josh said, staring ahead.

The car slewed across the road towards the crash barriers for several frightening seconds. Anna instinctively flung her arm across Josh.

'Get down! Oh my God, no!'

She remembered letting go of the steering wheel and covering her face. The noise and sensation of the impact was quite terrifying. At first, it seemed to Anna that a bomb must have exploded. Then she remembered nothing, nothing at all.

Chapter Seven

Jack

Jack was staring at the photograph of his wife above the fireplace. It had been taken two years ago, around the time she must have started her affair. Patricia Lloyd-Marshall. Sweet little Patsy with her long, chestnut hair and her flirtatious eyes. How he loved and hated her.

'I don't want to discuss anything with you now, we'll only argue,' she said, putting a little white card onto the coffee table. 'This is my solicitor.'

Jack picked up the card and handed it back. 'And I've told you, I'm not listening to anything you say till I've got my daughter back,' he said, struggling to stay calm and in control because Oliver was upstairs and probably listening.

'How can you do this?' he went on. 'Have you any idea what this is doing to me? Worse still, what it's doing to our children?'

'What? Oliver is already way out of control.'

'And this is your way of dealing with it?' Jack said, trying not to shout. 'To leave him? To keep Lottie away from me? It's unbearable not being able to see her.'

Patsy looked away for a moment. Jack could hear his blood pounding through his head as he waited for her to say something. She was the only one who could put everything right. She had all the power. She had his daughter and she knew she could twist the knife whichever way she pleased.

'You just don't get it, do you, Jack?' She replaced the card on the table. 'You must realise I don't love you anymore.'

Her coolness flared his temper. She was acting as if she was explaining something to a small child. He got hold of her Chanel jacket and pushed his face closer to hers. She didn't flinch.

'I've already worked that out. The part I don't get is why you are torturing me with Lottie?' he said, close to tears.

He completely lost his temper and shoved her backwards into the wall cabinet. 'You know what? You're the one who's out of fucking control! You should be burnt at the *fucking* stake, you witch!'

Patsy's face cracked ever so slightly and she was about to retaliate when Oliver appeared at the conservatory door. 'Will you two just *shut up!'*

Silence fell. Jack collapsed into a chair. Satisfied, Oliver gave them both a look of utter contempt and went back upstairs.

'I knew it was a mistake to stay,' Patsy said, snatching up her handbag and keys. Jack waited till he heard the front door slam, followed by the gentle rumble of the Mercedes as it pulled off the drive.

Lighting a cigarette, he paced up and down in the conservatory, aware that the telephone was ringing, but it took him a moment to feel able to answer it. It was Danny, in a jocular mood.

'Not now, Dan.'

'Why? Is the beautiful Anna giving you an Indian head massage?'

'What?'

'Only it's not your head you need massaging really, is it?'

'I don't know what you're prattling on about, just get to

the point.'

'One of these little dogs doesn't look too good. Is Anna still there?'

'No, she left a couple of hours ago,' Jack said, glancing at the clock.

'Oh, she should be back in a bit then.'

Hanging up the phone, Jack climbed the stairs and knocked softly on Oliver's door.

'Get lost, Dad.'

'Ollie, talk to me. Please,' he said, leaning his forehead on the door, but there was no response. Feeling a wave of exhaustion, Jack went to his own room and lay on the bed. He wanted a Scotch but he didn't dare start drinking in case he needed to take a sedative. Trying to ignore cigarettes was becoming a losing battle and he easily managed to chain smoke half a packet while staring at the television with the sound turned down before the phone rang again.

'Danny? For Chrissakes what now? Phone a bloody vet.'

'She's not back. Anna, she's not back.'

Jack struggled to prop himself up and put his cigarette out. 'Have you phoned that friend of hers, Hilly?'

'Yeah, just now.'

'What about Alex?'

'No joy there, he's away looking at caffs. I don't know what to do. Do you think she's stopped somewhere?'

Jack realised what Danny was on about. A sensation like cold water trickled down his spine. It was almost one in the morning.

'I'll check it out.'

'Dan, call me back?'

When the phone rang again later, it was Hilly. Jack didn't recognise her voice at first because she was so shocked everything was coming out disjointed. The police had recovered her car – or what was left of it. The Peugeot had crashed into the motorway barriers near the Chester exit.

'I'll go to the hospital. I can be there in half an hour,' Jack said, but Hilly put him off.

'No, Jack. There'd be no point. They wouldn't let you see her. Anyway, the road conditions are terrible. We've managed to get hold of Alex,' she said, then paused. 'I'll call you in the morning when I find out where they are and what ward. OK?'

Oliver found him retching in the bathroom.

'Dad, what's the matter?' he said tentatively.

'Nothing, I'm all right,' he managed to say, and sat on the edge of the bath, realising that was what Oliver said when it was something serious. Naturally, Oliver wasn't convinced and uncharacteristically broke down in tears.

It had been years since Jack had seen his son cry like this. He got up and caught hold of him. 'Ollie, it's OK.'

'This stuff with Mum … my fault,' he said between huge, broken sobs.

'Absolutely nothing is your fault,' Jack said, struggling to hold him up. At a solid five foot six, Oliver was no lightweight. 'It's Mum and me, we've let you down. I'm so sorry.'

'You're not going to get a divorce, are you?' he said, gasping for breath.

Jack buried his face in Oliver's hair and closed his eyes. 'Ollie, don't. You'll start me off and I won't be able to stop.'

Oliver did stop sobbing eventually, and fell asleep on Jack's bed. Jack covered him with the duvet and lay down next to him. He felt completely wrung out and stared at the ceiling for five hours, although he must have eventually slept because it was light when he opened his eyes. The headache and sore throat kicked in with a vengeance, but the reason he'd woken was because someone was at the front door

It was Maria. 'Happy New Year!' she said, her words tailing off as she took in Jack's dishevelled appearance, 'You look like you've slept in those clothes.'

'Well, I've lain down in them and not really slept, to be precise.'

'Is this not a good time?' Maria said, following him into the kitchen, glancing in at the messy sitting room as she passed and looking pointedly at the overflowing basket of ironing on the stairs.

'No, but I don't think there are any good times in the immediate pipeline anyway,' Jack said, and sneezed twice. 'How are you?'

'I've come for a reference,' Maria said, her eyes everywhere; taking in the half-dead plants and the overflowing bin. 'Patsy's gone … hasn't she?'

'Is it that obvious?' Jack said, trying to fill the kettle over the pans in the sink. 'Look, Maria, you can have a reference but do you think there's any chance of some part-time housekeeping, just till you find something else? I could really use some help.'

'You're not kidding,' she said with a funny little smile, and took off her coat.

The call he'd been waiting for came while Ollie and Maria were eating scrambled eggs in the cleaned up kitchen. Jack picked up the phone in the sitting room so Ollie wouldn't hear.

'Jack? They're both sort of all right,' Hilly said.

'What do you mean, sort of?'

'Anna's really badly shaken, mild concussion, cuts, and bruises, but Josh has a shattered wrist and they think maybe a fractured collar-bone.'

'Shit!'

'That's what I said, but if you could see the state of my

car you'd say thank God.'

'I need to see her.'

'Well, don't go today, they're both out of it and Alex is playing *Holby*,' she said, then lowered her voice. 'I happen to know that Alex has a meeting tomorrow afternoon.'

Jack broke the news to Oliver, who was predictably pedantic but didn't want Jack to go in to the office, which was not like Oliver at all. He sat on the bed while Jack showered and shaved.

'How long are you going to be?'

'Not long feeling like this,' he said, swallowing some painkillers and a lot of water. 'Why don't you come with me?' he said, hunting for shirts and resorting to dark green silk. 'We'll go for some lunch at that tapas bar.'

Ollie nodded in agreement but looked at the floor. 'It's Josh's birthday today.'

Jack rubbed Oliver's shoulder, not knowing what to do about this relationship.

At the office, Clare was frantic and took his mind off anything domestic. 'The computer lost some of the tax returns and I think I've made a big mistake on the Paul Glaser account. Sorry, is there any chance you can have a look?' she said, cringing behind his back.

'No, you're sacked,' Jack said, going through his post.

'Same punishment as usual then,' she said, grinning at Oliver. 'Mr Dodds said to tell you that there was a mistake with the number of gnomes on his inventory.'

'Oh, for Chrissakes!'

'There's a postcard from Jean somewhere in that pile. Nice shirt, by the way.'

'Get her to come back,' Jack said, pulling up the Glaser account on his computer and frowning at the jumbled information. 'She never lost stuff or crashed the system.'

At least the office banter raised something approaching a smile with Oliver.

'Why is it showing three different addresses?' he said, looking over Jack's shoulder at the screen.

'Because the client has two properties here which are both tenanted, then the New York address is his own. Just add up the rental taken from last July to this month on the Broad Walk flat, then subtract full management fees. It doesn't look right,' Jack said, hiding the calculator under a file. His phone buzzed.

'You're not going to believe this,' Tim said on the other end.

'Why do I hate that line so much?'

'Margaret's pregnant!'

'And you want to break my nose, right?'

Tim laughed. 'What are you doing at the moment?'

'Wondering why I've paid the equivalent of a small house to educate my son and he can't add up,' Jack said, frowning at Oliver's calculation.

Oliver was incensed and crashed out of the office. The other telephone line began to ring and Jon motioned that he wanted a word with him from the doorway.

'Speak to you later,' Jack said, resignedly to Tim. 'Love to Margaret.'

It was a full ten minutes before Jack went after Oliver, who was scanning through Jon's magazines in the staff room.

'Ollie, it was a joke.'

'Jokes are meant to be funny,' he said, fighting back tears again.

Jack sat down and searched for the obscure skills required for dealing with the teenage psyche, but decided he just didn't have the stamina for it.

'What's all this about?' he said impatiently, knowing he was going about it the wrong way.

'Light a fag first then I'll tell you, otherwise you'll go off the deep end.'

If he'd not felt so sick and tired and in need of a small

breakdown himself, Jack might have laughed. He lit a cigarette and looked at the ceiling, wondering exactly how much nicotine it needed to take the edge off. *Please God, don't let it be drugs or pregnancies.*

'Do you think her breasts are real?' Oliver said suddenly, throwing a magazine over. Jack picked it up and looked at the picture critically, playing the same tactics.

'No, definitely not.'

'How can you tell?' Oliver said.

'We'll talk about that when we've got the serious stuff out of the way. You first.'

It transpired that Oliver was so far behind with work at school that they'd given him written warnings to sort himself out. He'd failed all his mock exams, although his results had been forecast as A star last year.

'Ollie, why?' Jack said, breathing a private sigh of relief.

Oliver struggled to tell him the next part. Last summer he'd seen his mother and another man in a parked car.

'They were, well, they were together, you know.'

'Go on.'

'I was with a couple of the other lads, and they saw them as well and it all got out of hand, the jokes and everything,' he said miserably. 'So I started bunking off a lot and the school phoned Mum and she went ballistic. Since then, everything's gone wrong,' he said, his voice full of emotion. 'You've even gone and had a row with Josh's mum.'

Jack stood up and went to the window, wondering how it was possible that one adult failing could do so much damage to the other lives entwined in the same web. Patsy's affair was like ripples on water. As time went on, the effect grew and became all-encompassing.

He looked back at Oliver's tear-stained and confused face, and put his cigarette out. The rest of the staff wouldn't be pleased about the default on the smoking ban, but Jack couldn't even be bothered to waft the smoke around or hide the forbidden ashtray.

Oliver got shakily to his feet, expecting the worst.

'Come here,' Jack said, and folded his arms around Ollie, surprised he didn't resist, but Oliver seemed to crumple, his face buried in his hands.

Someone tried to get into the staff room but Jack blocked the door with his foot.

'Not now,' he said through the little gap, and the door closed again. It sounded manic on the other side, with several phones ringing and a lot of chatter, but this was more important.

'Why doesn't she come back?' Oliver said into Jack's chest. 'She wanted me to live in France, Dad. I'm not living in bloody France!' he said angrily. 'I hate her for this.'

Hate her? Jack thought; I want to kill the bitch. I want to cut Philipe's genitals off and hang them in a public place.

'Ollie, you're not living anywhere but with me, OK? I love you. I need you with me.'

Jack wondered whether he was asking too much, if it sounded like he was asking his son to take sides in an emotional tug of war, but it also struck him that Oliver was begging to be told what to do. He didn't want monumental decisions, he wanted it taken away and passed back in smaller chunks. He wanted his dignity back.

'I can't get everything back to how it was before, you know that. As far as everything else is concerned, you'll just have to trust me,' Jack said, 'Look, just do your exams then leave school.'

'No way. I'll never catch up!'

'Sure you will. You can drop French for a start.'

'That's a better joke than your last one.'

'Is it a deal, then? Have I got a trainee manager for the summer?' Jack said, holding him at arm's length and searching his face. 'But I'm warning you, I'm not an easy touch here, not like at home.'

The look on Oliver's face was one of pure transformation. He was so overcome that it made Jack feel practically euphoric. At last he'd got something right; his instincts were spot on. He knew then that Oliver was with him in all the ways that mattered.

'I never wanted to do A levels and all that stuff Mum went on about,' Oliver said, wiping his face on his sleeve.

'I know,' Jack said, ashamed by the amount of hidden strain his son had carrying. 'Just so long as you don't expect any preferential treatment,' he said, handing him Clare's box of tissues. 'You'll get all the rubbish jobs at first, like counting Mr Dodds' gnomes.'

But now Oliver was laughing and crying at the same time. 'I don't care!'

Jon knocked for about the third time and poked his head round the door. 'What's this, *The Jeremy Kyle Show*?'

'Hey, Dad,' Oliver said, 'you were going to tell me about silicone tits.'

'Um … have I missed something?' Jon said.

When Jack and Oliver returned home in the middle of the afternoon, Maria was still trying to plough through two weeks of housework and clear away the Christmas debris. A strange-looking pie sat on the kitchen table. It was difficult to decide whether it was meant to be sweet or savoury.

'Ugh, what *is* that?' Oliver said, lifting the lid with a fork and poking its innards.

Jack was just relieved he didn't have to start washing and ironing shirts. All he wanted to do was collapse somewhere and sleep, but Maria had stripped every bed in the house, cheerfully throwing duvet covers down the stairs and opening all the windows.

'It's like having Gran here,' Oliver said, scowling again.

'Do you want to do all this stuff then?' Jack said, waggling a duster in his face.

'No way. And I'm not eating that pie, either.'

Jack slept for about fifteen hours and woke to find the television still on and several previously hot drinks on the bedside table. It seemed barely credible that he only felt marginally more alive.

On the way to the hospital in Chester, Oliver got a call from Patsy.

'Don't tell her what we discussed yesterday,' Jack said quietly, hating all the subterfuge, but Oliver didn't let him down.

'She wants to speak to you,' he said after a while, and held out his mobile.

'I can't. It's breaking the law, and anyway, I'm driving ninety-three miles an hour.'

Oliver relayed the information, then disconnected the call. 'She said to tell you that you're well over the speed limit as well. Said she'd call you tonight.'

'Huh … can't wait,' he said under his breath.

At the hospital, they found Josh easily, looking bored beyond comprehension and restricted by a plastered shoulder and a sling, although he cheered up a bit when he saw Oliver with a bag full of electrical games and gadgets. Following Josh's hazy directions, Jack found Anna on the other side of the building.

The ward was busy with visitors but Anna was alone and asleep. She was lying on her left side and her hair was loose and tumbled over her shoulders and fanned across the pillow. There were lots of cuts and bruises on her right arm and the side of her face.

Now that he had actually seen her, peaceful and breathing, the anxiety subsided. Jack sat on a chair by the bed, picked up her hand, and studied it. One of those hospital plastic bands was attached to her wrist with her name on it. She didn't stir for a long time, and when she did, it took a while before she recognised him.

'Jack, what are you doing here?' Anna said groggily, and tried to sit up.

'Why do you think? I had to see you.'

'I'm all right,' she said, holding her side. 'Don't look at me like that, and don't make me laugh because it hurts. I've got a cracked rib.'

Unable to resist any longer, Jack sat on the bed and gently held her in his arms. 'God, Anna, you really scared me,' he whispered into her hair.

'Ouch,' she said, and tried her best to hug him back.

'I feel really bad about all this,' Jack said, pulling up the pillows behind her. She sank back gratefully and took his hands. 'Why? You weren't within fifty miles of the place.'

'But you were upset when you left. I'm sorry,' he said. 'And whatever you might think, I don't want to mess up your relationship with Alex. I don't.'

'It's all right. I know that,' she said, holding his eyes for just a second.

'So what happened?'

'I can't remember very much. I keep waking up in the night feeling the sensation, though. It's horrible. Have you seen Josh? He's been in quite a lot of pain and I couldn't be with him yesterday. He didn't want Alex, or his gifts, and sent him away,' Anna said, twisting her fingers through his. 'Jack, what if something really awful had happened? He's all I've got.'

'But it *didn't*, and he's OK. When I left him just now with Ollie they were filling those menu cards in. I think the bloke in the next bed's getting curried meatballs for his breakfast.'

Although she smiled at him, her eyes were teary. 'I'm going paranoid in here, aren't I?'

‘No,’ he said, his heart twisting for her, ‘It’s probably shock. I know a bit about that.’

He told her about Oliver’s emotional exigency, and after a while she interrupted him.

‘You know, I went through all this with Josh and his absent father a few years ago. It’s not easy.’

‘I think the boys have a lot in common – paranoid parents for one.’

‘They talk a lot. That’s good.’

‘So you won’t mind if I give Josh a birthday present?’ Jack said, and placed a box on the bed. It was an expensive internet phone. Anna turned it over in her hands.

‘No, I don’t mind.’

‘I’m not using this as a weapon against Alex,’ Jack said, eager for her to understand his motive, but Anna was two steps ahead of him.

‘Josh is *my* son,’ she said, a touch defiantly, as if a decision had long since formed in her mind well before Jack had put it there.

On the way home, Oliver said little, and Jack kept going over his conversation with Anna, enjoying the fact that they had come to the same conclusion about their respective sons. This was something Alex had no perception of, the lone parent bit. The compromise with them being friends was that it would have to be low key, but Jack had agreed.

‘I’m not belting up and down the A55, I don’t have the time, and anyway, you’re moving.’

‘Yes, and after this, I don’t really have the inclination,’ she’d said and Jack could understand if she never wanted to get in a car ever again. Nevertheless, he suspected the low key aspect had more to do with Alex than Anna’s inclinations. Despite her softness, she was one of the most tenacious people he knew.

And yet, there had been nothing tenacious about her lying in that hospital bed.

'I just want to go home,' she'd said, holding onto his hand, but Jack felt if he'd stayed any longer he'd have undone all his good intentions and made a complete fool of himself. He'd wanted to pick her up and carry her out of there. He wanted to be there when she woke in the night, he wanted to be the one who held her and kissed the tears away, but he couldn't do any of those things.

He told Oliver about the phone, and the compromise.

'You were ages talking to Anna. Why can't you sort things out with Mum like that?'

Jack gave him a double take. 'What's happened between your mother and me is a bit more serious. Come on, Ollie, you know that.'

Oliver stared gloomily out of the window.

'Ollie, don't blank me. I hate it.'

'There's loads of stuff I hate.'

'Me too,' Jack said, then sighed and focused on the road ahead. 'It'll get better, I promise. I'm doing my best.'

After a moment, Oliver said, 'Yeah, I know.'

Just before eight, Oliver announced he was going out. He wore cream chinos, a red baseball shirt, and a black leather jacket. And he must have had a bath in Jack's aftershave because there was a cloud of it all over the house.

'Where are you going? You look too cool for just the lads,' Jack said, frowning over the top of his *Financial Times*, legs up on the coffee table and the television on too loud – all the things that drove Patsy wild.

'Spider's.'

'What sort of answer is that? Who's Spider?' Jack said, aware that he sounded uncannily like his father used to. Oliver groaned and ran a hand through his hair.

'Dad, you always say that! John Webster, number fourteen.'

Jack went back to his paper. 'Back by midnight.'

'Aw, come on, Dad.'

'Midnight,' Jack said, feeling the scowl on Oliver's face burning a hole in the back of his head. He checked his stocks and shares. 'By the way, you're using too much Armani. Less is more, and that applies to most things,' he said, but the front door had already slammed.

Isabel called him to say that they'd bought a three-bedroom cottage in Dwygyfylchi.

'Where the bloody hell is that?' Jack said, walking about with the phone jammed under his chin while trying to pour himself a drink.

'It's down Mountain Road, a bit further on from where you turn for Gwern Farm. And I've told your father this is the last time I'm moving.'

Jack told her about Anna and Josh, and she was shocked. 'Will you go and see them when they get home?'

'Yes, of course I will,' she said. 'Now, have you any good news?'

'My shares in Durex have risen. That's about it.'

'What? Oh, Jack, stop it!'

'It's not a joke. Danny gave me them in lieu of debt last year.'

'Oh. Talking of your brother …'

'What's he done now?' Jack said, wandering into the conservatory, drink in hand and swishing the ice round.

'Gone back to university and finished with Gina. Your father isn't pleased because she keeps weeping into the photocopier.'

'Nothing new, then. I did try to warn her.'

Patsy called immediately after Isabel rang off. 'This line's been engaged for ages.'

Jack wordlessly topped up his drink.

'I want to know why you've cancelled our joint bank account,' she said.

'I can't believe you just said that.'

'You had no right to cancel it without telling me!'

'Really? Like you cancelled our marriage without

telling me?' he said, pacing about again. He could feel his anger surging already. 'Like you cancelled me, without telling me? Like you cancelled my bloody life without telling me? Do you want me to go on?'

Patsy disconnected.

The house was too big, too quiet. Jack prowled round the rooms restlessly, then fell asleep on the sofa. The noise of the front door and footsteps going upstairs woke him in an instant. It was ten to one in the morning.

When he looked in Oliver's room, his son was still fully dressed with the duvet pulled over him, obviously feigning sleep. Jack tiptoed round the bed but Oliver couldn't quite pull it off and started to shake with suppressed laughter.

'Dad, how come you're such a light sleeper?'

'Years of experience,' Jack said, relieved that Oliver was actually laughing.

It was after two when Jack finally went to bed. Shortly after falling asleep, he woke in a sweat, thinking about Anna, then realised he'd been dreaming. But it was all mixed up with odd sensations. He'd been vividly aware of her body alongside his – or had it been Patsy? There had been the premise of something sexual and everything was moving as if in a film, frame by frame, and the next moment he was falling and out of control. Anna's accident was in there somewhere.

'He's all I've got,' she kept saying, hanging onto his hand, and he was getting in a state because he couldn't work out who she was talking about, and her legs were trapped in the car. Sleepless, Jack turned over, and wondered if she was awake in the hospital.

Typically, when the alarm went off, he was in a deep slumber. He must have thrown the clock on the floor and gone back to sleep, because it was Maria who finally brought him round.

'Jack, I'm really sorry but the office are on the phone,'

she said.

'What … what for?'

'They say there's a Chinese man waiting for you.'

'In the middle of the bloody night? Have they all gone mad?'

'Oh God, I don't know!' Maria said indignantly and shoved the phone at him. 'Here, you deal with it.'

Jon's voice came over the line. 'Jack? Mr Wan's here with his interpreter.'

It took several seconds for the penny to drop and to realise it wasn't the middle of the night after all – it was after nine o'clock.

'Are you coming in or not?' Jon asked.

'Give me twenty minutes,' Jack said, then passed the phone back to Maria.

'Don't tell me, coffee and a shirt,' she said.

At the office, Mr Wan was the epitome of graceful good manners. His interpreter was not. Tall and intimidating, in a tightly belted raincoat with swept-up ash blonde hair and carrying a leather briefcase decorated with padlocks.

Jack apologised for being late and offered his hand, but she was either deaf or just bloody-minded and simply gave Jack a scathing look.

'Stephanie Harrison,' she said icily, by way of introduction. 'Look, Mr Redman, can we get on with this? My client has a very busy schedule and now we're running late.'

Jack used his own car instead of the company vehicle, and Mr Wan said something to Ms Harrison, who then relayed it to Jack. 'He says it's a *nice* car,' she said.

'Tell him it's an Aston Martin DB7 coupé, circa 1994.'

'No problem.'

As he negotiated the busy Friday traffic, Jack was aware of mildly dirty looks from the woman in the passenger seat.

‘I take it you are aware of the requirements?’ Stephanie Harrison said.

‘He wants a two-year company let with full management, doesn’t he?’

‘Yes, but it has to be the right property,’ she said haughtily. ‘We want something with a very high specification. He’s very particular.’

‘And you don’t think Redman Estates has anything to offer?’

‘I didn’t say that.’

No, but you’re implying it, you snotty cow. Jack wondered whether to take them to see the council flats just for the hell of it, but decided under the financial circumstances, he’d better be professional. And anyway, Mr Wan was actually very ingratiating and smiley, it was just his sidekick who was irritating.

He took them to see four properties, all very high calibre and all of which Ms. Harrison found fault with.

‘I’m sorry, none of those will be suitable,’ she said, giving the brochures back to Jack with a patronising smile. Although he was glad to see the back of them, it irked him not to get the business.

At home, Maria was still there, scrubbing the cutlery drawers. Jack went for a shower and when he returned she was putting all the knives and forks into separate compartments. He poured her a glass of wine.

‘Maria, will you stop doing that? It’s making me nervous. Where’s Ollie?’

‘Swimming with the Webster’s, I think. I was just filling in time till you got back,’ Maria said, draining her wine.

‘Why?’ Jack said, refilling her glass and not liking the way the conversation was going.

‘I’ve got something to tell you. Well, show you,’ Maria said, but she wouldn’t look at him and kept wiping the work surfaces. ‘I don’t know whether this is anything to do with me, or you might already know, but I thought I'd mention it to you anyway. I mean show you.'

'Why do I get the feeling I'm not going to like this?'

Maria looked a bit awkward, then fished about in her dungaree pocket and slid something on to the kitchen table. 'I found these in Oliver's room, behind the chest of drawers.'

They both looked at a box of neon glow-in-the-dark condoms. Maria blushed when Jack shook out the contents, counted them all, and read the back of the packet.

'I think the lime green ones are missing.'

'Aren't you shocked or anything?'

'No, I don't think so. I don't know. Not sure,' Jack said, idly reading the instructions, which didn't look to have been unfolded before. 'I need to think about it.'

'Right you are then,' Maria said, shrugging on her coat, glad to be going. 'I'm back at college on Monday, shall I come by after?'

'Whatever you think,' Jack said, deep in thought, 'I expect the cutlery drawer will need doing again by then.'

Minutes after she'd gone, he heard Oliver's key in the door. Jack shoved the condoms back into the box, dived upstairs, and neatly dropped them back behind the chest of drawers.

'Dad, I'm starving. What is there?' Oliver said, hanging on the fridge door as usual.

'Nothing if I keep getting bills like these,' Jack said, finally opening the post and trying not to pant too obviously. There was a red statement for Patsy's credit card, and an astronomic telephone bill. Jack threw it across the table to Oliver.

'You can pay for half of that out of your allowance. I know those calls aren't mine.'

'Will you let me off if I make a stir-fry?'

'Yeah, go on then.'

The school skiing trip to Chamonix began on Sunday night. They were late getting to school because Oliver had only started packing half an hour before. There was a list of suggested luggage and a list of prohibited items, but Oliver had his own ideas.

The coach was waiting in the school grounds to take them to the airport. They had only been on the premises for ten minutes when Oliver was pulled up by his form master for wearing Levis with big holes in them, and attempting to conceal his earphone lead down the back of his pants. The familiar deafness to instructions and the tapping foot gave it all away.

Adrian Clark, the school principal, gave Jack a strained nod of recognition, then decided to stroll over.

'Mr Redman, I need you to come and see me, perhaps next week?'

'I wonder what that can be about,' Jack said to himself after Clark had disappeared. His neighbour, Susan Webster, spotted him and wandered over. She gave him a wry smile. 'Been getting into trouble, Jack?'

'I'm always in bloody trouble,' he said, then leant against the car door and offered her a cigarette. 'Don't let Clarky see, I think it's two days detention for smoking.'

'Actually, it's three,' she said, and produced a lighter.

They watched the ensuing chaos as ten teachers with clipboards and torches attempted to get eighty lots of luggage and as many adolescents onto two coaches. There seemed to be some bitter argument between two girls as to who was sitting next to Oliver, who was laughing and enjoying the attention. Susan Webster nudged Jack's arm.

'He's very popular with the fairer sex, your son.'

The slim girl with the spray-tanned midriff and pierced navel must have won because she claimed the window seat and whispered something to Oliver, who got told off for putting his arm round her and kissing her. She was incredibly pretty, all giggly and bouncy with a lot of bare flesh. She had a big mouth, a lot of fluffy blonde hair, and slanting cat's eyes. When she saw Jack and Susan through the window, she waved furiously and smiled rather wantonly at Jack, or so it seemed at the time.

'*Bloody hell*,' Jack said, laughing and turning to Susan. 'I wouldn't mind sitting next to her myself. Who is that, anyway?'

'"That" is my *fifteen*-year-old daughter Amy,' said Susan Webster, watching him carefully.

When the ground didn't swallow him up, Jack decided it would be better to just go home and close the door. He did his customary prowl around the huge house, too dark and quiet for one person. He glanced behind the chest of drawers in Oliver's room, only to confirm his suspicions.

Over the weekend, Jack had agonised over what to do, if anything, on discovering his son's sexual liberation. He really wanted to avoid anything likely to be confrontational. After the shock of Chelsey's appearance when he was nineteen, Jack had never trusted condoms again. The thought that Oliver might not have even read the instructions played on his mind, but it wasn't an easy subject to drop into conversation. Patsy used to say he was utterly paranoid about condoms and did he think she was going to take dangerous pills forever?

On Saturday, he'd gone into Manchester with Oliver to shop for clothes. Jack had only been allowed to go because he'd been paying, but it gave Jack an excuse to be with him and keep his instincts sharp. Oliver was not an easy companion. He alternated between being arrogant or being pathetically insecure, depending on which way the wind was blowing, but would then astonish Jack with some mature observation. He was a ruthlessly careful shopper and drove Jack insane when choosing clothes, but he had good taste for his age.

'Ollie, do you want me to just walk behind with my credit card?' Jack had said, after Oliver had ignored his choice of shirts for about the fifth time.

'Yeah, if you want,' Oliver had said, taking him seriously.

After another two hours, Jack was bored and broke. 'This has to be something you've inherited from your mother.'

'No, Dad. I like clothes, Mum's hooked on labels. It's totally different.'

Later though, when Jack discovered Oliver should have done a project on the Northern Hemisphere and read something by Daniel Defoe over the Christmas holidays, he'd been moody and childish again.

'I knew you'd have a go at me,' he said, making a paper aeroplane out of a school letter Jack should have had a month ago. 'I can't do it.'

'Rubbish. You can read. can't you?' Jack said, throwing a copy of *Moll Flanders* at him and unfolding the aeroplane. The school fees had increased.

'What's it about?' Oliver said.

He was lying on top of his unmade bed with his arms behind his head and his feet skewered halfway up the wall. Jack folded up the letter again and made another aeroplane.

'*Moll Flanders*? She was an artful whore in the eighteenth century.'

It was around two in the morning when Jack went to switch off his son's bedside light. Oliver was still fully clothed and turned over in his sleep when Jack threw Lottie's Barbie duvet over him. *Moll Flanders* fell to the floor with a thump.

Now that Oliver had gone away for ten days, Jack felt ridiculously lonely and fretted about the lure of Amy Webster. He wondered if Josh was as sexually active as Oliver appeared to be, and if so, how did Anna handle it? But he couldn't talk to Anna.

He rang his sister, aware that he was wearing a path in

the carpet between the conservatory and the drinks cabinet in the sitting room from pacing up and down with the phone. Kate laughed so much at his faux pas with Susan Webster that Jack almost rang off.

'Hang on, I need a tissue,' she wailed, and banged the phone down.

When she came back she said, 'Come on, Jack, you must see the funny side.'

'Not really, no. She thinks I'm some sort of pervert.'

Kate was only slightly more attentive when Jack told her about the stash of condoms.

'Look, Jack, Oliver's a great-looking lad. He's bound to get the come on from some of these girls. At least he's got the sense to be using something, and my guess is he knows exactly what he's doing in that department,' Kate said. Jack got the impression she was holding her nose. 'What colours did you say they were?'

'I thought I knew what I was doing, and look what happened,' he said, spilling a lot of tonic water. 'For Chrissakes, he's only fifteen!'

'Sixteen next week.'

'Oh well, that makes all the bloody difference.'

His sister only began to take him seriously when he told her about the emotional stuff, but she stopped him when he started to sound negative.

'It sounds to me like you're on top of the situation. Oliver knows he can talk to you now. It's good he's opened up about it all,' she said, and Jack knew she was talking from experience. 'Look, I know it's hard going now, but it will pay off … eventually.'

'And I go grey and get an ulcer in the meantime?'

'Welcome to the club. You're a single parent with a mixed up teenager.'

For the sake of needing to talk, he called Danny.

'If you want my advice, I'd just go and get laid and bollocks to everything,' he said, which was Danny's standard answer to whatever life threw at him. 'Some of your staff are worth a second look.'

'I'm not even going to bother responding to that.'

'Well, it's always worked for me,' Danny said.

'I doubt whether Gina would agree,' Jack said, then had a sudden thought. 'I don't want you giving Ollie any of your deeply profound advice either.' He paused to add a lot of gin to his tonic water. 'Did you get to see Anna?'

'Yeah, on the way up here.'

'How did she seem?'

'Well out of it. She's got some kind of complication from a broken rib. Fish was there with a bunch of flowers. Said he was going to see Dad about some American taking a look round the farm with some surveyor.'

'Starkey's been up again? When?'

'Yesterday morning. Look, what's the score with this?' Danny said. 'Why do I get the feeling that you and Anna babes are still a bit spoony?'

Jack rang off and punched in his father's number. Leo answered with his usual abrupt greeting.

'Redman.'

'What's going on with Gwern Farm?'

'Jack. Joy at last,' he said, warming to his subject. 'I was talking to Alex Farnham, you know … Anna's intended? Well, he's got things moving. He's been up there today with Max Starkey and his surveyor. Reckons the place needs underpinning, rotten joists in the roof, the lot. Well shot of the place for nearly a million, if you ask me.'

'It's not the cash that's the issue, and it's not what Anna wants,' Jack said. 'At least wait till she's out of hospital.'

'Don't you think you should be concentrating on your own problems?' Leo said. 'Have you spoken to Charles West yet?'

'No.'

‘Then do it. He’s expecting your call and make sure you take any relevant papers, wills, policies, house deeds, and the like. He’s very thorough.’

Feeling tense and depressed, Jack tried to beat Oliver’s score on Cyber City Cops, but couldn’t get anywhere near it. He didn’t understand the instructions for the obscure games Oliver downloaded off the Internet. Once he’d killed the light and sound on the computer, the house was heavy with silence.

Standing at Lottie’s bedroom door, Jack felt slightly desperate at seeing her depleted things, so he closed it and lay on his bed. Without Oliver and his problems, he was morose and unfocused. Whether it made sense or not, he was beginning to hate the house. Its beautiful richness was a mockery. It was empty and spiritless, with no love in it.

Making a decision, Jack found the key to the house safe and went down the cellar steps. His father was right; he had to get a handle on the legal stuff. There was no point in delaying the inevitable and he couldn’t cope with this inertia, as if he was waiting for her to come back. *Was* he waiting for her to come back?

Even if she did, and even if he wanted her, it would never be the same now. They’d gone through some tough things together but this had to be the end. He slotted the key into the lock and the little door swung open. It was completely empty.

Chapter Eight

Jack

In the night, he dreamed that Susan Webster was at the door with a heavily pregnant daughter.

'I'm not leaving until I know who's responsible,' she'd said, pointing a finger at Jack. 'I know it's either you or that son of yours.'

He'd woken then to find there was still two hours and forty minutes before his alarm went off. The sore throat and headache he'd had for about a week had developed into a nagging cough, so in the end he was driven to getting up to search the bathroom cupboards, but there were only Mr Men blackcurrant pastilles for toddlers and they were out of date.

When Clare saw him go into his office, coughing and sneezing, she trotted after him with a pile of paperwork and his diary for the day.

'Good weekend?'

'Fine. You?' Jack said, bringing up the Conwy properties on his screen.

'Yes, thanks. Don't forget you've got Mr and Mrs Worthing coming in to see you about a mortgage at ten and the manager of the Burnside Building Society wants to see you about first time buyer offers on the new Firs Estate.' Clare was not convinced he was listening but she ploughed on regardless. 'Jon wants to know if we can handle some commercial leases for Dunkirk and Sons … Jack?'

'Fine, whatever you think.'

'You don't seem very well,' she said, looking at the Mr Men pastilles on his desk.

'I'm not!'

Clare went out and closed the door firmly behind her.

On his computer screen, Gwern Farm was flashing as Under Offer, and the local advertising was cancelled. In seconds, it was back as Fully Available with full marketing. The next page showed Anna's details. Jack scrolled down to find Max Starkey's address, his contact numbers, and his solicitor. There was a letter of introduction ready to be printed and sent. In a moment of childish pique, Jack deleted the whole lot. The screen flashed up a message – archive or delete? Then it checked again – are you sure you want to permanently delete this? Yes, I'm bloody well sure.

When he called Charles West's secretary, she told Jack that Mr West was booked up for six months, but when Jack mentioned Leo she found an appointment for Wednesday. Doctor Musgrove was a lot more elusive.

'I don't want to see a doctor next week,' Jack said, then had to stop to cough. 'I might not be ill next week; I might be an emergency clogging up the hospital system.'

'Is that Mr Redman?' the receptionist said on the other end of the phone wearily. 'Come at the end of surgery, but you'll have to be prepared to wait.'

It was easy to get a meeting with Adrian Clark, and his secretary was very pleasant, but then Jack reasoned he was probably paying her salary. At four o'clock, on the way to Oliver's school, Jack remembered to be good and pulled over before he answered his mobile.

'What the bloody hell are you playing at?' Leo asked angrily.

'Hi, Dad, how are you? Yes, I'm fine, thanks.'

'Gwern Farm! You've swiped everything.'

'That system's always losing info. Probably needs rebooting.'

'I know what needs rebooting, and I know what you're doing and it won't work. It's going to take another week now to get hold of Max Starkey. Makes us all look like dummies.'

'I can't hear you, you're breaking up,' Jack said, and hung up.

Adrian Clark was a lot calmer than Leo, but looked ready to deliver a lecture. His office was big and tidy with a view of the playing fields and the new sports hall.

'Oliver is very talented in music. He's also very talented in a lot of other directions, but unfortunately we don't offer a qualification for the Internet, or wit and wisecracks,' he said with unexpected humour. He peered at some files. 'Until last summer he was easily achieving A grades in all his subjects.'

Since Clark seemed to want an explanation from him, Jack thought he might as well get to the point. 'His mother and I have separated.'

Clark looked over the top of his spectacles and locked his hands together in a triangle.

'Ah …' he said, then got up and went over to the window.

'He still wants to do his exams in June.'

'He's so far behind with coursework he'll be cramming every weekend and every evening, just to keep pace,' Clark said, turning to face Jack.

'You don't think he can do it?'

Clark sat down again and twiddled with his pen. 'I think he's more than capable. The big question is, does he want to do it?'

'I think he does.'

'But on his terms?'

'No, on my terms,' Jack said, coughing so much by then that Clark had to get him a glass of water.

Driving home, Jack felt deflated by the meeting. He'd got what he wanted in the end, although there was so much owing for fees and the Chamonix trip that Clark was twitchy in case Jack wasn't going to settle up.

While he was sitting in the waiting room at the doctor's, Clare rang him on his mobile. 'Are you coming back today? Only I'm stuck here on my own and it's really busy. Jon's out and Carol's rung in sick, and have you got the client paying-in book? I've looked everywhere for it.'

'No to the first question, yes to the second,' Jack said wearily, then waited an hour to be told he had a cold because he was run down, and it was a knock-on effect from everything else and the best thing he could do was to rest.

'No chance of any hard drugs, then?'

'Go home and go to bed,' Doctor Musgrove said, clearing his desk for the day.

Jack went home and went to bed.

The following day, he rang Clare at the office and told her he wasn't coming in.

'What appointments did I have for today?'

'You'll have to hold while I get these other calls.'

In the background, he could hear the other two phone lines ringing and a lot of people around the desk. Jack waited for ages then got fed up and put the phone down. Clare rang him back a lot later, to confirm his diary was rearranged and under control, but she sounded close to tears.

On Wednesday afternoon, after a day and half of lying in bed suffering with about twenty years' worth of colds, Jack managed to keep the appointment with his father's solicitor, Charles West. The meeting was partly reassuring, in that West didn't see the missing legal papers as a problem, and he was pleased that Oliver was in situ with Jack in the family home, but all the implications of divorce were harrowing and complicated.

At home, Jack told Maria the full story about Lottie,

and that he was filing for divorce. She was quiet at first, then finally confessed to Jack that she knew something had been going on.

'I heard Patsy talking on the phone once and that day Lottie broke her arm I think he was there, at the hospital.'

The following day, Jack managed to get back into the office, determined not to let his personal problems and his deteriorating health interfere, but it was all creeping round his mind like a cancer. It had taken all his willpower not to interrogate Maria. He turned up at the office to discover the new assistant had started.

'She's called Tabitha,' Jon said.

'Has she got any experience?'

'Probably, but not in estate agency, but hey, she's a blonde, got great legs and a big chest.'

Jack looked at him askance. 'I hope for your sake that you're joking.'

'What's the matter with you? What's happened to your sense of humour these days?' Jon said, and slapped a file down on his desk. 'Maintenance invoices you wanted.'

Twelve hours later, Jack got home to a dark, empty house, but at least the phone was ringing. Jack was surprised to hear the deep crisp voice of Charles West.

'Redman versus Redman. I've had an e-mailed reply.'

'What, already?'

'They obviously want swift action for some reason. Have you thought about the private eye we talked about?'

'Yeah, I've thought of nothing else.'

Jack sat down, still in his coat, and found his cigarettes. It was all too fast, but then Patsy had had two years to think all this through. Redman versus Redman! It sounded like a Sunday afternoon film.

'Jack? Remember I said she'd go for the jugular to start with? Well, she has … the house and half the business.'

Jack took the phone with him into the conservatory and opened the door. Cold air rushed in and the security lights came on, illuminating the sweep of the lawn and the little copse at the bottom of the garden. Oliver and Charlotte had played there most of their lives, climbed the trees and fallen off the gazebo. Of course she wanted the house. Of course she wanted to live in it, but she wanted to live in it with someone else.

He watched his cigarette smoke evaporate. 'And … there's always an and with Patsy.'

'She's claiming full support for herself, your daughter, and your unborn child. She's saying she has no personal income,' Charles West said. 'She also maintains that you forced her out of the marital home and she wants to divorce you for emotional cruelty. Don't worry,' he added quickly, shuffling paper, 'That's a standard one. I did warn you it'd be grim. It's a case of think of a number and treble it. Then think of a load of shit and throw it.'

'I just want my daughter,' Jack said, staring at the black sky. 'She can have The Links.'

'That's not a good idea,' West said quickly, 'If you let her back in the house, she'll easily get custody of both children and have full control over the situation. All you'll get is the bill.'

'I want Lottie with me,' Jack said stubbornly.

'And you're unlikely to get her. We could try for shared residency since you've got the family home and the child-minder, but to be honest it doesn't really work for the majority of kids,' West said, then sensed that Jack had switched off.

'Look, let me get my private eye on it before we do anything. This French guy is an unknown entity. For all we know, he could be conning her out of your assets, and we could do with knowing what's happened to the money from the sale of the salon.'

'OK, OK,' Jack said, struggling to keep his mind on all the different issues. 'Do it.'

Knowing he wouldn't sleep, he tried ringing Kate, but

he only got the answering machine at home and her mobile was switched off. He knew Tim and Margaret were out for dinner. He deliberated for ten minutes over whether to call Anna, but what the hell; it was just a chat, wasn't it?

'Yes?' Alex answered, 'Gwern Farm.'

'It's Jack. Can I speak to Anna?'

'At this time of night?' he said curtly. 'I hope it's important.'

Presently, he heard Anna walk across the slate floor of the kitchen and pick up the receiver. They exchanged the mundanities of their flagging health. She sounded as low as he did, but she wouldn't let him ring off.

'No, don't go. After a few days in that hospital I'm desperate for conversation. How's Oliver?'

'Gone to Switzerland with a coach full of babes and his pockets full of condoms.'

She laughed and it gave him a buzz, making her laugh when she was so down, so he told her about the Susan Webster incident as well, but then he ran out of funny stories.

'And what about everything else?' He told her what had happened after the concert and she sounded confused.

'So Patsy's gone back to Paris?'

'You didn't think I'd want her to stay, did you?'

There was a long, thoughtful silence from Anna. 'So what happens now?'

'An expensive, messy divorce.'

She was shocked, and listened with a mixture of empathy and disbelief as he related the gist of the conversation he'd had with Charles West. All the time he was talking he could hear Alex or someone making cups of tea, or something that rattled crockery and noisily running water. Then silence, and he imagined Alex lying in wait upstairs for her, watching the clock creep past midnight and holding two cups of cold tea.

'Anyway, I've talked about me for long enough,' Jack

said. 'Talk to me about you. I believe Alex has been busy?'

'He's made an offer on a place in Cornwall,' Anna said carefully.

'So you're in a corner now with the farm? It's the American or nothing?'

'Well, we don't want to lose the Cornwall place.'

'So you've agreed to sell to Starkey?' Jack said, convinced she was compromising herself and annoyed she couldn't see it, or didn't want to.

'So what was the point of me doing the sales brochure and blanking this guy, when you just go ahead and accept anyway as soon as they put a bit of pressure on? Alex had it sorted all along. He sounds like another version of Patsy.'

'Don't be like this,' she said.

'All this happened when you were in bloody hospital!'

'Jack, just leave it.'

After he'd put the phone down, Jack swore at himself for messing up their relationship yet again. But what relationship? Anna was lost to him a long time ago, and he only had himself to blame for that as well. He knew he couldn't call her any more, even if the loneliness in his heart was breaking him up.

The Susan Webster dream happened again, mixed up with blackcurrant Mr Men and Mr Wan. He woke in a sweat when he fell down some stairs, to find Stephanie Harrison at the bottom, breaking his fall. Jack tossed and turned, wondering about the philosophy of dreams and if they meant anything.

Unrested and ready to kill someone, Jack got into the office early, but Clare had beaten him to it and was already frowning at her screen.

'Get me Mr Wan's assistant,' Jack said.

'Sorry, who?'

'The one with the flick knife in her knickers.'

Presently, Stephanie Harrison came on the line. 'Mr Redman, how nice,' she said smoothly.

'I've got another property for you.'

'Details?'

'A Victorian six-bedroom detached, fully furnished. Initial six month let then standard contract with two-month notice to quit.'

'Price?'

'Two grand.'

'Availability?'

'Soon. I'll pick you up in half an hour if you want to see it.'

'All right. Prestbury Hotel. Oh, and Jack?'

'Yeah …?'

'In the Aston Martin.'

Cheeky bitch. On the way to the Prestbury Hotel, Jack went over his conversation with Anna. She'd been a sweetheart to him over the phone, listening to all that crap about Patsy, and he'd repaid her by insulting Alex and letting his personal feelings get in the way of her business, as well as wanting her to be available to him. While he was waiting for Stephanie, Jack called Interflora and sent her a dozen white roses, and a dozen white lilies.

Stephanie Harrison was so impressed with The Links that Jack didn't need to say anything except watch her wander through the house. A weak shaft of sunlight dappled the golf course and the garden, just reaching into the conservatory.

'What about all these things?' Stephanie said, making sweeping motions towards the coffee table, which was covered with newspapers and an empty beer can. 'When are the present tenants moving out?' She looked at him very closely with her china blue eyes.

'Next week.'

'All right,' she said, trailing her hand across the linen sofa. 'Yes, it's perfect.'

'I'll get a contract drawn up and drop it round to the hotel,' Jack said, all business-like and pretending to check paperwork. He didn't want to give away any emotional clues to this woman, but it was difficult when his daughter's school photograph smiled down at him from the wall. It was Lottie's home too …

Back on the office forecourt, Jack had to sit in the car for a while because he felt so shaken. He hadn't counted on feeling quite so bad about letting the house go. Still in the car, he called Charles West and ran the idea past him, just in case he was making a big blunder because his judgement was so haywire.

'I take it you can give reasonable notice to regain possession? Just in the event of us swinging it our way with your daughter?'

'Shouldn't be a problem. To be honest, I'm more concerned about Patsy and Co. going in there than Mr Wan outstaying his welcome,' Jack said, 'And anyway, I don't want to be there anymore.'

'Get a copy of the contract to me, and your new address, this time preferably one with a substantial rent or a mortgage.'

New address? Jack hadn't thought about that.

In the office, all the phones were ringing. There was no sign of Clare and the new girl was in a panic on the front desk, trying to do everything.

'This is Jack,' Jon said to Tabitha. 'He thinks he's the boss.'

'Where's Clare?' Jack said, picking up one of the phones and handing another to Tabitha, who was mercifully small and dark with normal-sized breasts, but looked ready to run.

'Gone to get some keys cut,' Jon said. Jack finished the call, found the right screen on the computer for Tabitha, and followed Jon into his office. He slid the tenancy application for The Links into Jon's in-tray.

'What keys?'

'Full set of office keys,' Jon said with a shrug. 'She said she lent them to Patsy ages ago and she's fed up with trying to get them back.'

When Clare returned, she removed her coat and threw a receipt into the petty cash tin, then saw Jack going through everything in the safe.

'I haven't done any banking because you've had the book,' she said frostily. 'I have tried asking for it but I don't get a civil answer.'

'Why the fuck did you give Patsy a set of fucking keys?' he yelled at her.

'Why shouldn't I?' Clare yelled back. 'She's your wife. I can hardly refuse!'

'You must have noticed there's about three grand missing!'

'I haven't noticed anything because I haven't had any keys,' she said. Then her eyes suddenly filled with tears and she had to take a deep breath. 'And if you shout and swear at me any more, Jack, I quit.'

Unable to move or speak, he watched Clare march to the staff room and slam the door. Tabitha was trying to listen to what was going on and deal with four enquiries at the same time.

'Isn't The Links your house?' Jon said, reading the application form.

'I want all the locks changing on this place, including the alarm code,' Jack said, 'and I want the same job done on my property. Then you can check out Mr Wan.'

'What's going on?'

'Nothing! Just get on with it, will you?' Jack said, already heading for the door. Minutes later, on the way to his first appointment, it struck Jack that his behaviour was becoming intolerable. He was even beginning to dislike himself and the thought that his staff were beginning to dislike him because of something Patsy had initiated was, in a way, a signal of defeat. By the time he'd got through his last appointment, he was full of remorse.

'Jon, I know it's late,' he said, sitting in his car later that day. 'Will you and Clare wait there for me? I need to talk to you both. Is Clare all right?'

'Not sure. You might need to do some serious grovelling.'

When Jack reached the office, it was well after six and Clare was still at her desk filling out forms with a couple of first-time buyers. When she glanced up at him she looked as though she'd sobbed her heart out and was utterly exhausted, but she was still there, chatting to his clients and pretending she had hay fever in January.

Jon, who was setting up the contract for The Links, slung two bunches of keys across his desk.

'There you go, one office set and one house set. The new alarm code for here is double C followed by triple six, the sign of the devil. Clare's idea, not mine,' he said, accepting one of Jack's cigarettes, 'The double C is her bra size I reckon.'

'Don't tell me – your idea, not hers,' Jack said, and thumped a bottle of wine down on the desk. 'Did you check out Mr Wan and Sangwang Electronics, or whatever he's called?'

'Yep, no problem, good for half the cash up front as well,' Jon said, pushing some letters and cheques over to Jack for signing. 'Oh, and you had a message from a woman with a very sexy voice,' he went on, looking at his notepad. 'Anna Williams.'

'What did she want?' Jack asked quickly.

'She didn't want to speak to you but wishes to thank you for the flowers,' Jon said, with a smirk. 'How many women have you been upsetting?'

'All the ones that mean something to me.'

'That sounds a bit heavy. I take it that includes Patsy?' Jon said, pouring most of the wine into two coffee mugs.

‘Not exactly, no,’ Jack said, and went on to explain why he was letting his house to a Chinese Managing Director and his family.

‘Bloody hell!’ Jon said eventually.

They’d got through all the wine and Jon had gone home before Clare had finished with the couple at her desk. She locked the door behind them then went back to her computer and ignored Jack, until he leant across and pressed save and escape on her keyboard.

‘I wanted to finish that! Why do you have to be so patronising?’ she said, pushing her chair back and getting to her feet. She threw her pen down and began to go through all the paperwork on her desk. There was too much of it, Jack thought. He’d thrown her in at the deep end without the smallest of floats and he knew what that felt like.

What he really wanted to do was throw his arms around her, but this was work and there had always been a strong unspoken code of conduct between his staff. Somehow, all of that seemed irrelevant when her tears began spilling onto some washing machine invoices.

Jack took them out of her hand and the beaten way she looked at him reminded Jack of his own larger scale war. It felt natural then to hold her and worry about the consequences later.

‘Clare, I’m so sorry,’ he said, pulling her into his arms.

She didn’t say anything, but he knew he was forgiven by the softness of her body language. It struck Jack that he was on dangerous ground on several counts, but the other immediate feeling that came to him was that the whole touching experience felt relatively safe and under control. He could tell she didn’t presume anything by his actions.

When he’d held Anna and kissed her, the feelings had been so overwhelming that at first he’d tried to fool himself that it was only because he was so vulnerable. If she’d wanted him to make love to her across the bonnet of the car, he probably would have done so, but it wasn't just sexual with Anna. There was something else, something in her eyes that made him want her arms around him for ever.

'It's not just your foul mood,' Clare said, finally sitting down and wiping mascara from under her eyes. 'It's this job of Jean's.'

'Don't you want to do it? It doesn't matter if you say no,' Jack said, wondering what he was going to do if she did say no.

'I want to do it, but I don't understand the tax invoices and the computerised payroll is a nightmare.'

'I can't do that payroll thing either,' he said. 'Would it help if I did the tax and banking for a while?'

'Well, yeah, it would,' she said, 'but what about the payroll?'

They lit cigarettes. 'Give Jon the payroll.'

For some reason, and one that Jack wasn't sure he wanted to know, Clare found the idea of Jon doing the payroll helplessly funny.

'I'm sorry,' she said, holding her nose in an effort to stop snorting. 'It must be nerves. So, are you going to tell me why you've had a personality change?'

'Yeah,' he said, handing Clare her coat, 'but over something to eat. You choose and I'll pay by way of apology.'

'The Mandarin?' she said, applying lipstick.

'I can't. I'm banned for unruly behaviour.'

Oliver woke him in the night with a phone call. The reception was extremely poor.

'Dad, it's me.'

'What's happened?' Jack asked in a panic, already working out how he was going to get to Switzerland. 'Are you OK?'

'Yeah. Snow's really fast. Tommo did his wrist in.'

'Who?' Jack said. 'Why are you calling so late?

Shouldn't you be in bed? I mean, shouldn't you be asleep?'

'Well, yeah, but we have to wait till the olds are all snoring before we can use the hotel phones,' Oliver shouted. 'No one's got a decent signal on their mobile. Anyway, Dad, you've got to pick us up at five on Tuesday morning. Amy asks can you drop her off?'

There was a lot of muffled laughter in the background.

Jack groaned at the thought. 'Five? Bloody hell, yeah, OK.'

'What? Shout!'

Thoroughly awake from shouting, Jack tried to get back to sleep, but snatches of conversation kept meandering through his mind. Clare had given him some herbal sleeping pills, which tasted of liquorice and did absolutely nothing.

'You've got to take them for a month,' she'd said.

'That's no good. I need instant knock-out.'

She'd laughed, and pretended to hit him over the head with her handbag, but even that had been better than sitting in the house alone all evening. Clare had cheered up a lot after he'd taken her out to dinner and he'd told her about the farce that roughly translated into his life, but at least she was on his side again.

Of course, he hadn't gone into the same details and depth he had with Anna.

'I don't think I'll ever be able to love and trust anyone again after this,' he'd said to her.

Anna had disagreed and quoted an odd little Celtic verse to him in Welsh. The strangeness of the language, and the animated way she pronounced the words, made it doubly evocative.

'What does it mean?' he'd said to her.

'"I believe in the sun even when it isn't shining, I believe in God even when he is silent and I believe in love … even when I cannot feel it."'

Jack had thought it a bit corny at the time, but now, in the dead of night with the rain coursing down the windows, he couldn't stop thinking about it.

Couldn't stop thinking about her.

In the morning, Maria found him energetically stuffing Patsy's clothes into bin bags.

'Don't ask me what I'm doing because it's really obvious. I need you to do me a big favour. I want you to pack Lottie's stuff into some boxes and put it all in the cellar,' he said, then held up one of the bags and Patsy's Chanel suits fell out. 'And I want you to take all this lot to a charity shop. Don't ask me if I'm sure because I am.'

'Right you are,' Maria said, watching him drag handbags and shoes out of the wardrobes and throw them into a big pile.

Jack left her sorting through the mess and went in to work.

'It's not your Saturday in,' Jon said suspiciously. 'Where's Clare?'

'I've given her time off,' Jack said. 'I'll cover for her till Tuesday.

Jack spent all day with Tabitha on the front desk, showing her the telephone and computer system and trying to prove that he was not the raving lunatic she was beginning to suspect him to be.

Tim rang him later in the afternoon. 'Are you doing anything tonight?'

'If you don't count planning manslaughter and crimes of passion, then no, nothing much,' Jack said, feeling Tabitha's eyes boring into his back again.

'Come to the house. We're having a few people round, mostly business.'

'What's this in aid of?'

'I've just landed a big accounting contract. You know us, any excuse for a drink.'

Jack thought about the house strewn with packing cases and Lottie's toys in the cellar, then compared it with an evening of trying to be sociable, and wondered which he could stomach the most easily.

'I dunno, Tim. Can I see how I feel later?'

'Sure. Be good to see you though.'

Seven hours later, Jack parked the Aston Martin behind Tim's BMW. The house was jam packed with throngs of people, and every way he turned, someone knew him and asked where Patsy was.

'She's gone to a trade fair,' Jack said automatically, almost shouting above the music and several different conversations. The woman asking must have been one of Patsy's best customers. She had that over-groomed appearance that was beginning to haunt him.

'A what? What did you say?' she shrieked, her false nails digging into his arm.

'A trade fair.'

'Oh!' she said, laughing too much and spilling her drink. 'For a moment I thought you said she was having an affair.'

Jack looked at her perfect red mouth and suddenly wanted to close it. 'Actually, you were right the first time,' he whispered into her ear. 'Excuse me.'

Tim pushed a large Scotch at him. 'Jack, I can't believe how many people have turned up. How's things?'

'Business things are OK if you don't count half the staff having nervous breakdowns.'

'And personal things?'

'Not now, too much to tell you.'

'Lunch next week?'

Jack nodded. 'So who's this company entrusting you to count all their money?'

'Chinese firm called Sangwang Electronics,' Tim said, looking over Jack's shoulder as if he'd just spotted someone. 'In fact, I'll introduce you to their PR; they're looking for property leases.'

Jack turned round to see Mr Wan's interpreter standing close by. She wore a sheer silver dress with a slit up one side. Tim gave her a big business smile.

'Jack, this is Stephanie Harrison.'

Jack said, 'We've met.'

'Hello again, Jack,' she said, and offered her hand, obviously a lot more polite after dark and in party mode. 'Have you a firm date for me yet?' she said, still holding on to his hand. Jack wondered whether he was imagining the sexual reference.

'No, not yet.'

Tim topped up Jack's glass with a laddish grin.

'I'll just go and circulate, shall I?'

'This house,' Stephanie said, holding the eye contact. 'The Links, it's yours, isn't it?'

'What makes you say that?'

'You have beautiful children. They have your eyes. Are you divorced?'

'None of your business. Do you want the house, or not?'

'Of course,' she said, then put her mouth to his ear. 'I want to sleep in your bed. In fact, I quite like the idea of you being in it as well, in just your faded tan and your Rolex.'

While he was trying to work out how the conversation had leapt from one galaxy to the next, she sauntered away as if she'd been discussing shop or last night's film.

When Stephanie was safely out of the way, Tim came and re-filled Jack's glass.

'That's me well over the limit,' Jack said.

'Get a taxi.'

'Tell me if I'm hallucinating, but I've just had a very non-business proposition from Ms. Harrison. Do you think she's drunk?'

'Nope … she doesn't drink,' Tim said. 'So what are you going to do?'

'Do? Nothing.'

'Nothing. Why not?'

'She's just playing games,' Jack said, draining his glass, then looked at Tim's blank face. 'I'm all over the place as it is, and anyway, I don't like her.'

Two hours later, Stephanie Harrison drove him home in the Aston Martin, with his Sade CD in the player.

'I just love this car!' she said.

When they got to The Links, she ran in through the door, flung her shoes off, and let her hair down. 'I just love this house.'

Lured by a certain measure of curiosity and a lot of alcohol, Jack followed her upstairs, where she lay across his bed like a mermaid.

'Everything in this house is exquisite,' she said, patting the silk pillows. 'Who has the creative flair, or did you pay someone a lot of money?'

'Both. My wife.'

She laughed, 'I like you, Jack, but you don't want to have sex, do you?'

'I don't know,' he said, noting that he'd slipped from no to don't know in a very short space of time. That was probably just his flagging ego having its say.

'I'll have to make up your mind for you then,' she said, slithering across the bed and putting her mouth on his. She began to unbutton his shirt.

'Why are you doing this?' Jack said, peeling her out of her silver skin and finding no underwear. 'If you want ten per cent off, it won't work.'

She laughed with faint scorn, dropped her earrings into his hand, and pressed her nakedness against him. 'Are you past the "don't know" stage, yet?'

'More or less, but don't expect deep and meaningful.'

'I don't do meaningful,' she said. 'Deep will do.'

‘Are you always this coy?’

In the morning, Stephanie was entwined around his body and planting little butterfly kisses on his face. Jack wondered if he’d been set up. Maybe he’d get some big glossy pictures in the post and a nasty letter. Maybe he should find out who fixed her hair.

‘Have you got a raging hangover, darling?’ she said.

‘What do you think?’

‘You know something? You’re bloody awful to sleep with,’ she said, back to being as annoying and sassy as before.

‘Clear off and leave me alone then.’

‘What I mean is, you’re a restless sleeper and thrash about too much,’ she said, leaning across him. ‘You’re quite good at sex, though. You can be quite rough if I push you. I like that.’

‘I don’t remember anything about it. I don’t even know who you are,’ Jack said, and opened one eye. Stephanie Harrison loved every moment.

There was a commotion at the front door. At first it was the fumbling of keys and then a furious ringing of the bell and a muffled thumping, like bags being thrown into the porch. Then someone shouted through the letterbox.

‘Dad! Open the door, will you? Come on, its freezing out here!’

Jack peered through a gap in the curtains and saw Chelsey’s car on the drive.

‘Steph, get up. Now!’ he said, quickly pulling on a pair of Levi’s and a sweatshirt. Then had to hold his head because it was spinning. Stephanie was stretching like a cat in slow motion.

‘Put some bloody clothes on,’ he hissed. ‘My daughter’s here.’

‘Stop panicking, go and answer the door. Well, go on.’

Still panicking, Jack answered the door and Chelsey fell into his arms, boyfriend and bags bringing up the rear.

'Why have you had the locks changed?' she asked. 'Do you know you've got that sweatshirt on back to front?' she went on brightly, and marched into the kitchen, not seeming to notice the bareness of the walls. 'Where's Mum?'

'She's gone to a trade fair in Paris,' Jack said, feeling like some kind of mad contortionist trying to twist his clothes round to fit correctly without falling over. He filled the kettle and began spooning coffee into the percolator to try and focus on something, but Chelsey grabbed hold of his hand.

'Dad, stop that a minute,' she said, looking at Mike. 'We've got something to tell you. It's important, and if I don't tell you now I'm going to burst.'

'What?' Jack said suspiciously, unsure if he could handle anything exciting without passing out.

There was a short pause to ensure she had his full attention, then Chelsey took a deep breath and said, 'I'm pregnant!'

Chapter Nine

Jack

The baby was due in August. Jack wasn't surprised they wanted to be married – Chelsey had always been conventional and traditional.

'I'm pleased for you both,' Jack said, smiling at Mike and handing round the sugar. However, he felt let down, cheated almost, that Patsy was not sharing this stage of life with them, and had instead left him to deliver the blow that would rip his daughter's life apart. She sat on the arm of his chair, showing him photographs of Perth, telling him about New Year in Scotland and Mike's new teaching job in London.

He wondered if he should carry on bluffing for a while, but his nerves were so shot he found himself thinking that it would actually be easier if Patsy were dead. Perhaps this was the first sign that he was losing his mind.

They were in the sitting room. Jack had closed the door in the hope that Stephanie would discreetly find her way out without suddenly appearing in her knickers-free dress.

'I've got something to tell you too,' he said, suddenly serious.

'What is it?' Chelsey whispered, transfixed by his face. Somehow he managed to tell her without becoming incoherent. She was so devastated, he was worried for her. She sobbed and sobbed so much that Mike had to prise her off Jack and try to talk her round. Jack went outside and left them alone, feeling sick and empty.

Mike found him in the summer house.

‘She’s resting upstairs. She’s a bit emotional at the moment,’ he said.

‘I had to tell her.’

‘I know. She’ll be OK.’

But the mood was destroyed and instead of staying for a few days, they were gone by Monday morning. By evening, Jack felt so wretched that he broke down on the phone telling his mother.

‘She’s taken it really badly. What if something happens to the baby?’

‘Jack, stop it. Nothing will happen. You’re so stressed you’re imagining the worst.’

He ran a hand through his hair. ‘I couldn’t handle that. That would finish me.’

‘Why don’t you let me come down there?’ Isabel said. ‘I know you’re struggling with all this. It’s too much!’

‘No. Just phone Chel and make sure she’s OK, will you?’

‘Jack, she’s a grown woman and she’s got Mike. It’s you I’m worried about,’ she said, then lost her temper. ‘I don’t understand why this had to happen. Patsy just swans off and leaves you to pick up dozens of broken pieces.’

‘Mum, I don’t want to go through all this again.’

‘I know, I’m sorry, darling,’ she said, close to tears. ‘I think about you all the time.’

At half past four in the morning, Jack went to meet Oliver’s coach. They were late, and Jack sat in the car for fifty minutes listening to the radio, smoking too much, and thinking about Stephanie Harrison. She’d performed the perfect escape on Sunday morning, but maybe she’d had lots of practice.

It had been a strange experience, having a one-night stand after nearly twenty-five years of marriage. Although he had been well aware of what it was, Jack was still unprepared for the big feeling of nothing that followed. Stephanie made love like she was in a business meeting, leaving Jack with the impression that he was an experiment. She likely had an 'estate agent's performances' table somewhere in her briefcase.

It was good to have Oliver back. Jack watched him haul his bags off the coach, earphones in place, wearing a Technicolor bobble hat. Amy was as effervescent as before in a fake fur jacket and skin-tight PVC trousers. When she saw Jack, she gave him an excited smile and a bubbly little wave. She really was extremely pretty, and he had to keep reminding himself that she was only fifteen and her mother was already on his case. When he dropped her home, Susan Webster came out of the house in her dressing gown and gave him a very cool thanks.

He took Oliver out for breakfast. They went to a hotel and ordered half a bottle of champagne to go in the orange juice. Oliver was appreciative, but suspicious.

'What's all this for?' he asked, ordering full English with an extra sausage.

'I've got some stuff to tell you. And anyway, there's no food in the house.'

'Is Mum back?'

Jack shook his head. He waited till Oliver was a good way through his breakfast.

'I went to see the principal last week.'

'Nice for you,' Oliver said cockily. 'Are you not eating that toast?'

Jack pushed the toast over. 'I've done a deal for you, but you're on your last chance.'

Oliver chewed more slowly. 'Which is?'

'You've still got to do the compulsory subjects. Then music and computers if you want, but you can drop the rest,' Jack said. 'You can also drop pissing about.'

Oliver finished his breakfast thoughtfully and had the humility to look something approaching grateful. 'That's not a bad deal, actually.'

'What did you expect?' Jack said, refilling his coffee

cup. 'I negotiate deals every day. Clarky was a pushover in comparison.'

When he talked about moving out of The Links, Oliver went very quiet. Jack knew he was talking to his son as if he was another adult, but he wasn't a child, either. Somehow he had to find a way of explaining the reasons behind his actions, but in the end, Jack found it easier to tell the truth rather than try and fabricate something. The hardest part was asking him to lie to his mother by way of omission.

'If all this would make you really unhappy, then I'm not prepared to do it,' Jack said, 'I'll tear up the contract now.'

Oliver spooned a lot of sugar and cream into his coffee. 'Where would we move to?'

'I haven't thought about that yet. Any ideas?'

'You know how you always said that when I was eighteen I could move into the flat over the office?'

Jack nodded, guessing what was coming next. 'Go on.'

'Why don't we move there? I could throw *you* out then, when you hit forty-five.'

'Because it's an almighty tip,' Jack said, thinking about the photocopier and the archived files stored up there, but Oliver was animated.

'I could do it up. Go on, Dad, we'd be in the middle of town. It'd be cool.'

'I'll think about it,' Jack said, and when he looked at Oliver's face it struck him that he looked older, tanned from a week in the snow and trying to grow up, and although both their lives had been turned upside down these past few weeks, he was starting to feel closer to his once slightly remote son. Maybe this was his first sign of a silver lining.

'So what did you get up to in Chamonix?'

Oliver shrugged and drained the champagne bottle. 'Nothing much. What about you?'

'Same,' Jack said.

At work, Clare was back and helping Tabitha sort through the post on the front desk.

'How are you?' Jack said to Clare, trying not to feel too anxious by the sight of several large brown envelopes. He tried to rip them open and scan the contents without looking too frantic.

'I'm fine,' Clare said with a smile. 'You did all the tax and the banking yesterday, thanks.'

'If any more big brown envelopes come, I want to open them,' he said to Tabitha.

'Right,' she said, then nodded and gave him a sickly sort of grin.

On the way to lunch with Tim, Charles West rang Jack's mobile. 'Are you driving?' he said.

'Yeah, why?'

'Pull over.'

Once the car had stopped, Jack automatically lit a cigarette and opened the window.

'Go on, I'm listening.'

'Philipe Rouen, hairdresser to the up-and-coming stars. A real ladies man and, it seems, something of a con merchant. He's managed to move himself up the social ladder by preying on rich married women or those with successful partners,' West said. '*And* he's been known to deviate from the path of virtue in order to get what he wants. Nothing violent,' he added quickly, 'more manipulative, mind games, if you like.'

'My daughter's in the middle of this! I want her out of there,' Jack said, throwing his cigarette out of the window. 'I'll go to the airport now. Give me an address.'

'Jack, there's no point. What are you going to do, kidnap her?' West said, then lowered his voice. 'Look, I understand what it must feel like but you've got to play it by the book.'

Jack grunted.

West continued, 'The other item was the money from the salon. It's gone into Rouen's new hair and beauty development in Manchester. She obviously has every intention of coming back.'

'So what do I do now?'

'You wait.'

Jack rested his head on the steering wheel. 'This is really getting to me.'

'I think that was fully intended.'

At the pub, Tim was already there with two beers.

'You're late. Where have you been, giving Stephanie a market appraisal?'

'More like the other way around.'

'So Saturday was hot then? To be honest, you looked like you were being dragged off to the dentist.'

'I'm sure there's a joke about fillings in there somewhere,' Jack said, but he was thinking about the conversation with Charles West and trying to digest the information. Tim slid a beer over. 'You'd better fill me in on the serious stuff first.'

At the end of the day, Jack went to look at the flat over the office. Tim hadn't been sure it was a good idea, but then he had a strictly analytical mind, where Jack was more emotional and made decisions based partly on his gut feelings.

The rooms were big and old fashioned and full of office overflow, and it came completely rent-free. Charles West wouldn't like that bit, but there were other considerations, such as a feeling of belonging and giving Oliver a sense of direction.

Leo and Isabel had lived there when they were first married and the business was new. Since then, Jack, Kate and Danny had all used it at some point in their lives and the memories were good. They went back a long way, all the way to Anna, and if he was going to stay sane then he needed every good vibe he could get.

Jack sat on the cheap little sofa and tried not to look at it as a backward step, but more a temporary way of protecting what he had, which at present amounted to his son and the business. He went back downstairs and leant on Jon's office door.

'Is the money in place for The Links yet?'

'What? Oh, yes, it is,' Jon said, frowning at his screen. 'This payroll says I owe two hundred quid in tax and this month's salary is fourteen pounds sixty pence.'

'Sounds about right. Petty cash should cover it,' Jack said, aware that Clare was at her desk pretending to do paperwork but her shoulders were shaking.

'I want you to phone Stephanie Harrison,' Jack said. 'Get the contract signed and arrange it for Friday.'

Minutes later, Jon put the call through to Jack. 'Snotty cow says she'll only do business with you.'

When Stephanie came on the line, she was back to her daytime manner. 'Meet me in the Prestbury Hotel at eight thirty.'

'I can't do that.'

'Then the deal's off,' she said tartly, and hung up.

Jack arrived at the hotel a good twenty minutes late, but Stephanie was even later and strolled into the bar wearing a lime green trouser suit and a supercilious smile.

'I knew you'd be here, waiting,' she said, kissing him on the mouth. 'I'll have an iced mineral water with lemon.'

Once she had her drink, Jack slapped the contract on the table. 'I like to keep sex and business separate,' he said, offering her a pen.

'Do you? How boring,' she said, taking the pen. She slid it back into his shirt pocket then said, 'Dinner first. My shout.'

'I don't want any dinner.'

'I think you do.'

Stephanie walked into the dining room to a reserved table for two, knowing Jack would follow her, and ordered all the food and two bottles of wine. Then she filled his glass with Pouilly-Fuissé. Jack struggled to ignore it.

'You're so uptight, Jack,' she said. 'Are you still in love with your wife?'

Jack toyed with his avocado and chicken salad, wondering how to get this woman off his back without losing the contract. 'Of course I am. I want her back, if she doesn't bankrupt me in the meantime. Leasing The Links is only the start. I expect the car will go next.'

She smiled dreamily at him, like the cat about to get the cream. 'I don't quite believe that, but I *love* the idea of it all,' she said, and slid him the garlic-sizzled prawns. 'I'd much rather be faced with a challenge than a lot of easy, slushy romance.'

Jack drank the wine and resigned himself to mixing sex with business. Stephanie took him to her hotel room, where Jack searched the wardrobes and checked under the bed, with difficulty because he'd had far too much to drink. He fell over the trouser press.

'This time, I want you to think about me,' she said, lying amongst her discarded clothing. 'Will you stop fussing with those curtains and come here?'

Later, when he was ordering himself a taxi to get home, Stephanie slipped her arms around him. 'I suppose you want me to sign your bit of paper.'

'Only if you want to,' Jack said. 'I've got someone else interested, but I don't suppose you believe that.'

'No, I don't,' she said, but signed it anyway.

The following morning, Jack went to collect his car from the hotel car park, with the usual banging headache and a bruised foot from the man-eating trouser press. Stephanie had left a note on the windscreen.

'You still weren't thinking of me. Next time you will.'

Jack slung the paper in the nearest bin and ordered two-dozen red roses from Interflora. He was in the wrong time period of his life for casual sex with a control freak. He went home to pick up Oliver to make sure he went in to school. Susan Webster was reversing out of her drive with Amy. She gave Jack a barely there sort of smile but Amy was a lot friendlier and waggled her school tie at them through the back window.

'What's the score with Amy?' Jack said.

'I dunno. She's been chasing me for ages but I think she's got a crush on you now.' Jack just missed hitting the bumper of Susan's brand new BMW.

At work, Clare brought him two bottles of water as requested, along with his coffee and the diary printout. His day was full of appointments, which was good, but didn't leave him any time to sort out the flat.

'Clare, I need you to do something for me today,' he said, hunting for painkillers.

'How come you've got a hangover midweek?' she said, handing him some paracetamol.

'Thanks. Don't ask.'

When he told her what his plans were, she was understandably bewildered. 'All I want you to do is to get one of the removal people to shift all the office stuff out of the flat and all the files that are more than two years old to the cellars in the house,' Jack said, giving her a key. 'Then I want them to bring here all the stuff out of Ollie's room, and the suitcases out of mine.'

'For Friday? It's Wednesday now!'

Jack stuck his head round Jon's office door. 'Can you arrange the inventory for my house tomorrow? I'll cover any appointments for you.'

'That's a bit short notice. It's a full day's job. Where do you want me to redirect everything to, anyway?' Jon said, peering at his on-screen diary. 'Where are you moving to?'

'Here.'

When he returned to the office it was late afternoon, and Tabitha was struggling by herself with the phones because Clare was busy at Jack's house and Jon was busy with someone signing up for a rental property. Patsy's parents were sitting in the reception area, looking bored and disapproving.

Jack went straight to the front desk and began dealing with some of the enquiries while he tried to judge what mood Harry and Cynthia were in. After five minutes or so, they came over and cornered him.

'How much longer are you going to be?' Cynthia said.

'You can see how I'm fixed. Why didn't you ring me first?' he said, picking up another call. It was someone looking for a three-bed house with a garage, space for a caravan, and close to a primary school, all within budget. It was tedious and took a while to scan through everything, pull out the relevant brochures to go in the outgoing mail, then put the client details on the computerised mailing list.

When he went to grab the phone again, Cynthia put her hand over his.

'You'll have to wait,' Jack said. 'This is more important.'

'Is it? No wonder Patricia wants a divorce,' she said loudly.

Jon and Tabitha looked up for a second then resumed what they were doing. Jack told Cynthia and Harry to wait in his office, but they wouldn't have any of it and seemed bent on wearing him down.

When there was a gap in the calls and he was showing Tabitha how to access all the properties becoming vacant the following month, Cynthia planted her handbag down firmly on top of some files.

'We've had enough of this. We want to know what's going on.'

'Ask your daughter. She's got more time on her hands.'

'We have,' Cynthia said heatedly. 'She says you've thrown her out and she's pregnant with your child!'

'That's rubbish! Your daughter is a liar.'

The silence in the building was palpable until the door flew open and Stephanie marched in looking like Cruella de Vil. In her arms were two dozen red roses, which she flung haphazardly over the front desk, but mostly at Jack. She was so angry that Jack thought she might fly at his throat any second.

'Don't you ever send me flowers again!'

After a few moments, Jon broke the silence. 'Great timing, Jack.'

'There's nothing wrong with his timing,' Stephanie said, dusting her hands free of greenery. 'It's his little power games I don't like.'

On her way out, she slammed the door so hard that half the wall display fell down and snapped Clare's rubber plant.

'Do you think she's gone off me?' Jack said.

The clients with Jon started looking at each other and giggling.

'I know I've said this before, but this place gets more like *The Jeremy Kyle Show* every day,' Jon said, trying to get Harry and Cynthia to smile as well and grinning at Tabitha, who was picking up all the phones that weren't ringing. 'So, boss, how many women have you sent flowers to this week?'

Cynthia didn't see the funny side. 'You were saying?' she snarled at Jack, then gathered up her coat and bag. 'We've seen and heard enough, thank you.'

Jack put his head on the desk, face down into the heady perfume of the roses and waited till they'd gone.

At home, it was bare. Maria had turned up every day after college and packed all their personal belongings. She was stripping the kitchen cupboards when Jack got there, filling a bin bag with Lottie's out of date cake mix and some furry yoghurt she'd found in the fridge.

'There's penicillin on some of this stuff,' she said, emptying a carton of milk down the sink.

'I know,' Jack said. 'You will come to the flat with us, won't you?'

'If you want me to,' she said, packing bottles and jars into a box.

'It won't be as much work but I'd like to say that Lottie's child-minder is with me looking after Oliver,' Jack went on. 'I know that's a bit of a joke.'

Maria nodded. 'Whatever. It doesn't seem right though, you having to leave all this and live in a flat.'

His mother was of the same opinion.

'But your house is *so* beautiful. It's everything you've worked for,' she said to him over the phone.

Jack ignored the sentiment. 'Ollie's made up about taking over the top floor.'

'So Oliver gets the double room, a sitting room, and a bathroom, and you get the single next door to the lounge.'

'I don't need anything else. It's only temporary till I decide what to do,' he said, 'If Ollie's happy then my life is easier.'

'You'll never get away from that office,' Isabel warned. 'I've seen it all before with your father.'

Jack got her off the subject and on to Chelsey, but she was reluctant to say anything other than not to worry, which made him worry.

'Did you get to see Anna?' he said.

'Yes, yes I did. She's a bit depressed. Alex has to do everything for her. Jack, are you smoking?' she asked suspiciously. 'Oh, and they've set a wedding date for Midsummer's Day.'

'Have they? When's that?' he said sharply, not really wanting to know, and not liking the idea of Alex doing everything for her.

'You know, it's the longest day. In June.'

How bloody appropriate. 'Have you moved yet?' he said, sloshing gin into a tumbler.

'This weekend. I'm trying to persuade your father to have one of Anna's puppies. Have you seen them, Jack?' she said, in a gooey voice.

'Yeah. Cute.'

'There's a little black one that Lottie wanted. I'd like that one, for her. Jack, are you drinking?'

'Of course I'm bloody drinking and smoking, what do you expect?'

On Friday, Jack walked out of The Links with two remaining suitcases and a box, and tried not to think about the implications. Oliver had spent half of Thursday night frantically texting and making sweeping statements on Facebook about his change of address to his inner city penthouse; mostly in the hope that anything destined for his birthday on Saturday would not go astray.

In the office reception, Stephanie's roses had been sentenced to a vase but their heads were drooping, and Clare's rubber plant had been repaired with tape. Jack slid his house keys onto Jon's desk.

'I'm not available to whoever comes to get those.'

'I'd never have thought of that,' Jon said, munching toast.

'Have you managed to suss the payroll yet? Or do we have to phone Jean in bloody Australia?'

Jon stopped chewing then and looked almost sheepish. 'Tabitha's done it.'

Later that day, Jack made a start on unpacking in the flat. Although it was a bit depressing looking at furniture and carpets from the seventies, he did actually feel better knowing he could go downstairs and talk to someone. Being constantly available with a telephone extension from the main desk was something he would just have to live with for a while.

Jack slung his cases into the single room and opened the wardrobe to find an old, broken fax machine, plus a couple of Danny's old jackets and some records. He began to clear everything out, then noticed the pictures stacked on the bottom. Flicking through them, he stopped when he came across a long, slim print framed in limed oak. Turning it over, he was amazed to see the label still there. 'To Jack. All my love forever, Anna.'

Jack sank down onto the bed and stared at the pastel sketch, then propped it against the radio on top of the chest of drawers. It was difficult to be motivated after finding the picture, but then Maria arrived, full of enthusiasm, and tried to make some order out of the chaos in the kitchen. After a while, she declared that the oven didn't work and the washing machine leaked.

'Make a list,' Jack said, investigating the boiler, which refused to fire. Oliver turned up after school with two friends dressed in bin bags, a six pack of lager, and a big plastic bag from the DIY store.

'Me and Maria will have a couple of those beers,' he shouted after them. 'What have you got in that bag?'

'Just some stuff,' Oliver shouted down, then followed with, 'There's not enough plug sockets, Dad.'

Clare buzzed the telephone extension. 'It's OK, you can come out now. Someone's collected your keys.'

'Clare, I need you to get me one of our electricians and a plumber,' Jack said, not wanting to think about his keys, his house, and the solid oak kitchen he'd left behind. 'Buy me a cooker will you?'

'Are you serious?'

'Yeah. One that doesn't burn anything.'

In the morning, it took Jack a while to realise where he was. The orange and blue circles on the wallpaper, and his suit hanging on the curtain pole, reminded him. He'd not expected to sleep well and he hadn't, but he wasn't used to a single bed and had woken himself up several times from hanging off the edge, almost sweeping the contents of the bedside cabinet onto the floor. The traffic noise, especially the Friday night police sirens and ambulances, would take some getting used to.

Just after nine, still in his dressing gown and filling the kettle, the office extension buzzed.

'Jack, I'm *really* sorry to disturb you,' Clare said, in a hushed voice. 'Patsy's here and she's got your little girl with her.'

It took several seconds for this information to sink in. 'Send her round the back.'

Jack went quickly down the stairs, heart pounding, and opened the door. Patsy looked murderous, but he only gave her a passing glance as he lifted up his daughter. Lottie said nothing and seemed limp in his arms, her thumb planted firmly in her mouth; something she'd not done since she was two.

He carried her back up the stairs, and Patsy followed, her heels sounding hollow on the thin carpet. Once in the flat, Jack hugged Lottie to him.

'I've missed you so much,' he said, kissing her hair and her face, but she remained unresponsive. After a while, Jack sat her down on the sofa. She looked at him vacantly. When he asked her if she wanted a drink, she nodded and sucked the hem of her dress.

Patsy followed him into the kitchen. 'So this is where you're hiding!' she hissed, looking disdainfully at the purple wood-chip on the walls. Jack hunted through a cardboard box, looking for Ribena.

'I'm not hiding from anyone,' he said, then went through all the cupboards for a glass, ignoring one of the doors when it fell off.

'I want my house back. How dare you put tenants in it!

How *could* you?' she said, holding the bridge of her nose, her voice breaking with emotion. 'I want all my things back. All my clothes.'

'Try two doors down, Red Cross.'

Once his words had sunk in, her face drained to an angry pallor. 'You bastard!' she said under her breath, and flew at him with her fists.

'Don't be so fucking stupid,' Jack said, pushing her away. 'I can't believe you value all that designer crap more than our marriage.'

She started to cry, and not able to think of anything else to say, Jack went back to Lottie, pulling her on to his lap. The child flopped against him, holding the drink but doing nothing with it. When he tried to talk to her, she just shook her head or nodded.

After a few minutes, Patsy emerged from the kitchen with a repaired face. 'I've brought Oliver's birthday present,' she said, and placed something on the Formica coffee table. 'Where is he?'

'I'm here,' Oliver muttered, making a brief appearance en route from his room to the kitchen. He re-emerged with a mug of tea, barely said two words to his mother, and announced he had some studying to do. When Jack suggested he took Lottie to see his multicoloured room, she followed her brother as if he was a stranger, her thumb back in her mouth.

'How did you bribe Oliver to go back to school?' Patsy said, back to sneering at him.

'I negotiated and we reached a compromise, and if you mess him up I swear I'll *kill you!'*

Lottie came straight back like a little ghost and Jack went to pick her up. 'What's the matter with her?' he said, full of anguish.

'Nothing. She just stops talking sometimes,' Patsy said, and pulled her from his arms.

'It doesn't have to be like this,' Jack said, looking at his daughter's sad face. Something caught in his throat. 'Patsy, please.'

'I'll be in touch through my solicitor,' she said, 'I've got absolutely nothing else to say to you.'

When the door banged closed downstairs, it was like something closing inside his heart.

The extension buzzed. Clare told him that a lot of cards and a couple of parcels had arrived for Oliver. 'I'll bring them round, shall I?'

Jack wiped his eyes. 'Yeah, just give me a few minutes, will you?'

'Sure,' she said, tentatively. 'Jack, are you all right?'

'No, not really. Ten minutes, OK?'

The allotted time passed. Jack watched Oliver open his post while he forced himself to go through the motions of getting dressed. Danny had sent a card featuring blow-up dolls, which was bordering on obscene, until he glanced at some of the others from his friends, including Josh, and realised they were only marginally more tame.

Amy's choice was a tasteful, arty sort of nude but once Oliver had read the message inside he put it in his pocket. Harry and Cynthia had gone for a pop-up skateboard card.

'How old do they think I am, six? Great, loads of dosh from Granddad Lion, naff card as usual,' Oliver said, and propped a cheque against the plastic fruit bowl. Chelsey had sent an iTunes card and a happy birthday balloon.

'Did I tell you your sister's having a baby?' Jack said, trying to find a pair of shoes.

'Who is, Lottie?'

'Don't be so bloody stupid.'

'Dad, isn't it a bit weird, Mum and Chel having babies at the same time?' Oliver said, tearing open another envelope. It was the one from his mother. A letter fell out. Jack stopped tying his shoelaces for a moment. 'Yeah, I suppose it is.'

He gave Oliver his new guitar. It was just after ten in

the morning, exactly sixteen years since his son had come into the world. Jack had been present at all the births of his children, but Oliver had been the only one who was planned. Charlotte, his little princess, had been the result of a missed pill.

His relationship with Patsy had gone through a subtle change after Lottie, but sometimes Jack felt that this was the child he was closest to, maybe because she needed him the most. He felt the raw edge of it increasingly painful, and wondered if he was misreading the signals to imagine that Patsy was jealous of his bond with Lottie. Maybe she always had been.

'Are you all right, Dad?' Oliver said, thoughtfully strumming his guitar.

'Yeah, course I am,' Jack said, getting to his feet, determined not to be on a downer for Oliver's birthday. 'Didn't get much sleep, that's all.'

'What's the matter with Lottie?'

'I think she's probably confused, like we all are,' he said as he put his tie straight. 'Anyway, what are your plans for today?'

'I'm going into town with Beth to spend some of this cash.'

'Who's Beth?'

'My *girlfriend*,' he said, exasperated. 'Then it's party time later, that's about it.'

'Huh,' Jack said affectionately, making for the stairs, 'Don't overstrain yourself.'

'Hey, Dad!' Oliver shouted after him. 'Do you know you've got odd shoes on?'

Later, Jack took Tim for spring rolls and watered down beer at Oliver's party. The Mandarin had lifted its ban on Jack and Tim, with the proviso they didn't dress up as women. Jack had persuaded them to put on a DJ and some food upstairs for about twenty teenagers, but there was another proviso that they didn't become unruly, have sex, smoke anything, take ecstasy, smuggle in their own booze, or throw up anywhere.

'That's a bit of a tall order, isn't it?' Jack had said. 'They're all fifteen and sixteen.'

He promised to supervise, pay for any damage, and evict them all by midnight.

'What does he think they're going to do?' Jack said to Tim, 'Play pass the bloody parcel?'

'Any fit teenage babes coming?' Tim said, looking round the room.

'Plenty but they won't be pulling us, more like pushing us away.'

Right on cue, Amy saw them and trotted over dressed in a tight fluffy pink boob tube and a little silver skirt. She grabbed Jack's sleeve.

'I didn't know you'd be here. Come on I need a partner. Come and play pass the rude balloon with me.'

At the end of the evening, Tim admitted that he'd thoroughly enjoyed himself, to the point that his insides ached from laughing so much, and he'd hardly touched any alcohol. Jack listened patiently to all the highlights again as he walked back to the flat with Oliver. Once inside, he poured himself a large Scotch and a smaller one for his son.

'You never told me what your mother bought you,' Jack said, keeping his eyes on the ice cube tray, but Oliver knew what he was really asking.

'A watch,' he said. 'She's written me this really heavy letter.'

'What about? No, it's OK I can guess.'

'I miss Mum,' Oliver said sagely, taking the drink from Jack. 'but I don't want to live with her and this other bloke. I want to stay with you, do what we talked about.'

'Let's drink to that, then,' he said, hugely relieved. 'Happy Birthday, Ollie.'

On Thursday night, in an effort to regain his fitness and help him sleep, Jack went back to his local health club and slowly did twenty lengths of front crawl in the pool, but he was starting to feel tired after ten and his mind was still buzzing. Before December, he was easily swimming thirty lengths most days after work.

'You need to find a method of relaxation that doesn't involve cigarettes, drugs, or alcohol,' Doctor Musgrove had told him, and refused to give him any more sleeping tablets.

On his way out to the car park, while he was still towelling his hair and drinking water from a bottle, Charles West rang his mobile. Jack waited till he was in his car and had a cigarette before he continued his conversation.

'Patricia is very pissed off about the house,' West said. 'She's demanding seven hundred and fifty thousand as a settlement, plus a negotiable figure for maintenance.'

'What?' Jack said, stunned. 'I can't raise that in cash without mortgaging the company!'

'She says it's costing you nothing to live in the flat and you're pulling in two grand a month from leasing The Links,' he said. 'How do you want me to play it?'

'Fuck knows. What's the score with my daughter?'

Charles made a resigned sigh. 'I've asked for shared residency but she's blanked it totally. She says she'll accept arranged access only. To be honest, this is a grey area, Jack.'

'What do you mean?'

'Well, whatever we agree should happen becomes intransigent in practice.'

'So what are you saying?'

'I think you should agree to arranged access for now. We'll half the figure she's after as a starting point, but I'll need a full account valuation to back that up.'

At home, Jack looked at Anna's picture on the chest of drawers. It was a study of grass, leaves, branches, and sky, but the perspective was unusual. He could remember where the idea had come from. They'd both been about seventeen, lying in the long-faded grass of late summer under an oak tree and it was dusk. He couldn't recall what they'd been talking about, but snatches of conversation came back to him.

'There's always two ways of looking at things. Take us, lying here now,' Anna had said, taking hold of his hand, 'One man might look down and see nothing. The other, he'd look up and see the stars.'

Jack lay on the single bed and wondered if there were any stars at all beyond the dirty ceiling.

Chapter Ten

Anna

A heatwave started towards the end of May. The sky stayed Caribbean blue until the sun set behind purple mountains and burnished the dark sea with its fire. Hill tracks, where sheep lay inert and panting, were turned to dust and bare stone. Hilly's horses were exhausted in no time, their nostrils flared with effort, their flanks heaving and running with sweat.

'I'm not doing any rides in the afternoons,' she said, chewing a strand of grass. 'It's too uncomfortable. And the flies! I'm doing an early morning trek for novices and an evening beach ride for anyone who can stay on above a canter.'

'Sounds wonderful,' Anna said, closing her eyes against the sun. 'Put me down for the beach ride when you're not too busy.'

They were sitting on the untamed patch of lawn that just about passed for a garden at Gwern Farm. Early summer was the most spectacular season in the hills. The colour and profusion of foliage and wild flowers softened the less attractive aspects of the outbuildings, and the house basked well in the heat, its golden stones adrift in a haze of tranquillity. Insect noise was constant, the smells of jasmine and honeysuckle, wild thyme, and mint never far away. In contrast, the water in the lake had never been so low.

Further down the bank, the dogs were flat out under the trees, paws twitching in deep sleep. At times like this,

Anna felt the spell of the place close around her as she wandered dreamily down the little path to fetch the watering can.

'Are we still on for tomorrow?' Hilly said, rummaging in her bag for cigarettes then squinting at Anna as she watered the strawberry pots, poking at the hard earth around the forget-me-nots. 'Have you lost weight, you bitch?'

Anna looked up and frowned slightly. 'If I have, it wasn't intentional. What were you saying about tomorrow?'

'Wedding outfit. Chester,' Hilly said, watching Anna's face. 'You'd forgotten?'

'No, not at all. You know I hate shopping, and Chester will be hot and crowded.'

'Well, you can't get married in those old jeans.'

'Can't I? Not even if I patch the holes and wear a garter?'

Later, Alex rang from London. He was staying with friends for a week, while at a convention for The Catering Business, which was a good thing because neither of them had a clue about running a restaurant.

Alex told her about his day, but it was complicated and meaningless to Anna. He didn't ask about her current commission because he knew she was working on a painting for Leo and Isabel. It was a watercolour of the puppy, Snog, set in their cottage garden and she'd made a cameo print for Lottie alongside.

Anna had made two visits to their pretty cottage to sketch an outline drawing of the garden by the sea, and Isabel had told her all about Jack's on-going problems, which she had wisely kept to herself. Since his late night telephone call four months ago, followed by the flowers, Anna had hardly dared mention Jack's name to Alex.

It had been her first day home from the hospital and

she'd spent over an hour on the telephone to him. He'd pricked her conscience again with his opinions. She had tried to stay cross with him, but when the beautiful creamy roses and the white lilies had arrived with the little card, her resolve broke and she'd been overwhelmed with compassion. She'd even called off the sale, giving in to her mood swings and feelings of doubt. Anna blamed it on the accident and her age, having to deal with lots of major changes at a time in her life when other people were already settled. Alex blamed it on Jack.

But when the relentless winter rain had bled right through to the end of spring, the deterioration of the farm became paramount. Part of the barn collapsed and dry rot took a further hold upstairs. One day, back in April, Anna had stood outside in the rain. It was so wet she could hear the water running into the earth under her feet. The sky was thick, obliterating everything. Alex took her to see the place in Cornwall for the third time, and patiently talked her round. Max Starkey was a happy man again.

Anna loved Alex, but it was more a close partnership than a blazing passion, maybe because it had grown out of a long friendship. She admired the determination he had to pursue his dreams; nothing would deflect him from wanting this restaurant, and she knew he loved her intensely. Plus, she was almost forty-four. She couldn't expect those adolescent feelings of excitement to sustain a mature relationship, could she? Anyway, according to Hilly, their star signs were compatible.

Hilly had come across some ancient chronicles of astrology in Anna's sitting room and had since become hooked. 'So what's Alex then? I know you're a typical artistic, home-loving Cancerian, with a well-stocked larder,' Hilly had said, reading from the book. '"Intuitive and never impulsive, sensitive, protective and caring." You know you even have the physical traits? Big busted, shy but very sexual, expressive eyes, and strong bone structure.'

'Alex is a Scorpio, and I know what it'll say,' Anna said, peeling potatoes at the sink. 'It'll say he's overbearing and jealous.'

'It also says that they have a tendency to be hairy and bow-legged.'

Anna laughed and threw some peelings at her.

'No, to be fair,' Hilly went on, 'you're very compatible, according to this chart.'

'I already know that,' she said, starting on the carrots. 'Anyway, I don't believe all that stuff about predictions and planets.'

'I do. It's all in the stars. Guess who this is?' she said, flicking the pages back. "Has exceptional business acumen and will work to the point of exhaustion. Can pull a business back from the brink of bankruptcy. Likes to be in control. Competitive and enterprising and will take risks. Likes to drive a car with a great image."' She looked up. 'You can stop me when you've guessed.'

Anna said nothing, and threw the carrots into a pan.

'Romantic and soft-hearted, vulnerable to emotional hurts,' Hilly went on, watching Anna's back. 'Finds it difficult to relax, quick-tempered. Enjoys good wines and generally has good taste. Energetic, with a strong body and a dominating sex appeal.'

Anna turned from the sink then. 'OK, it's Aries.'

'Correct!' Hilly said, lighting a cigarette. 'Who do we know who's Aries?'

'Stop it, I know what you're doing!'

'Do you want to know what the compatibility chart says?'

'No,' she said, and turned back to the sink

In the morning, it was just as blazing and relentless as the days before. The post van had been early, and there was a distinctive red and cream envelope on the mat. Leo had said a few days ago that they were finally close to exchanging contracts.

Nevertheless, when she read the few words on the thick embossed paper, Anna had to sit down. She was still there, at the kitchen table in her dressing gown, when Hilly arrived to collect her.

'Aren't you even dressed yet?' she said, huffily. 'What's the matter?'

'It's Leo. He's dead.'

Hilly slumped down in a chair and dragged her eyes from Anna's to the sheet of paper.

'I was only talking to him a few days ago.'

'Do you want to leave the trip till another time?'

'No, no,' Anna said, getting to her feet, 'I'll not go at all if you don't drive me today.'

They set off for Chester in Hilly's new car, but the day was marred. Anna couldn't concentrate and kept complaining that her back and feet hurt and all she wanted was a pint. Hilly did her best to usher her in and out of changing rooms.

'It's no good,' Anna said, glancing over her shoulder into the mirror. 'My boobs are too big and I'm too tall. I either look frumpy or like mutton dressed as lamb.'

'Rubbish you've got a great figure.'

Towards the end of the afternoon, when Anna would have given up hours before and gone home, Hilly found a dark blue silk dress. It was too tight across the chest and too short but Anna had to admit, it had possibilities.

'It's gorgeous,' Hilly said. 'Do you think they'll alter it for you?'

'Well, I can't breathe so I should hope so.'

When the assistant said they could let it out and drop it down, Anna happily handed over Alex's money. 'Can we go home now?' she said to Hilly.

'No. Shoes.'

'No. Shoes when we collect the dress.'

At home, Anna read the letter again. It was just a photocopy, probably one of hundreds sent to clients, with Jack's scribble of a signature across the bottom. It said that the Conwy branch would be closed until further notice, and all business would be handled through Wilmslow.

Anna tried Isabel's telephone number but it was just the usual recorded message. When she tried Jack's office it rang for a good while before Clare answered. She was out of breath and her reply was rehearsed, as if she'd said it a dozen times already.

'Jack isn't taking any calls today. Can I take your name and he'll get back to you?' Clare took her details and disconnected quickly, probably adding her name to a long list.

Alex called to tell her all about stainless steel kitchen units and some state of the art food processors, then inquired if she'd found an outfit.

'Yes, but I'm not telling you what it's like. I'm afraid I've spent a lot of money.'

'That doesn't matter,' he said. 'Are you all right? You sound a bit fed up.'

She told him about Leo and he was sympathetic for a moment. 'Who's handling the sale of the farm, then?'

'Wilmslow office.'

'You mean Jack's dealing with it?'

'Well, I don't see what the alternative is. For goodness sake, Alex, he's just lost his father,' she said, feeling a lump in her throat now she'd actually said it. She took a deep breath. 'Anyway, it's all down to your solicitor now. I don't see how it can affect the sale.'

'It better hadn't.'

The phone rang twice again, but it was only the man about the cesspits, and a girl for Josh.

'Did you know about Oliver's granddad?' she said to Josh.

'What about him? Ollie's away on some mortgage

course, sounds dead boring,' he said then cringed. 'Why are you listening to that ancient version of "Gypsy"?'

The following day, Anna drove into town, parking on double yellow lines because it was so busy. Hilly was just coming out of the bank and trying to shove past a coachload of hikers with huge backpacks, but fell over a couple of buskers sitting on the pavement.

'Bloody tourists,' she said, grumpily.

'You say the same thing every summer,' Anna said, dragging Benson's muzzle out of a pile of kerbside fish and chips. 'We need the visitors. I've got loads booked in for B&B.'

'I suppose we may as well make some money out of them,' Hilly said, looking at the batter and half a polystyrene tray hanging out of Benson's mouth.

Errands done, Anna went to Leo's office. There was a brief explanatory sign on the window, and when she peered through the glass, only her reflection looked back. There was no Gina sitting at her desk, ready to wave or give Benson a forbidden biscuit out of Leo's tin. Benson looked at her reproachfully as she made him come away from the door. Unsure as to whether she was doing the right thing or not, but driven by a complicated need, Anna drove past the turning for the farm and continued down the twisting mountain road towards the cluster of houses and cottages on the other side of the pass.

Between the soaring mountains, the sea occasionally flashed a brilliant sapphire strip, only just distinguishable from the cobalt sky, while the gulls, high as could be, were bone white and noiseless.

Isabel's cottage was between a little caravan park and a row of detached houses that bordered the golf course and looked across the sea to Anglesey and Puffin Island. Anna took the finished paintings of the puppy from the Land Rover and tapped on the door. Kate answered and they recognised each other immediately.

'I wasn't sure if I should call,' Anna said, but Kate looked relieved.

'Oh, don't worry. I'm desperate for someone to talk to. Come in and help me drink some of this tea,' she said. 'Mum's asleep. At least, I think she is.'

Once in the tidy kitchen, Snog came to jump up at her legs, then dived on a shoe under the table.

'I'm so sorry about Leo,' Anna said. 'I've not been able to stop thinking about him.'

Kate stared into the sugar bag for a moment, then began spooning some into a bowl. 'Yes. It was a massive heart attack.'

'When? When did it happen?'

'Saturday morning. He was bending over to pick up a newspaper off the lawn, and that was it,' she said, then went through two cupboards looking for cups. 'Mum was here, and the ambulance was quick, but there was nothing they could do.'

She put everything on a tray and Anna followed her outside onto the patio. The puppy followed, dragging the shoe under its belly as if it were prey, then took it under some bushes. Kate pulled up some chairs to the table and poured the tea. She was attractive, bold in her manner as well as physically, and she still had the same long, bobbed hair. It used to be mousy when she was fourteen, now helped considerably with some artificial blonde colour, but it framed her strong features well, and although they were the same shape, her eyes were bluer, softer, and less flinty than Jack's and Isabel's. Anna couldn't help thinking they were not as seductive as Jack's eyes, perhaps because the tiny wrinkles of age never did look as attractive on a woman's face.

'How's Jack?' Anna said. She hadn't meant to ask quite so soon, but whatever she did, nothing more interesting or important would come into her mind.

'Oh, you know Jack. Grit your teeth and get on with it till you fall over,' Kate said, pushing the milk and sugar over to Anna. 'He belted down here on Saturday morning and managed to pick up a police escort in that car of his, although they had a job to keep up with him. They didn't believe him when he said it was life and death, wanted to give him a speeding fine.'

They exchanged a wry smile, and Kate put a cigarette to her lips and lit it with a gold lighter. She had dark red fingernails and no wedding ring. 'You know he's in the middle of a horrible divorce?'

'Yes, I know,' Anna said, holding her cup so tightly it was burning her hands. Kate gave a surreptitious glance up to the open bedroom window then lowered her voice.

'Mum thinks he's heading for a nervous breakdown and to be honest, I don't know how he's holding everything together,' she said, her voice beginning to betray her emotions. She sighed and wafted smoke away, but her eyes were full of angry tears. 'If that bitch Patsy turns up at my father's funeral I swear I'll tear her limb from limb for what she's done to my brother,' she said angrily, and spilt her tea. 'Oh, bugger!'

They were mopping up when Isabel appeared and accepted Anna's hugs and kisses of commiseration.

'I know what you've been talking about,' Isabel said to Kate. 'You mustn't take all of this business of Jack's to heart so much.'

'Oh, look who's talking,' she said scornfully, wiping the mascara from under her eyes.

'You'll have to excuse us, Anna, we're all upset,' Isabel said. 'You will come on Friday, won't you? It's family at the funeral and then everyone at The King Edward afterwards. Kate posted all the cards this morning.'

'Of course.'

Kate went into the kitchen for another cup and Isabel

took hold of Anna's hand.

'We're all driving each other mad, you know. Daniel phones me every couple of hours. I had Jack here all day Saturday, and he wouldn't leave till Kate got here on Sunday afternoon. They won't be able to keep it up for long. Kate's got three children and two jobs,' she said, hiding Kate's cigarettes under the edge of her chair cushion. 'And Jack! Jack's more in need of a support system than I am.'

Anna smiled sadly, unable to think of anything to say. When Kate reappeared with a spare cup, her mother waved it away.

'I'm awash with tea and coffee. Why don't you get out for a while? Anna will sit with me.'

'I'll go and check the arrangements at The King Edward,' she said, finding her bag and her car keys. She stood in front of Isabel with an outstretched hand. 'I know you've got them, Mother.'

Isabel handed over the cigarettes and gave Anna a tight smile. 'They all smoke too much.'

Anna showed her the watercolours.

'Oh, they're beautiful!' Isabel said. 'You are so clever, you capture every little detail.' She reached for a handkerchief. 'Isn't it silly, the things that make you cry?'

'I've always cried at daft things. Sometimes it's the small things that make the most impression, the things we remember,' Anna said, thinking about the little card Jack had sent with the lilies and the roses. *My Gypsy,* was all it had said.

'Now, let's have some nice news,' Isabel said. 'Tell me all about this wonderful man you're going to marry.'

He rang at teatime, just as she was bringing in the washing. Anna flung it all over the kitchen table and snatched up the phone. Somehow, she knew it was Jack before he even spoke.

'Sorry it's taken so long to return your call,' he said,

after she'd offered the formal commiseration and he'd responded in the expected way. 'I've just spoken to Kate. She says you've been round to the cottage.'

'They're driving each other mad, Kate and Isabel.'

'Always have done. Anyway, Kate's going home after the funeral. I think Dan's stopping with Mum over the weekend.'

'What about you?'

'Too much going on. I'm trying to sort out Dad's business affairs, and Ollie's got his exams coming up,' he said with a tired sigh. 'It's driving me nuts, trying to get him to stay focused.'

'Same here.'

Anna told him about Josh. They'd had arguments all week and Anna was dreading the start of exams because once they were over, it meant that the move to Cornwall would begin. Josh was adamant that he was not going to live hundreds of miles away from everything he knew.

He had real talent in Welsh language and local history, which gave Anna a secret flush of pleasure, but nowhere outside of Wales offered these kind of subjects at an Advanced Level, and Josh wasn't remotely interested in anything else. Alex had laughed at him and said what bloody use was Welsh anyway? Josh hadn't spoken to him since.

'Well, if you want me to be honest, I can't say I blame the lad,' he said, then immediately apologised.

'No it's OK,' Anna said, 'you're right.'

'Actually, your contracts are ready for signing.'

'Oh!'

A measured pause. 'Will you and Josh be there on Friday? I probably won't see you again.'

'Yes, we'll be there,' she said, touched he had included her son.

'Bye, love,' he said softly, and disconnected.

Anna finally replaced the receiver. The phone rang

again almost immediately.

'Bloody sodding tourists!' Hilly said.

I don't blame the lad. Your contracts are ready for signing. I probably won't see you again. Anna sat down slowly and twisted the telephone cord around her fingers.

'Anna?' Hilly said, 'are you there?'

'Yes, I'm here. What have they done now?'

'Only gone and cancelled on me. I've got too many horses tacked up for the beach ride. Do you want to take Blue?'

'All right. Give me ten minutes.'

When she got to the yard, Hilly's blue roan Arab cross mare was waiting for her, pawing the ground, whinnying and rolling her eyes because no one was getting on her. Hilly had to hold her steady while Anna clambered on.

'Are you sure you're up for this?' Hilly said, adjusting the girth and stirrups while expertly avoiding the mare's teeth. 'She's been a bitch all week. She's had both my girls off on those gallops across Tal y Fan. I hope you're in the mood for her.'

'Let's go.'

Once on the beach, the mare pulled relentlessly, the wind catching her mane and tail and whipping Anna's hair across her face.

'I can't hold her much longer, Hilly!'

'I hope you're insured,' she yelled back as usual. 'Go on, let her go!'

Anna let the wet reins slip through her fingers and the mare lurched into a gallop almost from a standing start. The sudden speed left her stomach behind, but Anna didn't care and kicked the mare on. After a few minutes, Blue settled into a powerful rhythmic pace along the edge of the sea. The tide was lazy with barely any movement, and occasionally the mare's hooves skimmed the edge of the surf and sent cascades of spray to rain down on them both, drenching Anna's legs. Then they were on silt, and the mare slowed, labouring in the soft ground.

Eventually, she allowed Anna to pull her back into a canter and they finally stopped, wheeling round to face the sea and wait for the others to catch up. The sun was dying over the horizon and the only sounds were hooves thundering on the sand, Blue's heaving flanks, the chattering of the oystercatchers and the screaming gulls investigating the day's litter. She should feel on top of the world. So why did she have so many tears waiting to pour down her face?

Isn't it silly, the things that make you cry?

After Anna had told Isabel about Alex and the house in Cornwall, she'd said, 'I'll miss you when you go. Do you mind if I confess something to you?'

Anna had replied, 'No, go ahead.'

'I know it was a long time ago, and I know I'm a sentimental old woman, but I was so disappointed when you and Jack split up.' Then she'd smiled wistfully. 'I haven't embarrassed you, have I?' she'd said, and looked directly into her eyes so Anna had to look away.

She looked down at the mare's restless hooves and tried to wipe away some tears on her sleeve, but Hilly caught up and noticed.

'There's something you're not telling me, Anna Williams.'

'I've got sand in my eye.'

'Sure.'

On Friday, the heat hit an all-time high, and it was difficult to dress for a funeral. All her dark clothes were heavy and wintry. In the end, Anna settled for a long, black cotton skirt. It had tiny white daisies on it, but with a black jacket it looked suitably sober.

Her hair was so long now that it almost touched the base of her spine, but it was easy to twist into a haphazard topknot without looking too untidy. No makeup necessary;

she was deeply tanned from painting in the garden and lying naked in the sun. Slipping her bare feet into a pair of mules, she shut the dogs in the barn and jumped into the Land Rover.

The hotel was so crowded that at first Anna didn't see anyone she knew. She refused the customary sherry and was ordering a beer at the bar when Danny came up behind her and slid his arms around her waist.

'I'll get that, gorgeous,' he said, hugging her as she turned round in his arms.

'Dan, how are you?' she said, planting a kiss on his cheek.

He shrugged and didn't seem to know what to say. 'I was supposed to get up and say this speech but my bottle went,' he said dejectedly, throwing a pile of loose change on the bar to pay for her drink.

'It doesn't matter,' Anna said, sipping her beer. 'Did anyone else volunteer?'

'Yeah,' he said, looking at his shoes, 'Ollie did it. He was brilliant.'

The funeral throng assembled in the main room behind the bar. Danny steered her over to Isabel, who looked polished and serene with a plate of untouched buffet food in front of her. There was only enough room to squeeze Isabel's hand across the table and find a space next to Kate, who introduced her to a lot of people she'd likely never see again. She vaguely remembered some of the staff from Jack's office. Tim was there, whom she didn't recognise at first because he was roughly twice the size he used to be, with half as much hair.

'How did it all go?' Anna asked Kate.

'As planned, apart from Danny's hiccup. He blubbed all the way through,' she said, playing with a forkful of food then finally abandoning it. Someone tapped her on the back, and Anna spun round, thinking it was Jack. It was Josh, who'd walked up from school.

‘I’ve found Ollie and we’re going down the quay,’ he said, draining her glass of beer.

‘Where’s Jack?’ she said to Oliver.

‘Dunno, down the road I think.’

Isabel overheard and exchanged a look with Kate, then leaned across the table. ‘I can’t believe he’s in that office. Do you think he’s all right?’

Kate just pulled a face and flapped her hand, so Isabel tugged Tim’s sleeve. ‘Go and find Jack, will you? He’s been acting really strange, I’m worried.’

‘He told me he wanted some time out,’ Tim said with a smile. ‘He’ll be along later.’

‘See?’ Kate said. ‘He’s not like Danny, so stop fussing.’

‘That’s why I’m worried. He’d feel a lot better if he was like Daniel and let some of it go.’

‘He’s too angry,’ Kate said, getting to her feet. ‘It’s stifling in here. I’m going outside for a fag. Are you coming, Dan?’

Danny and Kate left the table and everyone spread out a bit. A young, very pregnant woman looking hot and bothered sat in Kate’s empty seat. She looked at Anna under her lashes for a while, as if unsure whether to say something.

‘Are you Anna Williams?’ she said accusingly.

Anna looked at her properly. Chelsey. ‘Yes, why?’

‘I don’t know how you have the gall to turn up to my grandfather’s funeral.’

‘Why not?’

‘I know you’re having an affair with my father.’

‘I am not!’ she said, looking round to see if anyone else had heard, but it was too noisy with conversation and Aunt Beatrice was having trouble with her hearing aid.

‘You were in my mother’s bedroom waiting for him,’ Chelsey hissed. ‘You’re disgusting. I hate you both.

Oblivious to the tension, Isabel leaned across and

tapped Anna's hand. 'Be a love and go and find Jack, will you?'

Chelsey looked at her then, waiting for a reaction, but Anna was just glad of an excuse to leave.

She walked down the street in an agony of indecision, thinking it might be better to just go home, but she'd wanted to carry this alliance with Jack to a dignified end, one that she was in control of this time. She hesitated outside Leo's office, wondering how she was going to do just that, when Jack opened the door. Anna slid into the semi darkness.

'Were you looking for me?' he said.

'Isabel's worried. I was sent to find you.'

'I didn't realise how long I'd been in here.'

He sat in his father's chair and put his feet up on the desk, then took a cigarette out of its packet and turned it end over end before putting it to his lips. 'I've seen the boys. I had a walk down the quay with them.'

Anna sat in Gina's chair and took a critical look at him, trying to determine exactly what it was about this man that made her feel as if her life had been on freeze frame for twenty-five years. All she could see was that he was thinner, and even more tense.

'What are you doing here, anyway?'

'Thinking how to raise a million.'

'What on earth for?'

Jack laughed, but his voice, even his body, was full of bitterness. He lit the cigarette, and threw the lighter across the desk. 'On the strength of my proposed inheritance, my wife has seen an opportunity to up her settlement.'

He told her about Leo's will. It hadn't been read yet, but Isabel had told them all what was in it. Isabel, Kate, and Danny were well provided for, but it had been a well-known fact for years that Leo's business interests would go to his eldest son, and that included the Conwy office plus substantial properties and company shares, mostly because Jack was the only one who understood what they were all about. And now that Oliver was likely to be the protégé, it seemed doubly appropriate.

'I can't believe Patsy gets to benefit from your father's death,' Anna said quietly.

'Apparently, Patsy has claim to everything!' Jack said, getting to his feet and grinding out the cigarette. 'Even my peace of mind. Do you know that even my own daughter doesn't want me at her wedding? She won't even speak to me. Have you any idea what that feels like?'

She went to put her arms around him, but she couldn't bring herself to tell him about the exchange with Chelsey; he seemed too broken already. Although he hugged her back, he felt wooden, as if he was afraid of her closeness.

'Jack, please don't give up.'

'Why not? What's wrong with giving up?' he said, then seemed to soften and hung his head next to hers. 'I'm sick of trying to fight everyone. Sometimes I feel so ill I can hardly get out of bed.'

For some reason, he reminded Anna of the horse on the beach, labouring through the deep silt. 'I don't want to leave you like this.'

'Well, I'm sorry. I just can't summon the brave face required for saying goodbye to you, for wishing you a happy life with Alex.'

At first she thought he was being churlish, but when she looked at him, his expression was more complicated and at odds with his choice of words. Anna couldn't draw away and her throat was too constricted to speak, but he didn't seem to expect any kind of response. He stopped looking at her, picked up his cigarettes, and went to stare through the window instead. The chatter of people outside on the pavement filtered through to them, but Jack seemed unseeing and unemotional.

Through the reflection on the glass, the display of Gwern Farm looked back at her. Sold, Subject to Contract.

Anna picked up her bag and fumbled to open the door. Afterwards, she didn't remember running down the street.

Alex returned from London in the early evening. Anna collected him from the station and did her best to be interested in what he had to say. She'd made his favourite meal. The chicken was overcooked and the raspberry mousse wouldn't set, but Alex didn't notice. He was too busy talking.

'We need to decide on a new kitchen. I thought stainless steel,' he said, pouring wine. 'It's durable and more hygienic. I mean, this rustic look is all very well, but Health and Safety would have a field day in here.'

Anna looked round at her kitchen as if she was seeing it all for the first time; at the pheasants strung up in the larder and dog food all over the floor, and wondered if she'd change it in any way.

'What about the eating areas, have you had any ideas?'

'Sorry, no.'

'What do you think to a modern theme? Lots of white and silver?'

When she still made no comment, he looked at her more closely. 'Darling, what's wrong? You've hardly said or eaten anything.'

Anna sighed and pushed her plate away. 'Nothing, I'm tired.'

Alex carried on eating, but set his gaze on her. 'Come on, I know there's something.'

'Well, actually, I've had an awful day. It was Leo's funeral today.'

'I knew there'd be a Redman in there somewhere,' he said, throwing his napkin down, piqued because she'd taken the shine off his enthusiasm. 'Whenever you get these moods it's usually down to one of them!'

He apologised immediately.

The remainder of the evening was strange, as an outer

body experience might be, as if her spirit was watching herself go through the motions.

'Don't forget,' Alex said, when she was lying in his arms much later. 'Don't forget you have an appointment to go and sign on Monday.'

'I know,' she whispered, looking through the open window at the tumbling wisteria and the sounds of skylarks in the gorse.

Chapter Eleven

Anna

Anna's wedding day, at the height of midsummer. Swallows and larks darted over the rolling heather on the wild moorland above Gwern Farm.

She climbed the long, rocky track from Rowan up to Llangelynin Church, on the site of an old Roman road, and in places so remote as to be almost inaccessible. The dogs scrambled on ahead, tails high and noses close to the ground, exploring this unfrequented walk with unbridled enthusiasm, running back and forth with impatience. The climb was steep and Anna needed to keep stopping for water.

She came to the little stone church and lay on the rough grass amongst the bilberry bushes and slowly browning heather. There was no need to go inside. This was an ancient, consecrated place and Anna felt its spirit embraced not only herself, but everything she could see for miles and everything she could feel.

Old Farmer Jones called it *hiraeth*. There was no word quite like it in the English language, some Welsh just didn't translate well, but Anna understood it fully, as she lay on that remote hilltop with the wind tearing at her clothes, and a curlew crying over the marshes.

On the way back from Rowan, after such intense solitude, Anna felt the need for company and impulsively drove to Isabel's cottage. She didn't really know why. Maybe it was something to do with missing her own mother on such a bittersweet day,

‘Goodness, you look hot!’ Isabel said, opening the door. ‘Have you come for the cheque, for the paintings?’

‘Oh, no, I’d forgotten all about that.’

She followed Isabel into the cottage and saw Leo’s clothes and shoes strewn all over the sofa. The sounds of Vaughan Williams filled the room.

‘I’m sorry, you’re busy,’ Anna said, looking sadly at the suits and folded shirts, but Isabel just tapped her hand and turned the music down. ‘No, not really. Please stay, have some lunch with me.’

They sat at the little table on the patio and talked absently about how hot it was, knowing that neither of them was quite so trite as to discuss the weather. But then Isabel put her coffee cup down and looked shrewdly at Anna.

‘I know what today should have been,’ she said. ‘No regrets?’

‘No, none,’ she said, truthfully. ‘I haven’t shed a tear.’

‘Then you did the right thing, for all of you,’ Isabel said, with such conviction that Anna felt her heart gladden, and a huge well of relief began to wash away at some of the guilt. Isabel passed her the tissues with a sympathetic smile.

The previous month, on the day she was meant to sign her contracts for the sale of the farm, Anna had turned up ridiculously early on Isabel’s doorstep. After they’d gone through two pots of tea and toast, Anna had said, ‘I can’t marry Alex’.

Isabel had already guessed, and once the floodgates had inched open, it was as if all her other anxieties were desperate to get through the same gateway to freedom. Anna hadn’t realised how connected they all were. She’d talked all morning about the farm, about her mother, Josh, and Alex. Despite her own grief, Isabel had been supportive and remarkably astute.

That same afternoon, instead of driving to the

solicitor's in Colwyn Bay, Anna had gone into Redman Estates and told the new manager that she was backing out. She'd felt sorry for him because it was such a big sale, and it was his first day in the office. The worst bit, though, was telling Alex. At first he was furious because she hadn't signed the contract, but when he learned that she didn't want to marry him, he'd been inconsolable. For three weeks he'd followed her obsessively, trying to get her to change her mind, until she'd broken down in tears of angry frustration in the local butcher's shop. Anna vowed there and then never to become so hopelessly caught up in someone's hopes and dreams ever again. Marriage was not for her.

Isabel brought out some sandwiches and pulled the parasol over to shade the table. Midsummer Day was living up to its romantic ideal. It would have been a stunning day for a wedding.

'How do you cope with loneliness?' Anna said, wondering if the end of a long relationship carried some of the same criteria as bereavement.

'When they were all here fussing, I wanted them to go, and now I find it too much to be alone all the time,' Isabel said, pouring out some wine. 'I expect there's a middle ground somewhere. You'll get used to living alone again, but don't rule out another relationship. You're much too young and beautiful, and you're not the sort to be alone by choice.'

'Who is?'

'Well, Kate for one. She's as tough as old boots, just like her father.'

'What about Danny and Jack?' Anna said, knowing she was luring Isabel into a subject she felt both frightened and fascinated by.

She hadn't spoken to Jack since the funeral. He must know by now that the sale of the farm had fallen through, maybe even that the wedding had been cancelled.

Although, Isabel had given her word that their conversation would remain private until Anna was ready, and it seemed so far that she was an honourable confidante.

If Jack was aware of the whole story, he had chosen not to contact her, and at first she hadn't wanted him to. Now though, her feelings see-sawed between wanting him to know the facts and not being ready for him to say I told you so.

'Both my sons have got it right,' Isabel was saying. 'Their father's intellect and my emotional makeup and in fact, Daniel's the most sensitive underneath that chauvinistic act he likes to fool everyone with.'

'Really?'

'Oh, goodness, yes. Put him in front of *Bambi* and I can guarantee he'll have tears streaming down his face from just hearing the music,' she said, smiling at Anna's amusement. 'Jack lasts a bit longer, but not by much. He at least gets to the bit where the mother deer gets shot. But Daniel is *hopelessly* emotional. Leo and Kate used to tease him relentlessly,' Isabel laughed. 'Oh, is that my telephone?'

She went inside, killing the music. Anna collected the plates and glasses off the table and took them into the kitchen, then hovered in the sitting room. The conversation sounded upsetting and after a short while, Isabel came to find her. She looked ashen, and the light-hearted mood had gone.

'What is it?' Anna asked.

'It's Jack. He's had an accident. I have to go to him,' she said, distracted and darting about, busily locking the patio doors and pulling down the blinds in the kitchen. Then, as if she suddenly realised the hopelessness of the situation she sat down abruptly.

'I can't drive all that way. I have to feel brave to get in and out of the village car park,' she said, rummaging through her handbag, as everything began falling out. 'I'll have to get a taxi.'

'What kind of accident?' Anna said, trying to help her pick up lipsticks, keys, and shopping lists, but they both had shaking hands and kept dropping things.

'Clare said that apparently he was coming out of the pool in the health club last night and he passed out.'

'So, where is he now?' Anna said, 'still in hospital?'

'Oh no, he's discharged himself. The first anyone knew anything had happened was this morning when he turned up at the office in a cab.'

'I'll take you. I'll drive,' Anna said, handing Isabel her bag.

'Are you sure? We'll have to take Leo's car.'

'Fine,' Anna said, thinking nervously of the powerful BMW on the drive. Alex had tried many times to get her to drive down the dual carriageway after her accident, but to no avail. She'd needed a bigger incentive.

Leaving Isabel to pack a bag, Anna took Snog to Gwern Farm and shut her in the barn with her own dogs, fed and watered everything, and left messages everywhere for Josh who was taking his English GCSE exam. In less than an hour, they were heading down the A55.

Isabel was pensive and didn't notice how badly Anna was driving. The car handled differently to her old Land Rover but it kept her mind off the thought of the crash barriers near the Chester exit. Once past the fatal black spot, Anna relaxed a little and began to overtake caravans and fiddle with the air conditioning.

'I knew something like this would happen,' Isabel said after a while.

'Why did he pass out? Did Clare say?'

'According to Jack, it was low blood sugar. He'd swum a ridiculous number of lengths and not eaten all day.'

'That sounds like Jack.'

'Yes, but that won't be the full story. He isn't looking

after himself. You know he was diagnosed with a mild ulcer before the funeral?'

Anna glanced at Isabel. ' No, no, I didn't.'

'Clare said he seems exhausted, depressed,' Isabel went on, staring out of the passenger window. 'All this, on top of everything else, he must be feeling dreadful!'

Anna parked on the office forecourt and Clare trotted out. She pressed a key into Isabel's hand. 'He's in the flat. I haven't told him I've rung you,' she said. 'He'll go *mad.*'

'It's all right, you did the right thing.'

Anna followed Isabel up the stairs. She felt hot and tense from the journey and her insides were somersaulting. Jack was lying on the sofa in his dressing gown, a laptop across his legs, and Wimbledon blaring on the television. He did a double take at them.

'What the fuck are you doing here?'

'That's charming,' Isabel said, 'but not unexpected. Put that cigarette out.'

He stared at Anna with an expression bordering on incredulity, and at first she thought they'd overreacted because he only had a bandaged wrist, but when Isabel put her arms around him and he struggled to sit up, his movements were slow and obviously painful.

'You and Oliver are coming back with me,' Isabel said, but he just lay back against the sofa and put a hand over his eyes, as if the very thought of it was too much. There was something weary about him that had nothing to do with anything physical and Anna was reminded of the church above Rowan and her own personal crossroads.

'Pack some things and come back to the cottage. You need to get away from here for a while, and you need looking after.'

'No, Mum, I can't do that. Ollie's not back from a trip till tonight and he's still got exams.'

'Oh blast, I'd forgotten,' she said, still holding on to him. 'I'll just have to stay here!'

‘There’s no room, and anyway, I don’t need looking after.’

‘You do,’ she said, then went into the kitchen to cool off and rethink her strategy. They heard her banging down cups on the worktop.

‘Whose idea was this?’ he asked Anna. ‘I don’t need a rescue operation.’

She sank down into a chair, realising how tired she was. ‘Clare rang her.’

‘She shouldn’t have,’ he said in a low voice, and extinguished his cigarette. ‘Mum’s got enough to deal with and I don’t want her here now, not when I’m like this.’

Anna rested her head back and looked at the ceiling for a moment, and thought briefly about the wisdom of what she was going to say, but there didn’t seem to be any alternative.

‘You could come back to the farm with me.’

He looked up sharply. ‘What about Alex?’

‘Alex and I are no longer together.’

Isabel brought a tray into the room. ‘You’ve done wonders with this flat. I do like the plain walls and the dark wood floor in here,’ she said, pouring coffee. ‘When I’ve had this, I’m going to go and find that camp bed.’

‘Look Mum, you don’t need to do that,’ Jack said, looking directly at Anna for confirmation. ‘I’ll go back with Anna. You can stay and fuss Ollie.’

Isabel looked at them both, astonished. ‘Oh! Now, why didn’t I think of that?’

It took an age to get back onto the motorway because they hit Monday evening rush hour. Anna waited for Jack to make some remark about her driving, but he was engrossed in reading Leo’s papers and notes from the glove compartment. Then, within minutes of getting onto the motorway, he was struggling to stay awake and finally fell asleep against the passenger door.

Anna had never seen him so debilitated. He was much

weaker than she thought. When he was wearily getting dressed and throwing a lot of tablets into a bag, Isabel had taken her to one side.

'Anna, are you sure about this? Have you got guests booked in as well?'

'No, none,' she'd lied. 'I am sure, don't worry.'

Just as they were crawling through the traffic into Conwy behind someone with a boat on a trailer who didn't seem to know where he was going and a coach from France that became jammed under the archway, Jack woke up.

'Stop at the newsagents, will you?' he said grumpily. 'I need supplies if I'm to be held prisoner in the middle of nowhere.'

'No one's holding you prisoner, and it's not the middle of nowhere.'

She had to park on double yellow lines and he was an age buying sweets, books, cigarettes, and newspapers, while she fended off the traffic warden and waved on angry motorists. When he climbed, a bit shakily, into the car, he gave her an apologetic smile and some Jelly Babies. It was impossible to be cross with him.

At the farm, he sat in the cool sitting room while Anna unpacked the car and found cold drinks.

'I feel useless,' he said, fussing the dogs. 'I don't like you running round after me.'

'You haven't got much choice,' Anna said, throwing her shoes off and opening the French windows. 'Who says I'll be running round after you? There are eight people booked in, and Mrs Thompson's overweight spaniel to paint.'

'Can I ask you something?' he said, peering into the bottom of his glass. 'I need to know a couple of things. Did you call it all off or was it Alex?' He looked up and met her eyes.

Anna knew this was coming. 'I did.'

‘Would you have told me?’

She nodded. ‘Yes. I just wanted to get today over with. I wanted to get things straight in my mind.’

He gave her an imperceptible nod, then leant back and looked at her. ‘I didn’t know you’d backed out on the sale of this place. I couldn’t get my head round anything after the funeral. Didn’t know what was happening half the time.’

‘I can understand that.’

She gave him the double room at the back of the house. It was small and the window wouldn’t close because it had ivy growing through the frame, but it had well-behaved plumbing and a long view over the garden and down the misted valley towards Tal y Fan.

Jack sat for a while looking out, then lay across the bed, pleased that the temperamental television actually picked up Wimbledon once Anna had taped the aerial back in.

‘You should be having total bed rest and getting some sleep.’

‘There’s no way I can get to sleep at teatime with the sun blazing in and fifty bloody seagulls screaming outside the window,’ he said, folding his arms stubbornly.

‘Have you taken all your tablets?’

‘No. I’d be dead if I’d done that.’

‘Glad to see you haven’t lost your sense of humour.’

She left him alone and busied herself with the mundane tasks necessary to accommodate four Germans and a party of hikers. Tired as she was, she managed to prepare the rooms with a smile on her face.

A couple of hours later, holding a bundle of laundry, Anna looked around the slightly ajar door of her lilac room. The occupant appeared to be in a deep sleep. He was in the same position as before, with one leg propped up, but he had slid down the bed. Her young chocolate Labrador was lying across him and snoring. The dog looked up when he saw Anna, yawned, and thumped his tail. The television was making a loud shushing noise because the aerial had fallen out again and Jack's mobile was flashing. She quietly switched it off, then went to fiddle with the television, but only managed to make it worse.

'Leave that. I was watching it,' Jack mumbled, rubbing the back of his neck, 'and leave the phone switched on.'

'You were not watching anything. You were comatose,' Anna said, gently throwing the phone at him, but she was laughing to herself as she shut the door behind her.

It was Hilly's turn to buy the cakes. She complained about the queue and the lack of seats, then deposited a teapot and two meringues in front of Anna. They were in the village tearoom, a usual occurrence mid-afternoon every Tuesday.

'Did Alex phone you yesterday?' Hilly asked, squashing into a seat and pouring the milk.

'Sorry, what?'

'Alex, did he phone you?'

'Oh, yes,' she said, absently adding sugar and stirring. 'You'll never, ever guess who I've got in the lilac room.'

Hilly studied her face, then added tea to the cups. 'Go on, you'd better tell me. I've a feeling it's going to dominate the conversation.'

For a good while, Hilly listened avidly but made no comment, then poked the remaining cake.

'Are you having that or not? Only if not, I'll have it before it melts.'

'Have you heard anything I've said, or are you just here to gorge?'

'Yes and yes. Well, it's all I've got, the pleasure of food,' Hilly said and licked the back of her spoon. 'Anyway, now that your prickly scorpion has gone, you'll be concentrating on randy ram, and if that isn't being greedy I don't know what is.'

In the evening, Anna was arranging cut flowers from the garden for the bedrooms. There was an abundance of foliage everywhere, though she knew there was another, deeper reason – she was unconsciously avoiding Jack by making herself too busy.

She poked roses into an assortment of jars, and looked across at him sprawled on her sofa, watching *EastEnders* and drinking her strong beer. Her eye was drawn to his bandaged wrist and the way his shirt cuff was so unevenly rolled back. It made him look vulnerable. He'd spent the day falling asleep all over the house. The previous night he'd been awake after two in the morning, talking to her hens in the garden and reading some musty old school books he'd found in her bookcase.

When she'd arrived home from the tearoom, he was in the garden sitting in her deck chair under the old apple trees and reading *Gun Dogs-Effective Training Part One*.

'If I poach some salmon, will you eat it?' she'd said.

'In wine and tarragon?'

'What's this leading to?'

'Nothing. I've changed my mind.'

'About the fish?'

'No, about being looked after. I quite like it.'

She'd laughed, threw her shoes into the grass, and pinned up her hair. He'd caught hold of her wrist and pulled her onto his lap.

'What did you have a shower in?' she'd asked, her head close to his.

'Something out of a little bottle, why?'

'No wonder Hooper is in love with you. I think it might be dog shampoo.'

'I didn't think it lathered much.'

They were so natural together, and the simple, exquisite feeling of just being close to him took her by surprise. She'd wanted him to carry on holding her, looking at her with those tired eyes and making her laugh. She could remember the first time he'd made love to her, the hundredth time, and all the times after that. She'd never found the same passion and excitement with anyone else. She was wary of the chemistry now, unsure if it was in the present and real, or if it was all imagination and rose-tinted teenage memory.

Anna finished with the flowers. She picked up the outline sketch of Mrs Thompson's spaniel and went to sit next to him.

'It looks too fat,' Jack said, leaning against her shoulder.

'That's because *it is,*' she said, tapping the pencil on her teeth. 'You smell different. Nice.'

'Only because I washed off that bloody flea and tick shampoo you so thoughtfully leave in your guest rooms.'

She loved his sarcastic humour, becoming aware of a wide grin spreading across her face while she concentrated. He watched her draw for a while. 'Why did you ditch Alex?'

'I didn't ditch him,' she said, carefully drawing whiskers. 'It was more a combination of argument and circumstance.'

'Such as?'

'I couldn't … I couldn't let go of the farm,' she said, then stopped to look at him, wondering if he thought she was shallow or selfish to cite the farm as the number one reason, but his expression was serious, benevolent even. Encouraged, she bent over the portrait.

'I don't want to be married. I like my own space too much. And then there's Josh, we're both so happy here,' she said, making tiny additions to the feathering on the dogs paws. 'I didn't love Alex enough to change all those things.'

Jack lit a cigarette. Anna could feel him watching her, thinking about what she'd said, knowing he'd have an opinion.

'If he loved you, he shouldn't have expected you to make all those big changes. It was obvious you and Josh weren't happy. No doubt the cash from this place will be missed as well.'

She twisted round to look at him, feeling annoyed that he'd read the situation so easily and exposed all her fears, and, if he was so shrewd concerning her feelings, did he realise he'd been the catalyst? She wasn't ready for anyone, least of all Jack, to sit in judgement on her frail, confused emotions, but she now felt sure her eyes were giving it all away.

Jack put his cigarette down and folded his arms around her. 'I'm sorry,' he said. 'Anna, I'm sorry. I shouldn't have said that. What I really meant to say is, I'm glad you didn't go away. I'm glad you didn't marry him. The reason doesn't matter.'

She nodded into his shoulder. 'Me too,' she whispered, finding relief in acknowledging it out loud. He ran a hand through her hair, just once, and Anna would have given anything to understand what else was in his heart. Maybe he didn't even know. He probably felt as adrift as she did, if not more so. Anna only had five years of Alex to work through, and it had been her decision to end the relationship. Jack had had no choice but to dissolve his long marriage, leaving a lot of complicated threads dangling, something she needed to keep reminding herself of.

The telephone rang and the moment of intimacy was gone. She extracted herself from his embrace. He gave her a wan smile and went back to his cigarette. How ironic that it was Alex on the other end of the phone.

'You've been crying,' he said.

'No, it's nothing, I'm all right,' Anna said, stuffing tissues into her sleeve. 'I'm not in the mood for anything controversial, though.'

However, Alex was still hurting and struggling with the

issues they'd argued about. Bravely, Anna tried to persuade him to go into partnership with his brother and go ahead with the restaurant.

'But I still love you,' he said wretchedly.

It was dark and late when Anna finally said goodbye. Jack had gone to bed, leaving a note on the drawing of Mrs Thompson's spaniel. He'd found a copy of her quote and written across it in his barely legible scrawl, "You don't charge enough for your time. You did an hour on whiskers and paws. That's another twenty quid."

Saturday morning was just awful. Anna was so tired she knew she was going to snap at some point in the day. The whole week had been tense, busy, and hot. Jack had started to feel a bit stronger, but had nothing much to do.

'These gutters are like bloody Kew Gardens,' he'd said, straining his head out of the bedroom window and tugging at a trailing weed. 'I'll get a ladder. They need clearing.'

'You'll do no such thing! There's house martins nesting under there.'

Another time he'd asked, 'You know those people you've just put in room four?'

'What about them?' she'd replied, dusting the Welsh dresser.

'Better check how much they weigh. If it's more than thirty stone, there's a good chance they'll fall through the bloody floorboards. They're all rotten! They need ripping out. You know there's no point putting polish on that furniture? It's riddled with woodworm.'

The previous night, Alex had rung again and kept her talking till late, and the conversation went round and round in her head until she couldn't sleep. Then she'd heard Jack and Hooper going downstairs and making tea at some unearthly hour.

Anna must have eventually slept but woke agitated, already working out all the breakfasts she had to do. She'd never had so many paying visitors. The continuing good weather meant there was also a constant stream of tourists calling on spec for the weekend. They all wanted full cooked breakfasts before they went off into the hills to drop litter and disturb the livestock.

In the middle of her disorganisation in the kitchen, Jack appeared. Anna tried to work out which of his basic three moods he was in. He swayed from being his usual funny self, to sometimes not communicating at all and taking himself off somewhere. These two modes of behaviour she could happily live with, but his critical, irritable head was something she would no longer tolerate. It was as if he was taking out all his anger and frustration on her and she wasn't resilient enough to cope with him.

When she spied him watching from the doorway, Anna knew she was in for a dose of the latter and began to slam pans down and throw eggs into them with an aggression she hoped would serve as a warning.

'You know you're giving them too much food for what you charge?' he said.

Anna tried to get past him carrying three very hot plates. 'Jack, you're in my way,' she said, then gritted her teeth when he went to turn over the Welsh cakes on the hot plate before they were ready.

The German man who'd ordered extra eggs left them all because he said they didn't have yellow yolks and refused to believe Anna's explanation that free-range hens produced natural-looking eggs. He told her then, in very explicit English, that he would not be paying for his breakfast.

Anna tipped the whole lot into the dog's bowls, imagining they were going into someone's lap. She could sense Jack was itching to have his say. When she went to find the invoices, he'd already written out the bill for room two.

'What's this?' she said crossly.

He tasted her uncooked Bara brith mixture with a big spoon. 'What? Oh, it's Hitler's bill,' he said, adding a lot of sugar to the bowl.

Anna scanned the page quickly. He'd increased the price of the room, added VAT and a service charge, then deducted half the price of the breakfast.

'Stop interfering!' she hissed at him. 'He won't pay, it's much too high.'

'I bet you a fiver he does,' Jack said, stirring the Bara brith.

'He won't, and from now on you're banned from my kitchen.'

The German man paid his bill without question and told Anna her property was very beautiful, and did she know that not only was there a wide crack down the dining room chimney, but there was something nesting in there as well? Jack was waiting for her in the kitchen, leafing through all the other invoices he'd found on the hall table.

'If you charged for everything properly you might be able to do something about some of your repairs,' he said. 'As it is, you're not financially viable. How much do you pay for eggs?'

'Nothing,' she said smugly, and folded her arms.

'So how much does it cost to feed the hens?'

'About a dozen loaves of Bara brith,' she said, starting to enjoy herself. Let him work this little lot out. 'The hotel in town has them in return for poultry feed from their farm. Although not this time, because you've made it too sweet.'

'OK,' he went on, slightly exasperated. 'So how much do all the Bara brith ingredients cost?'

Anna shrugged. 'Well, I get all the flour and dried fruit in return for two dozen eggs every week from the man who has the flour mill in Llangollen.'

'You're being deliberately obtuse.'

'Yes, well, this isn't the same as the big city. Hard cash

is less important here,' she said, and began to load the dishwasher. 'And anyway, it's none of your bloody business. I don't tell you how to sell houses.'

'You'd probably give them away. Free apartment with every cream tea.'

Anna watched him shove the papers back into her old chocolate box and throw the broken lid back on.

'Why is "profit" such a dirty word to you?' he said darkly, making her feel at once dispirited, because she knew, in principal at least, that what he said was absolutely true. She watched him go moodily from the room, Hooper following, egg all over his muzzle.

Kate rang her after lunch. 'I believe you've got my big brother held hostage for the sake of everyone's sanity,' she said. 'How is he, anyway?'

'To tell you the truth, I'm not sure,' Anna said, glancing fretfully at the clock. 'We had a bit of an argument about my business methods, or lack of them. He went out somewhere and I've not seen him since.'

'Gone off in a childish stomp, has he?'

'No, not really. He was right, as it happens.'

'He usually is if it's anything to do with money. He's just like Leo.'

After the call, she went into Jack's room and flung herself across the bed, burying her face in his pillow. It had a faint masculine smell, something comforting like shaving cream. She allowed herself a moment of nostalgia, then turned on her back and looked at the peeling ceiling. The room was warm and flooded with sunlight, with an underlying aroma of lavender from the big bunch of herbs she had tied to the curtain pole.

She had decorated this room recently, in very pale lilac and cream, but the plaster was already falling off one wall and the window frame continued to be a source of amusement. In the summer, it was quaint and charming to have vegetation forcing its way through to the inside, like lots of other aspects around the farm, but the other eight months of winter, with the cruel wind and the endless rotting erosion of the Welsh rain, meant parts of the farmhouse would be in a serious state of collapse. The mountains were reclaiming it.

She sat up and looked at Jack's things, smiling at the diversity of what he was reading. Next to a book about Welsh industry in the nineteenth century, and a copy of *A Midsummer Night's Dream*, were a poignant mixture of items he'd found in his father's car, a driving licence, a notebook full of Leo's scribble, and some old photographs of Jack, Danny, and Kate. Two of Isabel all dressed up, one of Lottie dressed as a clown, and finally one of Patsy looking impossibly young with Chelsey at her feet and a cherubic Oliver balanced on her hip.

She put them back on the bedside table and read the labels on his assortment of tablets, all untouched apart from the painkillers which were almost all gone. He'd eaten all the Jelly Babies too, except the green ones. His watch crept to three o'clock and made a little beep.

Seeing his shirt on the floor, Anna snatched it up and went downstairs, calling Benson. She draped the shirt over the dog's nose, then watched him run round in circles outside, his nose practically scraping the ground, trying to pick up a scent. It took only seconds.

She had to walk briskly to keep up with the Labrador, following his waving tail along the track beyond the shrunken lake and climbing the fierce flank of Maen Esgob, where she and Jack had walked before Christmas. After a short distance, Anna was running with sweat, but she didn't care – she was just relieved that Benson was tracking so assuredly. After all the heavy thinking, there was something cathartic about hard physical effort. The dog waited for her to catch up, then bounded on, joyous at being useful.

It didn't take long to find him. He was sitting on a rock drinking water from a bottle with her brown dog beside him. The path had a steep gradient, dusty and slippery with tall dense bracken and dry brown heather encroaching on either side. For a time, all she could hear was the high-pitched drone of insects and her own labouring breath.

Benson reached him first, leaping up at his quarry with ecstatic pride. Anna felt something catch in her throat when Jack looked around and saw her. Gingerly, he made his way down, both dogs at his heels. He was red-eyed and looked utterly drained. He said absolutely nothing and neither did Anna.

As soon as he was close enough, she just put her arms around him, and it seemed he reciprocated with the same huge well of relief. The feeling it gave her was something she couldn't put into words. It was so immense she didn't have a hope of understanding it. She closed her eyes and buried her face in his chest because it was wet with tears.

When he did try to say something she pulled away and put her hand over his mouth.

'Don't. Don't talk,' she said brokenly. So he kissed her instead, all over her face and her hair, down her neck and across her bare shoulders, until he went back to holding her. Eventually, she took his hand and they followed the dogs. It was a slow, difficult descent and Anna was wearing sandals and a long skirt, Jack's shirt still tied round her waist.

Mid-afternoon, the heat was at its most intense and once back at the farm, Jack looked incapable of doing anything other than lying down, although he did his best to hide the fact. After splashing his face with cold water, he lay across the lilac bed looking exhausted.

'You shouldn't have gone up there,' Anna said, trying not to sound patronising because in truth, she was annoyed with herself for not going after him earlier. 'Climbing Maen Esgob in eighty degree weather is not a good idea.'

'Stop scolding me and come here,' he said, taking hold of her hand. 'Why is my dirty washing tied round your waist?'

She gave him a smile then and sat on the bed as he studied her blunt nails. After a moment, he said, 'I haven't cried like that since I was a kid.'

'You probably needed to, better than tablets, anyway,' she said, and tried to retie the damp, grubby bandage on his wrist.

'Anna, listen, I want to talk to you. I want to spend some time with you. Can't you get rid of all these bloody visitors?'

'No, I can't get rid of them,' she said, and gave up with the bandage because it kept unravelling. Jack threw it in the bin and took hold of both her hands.

'I want to get to know you again,' he said. 'I want to feel something other than bitter and angry, or sick and tired. Do you know what I mean?'

She knew what he meant. She threaded her fingers through his. 'I know. Just don't rush me.'

'No chance of rushing anything, *not* the way I feel.'

That evening, against her better judgement and after much deliberation, Anna refused any more bookings. Alex rang too, but this time she lost her patience with him.

'I don't know what else to say to you,' she said, in a low voice. 'I don't think you should keep calling me.'

Then it was Isabel, worried. 'Kate says he went missing.'

'He's OK. He's been on some kind of sabbatical. The downside being it involved a lot of mountain scrambling as well.'

'Get him to take those tablets.'

'I'll try,' Anna said, biting her lip and knowing that most of them were in the bin. When she asked Jack what they were he'd told her they were anti-depressants.

‘I don’t need them if I can have you,’ he’d said.

Then it was Oliver. ‘Can you get Dad on the phone? His mobile’s always out of signal down there.’

Anna trailed upstairs and glanced around the door, to see Jack in a rare, deep sleep, lying face down on top of the bed with shower-damp hair and wearing only an old T-shirt and boxer shorts. Hooper was chewing one of his expensive socks with enthusiasm. The dog stopped mid-chew and pricked his ears, trying to weigh up whether Anna was going to take it from him, as she usually did. Noiselessly, she closed the door and went back downstairs to the phone.

‘Sorry, Oliver, he’s flat out.’

‘Just tell him that all that advanced algebra he made me do never came up in the exam. Mum asks when is he going to reply to all the messages she’s left?’

At almost midnight, after a long, cool shower, it was still too hot to sleep. Anna wandered about the landing in her underwear and a cotton wrap, trying to open windows. Jack was awake listening to the owls with Hooper.

‘I don’t feel so good,’ he said, rubbing his face.

‘You’re surprised?’

Anna fetched him a glass of water and the last of his painkillers, which he took from her but placed down again, choosing instead to hold out his arms to her. With no hesitation she went to him, wanting to be close despite the heat.

As she lay with her back to him, he folded himself round her. He apologised for landing on her in such a pathetic state and then being a pain in the neck all week, but he was much less dogmatic. He shocked her when he said something about going home.

‘I don’t want you to go, not yet,’ she said, holding his swollen hand and wrist.

‘I was hoping you’d say that.’

A wide smile broke on her face. He couldn’t see her

expression but he must have sensed it because he played with her hair and kissed the back of her neck.

'How long have we known each other?' he said.

'Since primary school, I think.'

'Do you remember anything that far back?'

'Only that you stole my blue pencil case and it had my new felt pens in it.'

'Did I?' Jack said seriously. 'Did you cry?'

'No, but you did. I thumped you really hard.'

'You bitch,' he said softly and slowly turned her over, kissing her neck and her face.

When he found her mouth, she locked her hands round his neck and pulled him closer. He made her feel incredibly sensual, and the excitement of being close to him was just like it used to be. He only kissed her once, then held her as he slept. She listened to him breathing for a long time, remembering the other times they'd fallen asleep in the same way in borrowed tents under the stars, or in someone's single bed in someone's spare room.

Around dawn, she woke feeling cold. The space next to her was empty and the room was flooded with light. When she looked out of the window, Jack was sitting in the deck chair in the garden, holding Hooper on his lap like an overgrown puppy. She pattered down the stairs wrapped in a blanket from the bed and found her way across the dewy grass.

'Jack, what are you doing out here?'

'Nothing much,' he said, smiling at her and trying to light a cigarette without burning Hooper. 'Just thinking.'

'More thinking?' Anna said, and found another chair.

'This is an amazing place. It gets under your skin. On that mountain yesterday, I actually started to feel different, like I've never noticed things before,' he said, turning to look at her. 'You know what I mean?'

Anna nodded and smiled and listened to his disjointed conversation till the birds were in full cry and the sun had risen behind Maen Esgob.

'I've felt better, being here with you,' he said. 'Anna, I wish you'd let me help.'

He meant money. The other day, after he'd annoyed her by poking about in the loft and the cellar and pulling up floorboards everywhere, he'd wanted to loan her fifty thousand pounds to get the foundations partially underpinned and all the wood treated, and she'd refused.

'I can't afford a loan,' she'd said starchily, partly because it frightened her and partly because she hated the idea of being answerable to someone for all that money, and yet, there were few options open to her if she wanted to keep her corner of paradise. She didn't want to get involved with Jack's money for the wrong reasons. If she accepted his help, Anna wanted the money to work independently of their feelings for each other, whatever they evolved to be.

'You really feel something for this place, don't you?' she said, watching the insects in the parched grass and tracing dusty circles with a stick. She waited on tenterhooks for his reply, because it mattered deeply.

'Yeah, I do,' he said, then turned to look at her as if something enlightening had suddenly come into his head. 'In some ways it feels like I've come home.'

It was Anna's turn to buy the cakes. Hilly was bursting with curiosity and couldn't hide it.

'*Right!* I've looked forward to this for *days*,' Hilly said, all business-like with the cups and wagging her finger. 'You've had him a full week, so come on, let's have it. I know there's something going on because you've got a closed sign at the end of the drive.'

It had been Jack's idea of course, but she hadn't taken much persuasion, not after she'd sat and thought it through, and admitted that Jack was right about the hand to mouth money situation. She needed his advice, and of late,

Anna felt she was running to stand still or even slide backwards. There wasn't even a decent carpet to sweep it all under. Although she had never closed in the season before, it gave her some breathing space and stopped the endless stream of tourists bouncing down her pot-holed drive, looking for accommodation.

They'd sat and talked for two days, until Anna finally agreed, in principal, that Redman Estates should mortgage the farm, enabling the more serious repairs to get underway. Since then, Jack had been like a dog with a new bone; measuring things, making phone calls to surveyors, and wearing out Josh's calculator. He'd even bought her an account book.

'What's wrong with the chocolate box?' Anna had said.

'It's for keeping chocolates in,' Jack told her patiently, then tried to explain what she had to write in which column until her head had spun and she'd dragged him off to the beach. That bit had been nice, not having to clean rooms or cook for strangers or worry about the ceiling falling down. Just walking along the edge of the surf with him, with nothing much else to do except walk back again.

Although she wasn't quite ready to admit it, Anna was beginning to relax with the idea that someone else was looking out for her after years of being more independent than she sometimes would have wished. The only downside was that Jack was a loose cannon filled with ideas, and his mind went a lot faster than hers did with facts and figures. She was uncertain where all this involvement with her affairs was heading; how it would affect their romantic relationship if she decided to trust him with her heart again.

Hilly scraped a blob of custard off her plate with her finger. 'So, what you're saying is, he's going to be your sleeping partner?'

'Business advisor,' Anna said, then sighed and pushed her plate to one side. 'Oh, I don't know, Hilly, he's only been in my life a few days and he's already changing it.'

'But he's not changing *you,*' Hilly said, firmly. 'Now, have you anything more interesting to tell?'

'His *decree nisi* came in the post.'

'Did he celebrate?'

'I'm not sure it's something you celebrate,' Anna said, finally sipping her coffee. 'He's lost a lot of assets, and gained all this heartache with his daughters.'

'Patsy got what she wanted?'

'More or less. He couldn't live with the fighting any more.'

Hilly wiped her mouth with a napkin and looked levelly at Anna. 'Look, I know he's got the ex-wife and kids syndrome in a big way, but I still don't see what's stopping you two being together.'

'Me, I think,' Anna said, more crestfallen than she'd realised. 'I told him I didn't want to be rushed.'

Hilly made a scoffing noise and Anna stared at her cold coffee. In truth, being so physically close to Jack was driving her mad and she knew he felt the same. He was very affectionate in that he hugged her and held her hand, but he only kissed her when she initiated it and he always stopped short of anything else, with great self-control. It was all very frustrating and almost farcical because they'd had such a sexual history together. Trying to be platonic now was like trying to deny it ever existed.

She told Hilly, who said, 'Well, he must be in love with you to behave like that. I saw him this morning looking like unshaven sex on legs in that baggy sweater and those washed-out jeans,' she went on, all wide-eyed. 'He bought me a cherry soda.'

Anna frowned. 'Where?'

'Here, in town. He was wandering about the art gallery with a coffee and walnut ice cream and that brown dog of yours on a bit of rope.'

'Jack was?'

'Then he went into the newsagents. When he came out with a carrier bag I demanded to see what was in it,' she said, with a nod and a wink, enjoying Anna's curiosity. 'Anyway, that's how I know he's in love with you. Now, are you eating that cake?'

Chapter Twelve

Jack

He was watching her paint. She had a little book containing outline sketches, dozens of the same dog from different angles, some showing the swing of its coat, others the expression in its eyes. Then she blended all the impressions into one portrait so that all the tiny unique details of the animal were captured onto the canvas.

The whole process fascinated Jack. The little loft space caught the light naturally, the views across the mountains like nothing he'd ever seen. Or was it just that he'd never slowed down enough to look properly before?

It was late afternoon and the light was like a kaleidoscope through the building cloud. Anna was creating the effects on the canvas in front of her by looking and mixing the colour instinctively. She wore jeans and an old shirt splattered with paint, as was her hair, and little spectacles perched on the end of her nose. Benson lay on the floor with his head on his paws, watching her every move.

'I think there might be a storm in the week,' Anna said, concentrating on the deep shadows across Tal Y Fan. 'Where have you been? What are you up to?' she went on, finally turning round, brush in hand. 'Hilly said she saw you in the art gallery and the newsagents.'

'Traitor.'

'What's in that bag?'

'A present for you.'

He watched her clean off the brush and poke it into a

jar. She came to him, her dark eyes full of amusement. When she pulled out the blue plastic pencil case she was filled with pleasure, as he knew she would be.

'Is there something inside?' she said, unzipping it, and finding amongst the felt tip pens, a key. 'What's this about?' she said, with suspicion.

'It's somewhere to live while this place is a building site,' Jack said. 'It's one of the cottages down on the quay that belonged to Dad.'

'I see,' she said, then dangled the key in front of him by way of admonishment, 'and what were you doing in the art gallery?'

Jack grabbed her around the waist and enjoyed looking at her. She was so, so different to Patsy. Anna wasn't classically beautiful, but she had a kind of inner serenity, and her ways were so sensual.

'Don't look at me like that,' she said, but her eyes were saying the opposite so he carried on looking at her, loving her brown freckled face and her voluptuous body.

She laughed into his chest and hugged him back and the closeness of her was so overwhelming that Jack forgot what he was about to say, and kissed her instead, threading his fingers through her wild tangle of hair. She dropped the key with a noisy clatter and kissed him back eagerly.

Jack wanted her so badly he could have made love to her on the floor amongst the dust sheets and the old paints and brushes – anywhere, in fact. It was intoxicating to feel alive again, after months of nothing but misery. The tense anticipation between them was so tangible they sometimes struggled to hide it from Josh, who obviously thought they were a bit pathetic.

Later, Anna suddenly decided to have a barbecue before the weather broke. Hilly arrived with the local blacksmith and two bottles of homemade elderflower and apple wine. Anna took one look at the dusty bottles and burst out laughing.

'Oh no, not that stuff, it's lethal,' she said, passing a bottle to Jack to open.

'It smells like blackcurrant squash,' Jack said, sniffing the contents. 'Are you sure this is alcoholic?'

There was a resoundingly positive reply, so he filled everyone's glass. Hilly made a panic-stricken face at the amount. 'You look really well,' she said to Jack.

'Sleeping in the sun all day and eating like a pig has had quite a lot to do with it.'

Hilly laughed and offered him a cigarette, then leant closer. 'All that's missing now is the love of a good woman.'

Anna saw them huddled together and shouted across, 'Hilly! Are you being embarrassing?'

'Me? No! Jack was telling me about those awful, expensive pictures in the gallery.'

After food, Bryn the Smith was looking at some of Anna's paintings. 'How much do you reckon she wants for this one then?' he said, holding up one of her austere winter landscapes. Jack studied the picture. It was so vivid with life it practically leapt up and hit you in the face, although there was nothing much on the canvas, just a few sheep and some rundown farm buildings.

'It says here three hundred quid,' Jack said, pretending to find a price on the back of the frame.

Anna must have overheard. She lifted her head sharply and looked at him indignantly, then tried to mouth something at him behind Bryn's back, but Jack couldn't make out what she was saying. She looked furious though.

'I'll give her two-fifty for it,' Bryn said, then went back to looking at the picture. 'That's old Evan's place out by Foel Fras. It's right good.'

Jack agreed it was and took the money off him.

When everyone had gone home, Anna pounced on him. 'I can't believe you're interfering again. My paintings are not your business, and selling them to my friends at an inflated price during a social evening is appalling bad taste.'

'He wanted to buy it,' Jack said, handing her the money. 'And you still owe me a fiver.'

'What the devil for?'

'Hitler paid his bill, didn't he? Anna, listen,' he said, trying to catch hold of her arm before she flounced away. 'I've had an idea about the pictures.'

She wouldn't talk to him.

In the morning, Josh woke him on his way to school by slamming every door in the place and having an argument with his mother, just like Oliver. Jack could hear Anna reversing the Land Rover, and the dogs barking. The old grandfather clock in the hall chimed six times, although it was just after eight thirty. Then there was total peace, only distant bleating and the rising hum of insects. Even the gulls were quiet. The spirit of the place was like a drug. Jack closed his eyes again and wondered how long she was going to be.

When Anna had just turned up at his flat on her *wedding* day, he'd been speechless. His mother must have been sworn to secrecy to keep that little item to herself.

During the first few days at the farm, Jack had been frustrated with his physical state. He couldn't even remember falling over at the gym, just waking up in hospital with a mask over his face. When he'd finally come round, it was scary because he couldn't remember who he was. A paramedic told him he'd fallen down some steps and been out cold for over an hour. Then it was the nightmare of trying to work out whether the pain he felt was physical or mental. Once the drugs had worn off, he figured it was probably both.

He'd only gone down to the pool because he'd felt so miserable by himself. Oliver had gone away for a couple of days to a midsummer concert and it was the eve of Anna's wedding day.

Anna hadn't fussed over him. It was Josh who'd run up and down the stairs, ferrying drinks and food, and for three days all Jack had done was sleep. Then it was listening to the serene sounds of the farmhouse, watching the sky, and thinking. It was all he'd needed to pull him out of the dark pit he'd fallen into. Just knowing she was there meant the difference between feeling nothing and feeling everything.

His life had been mixed up, raw and angry, but the day he'd come down from the mountain and Anna had been waiting on the path was as if he'd turned a corner. What the hell, he didn't need self-analysis – he was in love with her. There was something within her, something that connected her to this wild place, something deep and emotive that he wanted for himself.

Half an hour later, Anna returned just as the post van arrived. Jack listened to their voices through the open window. They were laughing, chattering away in Welsh. Then the van pulled away and he heard her go into the shower.

She came to him quietly, unsure if he was still asleep. When he turned to look at her, she was wet, bundled up in a towel.

'Are you still cross with me?' he said.

She nodded her head slightly but without speaking dropped the damp towel to the floor and slid under the sheet next to him.

'I'm so, *so mad* with you,' she whispered and put her lips on his. She caressed and kissed him so passionately that for the first few seconds Jack thought he was in a dream, and their arousal was so instantaneous, it made him feel almost light-headed.

'Anna, Anna, slow down,' he murmured, but she moved beneath him like a beautiful, dangerous cat, pulling him into her body, and then there was nothing he could do.

The climax of their love for each other was fast, intense. When she at last lay still in his arms, it was difficult to tell if she was laughing or crying, but she wouldn't look at him.

'Anna … talk to me,' Jack said, and pulled her head back gently by her hair. He kissed her eyes and the side of her mouth, her neck and her breasts. 'Forget it … don't talk. Stupid idea,' he said, holding her to him, his mouth travelling down her body, feeling her respond to his touch till she wanted him again.

Afterwards, she caught hold of his face and searched his eyes. 'I want to lie in the long grass with you and be hopelessly in love and do all the things we did when we were seventeen.'

'Everything? Including the bus stop incident and the school shed?'

She laughed then, but her laughter turned almost to tears, and Jack was both moved and excited by the passion in her.

'I want all those feelings back,' she whispered.

She was still in his arms when he woke, not entwined about him but asleep on his bad wrist, which was excruciating, but he couldn't have cared less. Anna had put another bandage on it, more effective than the first one, only it was bright red and very long and not very medical looking. Hilly frowned at it suspiciously.

'Anna, isn't that Boomerang's tail bandage? The one he wore for the Rowan show?' And everyone had had a good laugh at his expense.

'Well, at least he was a thoroughbred,' Hilly had said, patting his arm, 'and he got second place for best turned out.'

Anna woke and stretched, then smiled at him lazily. 'You didn't tell me about your idea.'

'Too scared,' Jack said, trying to get the circulation

back in his arm. She made him tell her about using the Conwy office for storing all her frames and paintings while the farm was out of bounds, and about using the window to display some of her work.

'I thought maybe you could do some of the more interesting properties coming up for sale. That way I get a more interesting window, and you get a source of income with no overheads. Once you've priced them all properly, that is.'

She contemplated his words with a patient little smile, her head on one side and twisting tendrils of hair. 'You've got it all worked out.'

'No, not really. I'm helping you to be independent.'

'But I'd feel as though I was relying on you for everything,' she said, her eyes assuming a veil of hesitation. 'I'm not sure what you want of me, how it all fits together with us.'

'I don't want anything from you,' Jack said, 'I just want you to love me back.'

'That's too easy,' she said softly.

At the weekend, the storm broke and the sea rolled and crashed along the shore, tossing rocks and stones and small boats as if they were weightless. The mountains became ominous, dark and rearing, groaning and rumbling with thunder deep in the valley.

When the rain came at last they had just finished dinner at The View, a new restaurant on the far side of the Conwy Bridge.

'It seems another lifetime ago when we kissed in the car park,' Anna said, making him choose a pudding.

'Is that when you started to have doubts about Alex?'

'Deep down, I'd always had doubts about Alex, but you knew that,' she said, smiling at him over her wineglass.

'I was blown away with relief when you didn't marry him. It drove me insane when you were with him,' Jack said, wanting her to understand that he loved her for all the right reasons and not because she was second choice, a shoulder to cry on while he was on the rebound from Patsy, or anything else along those lines.

'I lay awake all night thinking about us after you'd been to see me in the hospital,' Anna said, pinching the pudding menu back with a mischievous smile. 'I remembered I first fell in love with you when you were eight, and you wore those blue dungarees at Richard Bickerstaff's party.'

'We should have got married then, saved ourselves a load of trouble,' he said, grinning, but a shadow crossed her face and Jack caught hold of her fingers. 'Anna, what I mean to say is, I know I made a mess of things before, and I don't expect it's going to be easy, but I don't want what happened with Patsy to come between us now. I want us to have a second chance.'

'We were young. We both made mistakes,' she said with a shrug, and looked away as if it didn't matter.

'That's not the point,' he stressed, 'I handled everything really badly.'

'No, you didn't. I never really told you how I felt. I kept it close to my heart, as if by saying it out loud all the intimacy would somehow be spoilt.'

Jack smiled but he was still determined to have his say. 'I bitterly regret how messy it got in the end, with Chelsey and everything.'

'I know.' She squeezed his fingers before she let go of them. 'But if we're going to have that second chance we need to move on, don't we? Now, are you having dessert or not?'

Back at the farm, Jack caught her standing deep in thought by the window, watching the rain stream down in torrents.

'Are you mad at me again?' Jack said, hopefully.

She turned round with a benign smile and came into his

arms. 'No, no, I'm just feeling a bit emotional, insecure, I think.'

'About?' As if he needed to ask.

'I don't know. Everything that happened to stop us being together. I've wanted you for so long and now that you're here, I feel a tiny bit afraid. Like something's going to happen to break us apart again.'

'I promise you, it won't,' Jack said. 'You were right about the moving on.'

She didn't trust him totally, or perhaps it was truer to say she didn't trust the situation. He couldn't really blame her, but Jack wanted to be sure of her feelings this time, of both their feelings, and since Patsy's affair, Jack was a bit paranoid about the word secret.

'I want you to tell me everything,' he said. 'Every secret worry and every secret fantasy in your heart. No secrets between us, OK?'

'No secrets.'

In the sleepless night, when the storm rattled the house, he went to her and loved her with almost wordless obsession, and it was just how it used to be.

On Monday morning in the lilac bed, Hooper woke him by licking his face and chewing his hair. Josh brought him a mug of coffee and a letter addressed to Anna.

'Mum says will you open it? She doesn't want to read it.'

Jack grunted with amusement and tore open the envelope. It was the surveyor's report he'd had done on the general condition of the farmhouse and a preliminary estimate. He scanned the pages, noting the horrific figures listed on the last page like a mobile phone number, then stuffed it all back into the envelope and placed it inside *Training Dogs the Barbara Woodhouse Way*.

'What are you reading that for?' Josh said and rubbed Hooper's tummy, so that the dog cycled his legs and assumed an inane grin. 'You won't train this one. He's got a hearing problem and gets confused with similar sounding words.'

They heard Jack's phone ringing downstairs and the dog pricked his ears.

'Go on, go get the phone,' Jack said. Hooper eagerly dived off the bed and thundered down the stairs. 'See?' Jack said.

Presently the dog returned with a filthy chunk of marrowbone and dropped it triumphantly on the bed. Josh collapsed with laughter.

'Yeah, well, he's just got a sense of humour, that's all,' Jack said.

Just as Josh was slinging the bone out of the window, Anna caught him.

'What on earth are you doing?' she said, then handed Jack his mobile and dumped a pile of bedding onto the chair.

'Nothing!' Josh said, and declared he was going to school on his bike. He looked at Jack with a smirk before he disappeared. Anna caught their exchange.

'He was never like this with Alex,' she said. 'What have you done with that report?'

'Filed it,' Jack said, looking at the missed numbers on his phone. It was Patsy again. 'We need some quotes. I suppose you want to use local people?'

'Will you deal with it?'

'Yeah, sure,' he said softly. 'I'll sort it when I get back to the office.'

At the mention of this, she was subdued and put her arms around him, as if he was going away on a long, dangerous sea voyage. Maybe he was.

There were several difficult things about going back. Leaving Anna after loving her gave him a sense of foreboding. Once on the A55, the BMW ate up the road, but Jack drove with his mind full of her. Thoughts of waiting for the dawn in her deck chair, talking half the night, making her laugh, making love by the lake, watching her paint and make pasta. Being with her, just knowing her, the last few days had been like a dream.

Speeding down the motorway towards his old life made him feel weary, nauseous, and wobbly, but he was hardly fully fit after just two weeks and his wrist was painful. Pulling into a service station, he sat and watched the traffic zip past.

Anna had been concerned about his health, making him promise not to work all the time, but he didn't need persuading. If he was honest, the investigations he'd undergone at the hospital concerning the ulcer, followed by the accident, had pulled him up short. Above all, it had made him determined not to go down the same route as his father. Maybe Patsy had been right. It was a bloody hell of a way to tell him though. He almost reached for a cigarette, then thought better of it. The car already reeked of cigars, a potent reminder of his father's heart attack.

In some ways, Jack was only just starting to think about Leo. When he and Anna had taken the BMW down to his mother's cottage to collect the Land Rover, his father's clothes had been strewn all over the lounge in black bin bags. The loss hit him then like a smack in the face, maybe because it was so final, knowing he would never actually be there again.

Anna had been brilliant by being there and just by being Anna. They were sitting together on the sofa. 'Do you remember what you said to me when I lost my parents, when we were both about six?'

He'd thought for a moment, but couldn't come up with anything. 'No, I don't remember.'

'"Don't be sad, Anna; you can share mine." That's what you said.'

He'd asked her about Josh's father. Jack knew she'd lived for a time in Italy after a holiday romance. She'd come back to Conwy after Josh was born because her grandfather had left Gwern Farm to her. What she hadn't told him before was that her continental Adonis liked to use his fists on her when he didn't get his own way. After Josh, she was told she could never have any more children, which didn't go down well with Mama Mia either.

It struck Jack how hard her life had been on her own, how she explained to Josh the absence of a father who was alive and apparently wealthy, but didn't seem to care. He could understand why Josh was jealous and protective of his mother. In her own way, Anna was telling him he was lucky to have had Leo.

Their own children had totally different criteria to learn, and Anna seemed more equipped to deal with it than Jack, maybe because she'd already been there.

'I don't want us to force any issues with them,' she'd said, 'It was a disaster with Alex. He tried too hard and missed the mark completely. I couldn't put Josh through all that again.'

Ironically though, it was Josh who started to come to Jack, with his maths revision and problems with the computer, but that was only because he didn't see Jack as a threat. They were careful to keep it that way, however comically furtive it became. Privately, Jack saw the absence of Josh's father as an advantage, but he paid for it by having Patsy permanently on his back in one form or another.

After they'd had the conversation about secrets, Anna had reluctantly told him about the incident with Chelsey at his father's funeral. Jack wasn't surprised. There had to be a solid reason why his eldest daughter wouldn't speak to him. It was as if Patsy was getting even with him by using Chelsey against him. This was payback time for Jack having Oliver all to himself. 'I don't know what to do about it!' he'd said, angrily. He couldn't even deny now that he was having a relationship with Anna. Later, he'd felt terrible and apologised to her. 'I'm sorry, love. I don't mean to take it out on you.'

She'd hugged him back, but there had been that shadow in her eyes again. Having a relationship with one person, and then having children with another, was a psychological minefield. Jack closed his eyes for five minutes, then remembered he had several of Patsy's unreturned calls stored on his mobile. The thought of getting back in the firing line with his almost ex-wife was worse than coping with anything physical. After months of bitter arguments he loathed speaking to her now, and it was only attempting to see Lottie that prompted the effort. He hit the speed-dial number reluctantly.

'It's me. What do you want?' he said, lighting a cigarette this time and opening the car window.

'Don't you ever return your calls?' she said, in a small voice.

'I've been away. Look, just get to the point.'

'Chelsey's had a little boy. He's in intensive care,' she said, her voice breaking down to a sob, 'He's six weeks early.'

Jack sat up and tried to gather his thoughts. 'Are they both OK?'

She wouldn't give him an answer. 'Jack, I want you to come and pick me up and we'll go down together. I can't drive, I've got high blood pressure and Philipe's away,' she went on, almost crying. '*Please,* Jack I want to see her, she is our daughter.'

'Are they both OK?' Jack said again, determined to ignore the rest of her conversation, obviously designed to draw on the same old emotional elastic as when they were married. She was only parting with the information because she wanted him to drive her there.

'Which hospital are they in?' he said angrily, but she wouldn't tell him. 'Stop playing stupid fucking games.'

'Don't you dare swear at me.'

In a fit of frustration, Jack switched his phone off and flung it onto the back seat. He'd find the information for himself, even if he had to phone every maternity unit in West London.

Half an hour later he was parking on the office forecourt. When he pulled open the rear door of the car to get his bags, Hooper jumped out with Jack's phone in his mouth. The dog wagged his tail, then followed Jack into the office, full of importance.

'Clare, I need you to go get me some plaid slippers and a pipe.'

'Any special reason?'

'Yeah, I'm a granddad.'

Used to his humour, Clare realised what he was talking about and told him he looked nothing like a granddad. 'You look great, actually.'

In the flat, the music was so loud that Hooper crawled across the floor and hid under the bed. Jack yelled up the stairs and there was a slight reduction in volume, followed by a grunt.

'You look much better,' his mother shouted, removing the cotton wool from her ears.

'Why didn't you tell me about Alex and the farm being cancelled?' Jack said, sitting down heavily and kicking his shoes off.

'Anna wanted to do it herself, in her own time,' she said, then looked at him closely. 'So what did you get up to? Whatever it was, it's done you the power of good. I didn't think pills alone work miracles.'

'I'm not responding to that. It's too loaded.'

'Oh, you don't have to,' Isabel said, going in to the kitchen. 'You had a phone call earlier from Mike. I knew you were coming home today, so I thought it best if I told you the news.'

Jack rested his head back and closed his eyes. Just as he'd begun to feel he was clambering out of the pit, this is where he fell in again. He listened while his mother related the story of Chelsey's ordeal at the hospital, but it was OK; the baby had been premature and they'd taken Chelsey in early only as a precaution. Trust Patsy to play the drama queen.

'So, I'm a great-grandmother!' Isabel said, emerging with a tray of tea and sandwiches. 'Oh, and Chelsey is going to ring you when she can.'

Jack frowned. 'Have you been meddling?'

'What if I have? Some things needed tactfully pointing out. Anyway, I think Chelsey's reached some of her own conclusions.'

'With your help?' he said. 'I need to know which hospital. I want to send her something.'

'All on the pad by the phone,' she said airily, then announced she was going to order a taxi and take the train home.

'What about Dad's car?'

'I can't drive it. It's too big,' she said, then sighed and admitted she didn't want it parked outside the cottage any more. 'You have it.'

'I don't need it,' Jack said, unsure if he wanted it parked outside the office either. 'What if I sell it, buy you something smaller?'

'Fine,' she said bravely, squeezing his shoulder. 'Yes, do that.'

Once she'd left, he rang Anna. 'Do you still want to share my mother?'

'I think I've been doing that for ages,' she said, but happily agreed to collect Isabel off the train at Llandudno. Then he told her about Hooper's cunning escape. 'Can I keep him for a bit?'

'I expect so, but don't give him curry, no matter how much he begs.' Jack looked down at the dog's doleful expression. 'Yeah, well, I'm not allowed curry either.'

When he told Anna about Chelsey she just said,

‘Congratulations.’

‘It doesn’t put you off, does it? Knowing you had sex with a granddad.’

She laughed. ‘You don’t look or feel like a granddad to me.’

‘No, but I’ve got the mind of a dirty old man. I can’t stop thinking about sex since I’ve been with you,’ Jack said in a low voice, aware that Oliver was straining to listen while pretending to revise his chemistry notes.

‘Who were you talking to?’ Oliver demanded later, as if Jack were several years younger. ‘It sounded like the sex chat line.’

‘Oh yeah, and what would you know about that?’ Jack said over the top of his paper, then hid behind it in case his expression wasn’t serious enough. He didn’t know which was worse; Lottie being too young to understand adult relationships, or Oliver and Josh in collusion and accurately interpreting their every move.

Waking up in the flat in the morning with the traffic noise roaring past the window was so far removed from the farm, Jack could almost believe he’d dreamt the whole thing. The worst part was turning over in bed still in a haze of sleep and not finding her warmth beside him, not being able to feel her arms around him. Not being able to pull her gently into the shower and watch soap running down her tanned body.

Living so far apart from Anna was going to be difficult, but she’d been adamant about the separateness of their respective lives.

‘Jack, you have two children at home and a business a hundred miles away from here,’ she’d said when they were lying on the local beach. ‘You’d be bored here, anyway.’

‘Oh, I don’t know. I could get used to being a beach bum.’

‘You sound like Danny.’

‘No, Danny can do it without sand. Danny can be a

bum anywhere.'

She'd laughed, but insisted that the distance between them wouldn't pull them apart, saying it would make them appreciate each other more.

'I don't want to make the same mistakes I did with Alex. If I've learnt anything, it's that I need my own space from time to time, and so do our children. Why make it complicated?'

On Saturday morning, Jack drove to the rented town house on the outskirts of Manchester where Patsy and Lottie lived with Philipe when he wasn't doing business in Paris, which was more often than not these days.

When Jack had first seen the house, he'd said in disbelief, 'Is this it?'

Patsy had turned on him. 'It's only temporary, till everything is sorted out.'

When Jack had looked down the narrow hallway to the poky kitchen and thought about the home his daughter used to have, his heart turned over.

'What's happened to the cash?'

'I know what I'm doing, Jack!'

'No,' he'd said darkly, '*He* knows what *he's* doing.'

The divorce settlement was practically finalised now, and The Links had sold quickly, releasing the cash to Patsy. It was the final severance, blowing away all those years of building a home and a family.

Once she'd admitted to adultery, it had been scary how quickly and easily their marriage had been taken apart. It was only his own stubbornness, and the astuteness of Tim and Charles West, who had saved him from mortgaging the business, even though it could be argued it had cost him his health and his peace of mind – but Patsy had changed too.

On one occasion, after he'd dropped Lottie back at the house, Patsy had followed him outside, snagging at his arm.

‘Jack, wait, I want to talk to you. I hate us being like this.’

‘Like what?’ he’d said angrily, turning round as he unlocked the car. ‘Nearly divorced?’

The look on her face was contrary to everything that had happened and it unsettled him, leaving her there like that on the pavement, pregnant and weeping. Over the last few weeks she’d been pathetic, clingy and attention-seeking instead of cold and calculating. He’d got used to her being nasty. Somehow it was easier to deal with.

This change of emotional tactic also manifested itself in access arrangements with Lottie, but only when it suited Patsy. She quickly realised the benefits of having Jack pick up Lottie whenever she felt tired and had swollen legs. He also got a call if she wanted to go out, as if he were a child-minder.

‘Don’t you want to spend some time with her?’ Patsy would say, usually when he was working or had a prior appointment, or was just dead on his feet.

‘Oh, so you don’t want to see her,’ she’d say. ‘I’ll tell her that, shall I?’

‘If you tell her anything like that I swear I’ll have you certified as an unfit mother.’

By then, Patsy and Lottie would both be crying down the phone and Jack would have to tear up there, frightened for Lottie in case Patsy really was becoming unhinged. Then, when the weekend came round and Jack went to collect Lottie as planned, Patsy would play power games with the whole situation by simply not being in. Charles West’s prophecy of access being somewhat intransigent in practice suddenly hit home hard. It seemed the goalposts had moved considerably since the money was in place.

Jack pulled up outside Patsy’s house. It looked shabbier than ever. Her Mercedes, the car Jack had bought for her fortieth birthday, looked very out of place. He noted with some relief that Philipe's car was absent. The less Jack saw of his smug face the better.

Patsy came to the door, looking huge for six months, white and worn out. She'd never had an easy time being pregnant.

'Oh, it's you, come in,' she said blandly, leaving the door open so he'd follow, then throwing herself sloppily onto the sofa in the lounge. It was dusty and messy, with the previous week's newspapers all over the floor.

'Sit down, will you?' Patsy said. 'Charlotte won't be long. Did you have a nice holiday? You said you'd been away,' she went on, determined to make conversation.

'I slept for most of it and took a lot of pills,' Jack said, drumming his fingers impatiently on the wooden chair arm and watching her. 'I spoke to Mike by the way, and my daughter and her baby are both fine. I don't understand why you have to keep using Chelsey to punish me.'

To his surprise, she nodded in agreement and reached for a tissue, but she wouldn't meet his eyes. 'I'm sorry, and I'm sorry I let Chelsey think you were to blame. Anyway, she knows everything now.'

'Sorry? You say sorry when you bump into someone in the street. Why did you lie about Anna? To get at me, make yourself look better or what?' he said, then realised he didn't really want to know, as there was likely a complicated answer. 'As it happens, I am in a relationship now.'

'Not with Anna Williams?' she said, absolutely horrified.

Jack just didn't get it. If he'd said he was having an affair with two schoolboys she couldn't be more shocked.

'What's the problem?' he said, getting to his feet.

'I don't want Charlotte dragged into another love triangle.'

'Why? Do you think you've got exclusive rights to a relationship?'

Fighting the temptation to launch into a full scale attack, Jack went to the window and looked stonily at the view of the river and the warehouses.

'Anyway,' he went on,' Anna and I don't intend to live together. I reckon you've done enough damage to our children all by yourself in that department. Anything I do is none of your business,' he said, noting the ashtray was already full of Philipe's little French cigars. The idea that he was smoking around a pregnant woman – and Lottie, come to that – was incredibly distasteful. Jack marched upstairs, lifted Lottie up with her half packed bag, and left without another word.

'Mummy's been visiting Auntie Natal,' Lottie said when they were speeding back along the motorway. 'Who is she? Mummy says Philipe s not very nice to her any more, and she's always crying down the phone.'

'She'll be fine when she has the baby,' Jack forced himself to say.

'I don't want a baby. Babies stink.'

Early evening, in the car on the way back from dropping Lottie home, Jack called Anna and tried not to go word for word over the conversation he'd had with Patsy.

'I can't understand why she's so pissed off about us seeing each other,' Jack said. 'I mean, she was dumbstruck! I dunno, I just can't make it out. At least this mess is sorted out with Chelsey.'

'Well ... maybe it's just her hormones,' Anna said, then changed the subject. She told him that Josh had gone to an end of exams party.

'Same with Ollie, he's round at the Websters, playing with fire.'

'Jack, I miss you,' she said. 'I'm not going to last till next week.'

'What are you doing right now?'

'Finishing that painting of the watermill.'

'I miss you too,' he said, and disconnected.

Just over an hour later, he was tapping on her door.

'You're mad,' she said, and fell into his arms.

It was approaching dusk when he woke, and she was still entwined about him. He wondered how long she'd been lying like that, watching him.

'I really do feel like a granddad now,' he said, feeling the effects of the day catch up on him. It wasn't much of a thrill knowing he had to drive all the way home either, this time without the anticipation of seeing Anna.

'Well, I don't feel like an old woman,' she said, 'though I might sound like one if I say I'm uneasy with the idea of you barely recovered, belting up and down the A55.'

'With a hard on, don't forget that bit.'

'I don't think granddads do that sort of thing.'

'Listen, I've had an idea,' Jack said, then smiled when Anna grabbed a pillow, ready to push it over his face. He caught hold of her wrists and said, 'I've been thinking of just working three or four days in the office so I can help you here, and it would give us some time together. What do you think?'

She lowered the pillow. 'I think that might be fun, only if you *promise* not to help in the kitchen.'

It was after midnight when he finally left. Oliver rang him just before the Chester intersection. 'Dad, where are you? Come and pick me up quick, will you? I'm at Spider's.'

'I don't do quick. Anyway, I'm forty minutes away.'

Oliver groaned. 'Amy's gone and had a fight with Beth, and Beth threw a toaster at me!'

'What have you done?'

'Me? Nothing!'

'Yeah, yeah. Get a taxi if you're desperate.'

Jack kept to the speed limit. He was a changed man,

and anyway, he couldn't risk another fine. It had been a hell of a long day, starting from swimming with Lottie and running round the forest with Hooper, then hurtling down the motorway to Anna, but it had been worth it. Shattered was OK if you felt happy.

As the sun had gone down, they'd eaten pasta and wild mushrooms in her garden and shared half a bottle of wine, until a few stars studded the navy blue sky and bats began to flit across the silver lake. Anna had been fine about the part-time idea. It meant he would be forced to slow down in the office. He'd have more time for Lottie, and when the renovation was finished at the farm, Jack was looking forward to getting the B&B properly established.

At the flat, Hooper was energetically chewing some suede shoes and Ollie was in the bathroom, dabbing ineffectively at his forehead.

'Dad, take a look at this. I think it might need stitches,' Oliver said, then pulled down the front of his shirt and made a wild face into the mirror. 'What do you think this is? It looks like jaundice!'

Jack frowned and pulled Oliver's head into the light. 'Don't be such a girl. There's hardly a bloody mark.'

'What about the yellow?'

'Looks like vindaloo to me,' he said, pushing Oliver's head away. He switched the shower on and kicked his shoes off. 'Although I have to admit it's got me stumped as to why it's so deeply ingrained into your neck. What condition's the Webster's toaster in?'

'In bits, like my head.'

'Little job for you tomorrow then,' Jack said, throwing his shirt off. 'You can buy a new one. It serves you right for sleeping with both of them.'

After a short, contemplative silence Oliver said, 'I never.'

While he was showering, it came to Jack that Oliver's love life had resonations with his own historical triangle.

He turned the water off and wondered whether this was the right time to say something prophetic.

Oliver was in the lounge, flicking through the television channels and eating microwave pizza.

'Ollie, this fight with Beth and Amy,' Jack said, still drying himself. 'Are you messing them about?'

'No,' Oliver said at first, then put the pizza down. 'Well, a bit.'

Jack grinned at him and opened a can of beer. 'You know you could end up losing both of them and you'd look stupid?'

'So?' he said, belligerently. 'Look, what is this?'

'A bit of advice. I made the same mistake with your mother and Anna when I was eighteen.'

He was interested then. 'Yeah? And?'

'Well, I was seeing both of them and got myself in a mess,' Jack said. 'Your mother got pregnant, and it was an even bigger mess. From then on, my life was decided for me.'

Not knowing whether he'd put the contraceptive issue across in the right way or not, Jack went into the kitchen to get a glass and buy some time. Oliver followed him and leant on the door jamb. 'So, what are you saying?'

'Well, I'm not saying I regret marrying your mother, and I certainly don't regret any of my kids, even though only one of them was planned, but now, the way it's ended leaves me feeling that perhaps I was coerced into the wrong choices,' Jack said. He poured out the beer and decided to get straight to the point with the morality lesson. 'Apart from all that, I'm not happy about you sleeping with Beth *and* Amy.'

'But I like them both.'

'Tough,' Jack said, and shoved the rest of the beer at him. 'Unless you have their joint consent?'

'Oh yeah, Dad, as if!'

'So you know what to do. And anyway, Amy's not

even sixteen, she's underage.'

'She keeps chasing me! She's sex mad.'

Jack laughed loudly and went into his room. Oliver followed him and leant on the doorjamb again. 'So, are you seeing anyone then?'

Jack brushed his damp hair and looked at Oliver through the mirror. 'Would it bother you if I was?'

'No,' Oliver said firmly, 'but I reckon you could use some advice.'

'Such as?'

'Make sure you use protection.'

Jack was disturbed in the morning by Beth shouting something about curry through the letterbox. He dragged Oliver out of bed and to the front door, still wrapped in his duvet and groaning. 'Dad, no, don't let her in. Has she got a toaster?'

'Just sort this mess out,' Jack said crossly, and snatched open the door. Beth stepped into the tiny hall, made even smaller due to Oliver's duvet.

Jack went back to bed with the papers and a subdued Hooper, no doubt full of shoe. In the lounge, Beth and Oliver launched into a heated argument, followed by a long, suspicious silence and then a lot of giggling. After a while, Oliver poked his head round the door and said they were going out, and did he know that the dog had sicked up a lot of shoe behind the curtains?

After they'd gone, Jack's mobile rang. 'Dad? It's me.'

It was Chelsey, and she sounded young and far away.

'Are you OK? You and the baby?'

'Yes. Yes, fine. He's only in intensive because he was early,' she said, then trailed to a halt. 'Dad … I want to say sorry. I've been horrible to you.'

'Forget all that, it doesn't matter now,' Jack said, sitting down on the arm of the sofa. 'Chel, I want to see you. I need to talk to you. Can I come and see you next week?'

'All this way? Are you sure? Gran said you'd been ill with stress.'

But Jack was thinking about the baby, his grandson. 'What are you calling him?'

'Sam,' she said, brightening. 'Samuel Jack McDougal.'

After he'd put the phone down, Jack wondered if he'd sometimes underestimated the effects of his divorce. Chelsey was different to his other children. She had no hard edge. She'd always needed everything in its rightful order, her crayons, her makeup, her parents, her feelings, everyone's feelings, in fact. Discord made her ill. It had made *him* ill, but his life was slowly clearing, like a river being dredged. It was as if all the rubbish was slowly sinking to the bottom, and for the rest of the day, Jack allowed himself to feel slightly euphoric.

Another good thing happened on Monday morning. Jean turned up out of the blue, out of the deep Australian blue, with a boomerang for Jack and a hearty embrace. She was shocked to hear about Leo, but the office was too busy to have any sort of conversation because Jon was on holiday, and interruptions were constant. Hooper was sitting up in Jack's chair wearing a tweed waistcoat and howling at the phones, while Oliver was trying to make sense of the key booking-in system.

'You don't fancy a job share with me, do you?' Jack said, partly as a joke.

'Actually, I'd love one,' Jean said, marching into Jon's office, 'but that dog will have to go, and that son of yours needs a firm hand if he's to learn anything.'

'I couldn't agree more,' Jack said, turning round the pornographic calendar on the back of the door. 'Is that a serious offer? I could do with taking a couple of days off next week. I want to go and see Chel and my grandson.' It sounded odd, saying the word "grandson".

'From what I hear, you haven't been taking enough

time off,' Jean said, hoicking the chair up to a better height. 'I've got the opposite problem to you – I'm as fit as a fiddle and bored rigid.'

In the middle of the night, the phone rang and when Jack eventually picked it up, the voice was unfamiliar. A wrong number, he presumed.

'It's Manchester General,' the woman said again. 'I need to speak to Mr Redman.'

'Speaking.'

'I'm sorry to tell you but your wife's been rushed in. She's rather poorly.'

'What wife?' Jack said, then realised the inanity of what he'd said. He ran a hand through his hair and the woman sighed and shuffled some paper. 'Mrs Patricia Redman … of River Street?'

'No, you don't understand, she's practically my *ex*-wife. You need to call her partner or her parents,' Jack said.

'Well, she's asked me to call *you,* since it's your baby she's having,' she went on, as a disapproving tone creeped into her voice. 'Your little girl is with her, and she's very distressed.'

'Lottie?'

'I think it might be appropriate if you were to at least come and collect her.'

Jack laboriously got dressed and scrawled a note for Oliver in case he woke up, something about going to pick up Lottie from River Street.

It was after two in the morning when he finally got to the maternity section of the hospital. The sister in charge told him that Patsy had had some kind of seizure called eclampsia. Jack followed her down the dark ward. 'How serious is it?'

'I'm afraid it can be life-threatening. Patricia will have to stay with us for the remainder of her pregnancy,' she said, and showed him where Patsy was. Lottie was asleep, but glued to Patsy's arm and Jack had to prise her fingers off. As he picked her up, she fell like a little doll over his shoulder, clutching his leather jacket and Dudley the dog. When Patsy opened her eyes and saw him, she grabbed his hand.

'Jack, don't go.'

'I have to,' he said gently, then sat on the chair by the bed. 'I need to get Lottie home. She can't stay here.'

Patsy looked like a ghost, sedated and slurring her words. 'Please don't leave me, Jack. I'm really scared.'

'Where's Philipe?'

'I don't know and I don't care,' she said, flapping her hand. 'We had a stupid row.'

Jack looked at the ceiling and counted to five. 'Do you want me to call your parents?'

'No, no, it's you I need. You always looked after me when I was pregnant before,' she said, choking back tears. 'You were so sweet.'

'Yeah, well, this time it's a bit different.'

'No, not really. Philipe told me last night that he could never father children. He had a vasectomy years ago, even showed me the papers.'

'What are you saying?'

'I admit I wasn't sure it was yours at first, but I am now,' she said, clutching his hand again, her eyes swimming with fear and determination. 'Jack, I know you don't want a baby, but it'll be different once it's here.'

Jack stared at her. The idea that she was carrying his child was grotesque now he was in love with someone else. The slim chance that the baby may have been his was something he hadn't really wanted to get to grips with. Now it had come back to haunt him.

Away from the miseries of the hospital, Lottie became more animated. 'Is it after midnight now, Daddy?'

‘Yeah, it’s Tuesday now,’ he said, concentrating on the road.

‘Then I can’t wear these knickers anymore,’ she said, folding her arms. ‘They say Monday.’

‘No one will know.’

While Lottie slept fitfully in his bed, holding Anna’s dog in a tight embrace, Jack chain-smoked the remainder of the night away. It seemed Patsy had fought for supremacy in their relationship right from the beginning and she still had the last word. Although she was no longer in his heart, their children would be there forever. The ultimate power.

Chapter Thirteen

Anna

It was Anna's turn to buy the cakes, but Hilly announced she was on a diet.

'I'll just get coffee, then,' Anna said.

'Why aren't you having a cake?' Hilly said, wondering where to sit. It was September so there were lots of free tables and no queues. 'You don't need to lose any weight, you're all bronzed and about a stone lighter. You obviously lived on love in Spain.'

'I did, and it was wonderful.'

'Go on then, make me sick with envy and tell me all about it. And I don't mean the bloody scenery. Oh, and where did you get that stunning necklace?'

'I'll start at the beginning, shall I?' Anna said.

Spending the whole of August at Isabel's villa had been Jack's idea, of course. Early one morning at the beginning of July, he'd turned up on her doorstep. She loved his spontaneity but on this occasion, there had been a hint of unease about him. Reluctantly, he'd told her about Patsy being in hospital.

'It means I've got Lottie for at least six weeks.'

Anna had been angry and disappointed at first. Even from the confines of hospital, Patsy had managed to sabotage what time they would have together, but then Jack had dropped an even bigger bombshell about being ninety-nine per cent sure that the baby was his.

'She could be lying about Philipe,' Anna said. 'Or he could be lying to her.'

‘I know! It’s just another mess.’

‘It’s history repeating itself,’ Anna had said heatedly, but he’d quickly taken hold of her hands and pulled her to him.

‘No, there’s a fundamental difference. I don’t love Patsy. I love you,’ he said, then searched her eyes. ‘We need to get away for a while. Come with me to Majorca, to the villa.’

At first she’d refused, but when they’d talked about it, Anna realised how easily and simply it would solve everyone’s dilemma. It sounded idyllic – a private villa surrounded by a garden with its own pool, thousands of miles away from Patsy.

Josh and Anna hadn’t had a holiday for eight years. Once Jack had reassured her that he’d put Jon in charge of all the work at the farm, it would be something of a relief to get out of the dust and stop hovering between the farm and the cottage on the quay. Since the hens were already farmed out, Hilly easily agreed to have all the dogs.

Isabel was desperate to go. The villa had stayed empty since the beginning of the year. Since Leo’s funeral, there were matters to sort out, then Oliver had apparently got himself a complicated love life and was so stressed out after the exams and Jean’s training that Jack reckoned he needed a break.

‘He’s worked really hard, and he’s had a rough time. We all have.’

In the end, Anna couldn’t disagree, although she had been nervous at the thought of being round Jack’s children for weeks at a time. But the villa was big and Isabel had been a constant buffer to Lottie’s odd little ways. Josh and Oliver discovered the local water sports and some beach babes, much to Lottie’s interest.

‘Anna, Oliver puts his tongue down other people’s throats, that’s not proper kissing, is it?’

Oliver had exploded. ‘Dad! Will you tell her to stop

spying on me?'

'No,' Jack replied calmly, and went back to his paper. 'I need all the help I can get.'

'You shouldn't be kissing strange girls anyway,' Isabel said.

Jack quickly interrupted, 'Mum, don't go there, he'll run rings round you.'

Compared to Josh, Oliver was a handful and despite the easy relationship Jack had with his son, Anna was sometimes glad of his intervention. Although Oliver had the ability to get everyone in stitches, he sometimes sailed so close to the wind he'd have everyone cringing and waiting for Jack to hit the roof.

The villa had two twin rooms and two singles. 'We'll have the singles if you like,' Jack had said, 'then we won't upset anyone.'

A week later though, when they were all enjoying a barbecue in the garden, Oliver was complaining about the room he shared with Josh.

'Hey, Dad,' he shouted across the pool. 'Why don't you and Anna have our room, then Josh and me can have the singles? Save you creeping about on the landing as well.'

'That's none of your business,' Jack had said crossly. 'No one is changing rooms.' Isabel had lifted her eyes over her book and exchanged a look of amused despair with Anna.

But Josh had witnessed the whole set of exchanges unhappily. Without saying a word, he'd set off down the road towards the village. Jack had gone after him, but it was three hours later before they returned, by which time it was dark and they were both sniggering and falling over things in the porch.

'Where the hell have you been?' Anna said to Jack when Josh had gone unsteadily to bed. 'What did you say to him?'

Jack had shrugged. ‘I caught up with him and we went to a bar.’

‘And?’

‘We played some pool and I told him I loved you.’

‘Is that it?’

‘I told him that nothing would change at home,’ Jack said, kicking his shoes off. ‘I told him I wasn’t going to marry you or take you away, and that seemed to do the trick.’

After this, Josh seemed to be trying out the whole scene in his head. Although he’d liked Jack from the start, Anna wondered if they were being too fast and up-front but Jack had hotly disagreed.

‘He has to realise that you have a need for someone other than him.’

‘I thought we’d agreed to keep the children out of our relationship?’

‘I know, but it’s impossible, isn’t it? By the time they’re all off our hands I’ll be on Viagra and claiming a bloody bus pass.’

As the days went by, Anna had to admit she admired the way Jack was with their respective offspring. He appeared to be laid back, but had a subtle way of getting them to toe the line. Maybe he was just naturally on their wavelength, even childish sometimes. Whether it was laddish behaviour in the water or a serious game of chess, he seemed to get the balance right.

Anna watched her sensitive son with interest and a certain measure of fear for his fragile trust. Sometimes, for no explicable reason, seeing Jack interacting with her son would bring on an emotional rush of tears.

‘What’s the matter?’ Jack said, full of concern but genuinely puzzled.

‘Nothing really,’ she said, wiping her eyes. Jack wasn’t fooled and sat down beside her.

‘I don’t believe you.’

Anna tried to explain something she hadn't really understood herself; something so deeply rooted in her need to be independent, but she had begun to realise that she couldn't save herself, let alone Josh from the risk of the hurts and disappointments that went with relationships.

'Just don't let him down, will you?'

Jack had understood then and held on to her for a long time.

Jack and Josh inevitably moved that bit closer simply by living under the same roof and through their shared passion for water. Very early one morning, Anna had found a note on the kitchen table explaining they had gone diving and would be gone for most of the day. Anna was anxious about Oliver and Charlotte's reaction, but they harboured no jealousies – they were used to sharing their father.

Oliver said he'd rather sit in a car wash than look at fish and rocks under the water with a tube in his mouth, and Lottie's reaction was roughly the same, to both her brother's comment and the contents of her father's note.

'Ugh, how sad,' she said, then offered Anna a blunt crayon. 'Anna, will you show me how to draw dogs doing a wee-wee?'

It had been a strange day without Jack and Josh. After lunch, Isabel had driven into town, leaving Anna with Jack's children. Oliver seemed to accept Anna as his father's partner, with the fortunate spin off of having Josh around as well, and it became no more complicated than that.

Lottie was far more complex.

Anna had taken the little girl to the local market, and was quite astounded at her intellect and perception of the world around her. Alone with Anna, she was sweet and entertaining, but if Jack was around as well, Lottie constantly needed her father's love confirming. When it came to adult love, she'd learnt that it changed things, and not always for the better.

‘Love is this,’ she’d said, and squeezed Anna’s hand as hard as she could. ‘I love my Daddy this much, till it hurts.’ Anna had looked away because there were tears in her eyes.

In the night, Lottie would have strange nightmares featuring her grandfather, or the events leading up to her mother being in hospital. One night, she flung open Anna’s bedroom door.

‘I miss Grandpa Lion,’ she cried, and ran to Jack, who mercifully still had some clothes on and was sitting on the edge of the bed.

‘Yeah, me too,’ he said, catching hold of her. ‘Lottie, you can’t just barge into Anna’s room.’

‘Why not? You do.’ She gave Anna a carefully rehearsed look before throwing her arms protectively around her father. Anna understood her, but didn’t always have the patience in reserve.

It was Isabel who had the real knack with Lottie, and was usually successful with some skilful intervention. After three weeks though, Lottie became tearful and difficult and wanted to speak to her mother to see if the baby had arrived. Jack spent almost an hour trying to get a connection to the hospital, only to be told that Mrs Redman was in theatre having an emergency Caesarean.

Patsy returned the call two days later, just as they had all sat down to a meal, and she wanted to speak to Jack first, which she did at great length. The conversation appeared very one-sided, because Jack hardly said anything and mostly stared at the floor. Oliver didn’t want to speak to his mother at all, so eventually Jack silently passed the receiver to Lottie, then disappeared outside with a packet of cigarettes and a set face. Isabel looked at his plate of cold food then shot a despairing look at Anna.

‘What now?’ she sighed.

Later that evening it transpired that Patsy had given

birth to a boy, and had stopped the divorce proceedings because it was obvious the baby was Jack's and she no longer wanted to become divorced from him. No one had very much to say on the matter except Lottie, but it blighted about two days, and the whole thing knocked Jack slightly off kilter.

'Don't let her get to you. It won't change anything between us,' Anna said, removing the bottle of Scotch from the table. 'Only if you let it.'

'How can it not get to me? I don't want to be still married to her and I don't want any more kids with her.'

He'd been moody and angry, and Anna had been fed up with it and a little hurt by his misdirected wrath. She wandered out into the garden, but after five minutes Jack had caught up with her.

'Sorry,' he said miserably, and put his hand in hers. 'All this stuff going on with Patsy, it makes me mixed up, as well as this emotional warfare with Lottie. It must do your head in too. I'm sorry, love.'

Anna had said nothing but she returned his kisses and held him close. Over his shoulder she could see his mother hovering behind the curtains in the villa. When they'd gone back inside, Isabel was waiting for them, wearing her single-minded face.

'*Right,*' she said, removing her spectacles and putting her tapestry to one side. 'I'm travelling back with Lottie and the boys at the weekend. You two can have the last ten days *alone*.'

So Jack and Anna had taken them to the airport. The boys were already becoming bored and promised to behave themselves in the cottage on the quay. Lottie had been on her best behaviour, lured away by her grandmother's promise of riding the ponies at Hilly's and seeing all the dogs again.

'Now you can have a proper holiday,' Isabel had whispered to Anna. The ten days alone had been like they only had ten days to live. Anna had vivid memories of the place now, caught in her sketchbook and camera and waiting to be put on canvas. Their private time together was recorded nowhere except in her heart. It had been ten days of wandering through olive groves and little villages, making paella and tasting sangria in local bars.

One evening, she found Jack trying to gut the sardines they'd bought at the market. Anna had grinned at the mess, then crept behind him and slid her arms around his waist so she could watch what he was doing.

'Go away, I can't concentrate,' he said, frowning at his mother's copy of *Mediterranean Fish*. 'Stop laughing. You know my talents lie elsewhere.'

'Actually, your son is better in the kitchen than you are and he'll eat anything. It's bliss feeding Oliver. Josh and Lottie are a combined nightmare,' she said, pinching olives out of his salad.

'Who said you could talk about the kids? It's one of the many banned subjects remember? I thought we were pretending to be rich vagabonds.'

'You haven't put enough lime juice in that salsa.'

'Go away, will you? Open the wine or something.'

'No, it's payback time in the kitchen.'

He'd got hold of her then. It had started as a playful kiss and somehow turned into something mad and sexy.

They had made love everywhere. Jack had been at his best once he'd relaxed again; funny and affectionate but at the same time driving her insane with the need to stay in tune with what was happening in the office, and trying to buy English newspapers with stocks and shares in. They'd had one little argument when she'd purposefully unplugged the computer in the villa, and he'd not spoken to her for a couple of hours, but it had been worth the clash of temper just to make up with him afterwards. He was always passionate with her after they'd disagreed, wanting to be close to her again.

When Anna had finished relating it all, Hilly was already on a second forbidden almond slice, but reminded Anna she'd left out the bit about the necklace. Back in June, Jack had asked her what she wanted for her birthday.

'I'll only tell you if you promise me you won't laugh,' she'd said to him.

'Promise.'

'I'd like some mallards and a pair of Aylesbury ducks,' Anna said, then laughed and threw her arms around him because he was speechless. Later, Jack warned her she'd have to think of something else as well. She hadn't of course, so by way of compromise he'd bought her the necklace when they were in Spain because it was the first time he'd ever seen her admire a piece of jewellery.

'I've never seen you like this,' Hilly said.

'I don't think I've felt like this since I was seventeen.'

'For a while you had me worried. All that stuff about Patsy and the kids made it sound like the holiday from hell.'

'It wasn't,' Anna said. 'A lot of issues were resolved and we moved on.'

'But it was better without them?'

Anna smiled and rooted in her bag. 'I don't need to answer that, do I?'

She slid an envelope across the table to Hilly. 'And here's another issue, now resolved and waiting to be moved on.'

It had arrived just that morning, a letter from Chelsey. It was a mature, reassuring sort of letter, full of apologies for any past misunderstanding, and she'd included a photograph of the baby and an invitation to the wedding. Chelsey had tactfully made a point of explaining that there would be hundreds of people there, removing the idea that Jack and Anna would have to sit at a table with Patsy and Philipe. 'I'd really like to meet you properly,' the letter ended. 'You've made such a difference to my father, but

I'll understand if you feel you can't.'

There was even a dinner menu, outlining the choices Anna could make. It was lavish and expensive, mentioning vintage this and that. Jack had already told her it was going to be a traditional affair; the service at an ancient atmospheric church, then at Oxford Hall, a prestigious country hotel surrounded by acres of landscaped grounds with peacocks, weeping willows, and fountains. Normally, the place was booked for two years ahead but Mike and Chelsey had been lucky to secure a cancellation.

'Very classy. Nice letter, too. Thoughtful,' Hilly said, after she'd read everything and glanced at the photograph of Sam. 'So, are you going?'

'I don't know.'

'What's putting you off?' Hilly said, then became exasperated at Anna's blank expression. 'Look, she's had her turn with him, it's your go again now.'

Anna laughed at her daft philosophy, but the amusement died. She really didn't relish the thought of crossing paths with Patsy again, this time with her lovechild in tow. Some of the old issues had an uncanny likeness to the present circumstances, and Anna was wary of her presence, making it a lot more strained. Plus there was bound to be some underlying conflict, especially given the emotive conditions of a family wedding.

'It'll mean a weekend away at the end of October,' Anna said doubtfully. 'Josh doesn't want to go.'

'Fine. I'll keep an eye on Josh and the animals,' Hilly said, draining her coffee. 'Come on then, you can't wear any old thing to a society wedding, and you can't let Patsy take centre stage all the time,' she went on, pushing her chair under the table. 'I'll pick you up in half an hour and we'll go into town. With a few fine adjustments I could make you look like Catherine Zeta-Jones.'

'By "fine adjustments" you mean liposuction, a face lift, and a wig?'

Back at the farm, it was slowly becoming more habitable on the ground floor. Anna called Jack on his mobile, but she had to shout because there was someone hammering nails in the floorboards upstairs and sawing the bottoms off the new doors.

'I had a really sweet letter from Chelsey, and an invitation.'

'I know,' Jack said. 'So, are you coming with me? Don't worry about Patsy causing any trouble, she'll be too busy with everything else. Anyway, I think she's got the message about us now. She's barely spoken to me since she came out of hospital.'

'Don't you think that's a bit strange?'

'I don't know and I don't care, to be honest.'

Since the start of the school term two weeks ago, Lottie had been back at her old school and was either staying with Patsy's parents or on Jack's camp bed because Patsy was still very unwell and seemed to be constantly in and out of hospital. Jack thought it was great because Lottie was more settled and he didn't have to deal with Patsy.

'You promise you won't lose your temper with anyone?' Anna said.

'I've already promised to be good, no fighting or throwing food.'

Anna grinned and chewed her bottom lip. 'OK,' she said softly, then had to repeat it much louder. 'OK!'

'I'll reserve a room at the hotel for us,' he shouted back, obviously pleased.

When Hilly arrived, Anna was ready. After talking to Jack and reading the letter again, her confidence was restored.

'All set?' Hilly shouted from the car.

'Yes, but I want to go to Chester,' Anna said, looking forward to it. 'I want something with attitude.'

The day before the wedding, Isabel collected Anna in her new car, a small, blue version of Leo's old car. She was driving them, very slowly, to Jack's flat.

'Well, this is a nicer occasion than last time,' Isabel said, admiring Anna's outfit before she hung it carefully next to her own silvery lilac suit and peeped inside the hatbox.

Jack wasn't ready, of course. He was still in his office, a phone jammed under his chin and tapping something into the computer. Eventually, Anna prised him away, only to have him continue business on the office extension in the flat.

Isabel was trying to make sandwiches and complaining about the lack of anything nutritious in the cupboards and Oliver was complaining that he had to wear a suit.

'Uncle Danny won't be wearing a suit. He'll wear white Levi's.'

'He better hadn't!' Isabel said, frowning at some of the items in the fridge and putting most of them in the bin. The phone calls continued in Jack's car, all the way down the Ml into London. Tim rang to say he wasn't getting any sleep with the new baby.

'Huh, that's nothing. Wait till she's getting married,' Jack said. 'You won't get any sleep then either, better start saving now.'

'Great. In the meantime, we'll be needing a bigger house with a garden.'

There followed a fully animated conversation which progressed onto stocks and shares and other financial mumbo jumbo.

The hotel was a welcome sight. It looked like a stately home, with castle-like turrets and a lot of red deer running about. Jack and Oliver were engrossed in a mild argument about someone's invoice, which lasted all the way down the three-mile-long drive and only ended once Jack had parked the car and Anna told them both to shut up.

The minute she stepped inside Oxford Hall, any irritation from the journey was dispelled. It was incredibly romantic, like a film set, and their room was just fabulous. Anna threw herself across the huge bed, stretching after the long journey.

'I feel scruffy in these jeans,' she said, glad now that Hilly had persuaded her to buy the more formal outfit with the little hat and sexy top.

'You look great, sort of animalistic,' Jack said, throwing himself down next to her. 'Perfect sort of attire for a food fight. I reckon there's already some chicken feed and marmalade on there.'

She gave him a look. 'Promise me there won't be any nastiness?'

'Only if they start something first.'

'That's exactly what I'm worried about!'

'Come on, I'm joking,' Jack said, and folded his arms around her. 'Look, I don't care what they throw at me; food, babies, bills, insults … I can handle it,' he went on mildly and reached for his cigarettes, then remembered the smoking ban and pressed them into Anna's hand. 'I want you to be really strict with me and these things. You keep them and ration them out.'

'No,' she said, and plonked them back onto his chest. 'You have to learn the art of self-control.'

He lit one immediately and Anna had to hide her smile; then he ran the water in the corner bath for her, emptied in the little complimentary bottles of oil and foam, and opened some very cold wine.

'This is lovely but I could murder a cup of tea,' Anna said from the bath, carefully placing the glass on the side. He made tea; they shared the bath, then finished the wine.

Anna watched him getting dry. He was still tanned from Spain and she liked the shape of his body. Years of swimming had done him a big favour. She went to him bundled up in the hotel towels and he unwound her out of them. Her hair fell out in a long, messy tangle. He only had to run his hands through it and she was lost.

'Don't ever cut your hair,' Jack said, kissing her neck and her breasts, making her spine tingle. 'It's wild, I love it,' he whispered, carrying her to the bed. He pulled her close into his body, and loved her so deeply the thought of it all later made her insides feel golden and molten.

Afterwards, when they were lying there, feeling mellow and staring at the chandeliers, he said, 'You feel thinner. You've not been losing weight on purpose, have you?'

'No, it just happened. I'm not *thin.* I've still got an old-fashioned body ravaged by childbirth and sliding downhill into middle age.'

'That's rubbish. That's not how I see you,' he said, looking at her, his head propped on his hand. 'Can I ask you something? Something we've never talked about?'

'We've talked about everything, haven't we?'

'You said you couldn't have any more kids after Josh? Does it bother you?'

Anna wasn't sure how to answer him, unsure of the intention behind the question. She sat up and pulled the bed linen around her shoulders. It was the one thing she felt cheated of, having a child with someone who loved her. She didn't want Jack to see her face, didn't want him to feel he had to come up with a solution.

'Well, it did at the time. It did for a long while, but not anymore. I'm past the maternal yearning stage. I'm too old for babies now.'

When she turned to look at him, although she was smiling, she couldn't quite hide that deep-down gut feeling, and he knew. He knew her too well.

'Perhaps we want too much from life,' Anna said. 'We want it to be perfect and that makes us eternally unhappy.'

'Yeah … I'll go along with that,' Jack said, and gave her a thoughtful smile, then handed her the menu. 'Choose something expensive.'

They ate dinner in the room, partly because they couldn't be bothered with the formality of the dining room, but mostly because they preferred the intimacy of being alone. Much later, Jack suggested they went downstairs to see if Kate and Danny had arrived, and check out what Oliver was up to.

They were all in the bar, sitting by the long windows which overlooked the deer park.

'I don't know what you two are on,' Kate said, 'but it sure beats the hell out of Sanatogen.'

Danny hugged Anna a lot and kissed her several times until Kate said he was overdoing it.

'It's not fair,' Danny whined. 'I'm all alone.'

'You could have brought someone,' Jack said.

'She's got domestic problems,' Danny said gloomily, then pinched Jack's lighter and sloped off to the games room with Oliver.

'What's the matter with him?' Jack said to Kate.

'I think he's in love,' she said, sipping her gin and tonic.

'That's a first. Who with?'

'A forty-year-old married woman with four children. I think the domestic problem might be her alcoholic husband.'

'Oh, for Chrissakes,' Jack said.

'Don't tell Mum,' Kate said darkly.

Mike found them and ordered another round of drinks. 'I'm staying here tonight in the hotel,' he said. 'Actually, I've been thrown out of the flat, bad luck and all that. There's no room anyway. Patsy and Lottie are there, and Chel's got Philipe doing everyone's hair.'

'It must be chaos, with two babies in the house as well,' Anna said, relieved at least over Patsy's immediate whereabouts.

'Patsy's left baby James with some friends back home,' he said, draining his glass and getting to his feet. 'I need to go and check who else has arrived from afar. My best man, hopefully. Jack, I hope you've got a speech sorted out,' he went on, 'Chel said she doesn't want any dirty jokes, references to divorce, smutty sex, or children out of wedlock.'

Kate snorted. 'There's no point in having a speech then, is there?'

Jack frowned. 'What? What speech?'

'Father of the bride usually says a few words?'

'You mean like, please collect your individual accounts from reception before you leave?'

Everyone laughed and Danny reappeared, waving his mobile phone and looking a lot more cheerful. 'She left me a message' he said, sitting next to Anna. 'She works in the Spar shop and I go in and buy stuff I don't really need.'

'What message has she left you, Dan?' Jack said. 'Special offer, buy ten of anything and get a scrubber free?'

'No, *actually*,' Danny said, fed up with everyone laughing at him. He held the phone close to his ear, re-running the message. 'She says she can't live without me and she's leaving her husband.'

Because no one said anything, he scraped his chair back and sauntered back to the bar, the phone glued to his ear. Once he'd got out of earshot, Kate said, 'Oh God, don't tell Mum.'

The speculation about his brother's love life continued back in the hotel room.

'Dan's really clever, you know. He's got a degree in law and yet he behaves like a big kid,' Jack said, throwing loose change out of his pockets, trying to make tea and opening all the wrong packets.

Anna crept behind him and slid her arms around his waist. 'That's part of his appeal,' she said, moving the soup out of his reach before that went into the tea as well. 'I think Isabel is amazing, having another child when she was forty plus. Was he planned?'

'Danny, planned! You don't plan someone like Danny.'

She laughed at his sarcasm. 'I wonder how many unplanned people there are in the world?' she said. 'We know quite a few, and I was one.'

'Some of the best people I know were mistakes,' Jack said.

Anna woke first, with a mild hangover, and wondered where she was. Sunlight, streaming through a gap in the brocade curtains, made a triangle of light across the pale carpet. Jack lay face down next to her, still asleep, and the same sliver of autumn sun highlighted the hairs on his arm. The sheets had all slid slowly down the bed. Anna shivered and pulled them back, knowing she'd probably disturb Jack because he was such a light sleeper.

'Don't wake me up,' he muttered into the pillow, then turned to face her. She nestled into the warmth of his body and played with his hair. She loved the way it lay at the nape of his neck.

'Jack, I think you should know what time it is,' she said, noticing the little clock by the bed. 'It's after eleven.'

They missed breakfast but managed a room service brunch as they got dressed.

'What time is it?' Jack yelled from the shower.

'Late!' Anna said, carefully pulling on the fine stockings Hilly had made her buy. The suit was blue linen, her best colour. It had a long, narrow skirt with a slit up one side that just showed the tops of her stockings when she sat down. Then there was a long jacket and a sleeveless, strapless white top to go underneath, which showed a modest amount of cleavage.

Anna was trying to pile her hair up, holding the pins between her teeth, when she realised Jack was standing there, watching her and chewing a toothbrush. She finished her hair, pulled a few long tendrils down and turned away from the mirror. Still, he didn't speak.

'You're making me nervous,' she said, smoothing down the skirt. 'You don't like it, do you?'

He removed the toothbrush. 'You look absolutely bloody fantastic.'

Kate disturbed them by knocking on the door and asking if Jack knew what time it was.

She looked ultra-chic in a short black dress, white jacket, and a little black hat with a floaty white feather in it.

'Wow, you look gorgeous, Anna. Where's Jack?' she said suspiciously, then saw her brother, still dressed in a towel with damp hair, and almost fainted. 'Oh, for God's sake, get a bloody move on! The poor girl will think you're not turning up.'

Jack went back into the bathroom, then shouted in an exaggerated Scottish accent, 'Do you think old man McDougal will be wearing the family tartan?'

'I hope not,' Kate said. 'I don't like men in kilts, do you, Anna?'

'Not as a rule,' she said, applying dark pink lipstick and a little blue pillbox hat. She glanced in the bathroom for signs of progress but there was hardly any. 'I think it's probably better than a bath towel with Oxford Hall stamped on the back, though.'

Kate agreed. 'Where's Dan and Ollie? I haven't seen them yet.'

'Next door,' Jack said, finally emerging in his suit, but with the shirt still hanging out and only one shoe on. 'Kate, go and tell them the sailor suits have come. Tell Ollie he's got the one with the short pants.'

They laughed, found his missing shoe, and told him to *hurry up*. He kissed her before he went, finally looking complete in Armani grey linen and a dark cream shirt. Anna straightened his tie, because Jack said it was the traditional thing to do.

‘Have you thought of a speech yet?’ Anna said.

‘No, no I’ll think of something later. How do I get to Chelsey’s flat from here?’ he said to Kate as she bundled him out of the door.

Anna set off for the church in a white London taxi with Kate, Isabel, Danny, and Oliver. St Bartholomew’s was big, already half full and humming with anticipation. For the first few minutes, Anna was transfixed by the front of the church. In the centre stood a single white statue of Christ flooded with an ethereal shaft of light. It seemed to epitomise all things spiritual, from the coloured leaded windows high in the ceiling, to the beautiful waterfall of white lilies, blue hydrangeas, and freesias covering the altar and festooned on every pew. Their scent was just discernible amongst the more cloying, though not unpleasant, odours of old wood and polish. On the opposite side of the church, Mike was already looking nervous because there was no sign of Jack and his bride-to-be, although he seemed better once he’d caught sight of Anna and Isabel. After another few minutes, his best man trotted over.

‘They’re twenty minutes late.’

Danny leant across. ‘It’s all off,’ he said with a solemn little nod.

Isabel gave Danny a withering look. ‘I’m sure they’ll be here soon,’ she said to the best man. ‘Jack set off in good time, didn’t he, Anna?’

There was a well of relief with everyone chattering and laughing. The atmosphere became hushed and expectant, with only the sounds of a crying baby filtering through the beginnings of the wedding march.

‘About time too,’ Kate said to Anna. Anna began to feel nervous. There must have been almost two hundred people in the church. After a few moments, she could sense Patsy standing just behind her, but Anna couldn’t resist turning around to look at Jack and Chelsey as they came down the aisle. Her eye was drawn to Jack first, then the bride. Lovely, very understated Anna thought.

Her dress was the sort of classical simplicity that didn't suit very many people; an almost plain strapless, fitted bodice, save for some tiny details and beading, then a sleek, sheer drop to the floor. There was no veil or train to the dress, but Lottie followed behind in an almost identical dress, with a shallow basket of long-stemmed white roses.

The three of them looked so relaxed and were walking so slowly because Lottie was insisting on giving out flowers to all and sundry along the way instead of at the end of the service. Because it was so childlike, and such a contrast of mood to the solemnity of the church, it was all very touching and no one had the heart to stop Lottie or hurry them along.

Kate passed tissues to Danny and Isabel.

At the end, when everyone turned to follow Mike and Chelsey out of church, Lottie managed to find Anna.

'I saved you the last one,' she said, handing the rose to Anna. 'I picked the thorns off because I'm saving them all to put in MacDonald's sporran.'

'Oh, thank you, sweetheart,' Anna said, laughing with Kate. When she looked up, Patsy was staring at her with malevolent eyes.

Outside was confusion as to who was going in which car. Chelsey and Mike were caught up with the photographer and there was no sign of Jack or Patsy. Isabel and Kate were swept along with the crowd, bumping into old relatives and being introduced to new ones.

Anna found Danny. He was holding Lottie up so she could throw confetti from higher than anyone else, but when the time came, she wanted to tip it all down the back of Oliver's neck instead.

'Will you get her away from me?' Oliver said,

alternately scowling and talking on his mobile, one finger in his ear to try and block the peal of bells. 'I'm trying to have a conversation here!'

At the hotel, Chelsey and Mike were welcoming everyone in.

'I'm sorry I haven't had a chance to talk to you,' Chelsey said, passing Anna a huge flute of champagne. She had her long, blonde hair twisted up in a complicated knot and entwined with little sprigs of blue lavender. Philipe had excelled himself.

'I'd really like a photo of you and Dad, would you mind?' Chelsey said.

'No, no, course not.'

Jack found Anna a little later talking to Josh on one of the pay phones near the dining room. She knew it was his hand on her back, then he put his arms around her and knocked her hat off, dislodging her hair so it partly tumbled down. She put the receiver down and turned around in his arms.

'There you are. Where have you been?'

'Standing about, doing pretend family photographs. Come with me,' Jack said, and took her by the hand through the terraced garden. A noisy group of guests mingled on the lawn below as waiters strolled about with silver trays.

'Why were you so late getting to the church?' Anna said, trotting down the steps after him and holding her hat, but before he could answer, the photographer pounced on them and made them stand under a cluster of oak trees, still in the blush of autumn colour.

'Oh, they look like film stars!' Isabel said, 'Catherine Whatsit Jones and that Douglas man.'

When Jack caught Anna around the waist and quickly kissed her, the film shuttered into life. The photographer kept them busy for a good while, considering there were only supposed to be a couple of prints. 'Thank you both, you're very photogenic,' he said graciously, folding up his tripod at last.

'I'd like some of those pictures,' Isabel said as everyone wandered back to the hotel. Jack became involved in conversation with Uncle Robert, and Anna found herself walking alone. Patsy caught up with her. Her hair had grown to a long bob but otherwise she physically didn't seem any different.

'Don't you dare cause any trouble, Anna Williams,' she hissed. 'Just remember, I can have him back anytime I want.'

It was like they were seventeen and eighteen again, although this time the stakes were much higher. Anna stood still and let Patsy march past, then watched as she went quickly up the terrace looking more like the bride's sister than her mother in a short, green suit the same colour as her eyes. But there was something different about them. They were heavy with heartache, desperate, even.

Kate came alongside her, carrying her shoes. 'What's she said?'

'Oh, you know Patsy. She has to take centre stage.'

'She was watching you and Jack do those pictures,' Kate said, holding on to Anna's arm and struggling to put her shoes back on. 'Everyone was talking about you two and the next wedding. You know how people are,' she went on. 'You should have seen Patsy's face. Same colour as her suit.'

They went in to the dining room, where Anna glanced round diplomatically. The tables were circular, with no traditional top table. Chelsey and Mike appeared to be sitting with friends, which was unusual and a bit sad, but Anna couldn't really blame them under the circumstances. Patsy and Philipe were on the far side of the room with Patsy's parents and Lottie.

It was very formal, with swathes of white linen, silver cutlery, and crystal. Someone tinkled on a grand piano, and Danny wanted to know if he was actually playing something or just practising.

'Even I could do that,' he said, plonking a pint of lager down on the table. 'Same sort of thing they play in Sainsbury's on a Friday night.'

Anna found herself between Oliver and Danny. Kate and Isabel filled the other places, and Jack was opposite, with his back to Patsy and Philipe.

A nouvelle cuisine starter arrived. Oliver asked Anna what it was, then answered his mobile phone with a feverish urgency.

'Switch that off,' Jack said, 'You're worse than me with that bloody thing.'

'It's Amy, she's at the station,' Oliver said, reading a text message. 'Can you lend me thirty quid for a taxi, Dad?'

'No. You've got more cash than I have after this little lot today,' Jack said. 'You're as bad as Danny.'

Danny heard his name and looked up. 'Actually … actually, I was going to ask for a little loan,' he said in a small voice, then hid behind his menu.

'Why? You earn three times as much as me,' Jack said, then frowned. 'Just a minute, why is Amy at the station?'

The wine waiter arrived. Jack ordered three different wines and a pint of beer for Anna.

'Have you worked out a speech yet?' Anna said, in an attempt to distract him from the wine list and give the waiter time to recover.

'This tastes better than it looks,' he replied, spearing chargrilled mushrooms, then just managed to stop Oliver setting fire to the table linen while he attempted to light the candles. 'No, I haven't thought of a speech yet.'

The three women looked at each other in disbelief.

'I don't believe you,' Kate said, and checked his pockets for bits of paper, but there was nothing.

'You know me,' Jack said, 'I'll just say what comes

into my head.’

‘That’s what we’re all worried about, Jack,’ Anna said, and only managed to give him a smile when he gave her one first. He looked at her for a long time, long enough to take her back to the hotel room and the tangled sheets and golden, molten sunlight.

After the food, Samuel Jack made an appearance in the arms of Mike’s mother. She passed the baby to Oliver, who was horrified and held him at more or less arm’s length.

‘Dad, do something,’ he said when the baby became restless. ‘It’s going to start thrashing about.’

When the coffee and champagne came round, the best man stood up, told a lot of smutty jokes, and made embarrassing remarks about Mike.

‘I hope you’re not going to say anything like that,’ Isabel said to Jack.

She held out her arms for the baby, who was beginning to object to Oliver’s idea of a lullaby, but Jack took Sam with him to the little table reserved for the speeches and the cake. He stood in front of a hundred people, with no sense of fear or hidden sheets of paper, directly in front of Patsy and Philipe.

‘My daughter didn’t want me to tell any dirty jokes, but all the best ones have been done anyway,’ he said, smiling at Chelsey. Then he looked pointedly at the baby. ‘And as for sex, well, that’s already been done as well.’

This caused a lot of whoops and table banging amongst the younger guests, but even Isabel laughed.

‘So that just leaves divorce and children out of wedlock.’

The silence was so profound then, all they could hear were the candles flickering and the funny little broken cries from the baby, trying to touch his grandfather’s face. Someone gave a low, sardonic laugh. Was it Philipe? Anna looked slowly across the candlelit room to their table, where Patsy was staring at Jack as if in a trance. Philipe was leaning back in his chair with a sanctimonious expression.

'I've done both of those and everyone presumes you've made a mistake,' Jack said, then stopped to move the baby to his other arm, smiling at its flailing arms and legs. 'But the only mistake is to stop loving.'

When the words had had time to sink in, there was the most tremendous applause, then the room settled down again to the general buzz of conversation and noisy laughter. Mike got up for Jack to sit in his chair, and for a while he sat there with the baby, Chelsey hanging onto his arm and his every word.

Anna, with a sizeable lump of something emotional and complicated in her throat, looked across the tables again. Patsy met her eyes for a split second, then went hurriedly from the room, a napkin held to her face.

Chapter Fourteen

Jack

When Jack finally got back to the table, his mother was in tears and Anna was on the verge of something similar – but Anna had been on edge all day.

'What's the matter?' he asked his mother.

'Oh, nothing wrong,' she said. 'I just wish your father could have been here.'

He tried smiling at Anna, but she looked distracted so he sat in Danny's empty seat and held her hand under the table. 'Are you OK? I feel I've neglected you all day.'

'No you haven't, there were things you had to do.'

Jack realised she had a perfect view of Patsy's table. Having to contend with his family all day was hard enough, since they could all be overpowering, but there was his ex-family as well, who were not so much overpowering as completely overwhelming. Kate had told him that Patsy had already been on the warpath.

'This isn't very easy, is it?'

'Jack, I'm all right, really.'

Before the wedding ceremony, when Jack was at Chelsey's flat, Patsy had got her claws into him. She'd started by arguing about maintenance payments for the baby. Philipe had ignored them both, convincing Jack that something was going off. When Philipe was outside with Lottie, waiting for the bridal cars to arrive, Patsy hadn't wasted any time.

'I want to show you the photographs of James. He looks like you.'

‘Patsy, not now. Not today.’

Then Chelsey had come downstairs and all the attention was focused on his daughter. Presently, Patsy, Philipe and Lottie went to church in the first car, and Jack was left alone with Chelsey.

‘Dad, I want you to promise to talk to Mum,’ she said full of concern. ‘I’m sure there’s something wrong, and she can’t cope with the baby. She’s left him with friends.’

‘Not my problem.’

‘You know Philipe’s talking about going back to Paris? He’s told her there’s no way that James is his.’

‘Chel, I don’t want you worrying about this today,’ he said, then he saw the anxiety in her face and relented. He knew deep down he couldn’t, wouldn’t, escape the paternity issue.

‘Can’t you have a DNA test?’ she said.

‘Yeah, I expect so.’

Then at the hotel after the welcome drinks, Philipe had caught him coming out of the gents.

‘Ah! The proud father,’ he’d said.

He was a similar build to Jack, only a fraction shorter. He was very dark, with hypnotic eyes and a womanly mouth. Out of curiosity, Jack had asked Kate if she found him attractive.

‘He’s not my type but I can see why Patsy likes him. He’s loaded,’ she’d said, then added thoughtfully, ‘I quite like the French accent, but there’s something scary about his eyes.’

‘All this must be costing you,’ Philipe had said, then followed Jack and stood behind him at the bar, crunching peanuts.

‘Look, what is it with you and Patsy?’ Jack had said irritably. ‘You’ve both got what you wanted, so just piss off and leave me alone.’

‘Yes, I have what I want but I can’t speak for Patricia,’ he’d said. ‘You could have her back right now. I know she'd be willing to negotiate. Think of it as a return on your losses.'

'I'm trying to divorce the bloody woman, in case you hadn't noticed,' Jack said, then ordered a scotch with ice and told the barman to put it on the Redman account. After a few slugs of scotch he said, 'I don't want her.'

'Neither do I. I never really did,' Philipe had replied, then laughed and tapped one of his cigars on its box before he put it to his lips. 'I rather like your latest woman, though. Very tasty.'

Controlling his temper was not one of Jack's best assets, but he had to hold it together for Mike and Chelsey. He'd promised Anna – and he already had a police record. When he was seventeen, he'd beaten up some lad for drowning a dog in the canal. Anna had been distraught about the dog, plus Jack couldn't abide animal cruelty, and then when Chelsey was twelve, some weirdo had followed her home from school and exposed himself. The police couldn't find him, but Jack did. He'd received a warning after that. If he smacked Philipe on the nose, Jack reckoned the police wouldn't be quite so lenient, and once he'd started he knew he'd find it difficult to stop, but trying to interact on any level, or completely avoid Patsy and Philipe, was like being made to walk over glass or swim through treacle.

When they were doing the wedding photographs, Patsy had said to him, 'I've been talking to Oliver. He tells me he passed all his exams.'

'Yeah, he did OK.'

She'd started the conversation reasonably enough but then became all sentimental and weepy.

'I want you to know that I think you've handled Oliver brilliantly. I don't know how you've coped with everything on your own,' she'd said, her eyes running with mascara.

'Well, I didn't, did I? I ended up in fucking hospital,'

he hissed at her, still managing to smile and nod at Auntie Beatrice.

'Oliver thinks the world of you. All the children do.'

'Patsy, go away.'

She'd caught up with him again after the speeches. Jack had been called to reception to sort out some minor problem and she'd been there, dabbing at her face with a napkin.

'Jack, I need to talk to you.'

'What about?' he'd said warily.

She looked around the foyer then and indicated that they sit at some tables. Jack decided to comply; anything was better than a scene. 'This better not take long,' he'd said.

'What you said in there just now, about mistakes.'

'What about it?'

'The biggest mistake I ever made was to stop loving you. Philipe never loved me like you did. He used me.'

Jack stared at the floor with a grim expression. 'Patsy, it's too late for this.'

'No, no, it isn't! Please say we can try again. We were so good together. Lottie needs you, she's so unhappy without you, we both are. And then there's the baby. I knew I still loved you when I saw you holding Sam.'

She'd gone on in this vein for some time, her voice becoming less audible because she couldn't keep trying to talk, trying to cry, and trying to breathe all at the same time.

'I don't think I can carry on much longer without you,' she'd said.

He'd stared at her. Chelsey was right. If he really laid into her she might cause trouble, or she might become totally psycho and start cutting her wrists with the wedding cake knife. Then again, Patsy had proved herself to be a phenomenally good liar when she needed to be. Either way, she needed help.

'Let me think about it,' Jack heard himself say, hardly believing the charade he'd let himself play, hating the lies he had to say to save the situation, but she'd calmed down, and he'd been able to escape.

A live band and a DJ were setting up for ten o'clock. A lot of the older generation disappeared to be replaced by more of Mike and Chelsey's friends. The waiters began clearing the tables and moving them all into one corner so there was room to dance, although Lottie was still working her way through an ornamental tower of Pavlova with a soup spoon. Because she'd messed about through the meal, running to Jack one minute then darting somewhere else, she was hungry now and wouldn't let the waiter take anything away. Patsy was trying to supervise the mess and Philipe was ordering the most expensive champagne on the wine list and charging it to Jack's account.

'Did you hear that?' he said to Anna.

'Yes, and I know it's annoying but he's bound to take advantage.'

It was too hot for a suit and tie so Jack went back to the room to shower and change, mostly to give himself a chance to think without bumping into anyone and trying to remember which hat he was supposed wear. It was tougher than he'd thought, having Philipe pop up when he wanted a laugh at his expense, and then in between times Patsy playing the abandoned mother one minute and schizophrenic ex-lover the next.

On his return, twenty minutes later, the order and formality had vanished in the dining room, and there was a loud, pulsing beat. Jack saw Philipe trying to slip one of his business cards down Anna's top – only it didn't get that far because she whipped it away and dropped it neatly into his glass. Jack marched across and told him to move.

'I was giving her a consultation, Philipe said, fishing the card out of his drink. 'I was saying how much she'd suit short hair.'

‘Is that what you do to all your victims? Scalp them first?’

‘Not at all,’ he said effusively, ‘I’d love to cut it.’

‘You know what I’d like to cut?’

Anna pulled him away. ‘He was only talking. I can handle him.’

‘He was stirring.’

‘You made it ten times worse. Stop being so *macho*!’

‘Oh, is that what it is?’ Jack said crossly.

Oliver turned up with Amy, who was wearing a skin-tight animal print dress that plunged in every direction and showed a lot of skin.

‘Who’s that?’ Danny said with a slack mouth, his eyes transfixed.

‘Oliver’s girlfriend, still at *school*,’ Jack said, watching Philipe chat to all his relatives with a smarmy grin on his face. ‘A level Maths and Physics.’

‘No way!’

Amy gave Jack a foxy smile and a girly wave. ‘Hi, Jack! You look nice.’

‘Bloody hell,’ Danny said.

‘Come on, Dad,’ Chelsey said to him. ‘Come and dance with me, and stop glaring at Philipe. He’s very entertaining. Aunt Beatrice thinks he’s Sacha Distel.’

Reluctantly, Jack allowed himself to be led into the jostling throng of twenty-somethings on the dance floor. A tall redhead said hello to Chelsey, then smiled at Jack.

‘Is this your brother?’ she said, looking him up and down.

‘Oh no! This is my dad.’

When the girl had gone, obviously thinking it was a huge joke, Chelsey said to him, ‘I bet that’s done your ego good.’

‘I’m not sure if it’s embarrassing.’

‘Rubbish! It’s hilarious having my friends fancy you,’ she said, catching hold of his hands. She was wearing leather trousers and a silk shirt, her hair free of Philipe's braids. 'Actually, it's great having such a young dad,' she went on, and planted a kiss on his face. 'Thanks for today, I've loved it.'

Jack smiled at her, feeling the angry niggles evaporate. Everything was back in perspective when your daughter said something like that. Philipe could order as many bottles as he liked, but he'd never enjoy the pleasure that Jack had at that moment. He looked at the dancing guests and said to Chelsey, 'Which are the ones that fancy me, exactly?'

Lottie tugged at his trouser leg. She was in her element, dancing in her white dress, which was decorated with Pavlova, and she had a chocolate rim round her mouth.

'Daddy! I want a sticky-out dress when I get married.'

'You've got a sticky dress now,' Jack said, lifting her up. 'You can tell what's been on the menu just from looking at you.'

'I've had orgasmic chicken.'

He exchanged a grin with Chelsey; 'I think you mean organic.'

Patsy's parents came to find Lottie because they were leaving, and Jack was relieved she was staying with them. Jack kissed her goodbye, then left Chelsey dancing with Mike. When he went to find everyone else, they were all seated. Philipe was on the next table still working his way through a magnum of Coteaux Champenois.

'Here he is, the father of the bride!' Philipe shouted, and raised his glass.

'Why does he keep saying that?' Jack said in a low voice.

'Just ignore him,' Anna said.

'A very touching speech you made earlier, Jack,' Philipe shouted.

Isabel looked warningly at Jack, making it clear that any kind of retaliation was not going to improve things.

Jack drained the remains of his Scotch and slammed the empty glass down on the table, then sent Oliver for another one.

'Jack!' Philipe called. 'How does it feel knowing you've been had?'

Jack suddenly turned round and shoved Philipe's table so hard his drink slopped into his lap.

'Shut the fuck up and get out of my personal space!'

'I've been in nearly all your personal spaces now,' he replied, placing the champagne flute to his lips before looking across to Anna with a little nod. 'Except for one. I always save the best till last.'

'Jack!' Anna snatched at his sleeve, but it was too late.

He dived across the table and grabbed hold of Philipe, pulling and twisting the front of his clothes.

Isabel screamed, 'Jack! Put him down, let go of him! Danny, do something.'

'OK,' Danny said, and lifted Philipe's feet so that Jack got enough purchase to drag him slowly across the table, almost strangling him in the process. The front of Philipe's shirt slid through a pile of leftover food, and Jack made sure it went through the remains of Lottie's Pavlova until both his hands were entwined round his tie. Philipe plucked at it, struggling to breathe, his arms and legs flailing and crockery crashing all over the place.

Anna threw a glass of mineral water into Jack's face. 'Let him go, Jack.'

With a final shove, he released Philipe, who fell sideways, pulling first the tablecloth, then the whole table went down with him, and finally banging his head on the ice bucket.

'Nice one, Dad,' Oliver said, handing him another Scotch.

'Go outside and calm down!' Isabel snapped at Jack, then she smacked Danny round the head, absolutely furious. 'You!'

‘Ouch! That hurt, Mum.’

Jack sat down with his drink and concentrated on the contents. When he looked up, Patsy was gazing at him with an admiring little smile.

The DJ announced the departure of Mike and Chelsey. Jack pulled himself together and went to look for Anna. She was in the corridor outside, leaning against the wall. Jack placed his hands on either side of her. He knew how much she hated physical violence since her time with Josh’s father.

‘Sorry, I just lost it,’ Jack said.

‘You were provoked.’

‘I’ll kill him if he touches you.’

‘I know.’

Everyone spilled outside into the cold October air. Jack was caught up in the family farewells. Mike and Chelsey were going to the villa for a week and Mike’s parents were going back to Scotland with baby Sam. Someone had tied tin cans to the car and sprayed it with obscenities.

‘Did you do that?’ Isabel said to Danny.

Danny looked hurt. ‘No. I don’t even know what those words mean.’

Chelsey did the traditional thing of flinging her bouquet backwards, amid a roar of clapping and jeering. No one caught it, some even avoided it. It fell at Anna’s feet. Patsy watched with a set face.

‘Yours, I think,’ Kate said, and passed the bridal flowers to Anna. In the main room, the guests who were still around were becoming more rowdy but there was no sign of Philipe, and the mess had been cleared away. Oliver had taken Amy back to the station, and Danny was on the dance floor with the tall redhead, no doubt trying to convince her that he was Chelsey’s uncle.

Isabel announced she was going to bed. ‘It’s been a lovely day,’ she said, kissing Jack on the cheek then giving him a reproachful smile. ‘Apart from you and Philipe fighting.'

'We didn't have a fight. He fell off the table and spilt some of his dinner, that's all.'

Unable to find Anna, Jack sat on the fire escape at the rear of the dance floor with a cigarette and a mineral water, glad that at least Mike and Chelsey had got away without anything spoiling their day. All he wanted to do now was avoid Patsy and fall into bed with Anna.

He caught sight of Kate looking for him, and he knew there was something wrong from her face. She trotted across the dance floor to him, her shoes in her hand again.

'Jack, don't go off the deep end but Patsy and Anna are tearing strips off each other.'

He frowned and put his cigarette out. 'Where?'

'It started in the powder room but I think they've gone outside.'

'Stay here and wait for Ollie.'

It was raining slightly and the hotel security lights only lit the terraced garden. Beyond that, just outside the pool of light, he could see Patsy and Anna having a heated argument by the fountain. Or at least, Patsy was. Anna was a little more composed, still holding Chelsey's bouquet, but she wouldn't look at him. No doubt Patsy had filled her in on her latest fantasy that they were getting back together and living happily ever after with the baby, but he only had himself to blame for that.

Philipe was sitting on the low stone perimeter of the fountain, still wearing his food splattered suit and waistcoat, and smoking a little cigar.

'What's going on?' Jack said.

'Ah!' Philipe said, 'Here he is, thc missing link to this emotional little triangle.'

Patsy was flushed and excited. 'Jack, tell them we're going to be together.'

'No,' he said carefully, and took hold of Anna's arm. There was an ominous atmosphere and they'd all had too much to drink for this sort of caper. He didn't trust Patsy and he didn't trust himself around Philipe. 'Anna, come inside.'

'No, Jack,' she said, shrugging his hand off, 'I want this mess sorted out or you and Patsy will carry on like this forever.' She looked at Patsy. 'You think you can move people around like a game of chess.'

Philipe laughed heartily. He was standing on the fountain wall by then, leaning on the statue in the centre with one hand, and a champagne bottle in the other.

'And you are a mere pawn,' he said to Anna, waving the bottle around. 'In fact, you are all pawns. So I must be the king! I get the cash while you all fight for *amour*. Such a waste of effort.'

'I don't see it like that,' Jack said. 'I reckon you're a sad old git.'

'Me? No! I'm getting the next flight to Paris. I've almost finished here.'

'Almost?' Patsy said, horrified. 'You said you were leaving.'

'All in good time. I wouldn't have missed today for anything,' he said, looking down at her with a smile, only it didn't reach his eyes. 'Hey! Father of the bride,' he shouted at Jack, then frowned and put a finger to his lips. 'Only you're not really, are you?'

Patsy seemed to buckle. 'No, don't. Please. *Please,* Philipe.'

'What is this?' Jack said, looking from one to the other.

Anna looked shocked beyond belief. 'You *told* him?' she said to Patsy.

'Yes, she told me,' Philipe said. 'She wanted to purge her soul, but perhaps we should let Anna tell the story – after all, she witnessed the conception with the real father of the bride.'

'What the fuck are you talking about?' Jack said angrily, looking to Anna for some answers, but she was still staring at Patsy.

'Oh, surely you've worked it all out by now, Jack,' Philipe said. 'Patsy had her head screwed on marrying you instead of that no-hope of a flatmate of hers. Such a pity someone screwed you both twenty-five years later. An interesting story, though.'

Patsy flew at Philipe. 'You bastard!' she screamed, but he knocked her away like a fly.

'What's the matter, Patsy? What makes you think I'd keep your little secret to myself? It's far too good to waste.'

They watched him walk around the wall, like some curious circus act. 'Jack, tell me, how does it feel knowing you've been bringing up some loser's kid all this time?'

Jack looked across to Patsy, and he knew. He knew the truth before anyone said it, but he had to hear it. 'Is this true?'

'No,' she whimpered. 'He's making it up, they both are. Anna's jealous of us.'

'Is this right?' he said to Anna. She'd not lie to him. 'I'm not Chelsey's father. Is that what he's saying? Anna?'

Her eyes were huge and dark and full of emotion. When she nodded, he could feel his heart breaking with the deceit of it all. She made a move towards him, saying his name, but he backed away from all of them, not wanting anything to cloud his slow, painful thoughts.

Suddenly, a lot of little things made sense.

'Don't listen to her,' Patsy burst out. 'She's jealous of the baby. She can't believe we're going to be together.'

'Shut up, you're pathetic,' Jack said, all his focus still on Anna. 'You knew this all the time?' he said to her.

'Yes,' she whispered, tears starting to spill down her face.

'I see. And you didn't think to mention it at some point in the last twenty-four years? You know something? You've all got me going barking mad. You're as sick as each other.'

'Jack, please,' Anna said, still advancing towards him, but he made no move to touch her.

He looked into her eyes, trying to understand. They were the eyes of the woman he loved, his childhood sweetheart, the one person in the whole world he thought he could trust his life with. *No secrets*. He felt the shock kick in. It set his anger searing like a white light, but there was nowhere to direct it.

'Chelsey doesn't have to know,' Anna was saying. 'I'll never tell her.'

'No, but I might,' Philipe said, right on cue. 'What's it worth, Jack?'

He knew then. He knew where the anger was going. Jack took one stride onto the low wall and made a wild lunge for Philipe, who was taken by surprise and overbalanced. One leg slipped into about three feet of cold, dirty water, but he instinctively grabbed the front of Jack's shirt and swung him round.

The noise of them falling into the water was like a thousand firecrackers in the silence of the night, and the sudden drop in temperature after the alcoholic warmth of the hotel was a massive shock. It took Jack a few moments to recover, fighting to find his breath and get to his feet. Philipe was standing up by then, sodden and dripping and staggering about, but he was laughing like a jester.

'It must be worth quite a bit to keep Daddy's little girl sweet.' Jack hit him then. The whole day, twelve months, even years of anger went behind the blow, sending Philipe flat on his back. The water cushioned his fall and he dragged himself up, blood pouring from his nose. For a few seconds, he looked at Jack with drunken, unfocused eyes. Then Philipe made a half-hearted effort to retaliate, but he was like a wild animal that had been darted, and it was easy then to hold him still with one hand and plunge a fist into his fancy waistcoat with the other.

When Philipe didn't move, when he lay there in the water, floating like a dead fish with the weeds, Jack floundered about in the dark and grabbed hold of the front of his jacket, pulling him up. He weighed three times as much in the water and it took all Jack's strength to manhandle him over the side of the wall.

Jack stood in the fountain, gasping, dripping with filthy water, starting to shiver and cough. 'Who was it, Patsy?' he said, wiping the wetness from his face. 'Was it Banks? Simon Banks?'

She looked at him for a moment, her beautiful face inscribed with misery. 'Yes,' she managed to say, then looked at the ground.

There was no need for any more words. He could feel the pain of her confession mirror everything he'd been through. Jack felt a tiny flicker of pity, regret for everything that had been lost. At least she'd given up her futile act of innocence and dropped all the straws she'd been clutching. Jack left her sitting there in her crumpled Yves St Laurent suit, and strode across the grass, feeling the chill air attack his wet clothes. He looked back, and neither of them had moved. There was no sign of Anna anywhere.

Mr Carter, the hotel manager, wouldn't let Jack back in the hotel because he didn't want pond weed and dirty water all over his carpets. He stood protectively in the doorway and looked at Jack with distaste.

'Were you pushed or did you fall?' he said.

Jack stood on the terrace and shivered violently, pools of water beginning to form round his feet.

'I think some of your koi carp are dead,' he said, trying to stop his teeth from chattering, but Carter either had no sense of humour or he was in love with his fish. Judging from his expression, he probably had names for them.

'You'd better add them to the bill,' Jack said humbly, then added, 'can you ask my sister or my partner to come to the door?'

Kate's face suddenly appeared behind Carter's shoulder.

'Jack? Oh my God,' she said as her eyes travelled the length of his body, then watched as he pulled a packet of squashed and sodden cigarettes out of his pocket, along with his room key.

'Get me some clothes and a towel, will you?'

Kate scuttled away and returned with a pair of jeans and other items. Carter watched him get changed on the patio, while Kate wrung out his wet clothes and stuffed them into a plastic bag.

'What's happened? What's going on?' she whispered urgently.

'I'll tell you in private,' Jack said, glancing at Carter's face. 'Where's Anna?'

'Halfway home, and I can't say I blame her,' Kate said, handing him a sheet of hotel paper with a few words scribbled on it, the most prominent of which was overnight train. Jack pushed it into his pocket and felt something die inside him.

Once he was dressed, Carter suggested he come to the reception desk because he'd like him to sort out his bill, and there was someone to see him. Kate trailed behind him with the bag of wet clothes. At the desk there was a policeman talking into a radio, but he looked up when he saw Jack.

'Mr Redman? Jack Redman?'

'Yeah, why, what's happened?' Jack said, still rubbing his hair, which smelt strongly of stagnant water and fish.

'We've had complaints of a fight in the grounds,' he said in a bored voice, then grinned when he saw the water dripping out of Kate's bag. 'Had a bit too much to drink, sir?'

'What is this?' Jack said to Carter. 'A free whodunnit mystery weekend thrown in with every wedding?'

Jack strode angrily back to the fountain, with PC Henderson close behind. His head was all over the place. It was so full of big, serious issues that his mind had gone on random select and he wanted to laugh. Why did all this stuff keep happening to him? He should be falling asleep with Anna, all warm and dry. Instead, he was hanging around the hotel grounds playing Cluedo with PC Plod.

In the darkness, they could just make out Philipe, slumped over the fountain wall. His legs were still in the water and his arms dangled onto the grass. A pair of shoes floated about. Patsy got slowly to her feet when they approached, but PC Henderson was more concerned with the body.

'I reckon it was Colonel Green, in the fountain, with the fish,' Jack said.

PC Henderson narrowed his eyes. 'Quite the comedian, aren't you?' he said, then palpitated Philipe's wrist and lifted his eyelids. 'Who's this then?' he said to Patsy, cringing slightly at the mess Jack had made of Philipe's nose and teeth. The blood from his face was still dripping onto the grass. Patsy blabbed out all the details, their address, and his Paris address. No next of kin. When he called for an ambulance on his radio, Patsy looked from one to the other, a slow dawn of realisation on her face.

'He's not … he's not *dead,* is he?'

'Not yet,' he said calmly. 'And you are …?'

All the time she was talking, Patsy looked at Jack with frightened, reproachful eyes.

'Any other witnesses to this disagreement?' PC Henderson said, still jotting notes. Jack snapped his eyes on to hers, willing her not to involve Anna. If Patsy had any shred of moral fibre left in her, she'd do this for him. She owed him this. Amazingly, she shook her head.

'No, just me,' she said, still holding Jack's eye contact.

But then Jack wondered if he'd done the right thing. Patsy could say what she liked now, couldn't she?

They were taken to the police station in separate cars. Mr Carter had insisted Jack pay the bill before he went and presented him with an itemised invoice, the total of which looked like a mobile phone number with an overseas prefix thrown in. Also included was a table, an ice bucket, and six koi carp.

At the station, they questioned him for two hours about the incident, allowed him one phone call to Charles West, and then showed him to a room. It wasn't as nice as Oxford Hall and there was no mini bar.

The remainder of the weekend was quiet.

Chapter Fifteen

Anna

As Mondays went, the one following the weekend of the wedding was just about the worst Anna could remember. She climbed steadily. The path from Rowan to Llangelynin church was so different to last time in the blistering heat of midsummer. The mountains were dying, covered with dry, strawberry-coloured bracken and beautiful golden trees stripped almost bare by the wind, as if the splendour of summer had to be paid for. She understood this cycle of nature; that everything had to be paid for, that even in the basic structure of things there was a time for life and for death.

The dogs ran ahead of her, full of energy in the cold air, but Anna could only go slowly, without spirit. Then, when she reached the sanctity of the church, she found no comfort in the damp little building she had once found rich in things beyond the physical, something left over from its holy past. God, even. Whatever it was, it eluded Anna and she sat hunched on the edge of the plateau, trying to find a path through the muddle of her feelings.

After the wedding, she'd left the hotel and taken a taxi to the station, then sat half-asleep on a train for the remainder of the night. She'd left him, having an ugly confrontation with Philipe, with Patsy convinced they were fighting over her. The further away from Jack she travelled, the more bereft she felt. The confusion and the arguments with Patsy, the baby with the question mark over its paternity, and then the dreadful shameful guilt when it had all been revealed about Chelsey in that awful, humiliating way, had brought the emotions of the past hurtling back, just like before. The memory of it forced open all the old cracks in her heart and she'd just wanted to run away.

Arriving home as she did, in the early hours of Sunday morning, Anna couldn't hide the fact she'd had some sort of argument with Jack. At first, Josh had been sore about it and disappointed in her, then as time went on and they didn't hear from Jack, he'd been as miserable as she was.

'Just call him, Mum.'

'Not yet. I need to think about it and so does he. Have you heard from Oliver?'

'No, his phone's off. He's probably too embarrassed.'

'I'm sorry,' she said, feeling like the worst mother in the world.

By far the worst feeling, though, was missing the closeness she shared with Jack, when it was all she lived for. To think that maybe he didn't even want to talk to her was unbearable. The way he'd looked at her when she'd confessed to knowing the truth about his daughter would haunt her forever.

He'd never forgive her.

After forty-eight hours of not hearing from him, Anna was incapable of doing anything constructive because of the tears that kept raining down her face. These debilitating feelings were alien to her, but after two days, they were beginning to take shape. The realisation was simple; she had never loved like this before, and it was beating her. It was beating everything. Her head was full of him, things he'd said that had made her laugh.

'Anna! Those bloody puddle ducks of yours have been in the kitchen again.'

Then things he'd done that had made her cry.

'It's fantastic,' Anna had said to him when the farm was finished. There hadn't been anything very exciting to see, but the floor was solid beneath her feet and all the windows and doors opened and closed. He'd taken care that everything was as close to the original as was physically possible.

She'd said, 'I can never repay you … all that money.'

'I don't care,' he'd said, 'You don't owe me anything – you brought me back from the dead. There is no price on that.'

Everything around the farm reminded her of Jack now. Some of his things were in her room; a shirt and an old pair of denims that he'd worn to scramble around in the loft and pull up floorboards. He'd even made a line drawing of the foundations and the ancient drains because he was trying to explain to her how they'd done the underpinning and sorted out all the plumbing problems.

In her bathroom was a razor and a can of shaving foam. She wondered how anything so inanimate could be quite so evocative, threw them in the bin, then took them out again. Every time the phone rang, she thought she was having a panic attack, and every time she answered it, she was torn apart because it wasn't him. Even his doodles were on the notepad; daft little cartoon drawings of Hooper's expressions, and a lot of figures crossed out and added up. She didn't understand any of it but she rather liked the way it made him so different to her.

On Tuesday morning, Isabel rang her. Anna didn't quite know what to say.

'You must think I'm awful, just leaving like that.'

'Kate told me about this stupid fight. Are you all right?' Isabel said, concerned.

'No, not really.'

'There's something you should know,' Isabel said. 'Jack's been held in custody.'

'In custody! Why?'

'It's Philipe; he's still unconscious in hospital.'

Anna pulled out a kitchen chair and sank into it,

listening with a thumping heart as Isabel told her what had happened. The thought that Jack was stuck in a cell, thinking he'd been betrayed by everyone and wondering if he was going to be on a charge for manslaughter – or, even worse, murder – was for a moment beyond comprehension.

'I've spoken to Patsy,' Isabel was saying. 'They took her in for questioning, and as far as I can tell she's actually told the truth.'

'Which is? What did she say?' Anna said urgently.

'That Philipe is some kind of psychological manipulator and he antagonised Jack to breaking point. Charles West seems confident he's got enough evidence to have Philipe charged with fraud. If Philipe recovers, Jack should be OK.'

'What if he doesn't? If he doesn't recover?'

'Oh, Anna, I don't know,' Isabel said, her voice full of fear.

'Where are you? Are you at home?'

'No. We're at Mike and Chelsey's flat, waiting for news. Kate and Oliver are here with me. We had a key because we brought all the wedding presents back, leftover cake, that sort of thing,' she explained.

Anna wanted to jump on the next train, but Isabel talked her out of it. 'You have Josh and the farm to take care of, and anyway, it could be days before we hear anything. I promise I'll call you as soon as we have any news,' she said. 'I'm so glad Chelsey didn't witness any of this. She was so proud of him on Saturday.'

Immediately after putting the telephone down, Anna called Hilly.

'Don't go to the teashop, come here. Something's happened and I need to talk to you.'

Hilly dutifully arrived forty minutes later, with a serious face and a bottle of brandy. She took one look at Anna and hugged her, then stood back and looked at her face again.

'Go and get some glasses, big ones.'

At first, Hilly couldn't keep track of everything that had happened, because Anna told her Isabel's news first, then worked backwards at random. Finally, she told Hilly that Chelsey was not Jack's daughter. Hilly wasn't entirely surprised.

'I always had the feeling there was something you weren't telling me,' she said, pouring Anna another brandy. 'You know, when you first told me about you and Patsy sharing that house with Banks I got the feeling you knew.'

'At first, I wanted to believe Patsy when she said the baby was Jack's but it was too hard to swallow. Jack was the careful one. Simon was notoriously risky; he slept around and had this couldn't care less attitude.'

'Go on, get it off your chest,' Hilly said.

Anna got to her feet and went to look through the French windows, trying to remember the sequence of events clearly. It was so long ago, marred with the passage of time, and she'd wanted to forget, never dreaming it would all come flying back in her face and ripping at her heart.

It was quite some time after Jack and Patsy were married and the baby had been born that Anna discovered the truth for certain. She'd bumped into Simon at a club and he was roaring drunk. He told her that he was still seeing Patsy, that he'd had a blood test and it was a positive match with Chelsey. He'd thought that if he could prove he had a claim on Chelsey that he had a chance of winning Patsy back. He'd threatened to tell Jack about their affair unless Patsy agreed to the test. Patsy didn't want any trouble, and she was sort of curious, so she went along with it. It proved Anna's deepest fears.

They'd had an argument about it then because Anna blew her top and confronted Patsy. Patsy was furious that

Simon had spilled the beans – and to Anna! Bored with Simon by then and fed up with his big mouth, Patsy made him a cash offer he couldn't refuse to clear off. Realising that Patsy had no intention of leaving Jack and her comfortable lifestyle, Simon took the money and ran, grateful to be let off the potential financial hook of absent father. After that, Patsy only had Anna to worry about.

'All these years I kept her sordid secret,' Anna said, pacing up and down. 'To protect Jack and Chelsey, and then she tells Philipe!'

Hilly frowned thoughtfully. 'Do you think he'll tell her? Jack, tell Chelsey I mean?'

'I don't know. I don't know what he'll do,' Anna said, sitting down again, her mind racing. 'Does Chelsey have a right to know? If Jack doesn't tell her the truth, he could be faced with blackmail if Philipe recovers. That's the good news!'

'Somehow, I don't think Philipe will cause any more trouble,' Hilly said quietly, then leant forward in her chair. 'Look, love, you had no choice really. You made the best decision at the time, for the best of reasons. Blood ties are easy, it's what comes after that matters. You should know that more than anyone. You let Patsy give that little girl a decent father and a wonderful life. When Jack thinks about it rationally, he'll come to the same conclusion.'

'But you didn't see the way he looked at me,' Anna said, bursting into tears. 'He'll never forgive me.'

Anna was a lot more composed by the time Hilly had gone to do evening stables, and then Isabel called her to say that Philipe had made a partial recovery.

'Much as I dislike the man, I'm overjoyed,' Anna said. Isabel shared her relief, 'Charles West says it's likely Jack will be charged with assault.'

'When will they let him go?'

'We don't know yet.'

That night, Anna lay sleepless, as she knew she would. Conversations went round her head at least twice, somewhat pointlessly because it didn't help her conclude anything very much – but did she need to? Whatever lay ahead, she knew she wanted to be with him.

In the early hours of the morning, the telephone by the bed rang and Anna snatched it up quickly.

'Anna? I'm on the run,' he said.

'Jack! Where are you?' she said, already wide awake and pulling on a dressing gown.

'I need a hidey hole in the hills. Get the porridge on.'

'Jack, that isn't funny!'

'Wait till you see this suit with the arrows on.'

Had he been stood there in front of her, Anna would have thumped him. The strain of the past few days had almost been too much, and to hear him make daft jokes let loose tears of frustration. She didn't know whether to laugh or cry

'Sometimes I hate you, Jack Redman!' she said, knowing she meant the opposite.

'Hey, I've just driven seven hours to get to you!'

Then she realised. Anna dropped the phone, flew down the stairs, and pulled open the door. The dogs ran out and sniffed the sharp air. It was dawn and there were strands of barley sugar light behind the flooded hills. A mist lay suspended above the silken water of the lake, and he was there, leaning on the car door, holding his mobile phone.

'You hung up,' he said. 'Are you mad at me?'

THE END

Jan Ruth writes contemporary fiction about the darker side of the family dynamic with a generous helping of humour, horses and dogs. Her books blend the serenities of rural life with the headaches of city business, exploring the endless complexities of relationships.

For more about Jan Ruth and her books:
visit www.janruth.com

DARK WATER
PART TWO OF WILD WATER

BY
JAN RUTH

Jack Redman, estate agent to the Cheshire set and skilled juggler of complex relationships. Someone to break all the rules, or an unlikely hero?

In this sequel to Wild Water Jack and Anna return to discover that history repeats itself. Anna's long-awaited success as a serious artist is poised to happen, but her joy, along with her relationship with Jack, is threatened by old scores.

Simon Banks is a depressed and unstable man with a plan. He wants to wipe out his past by buying a brighter future, but Jack Redman stands in his way.

Will Jack ever escape the legacy of lies and deceit left by his ex-wife? Can Jack and Anna hold it all together, or will tragic repercussions from Jack's past blow them apart forever?

MIDNIGHT SKY

BY
JAN RUTH

Opposites attract? Laura Brown, interior designer and James Morgan-Jones, horse whisperer - and Midnight Sky, a beautiful but damaged steeplechaser.

Laura seems to have it all, glamorous job, charming boyfriend. Her sister, Maggie, struggles with money, difficult children and an unresponsive husband. She envies her sister's life, but are things as idyllic as they seem?

She might be a farmer's daughter, but Laura is doing her best to deny her roots, even deny her true feelings. Until she meets James, but James is very married, and very much in love, to a wife who died two years ago. They both have issues to face from their past, but will it bring them together, or push them apart?

WHITE HORIZON

BY
JAN RUTH

Three couples in crisis,
multiple friendships under pressure.

On-off-on lovers Daniel and Tina return to their childhood town near Snowdonia. After twenty-five years together, they marry in typically chaotic fashion, witnessed by old friends, Victoria and Linda who become entangled in the drama, their own lives changing beyond recognition.

However, as all their marriages begin to splinter, and damaged Victoria begins an affair with Daniel, the secret illness that Tina has been hiding emerges. Victoria's crazed and violent ex-husband attempts to kill Daniel and nearly succeeds, in a fire that devastates the community. On the eve of their first wedding anniversary, Tina returns to face her husband - but is it to say goodbye forever, or to stay?

SILVER RAIN

BY
JAN RUTH

Alastair Black has revealed a secret to his wife in a last ditch attempt to save his marriage.

A return to his childhood family home at Chathill Farm is his only respite, although he is far from welcomed back by brother George.

Kate, recently widowed and increasingly put upon by daughter, sister and mother, feels her life is over at fifty. Until she meets Alastair. He's everything she isn't, but he's a troubled soul, a sad clown of a man with a shady past. When his famous mother leaves an unexpected inheritance, Kate is caught up in the unravelling of his life as Al comes to terms with who he really is.

Is Alastair Black her true soulmate, or should Sleeping Beauty lie?

Printed in Great Britain
by Amazon